WINWTC099

✓

W9-CYC-270

DATE DUE

WILLIAM THE CONQUEROR

WILLIAM THE CONQUEROR,

AN HISTORICAL NOVEL ,

John Wingate

FRANKLIN WATTS 1983
NEW YORK

fiction

16 <u>95</u>

WATTS

10/83

DEDICATED TO
COLETTE, JACQUES AND NADÈGE

Verely, he was a very great Prince: full of hope to undertake great enterprises, full of courage to achieue them: in most of his actions commendable, and excusable in all. And this was not the least piece of his Honour, that the kings of *England* which succeeded, did accompt their order onely from him: not in regard of his victorie in *England*, but generally in respect of his vertue and valour.

John Hayward *The Life of King William The First, Sirnamed Conquerour,* (1613)

Contents

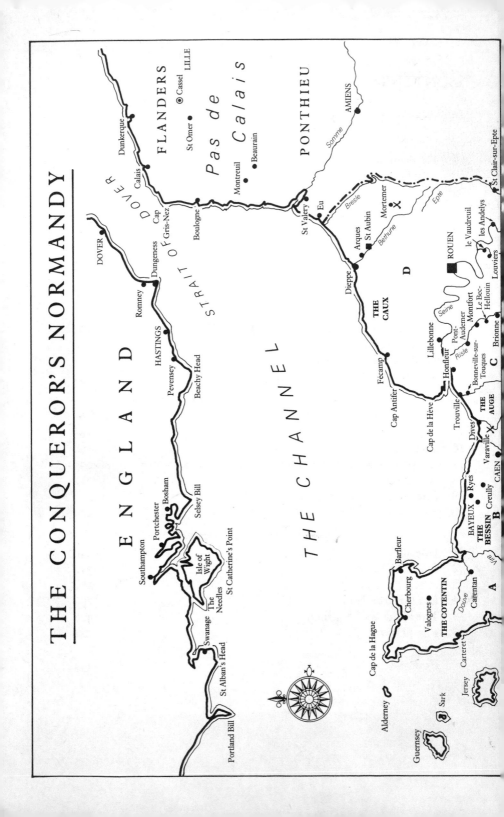

THE CONQUEROR'S NORMANDY

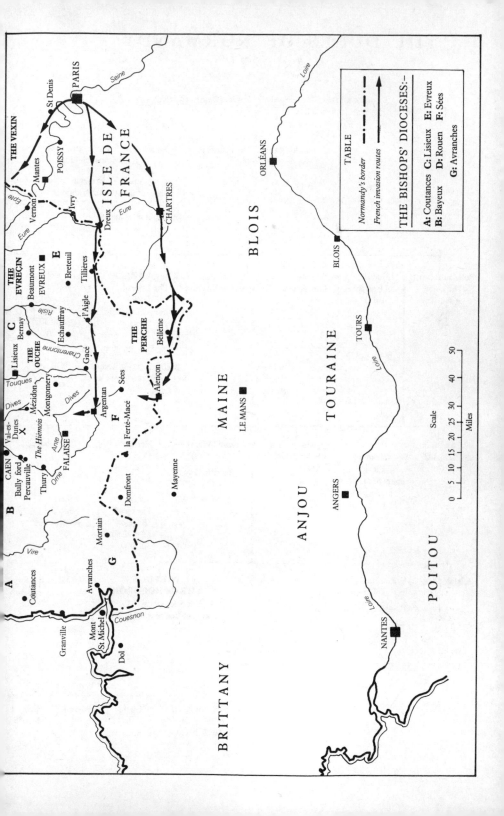

THE DUKES OF NORMANDY
911-1087

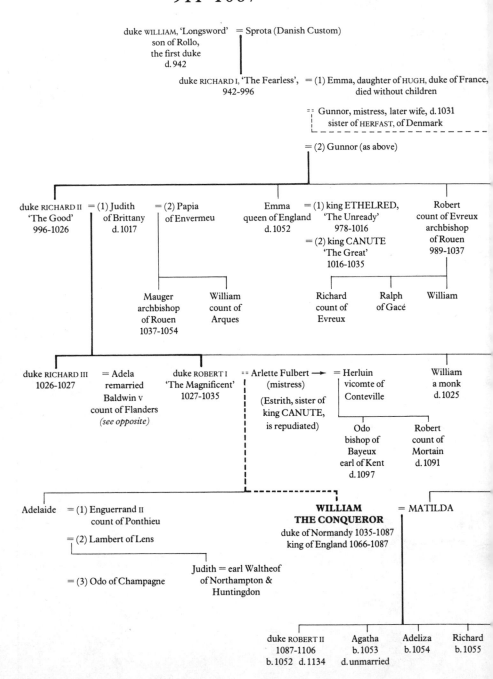

duke WILLIAM, 'Longsword' = Sprota (Danish Custom)
son of Rollo,
the first duke
d. 942

duke RICHARD I, 'The Fearless', = (1) Emma, daughter of HUGH, duke of France,
942-996   died without children

== Gunnor, mistress, later wife, d. 1031
sister of HERFAST, of Denmark

= (2) Gunnor (as above)

duke RICHARD II = (1) Judith = (2) Papia | Emma = (1) king ETHELRED, | Robert
'The Good'   of Brittany   of Envermeu | queen of England   'The Unready'   count of Evreux
996-1026   d. 1017 | d. 1052   978-1016   archbishop
  | = (2) king CANUTE   of Rouen
  | 'The Great'   989-1037
  | 1016-1035

Mauger   William   Richard   Ralph   William
archbishop   count of   count of   of Gacé
of Rouen   Arques   Evreux
1037-1054

duke RICHARD III = Adela   duke ROBERT I == Arlette Fulbert → = Herluin   William
1026-1027   remarried   'The Magnificent'   (mistress)   vicomte of   a monk
  Baldwin V   1027-1035   Conteville   d. 1025
  count of Flanders   (Estrith, sister of
  (see opposite)   king CANUTE,
  is repudiated)   Odo   Robert
  bishop of   count of
  Bayeux   Mortain
  earl of Kent   d. 1091
  d. 1097

Adelaide = (1) Enguerrand II   WILLIAM = MATILDA
count of Ponthieu   THE CONQUEROR
  duke of Normandy 1035-1087
= (2) Lambert of Lens   king of England 1066-1087

Judith = earl Waltheof
= (3) Odo of Champagne   of Northampton &
  Huntingdon

duke ROBERT II   Agatha   Adeliza   Richard
1087-1106   b. 1053   b. 1054   b. 1055
b. 1052 d. 1134   d. unmarried

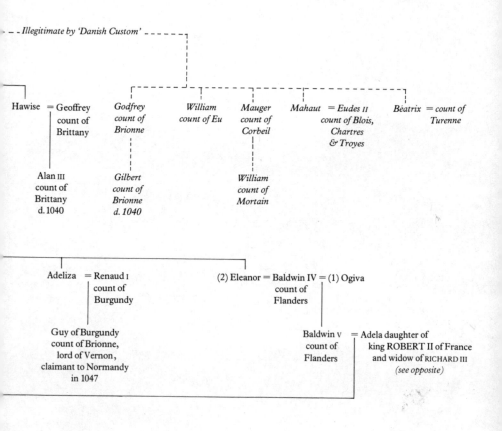

- - - *Illegitimate by 'Danish Custom'* - - - - - -

Hawise = Geoffrey count of Brittany

Godfrey count of Brionne

William count of Eu

Mauger count of Corbeil

Mahaut = Eudes II count of Blois, Chartres & Troyes

Béatrix = count of Turenne

Alan III count of Brittany d. 1040

Gilbert count of Brionne d. 1040

William count of Mortain

Adeliza = Renaud I count of Burgundy

(2) Eleanor = Baldwin IV = (1) Ogiva count of Flanders

Guy of Burgundy count of Brionne, lord of Vernon, claimant to Normandy in 1047

Baldwin V count of Flanders = Adela daughter of king ROBERT II of France and widow of RICHARD III *(see opposite)*

Adela b. 1057 = Stephen count of Blois

WILLIAM II 'Rufus' king of England 1087-1100 b. 1059

Cecily b. 1065 abbess of Holy Trinity, Caen

Constance b. 1067 d. 1090 = Alan IV count of Brittany

HENRY I king of England 1100-1135 b. 1068

Matilda b. 1074

Dramatis Personae

The English Royal Family

Edgar, king 935–975

Elfrida, Edgar's second wife

ETHELRED II, the Unready; king, 978–1016. Son of Elfrida and
    Edgar

Aelfgifu, Ethelred's first wife

Edmund Ironsides, son of Aelfgifu and Ethelred; king, 1016

Edward Atheling, the Illustrious of Hungary; son of Ironsides and
    grandson of Ethelred

Edgar Atheling, son of the Illustrious; great-grandson of Ethelred;
    d.1125

Margaret, the Saint; daughter of the Illustrious; great-granddaughter
    of Ethelred. Marries Malcolm III, king of Scotland

Matilda, daughter of Margaret and Malcolm; marries Henry I, king
    of England, fourth son of William the Conqueror

Emma, Ethelred's second wife. Daughter of Richard I, duke of
    Normandy. (King Canute becomes her second husband.) She dies
    in 1052.

EDWARD, the Confessor; king, 1042–1066; first son of Emma and
    Ethelred

Edith, daughter of Godwine, earl of Wessex. Wife of Edward the
    Confessor. Queen of England

Alfred, second son of Emma and Ethelred. Murdered 1036

Goda, daughter of Emma and Ethelred. She marries:
    1 Count of the Vexin. Their son is Ralph, the Timid, earl of
        Hereford, 1057
    2 Eustace II, count of Boulogne

The Danish Royal Family

Sweyn Forkbeard, king of Denmark, 986–1014
king of England, 1013–1014
CANUTE, the Great, son of Forkbeard. King of England, 1016–1035; king of Denmark, 1018–1035; king of Norway, 1030–1035. Marries Emma, widow of Ethelred, the Unready, king of England
Harthacanute, first son of Emma and Canute. King of Denmark 1035–1042; king of England 1040–1042
Harold Harefoot, second son of Emma and Canute; king of England 1035–1040
Estrith, daughter of Sweyn Forkbeard. She marries:
1 Robert I, duke of Normandy, who repudiates her
2 Earl Ulf, son of Thorkils Sprakaleg
SWEYN ESTRITHSEN, first son of Estrith and Ulf; king of Denmark 1047–1076
Asbjoern, second son of Estrith and Ulf
Bjorn, third son of Estrith and Ulf
Harold, first son of Sweyn Estrithsen; king of Denmark 1076–1080
Canute IV, second son of Sweyn Estrithsen; king of Denmark 1080–1086. Murdered
Olaf, third son of Sweyn Estrithsen; king of Denmark 1086–1095

GITHA, daughter of Thorkils Sprakaleg. Marries Godwine, earl of Wessex who dies in 1053. They have six children:
Edith, who marries Edward the Confessor.
Sweyn; dies 1052
HAROLD II, king of England 1066. Dies 1066
Gyrth; dies 1066
Leofwine; dies 1066
Tosti, who marries Judith, daughter of Baldwin V, count of Flanders; dies 1066

THE OSBERN FAMILY

Herfast, brother of Gunnor who was mistress and second wife of
  Richard I, duke of Normandy
OSBERN, the Steward of Normandy. Son of Herfast. Marries Emma,
  daughter of Rodulf, count of Ivry and half-brother of Richard I,
  duke of Normandy. Murdered 1040
WILLIAM fitz Osbern, son of Osbern. Steward of Normandy
  1040–1066; earl of Hereford 1067–1071; marries Adeliza, daughter
  of Roger I of Tosny. Killed 1071
William, son of fitz Osbern. Inherits Norman estates.
Roger of Bréteuil, son of fitz Osbern. Inherits English estates. Earl
  of Hereford, 1071. Deprived of earldom, 1075.
Emma, daughter of fitz Osbern. Marries Ralph of Gael (Brittany),
  earl of Norfolk. Deprived of earldom, 1075.
Osbern, brother of fitz Osbern. In England before 1066; bishop of
  Exeter, 1072.

The author wishes to acknowledge his debt to all those others who, historians and novelists alike, have over the centuries recorded the life and times of William I, the Conqueror.

It would be invidious to name those many friends, archivists and librarians who have helped him so much, but an especial expression of gratitude is due to Mademoiselle Le Cacheux, Conservateur en Chef, Directrice des Bibliothèques de la Ville de Caen and her Staff.

JOHN WINGATE

INTRODUCTION

For interminable centuries, the savagery of the barbarians from the East had cast its sombre shadow across the continent of Europe. It was Charlemagne who reversed the crimson tide, but after the great emperor's death in 814, his sons swiftly dissipated all that their father had achieved. Europe was again torn asunder by the continuous wars of rivalry and greed, not the least being the regular invasions of England and the northern seaboard of France by the Men of the North, the Norsemen, the 'Normans' whose forebears were the Vikings from across the North Sea. In their *drakkars*, their ferocious dragon-prowed long ships, shallow of draught and fine-lined, the pirates had penetrated the estuaries and moved up the rivers of northern France and England, pillaging and conquering. Eventually, bringing their culture, discipline and their women-folk from Scandinavia, they settled to colonize their conquered lands.

Seventy years before the first Capetian monarch was acclaimed King of France – and eighty years before England became one nation under King Edgar – a remarkable event occurred in the Norsemen's province of Normandy bordering the French kingdom.

In 911 in the Vexin at St-Clair, four leagues north of Vernon on the Seine, the pirate chieftain, Rollo of the 'Normans', was encamped on the left bank of the river Epte. Confronting him on the right bank was King Charles the Honest, of France. At this treaty of St-Clair-sur-Epte, Rollo placed his hands in those of the French monarch and swore allegiance to him as his overlord: no longer would the dreaded long ships raid up the French rivers. Without a word in writing, the duchy of Normandy was born, boarded to the east by the Epte and to the south by the Avre at Verneuil; the dense forests effectively created the vague, unmarked boundaries for the remainder of the province. Civilization began to glimmer once again upon the continent, after five hundred years of darkness.

William 'Longsword' continued the pacification started by his father Rollo, the process passing on from father to son: his heir, Duke Richard I of Normandy then ruled for fifty-four years, from 942 until 996. This great Duke Richard I cemented peace by marrying the daughter of the monarch of France, Normandy's powerful neighbour and overlord, King Hugh, the first of the Capetians. Richard I's royal spouse presented him with three children before she died: the future duke Richard II, 'the Good'; Robert, who was to become the formidable archbishop of Rouen; and the illustrious Emma who, in 1002, created 'the English Connection' by marrying, first, the feckless Ethelred, 'the Unready'; and then, on his death in 1016, her second husband, the great Canute, king of England, Norway and Denmark. Thus, since 1002, Normandy had been joined to the Anglo-Saxon kingdom founded by Alfred the Great's grandson, Edgar, England's first true king. When Richard I's wife died, he immediately married his long-established mistress, the charming Gunnor who completed his numerous family.

Duke Richard II, the Good, ruled Normandy for thirty years, from 996 until 1026. He linked his duchy to Brittany by marrying Judith, the Breton count's daughter who gave him two sons, Richard (his heir) and Robert, and two daughters, Alice and Eleanor. When Richard the Good died in 1026, he was succeeded by his first-born, Richard, at eighteen years of age the third duke of Normandy. This Duke Richard III ruled until his suspected murder, only a year later.

It is in this year of 1027 that this saga unfolds . . .

PART I

OUT OF THE DARKNESS

I

❧❀❧

FALAISIAN IDYLL

'Sire, you're reducing our Normandy to a state of anarchy.'

Steward Osbern shrugged his shoulders: he had expected no answer from this tempestuous, sullen youth slumped in the saddle of the white hunter beside him. But he was Normandy's new duke, Robert I, and was almost eighteen, having stepped into his dead brother's ducal shoes barely a month ago – 3 August in the year of Our Lord 1027. The wretched Richard III, a year older than his brother Robert, had been ineffectual but, egged on by his supporters, determined to defend his ducal crown when Robert rebelled against him from Falaise, this provincial capital of the Hiémois district. Though Richard III had succeeded in reducing the castle during the siege, Robert and his cronies continued to feud against Normandy's hereditary duke. But the disgraceful murder a month ago had left too many questions unanswered.

'Robert,' the thirty-four-year-old Steward of Normandy rapped, 'I'll not return to Vaudreuil until we've talked seriously together: you could have been confronted again by Archbishop Robert, but he's waiting in Rouen for my report on you.' Osbern ended angrily, 'He's better there in his palace. You should consider the old man.'

There was no hint of acknowledgement: the young face remained determined, the jaw clamped tight, the blue eyes fixed in front of him as he and Osbern rode ahead of their retinues down the the valley of the Ante, on their way back to Falaise after a poor day's sport. The duke had made a leisurely start after lunch, leaving the castle by the town gate and crossing the river by the mill at the foot of the craggy spur upon which the battered fortress was built. They had galloped up to the village of Jalousie and, when reaching the Duke's Wood, the party had worked round to the hamlet of La Cocquerie on the northern side. Unlike his murdered brother, the duke preferred falconry to the boar-hunt: for the first hour, Robert had been totally immersed in

5

watching his new birds, but now he had slipped one rein over the pommel of his saddle: he held the curb rein of his double bridle lightly in the fingers of his right hand to free his left for his favourite tiercel. The falcon had just killed, plummeting from a hundred feet to stun an unsuspecting partridge. Blood from the bird's leg smeared Robert's glove; he had snapped the jess to the leash around his wrist and, from the obstinate scowl on the youth's strong face, it was obvious that the evening's sport was terminated.

Osbern swore softly beneath his breath: he was not to be foiled by this petulant, moody youth, nor lulled into defeat by the tranquillity of this soft, September evening. Shafts of sunlight were piercing the drifting clouds to swamp the Duke's Wood in warm colour, to touch gold the first leaves of autumn: the bracken was already turning bronze where it lapped the fast water of the Ante river. The hunting party was trotting down through the meadows, following the left bank below the hamlet of Les Pres: the squelching of the hooves, the creaking of leather saddlery, the cawing of rooks in the elms at the edge of the wood and the shaking of a horse's head – these were the only sounds to disturb this peaceful evening.

'D'you hear me, Robert?' Osbern persisted. 'Your supporters are exploiting your tolerance of their despicable pillage. The most powerful lords are setting the worst examples by their feuding and land-grabbing. Your loyal knights are beginning to quit, preferring to seek their fortunes in Sicily and Italy, rather than have their women raped and their lands taken from them . . . *d'you hear me?*' the Steward rasped, furious at the youth's continuing insolence. No one could accuse this petulant new duke of indecision or vacillation, but he was like quick-silver, moody and unpredictable since that dramatic morning last month in the Andelys forest: his brother, Richard, had put the hunting horn to his lips and minutes later was writhing in agony upon the ground, killed by the poison which had been smeared on the silver mouthpiece. And Osbern watched the muscles twitching in Robert's face as he wrestled for control. The Steward rammed home his opportunity:

'You can't deny that it was *you*, sire, who first took up arms against Richard. He *may* have been weak in your eyes, but the people called you a traitor. You were more than lucky when he spared your life after besieging you here in Falaise,' and Osbern watched the tormented face. For an instant the brooding eyes flashed, momentarily meeting those of his illustrious administrator.

'I'm listening, Steward,' the duke snapped. 'You haven't finished lecturing me yet. Get on with it.'

'You'll hear me out, sire' Osbern said, his voice brittle. 'D'you refuse to admit you've looked the other way, while Montgomery grabbed the monastery of Bernay?'

The duke continued to glare ahead of his horse.

'And you know he's about to do the same at Vimoutiers with all the Church lands. The archbishop's been pestered by complaints from his clergy. Can you wonder he's furious with your connivance?' Osbern persevered, his words spoiling what had been a convivial day. 'And your friend, Humphrey of Vieilles, sacking Beaumont – you've allowed that too. Don't you care that the whole of the rich Risle valley is aflame, while the barons are grabbing what they can? Roger Tosny is fighting for what he can win at Conches, to prevent Beaumont controlling the region. Thurstan to the north at Montfort; and even your best friend, Gilbert, the middle at Brionne. Everyone knows you're in collusion with your friends in the desecration and grabbing of Church lands. The archbishop will tolerate no more of your complicity, Robert.' And then the young duke exploded at last, his eyes blazing as he faced his Steward:

'I'm not responsible for Tosny's cruelty. He's . . .'

Osbern cut in:

'You've made him your standard-bearer.' In the ensuing silence, the Steward's feelings of revulsion against the upstart Tosny needed no words.

'And Talvas, count of Bellême?'

Robert pounded his pommel with his right hand, his horse rearing, snorting:

'How *could* I have dealings with him?' he roared. 'They're a vile lot, Steward.'

Osbern forced home his advantage:

'I know, Robert,' he said kindly. 'You haven't stooped so low yet. But it'll come to it, if you don't enforce order amongst your friends. You could make a start with the lord of Beaumont: he's a sound man at heart, isn't he?'

'He'll support me to the death,' the duke said softly, his rage evaporating as swiftly as it had blazed.

'You'll have to act quickly,' Osbern said, turning to the bewildered youth. 'You're making many enemies. Your hold on the dukedom is precarious, you should know that well enough.'

7

'The English?'

Osbern nodded. 'Canute's a strong monarch. He's also king of Denmark.'

'And soon to be of Norway, they say.'

Osbern nodded again. 'Your danger lies inside Normandy: your dead brother's loyal supporters.'

'I know that, Steward. The foxes are everywhere, but I'll root 'em out. Yes, by God – and the archbishop won't like it.' An ugly smile was disfiguring the obstinate face.

'The old man wants only peace, Robert,' Osbern replied softly. 'That comes first, sire.'

'He's sixty-four.' Robert spat out the words.

'He had sons,' Osbern murmured.

'Ralph of Gacé?'

Osbern did not reply at once. 'Ralph's thirty-three already, Robert. His claim to the dukedom is almost as valid as yours.' The Steward was watching Robert carefully: the archbishop was Robert's uncle, brother of Richard II, the Good, dead only two years . . .

'Ralph's a crafty fox,' the duke murmured. 'You know him well, Steward: he's only a year younger than you.'

Osbern inclined his head and remained silent. Ralph of Gacé had a strong following, was gathering a coterie of the young about him, in particular Mauger and William, Robert's young cousins by his step-mother who both worshipped Ralph. Mauger was fourteen now, William twelve, only a few years junior to the young duke riding so disconsolately down this serene valley. Osbern could see the Ante river curving away from them: soon they'd be sighting the round tower of the castle.

'Your cousin Alan of Brittany is causing havoc in the west while you allow this mayhem to continue in the heart of your duchy,' Osbern persisted. 'He has a direct claim to your coronet, too.'

'From the wrong side of the blanket,' snapped Robert. 'Alan was born before grandfather married Gunnor.' He cut short his words, colouring as he realized his lack of tact. 'I'm sorry,' he said, remembering that his Steward was Gunnor's nephew and therefore also from the bastard line. 'Father often talked about her. Grandfather loved her very much.' For the first time this evening the Steward felt an easing of tension, as the young duke grinned.

'I'm glad we've had this chance to talk,' Osbern said. 'Clears the air.'

'You're a good Steward, my lord,' and Robert's sudden smile lit up

8

his youthful features. 'Ah! There's the castle.' The great tower of Falaise was coming into view behind the trees.

'One last thing, Robert . . .' Osbern said, ignoring the compliment. He realized only too well that the status surrounding his stewardship had been created entirely by his own efforts. Now he'd grab the worst nettle.

'Yes?' The duke looked up, his chin jutting as he spat the question.

'You know what they're insinuating,' the Steward persisted. 'That you were party to the poisoning of your brother.' Osbern waited for the outburst, his eyes on the young man. But Robert asked softly, staring straight at Osbern:

'D'you believe that, Steward?'

'It's a difficult rumour to combat, sire. What you couldn't win by honest warfare, you achieved by stealth.' Osbern added brutally, 'You stooped to poison . . .'

'You believe *that* . . . you?'

'They're even repeating it in your Falaise, sire. The gossip at last week's fair was of nothing else.'

'Richard used catapults in his siege of the castle,' Robert said, raising his voice. 'They even shot rotting corpses into the town. How could I combat *that* ?'

'You should never have started your feuding, Robert. Richard was an honourable young man. And you still haven't answered my question . . .'

Glaring at Osbern, Robert's eyes flashed with passion as he pounded his saddle-pommel. He swore obscenely, his young face twisted, the lips of his wide mouth curling in contempt:

'. . . and, *you* won't believe me, Steward. I did *not* connive at the crime. You're certainly well informed, damn your soul.'

'Who, then?'

'By the Holy Cross, how *can* I know? I can only suspect.' He added bitterly, 'My spies aren't so industrious as the archbishop's.'

'Who?' persisted Osbern. 'Let's have the truth, Robert: Gacé and his puppets?'

'You've answered the accusation, Steward,' Robert said, his anger subsiding. 'He's capable of anything to get what he wants.'

'That's one of the rumours, Robert,' Osbern acknowledged. 'One of my retainers witnessed the murder. He's reported all he saw, but the varlet suspected of smearing the poison vanished as mysteriously as he infiltrated Richard's hunting party.'

'Where'd he come from?'

'St-Evroult-de-Montfort.'

'Ralph's territory . . .'

'Neighbouring town. I've questioned my man personally. He's here today amongst my squire's men. He's my son's servant, so he's trustworthy enough.'

'His home town?'

Osbern's stern face softened. 'From Falaise, sire: a freedman. His father's a tanner here.'

Robert beamed, the storm spent. He leaned across and slapped the Steward's arm. 'Proof enough, noble lord. They love me here.'

'I know that, sire,' Osbern said gently. 'They'd have died to the last woman and child during the siege, if you hadn't submitted.'

Robert did not answer at once. His demeanour was calmer, his eyes steadier as he met Osbern's.

'I love Falaise, too, Steward. I've made it my home, my capital of the Hiémois. I hate Rouen and the patronizing old man who runs the city: I suspect he's aware of his son's treachery.'

Osbern let pass the unspoken question. They were threading through the final meadow and the ford was in sight, where the stream skirted the granite base of the tower looming over them. It was a relief to see that the moody young duke was himself once again, as he reined in his horse to bellow at his followers. He waited for them and together they all splashed across the ford. The track, baked hard by the summer sun, was snaking beside the stream which tumbled swiftly towards the first cottages clustered beneath the walls of the towering castle. Blue smoke was already drifting upwards into the pale sky of this soft September evening, when Osbern curbed his mount to allow his duke precedence. They were passing a group of cottages on their left; next they'd be skirting the communal, covered *lavoir* where the women washed the dirty clothes; and then the sparkling, gushing water of the fountain, where they rinsed the linen . . .

Osbern's thoughts were wandering: how soon could he courteously dismiss himself from the duke's presence and his youthful court? The Steward longed to be on his way back to Vaudreuil, the half-finished castle he was building for Emma on the heights overlooking the beautiful Eure and the Seine valley. His wife hated the partings during these tumultuous days and always waited anxiously, keeping their only son by her side. William (fitz Osbern, the people called him) was seven now and already embarking upon his martial training, the traditional career Emma sometimes resented for her son, however much she tried to hide her fears. Osbern had provided William with a personal servant, a young man named Walter Fulbert whom the constable had recommended for his loyalty and skill at arms. Walter was wooing a merchant's daughter in nearby Louviers, and so had a personal interest in guarding and training William to the best of his ability. Fulbert had left his home here in Falaise to win his girl, so Osbern had included him in his retinue for this visit to Falaise: the young retainer could see his family again, if only for a few hours . . . and Osbern jerked himself back to the present, as he noticed the duke reining in his horse. His falcon hooded, Robert sat motionless in his saddle, watching the gaiety of the scene before them.

The fountain was bustling with laughing, chattering women. The linen was being rinsed in the clear water, the girls shrieking with pleasure in the cool stream, unaware of the stationary horsemen whose approach was drowned by the babble of the river.

'God's truth,' the duke muttered, loud enough for Osbern to catch his words. 'Did you ever see a lass so comely?' His eyes had singled out one of the girls, taller than the others – and Osbern caught the lust flickering in Robert's eyes.

The golden-haired girl was standing in the water and holding up the linen for one of her companions. Her skirts were tucked high to avoid the water and she was naked up to her bosom. Her sturdy legs were long, her thighs rounded, as white as milk. Osbern sucked in his breath at the sight of her exquisite loveliness. He glanced behind him at the silent retinue, frozen in their saddles, grins of admiration on their faces. Then one of the girls glanced upwards.

The screams, the giggles of false modesty, broke the spell as the wenches ogled the silent horsemen. Splashing in the stream like frightened chicks, they gathered their linen, squealing with pleasure, their derisory laughter giving place to feigned shrieks of surprise. The lissom girl stood motionless, her eyes riveted upon the duke astride his white stallion. For an instant, she held his undisguised admiration, accepted the unashamed arrogance as he feasted upon her loveliness; then, without haste, she shook free her shift to conceal her nakedness. In the silence, the only sound was the music of the tumbling waters of the Ante.

'Who is she?' the duke called, not taking his eyes from her. But the spell was broken, the girls gathering their washing and scattering, the while revelling in the banter of their applauding audience.

'Does no one answer his duke?' bellowed Robert, swinging towards his companions.

The incident was becoming unseemly and Osbern nudged his horse forwards. 'Which gate, sire?' he demanded. 'They await my early return in Rouen.'

'A plague on you, Steward,' Robert rapped. 'I'll not stir until I have the maid's name.'

The horses whinnied as a rider began nudging through the duke's retinue. Osbern recognized his servant, Walter, prodding his ageing mare towards him. The young retainer's face was pale, anxious as he approached.

'My sister, sire,' he announced, nervously glancing about him. Making way for him, Osbern spoke quietly to the duke Robert:

'One of my men, sire: my boy's servant, the man from Falaise.'

'Your name?' Robert asked briskly.

'Walter Fulbert, sire: my father's a tanner in the town.'

'Tanner Fulbert of Falaise?'

Walter nodded, blushing with embarrassment: 'Arlette's my younger sister, my lord.'

Robert nudged his horse to make space for the nineteen-year-old retainer. 'Ride with me, Fulbert,' he commanded. 'I'll take the postern gate.'

Steward Osbern dropped behind, smiling to himself as he watched the two young men, one on the royal stallion, the other in his simple smock and leggings astride the old mare; both were laughing as they trotted towards the castle walls curving towards the postern gate.

Not since the discussion on his departure from home, had Walter endured such tension in the home of his family. By the duke's command, Steward Osbern had allowed Walter to remain in Falaise while these delicate negotiations dragged on, conducted secretly through the duke's two intermediaries. It was now the twelfth of September, five days since the duke had passed by the fountain, and Robert's go-betweens were becoming impatient. The pressure on them, as they emphasized during their last visit this morning, was becoming unendurable. Duke Robert was stricken with an over-whelming passion for Arlette – and Walter watched his young sister as she and their mother busied themselves with preparing for the evening meal in tanner Fulbert's spacious communal room.

Arlette had remained extraordinarily calm while father and mother, not helped by Walter's brother Osbern and his sarcasm, had struggled with their difficult decision. And now the meal was spoiled by the unpleasant atmosphere. Father sat in his place at the head of the long table, silent, morose, the stench from his tannery exuding from his working clothes. 'Osso', facing his father at the other end, was stoking the dissension. He'd taken too much cider, as was his wont.

'It's bloody disgraceful,' Osso said, tipping the rim of his bowl to his lips and sipping the vegetable broth. 'I'd have thought your brother would have stuck to his principles, father.' His laugh was ugly, coarse, Walter thought, as Osso added, 'Like all monks: bloody hypocrites.'

Father slapped the flat of his hand on the table. His eyes were blazing. 'You'll not talk like this of your uncle: being my elder son doesn't allow you the privilege.'

Arlette was cutting bread and hovering over Fulbert's first-born. She spoke angrily to her elder brother:

'Uncle's a holy man. Father won't act against his advice: you know that well enough, Osso. Why else has father ridden twice to see him in his hermit's hut? It's a long way to Gouffern forest.' And she slammed down the bread at the end of the table.

'If you go to the duke, you'll make a laughing stock of us,' Osso said, sucking down the dregs of his broth. 'Already the town's laying bets: you'll be the duke's whore, no better. He's a lecherous, spoilt brat, like the rest of his kind.' He looked up, leering unpleasantly as he eyed his shapely sister.

From his place between his father and brother who remained glowering silently at each other, Walter glanced up at Arlette:

'Uncle's a saintly man, sister,' he said. 'Heed him. Don't listen to Osso.' He smiled up at her, stretching out his hand. 'After all, it's the custom of our Viking ancestors, as uncle reminded us. Dad's brother didn't leave our home in Guilbray, comfortable and safe alongside Falaise, to become a hermit in the forest for nothing. He's a good man, a thinker who understands the ways of our forebears.'

'Well spoken, Walter,' father growled. 'We Fulberts should abide by the same customs as those of our masters.' He reached up and folded his hand over that of his wife who was standing behind him and clasping his shoulder. He stared at his first-born: 'You've had it too easy, son: you've never struggled as a bondman.' The ageing tanner was looking up at his wife. Walter watched her wise old eyes flickering round upon her family until they settled upon her daughter.

'When I was a maid,' she said, 'we never questioned these things. It was an honour for us to give pleasure to our lords.' She smiled: 'But I found your father first.' She leaned down and kissed the greying head, then added, ' "The Danish Custom", we call it. It's an honour and a duty and – ' she turned to look long at Walter, 'our finest dukes were fashioned thus, weren't they?'

Walter nodded, responding to his mother's need for assurance: 'Our priests have always supported the Danish Custom, Osso,' he said, turning to his mother. 'The system's worked well for Normandy.'

'Fornication, no other word for it,' the elder brother mumbled.

Walter ignored him: 'Rollo's slave-girl, Popa, gave him William "Longsword", our duke's great-grandfather.' Walter looked up at his sister who nodded her head, a half-smile on her red lips. 'A good bit of work, that.'

Father growled, 'Longsword's woman, Sprota, gave us Richard the First: "the Fearless", they called him.' He was staring angrily at Osso. 'Robert's grandfather. You couldn't produce better dukes than those.'

'I know my history,' Walter's brother replied. 'And Gunnor was his mistress until he married her. God, I've heard it all before,' he ended in disgust. 'Their brat was Richard II. "The Good", they called that one!' His laugh was ugly. 'Robert's father – what a dynasty!'

Walter grinned, refusing to take his brother seriously. The Danish Custom had been practised since the Norsemen's first invasion a century and a half ago: in these dangerous days, young men, valorous youths bred in a chivalrous tradition, were at a premium. The pleasurable duty of the Danish Custom, outside the marital bed, was joyously exercised by men and women alike. The resulting sons furnished the nobles' militia; provided leadership for the ducal army; satisfied the overseas demand for the prowess of Norman knights in Spain, in Sicily, in the Holy Land to vanquish the Infidel. The demand for young warriors was insatiable; popular, the *mores* of Denmark. And these sons, if not the first-born waiting for their inheritance, asked nothing better than to sally forth to adventure and fortune – a choice which Walter in his minor way had taken by himself.

Against his father's wishes, he had quit home eighteen months ago to chase Miriel, the girl he loved. They'd met in the draughty Falaise market two Novembers ago, when her merchant father had travelled the twenty-five leagues from Louviers to buy hides. Impulsively, Walter Fulbert decided to win her, by earning enough money near Louviers to pay for her *dot;* and also to meet the marriage fee demanded by the lord of Falaise for the release of a freedman to another's domain.

Through the influence of Miriel's father, Walter found work with Steward Osbern's constable in Vaudreuil castle, only a league and a half from Louviers. A year later he'd been charged to care for William, 'fitz Osbern' as they called him, the son and heir, 'son' of Osbern. Walter had saved sufficient deniers to cope with the marriage fee, but another year was needed to earn enough for Miriel's *dot*. Her mother was a haughty one; she would need a lot of convincing before allowing her daughter to marry a man below her station, so eventually he would buy his own horse instead of riding one of the constable's old mares.

The Fulberts had escaped so recently from serfdom – Walter's great-grandfather was a bondman – and Tanner Fulbert, having escaped from serfdom through the efforts of grandfather Fulbert, reinforced the family's new-found freedom. Though Walter's mother was the daughter of a serf, his father had worked his way up the social ladder through his enterprise.

Walter allowed the conversation between Osso and his father to drone on without any contribution from himself. Yes, he was thankful now he had left home to seek his fortune, even if eventually Miriel were to refuse him. Youth had little time in which to gain fame and riches: from booty won in battle, and from rewards earned in the service of your knight. A man's life expectancy was short. Brutal death stalked the duchy: from feuding or from lawlessness everywhere; on military service; or from natural hazards, for wild boars and wolves claimed their quota during the long journeys through the forests. This instinctive feeling that time was limited bore a profound effect on people's attitudes: a short life, but a full one. A man needed a family around him, sons to till the fields, fight the battles; daughters to provide children for their men to have sons – the cycle was complete.

Walter's generation found it natural and right that the girls, as their brothers, sought the best match they could. A woman required a hearth when widowed; her physical attraction was her only weapon with which to win a man above her station, so that she could escape the slavery imposed upon her by this feudal system.

If youths were shameless in their haste to beget children, the maids certainly matched their ardour. It was the girls' duty, as well as their joy, to pleasure their lusty lovers. This is the way we live, Walter mused, and we accept the consequences: if a wife fails to provide her man with children, she becomes an outcast; but takes it as the natural order of things when her husband turns to another for the provision of a family. The Danish Custom is, as Osso had sneered, a form of polygamy; traditions die hard – society and the Church accept the Custom without censure, though there are always the envious with their poisoned words . . .

Walter leaned back on the bench, a feeling of well-being seeping over him as the cider and mother's pork, cooked over the fire, took effect. He'd lost track of the argument, for Osso was leaving the house in a huff: he would not stay to be insulted when the duke's emissaries arrived to escort Arlette to the castle.

His sister was dressing in the parents' room, mother helping her. Walter could catch their murmurings and their laughter from behind the heavy door. Arlette was decking herself out in her finest things, and Walter felt glad for her, particularly since father, thanks to his hermit brother, had at last accepted his difficult role. Walter smiled to himself as he remembered Arlette's powerful argument with father, a logic which the Fulberts found hard to resist: Arlette intended to make it clear to the duke that, if she were to sleep with him and bear his children, he must advance the fortunes of her family. Fair enough, Walter thought: she was giving her virginity, so Robert must honour his part of the bargain. Harlotry, the vicious tongues in Falaise would wag, but Walter knew better: during the past few days his adorable sister had confided totally in him.

For weeks, it seemed, she had been watching the duke at his window in the castle keep towering above their small house. Apparently, as is the way with lovers, a clandestine system of communication had sprung up – and, Walter wondered, was it chance which decided the duke to take the lower road past the fountain, five days ago? And was Arlette's shameless exposure as unintentional as supposed? Walter was convinced that the interlude and its forthcoming consummation were *not* mere lust between these two vigorous youngsters. Unusually for his caste, Duke Robert was not, it was said, as promiscuous as his companions; he longed passionately for the beautiful Arlette. And Walter knew that his sister was totally immersed in her dream to give Robert the pleasure he craved – and children too, if nature took its course . . .

The sparks flew as father threw on another log. The chill of the September night was descending and if the fire was allowed to die the house would fill with smoke, for there was no chimney and the door was the only means through which the light entered. It was early yet to douse the embers, to take the logs outside where they could smoulder harmlessly.

'Things'll never be the same again, Walter,' the ageing tanner grunted. 'But I'm glad you're supporting your mother and me.' Then he added, scowling into the leaping flames, 'You're like your sister, so you've understood.'

'I'm glad for her, father.'

'My little girl: she's always been different from the others. Impulsive and ambitious, but she's got her head screwed on.' The latch on the parents' door clacked upwards. Mother, her face beaming, her grey hairs out of place, bustled towards them: 'Our Arlette,' was all she said. Tears of mixed joy and bewilderment were trickling down her cheeks.

The sister entering the room to stand facing her father by the glowing fire was, Walter admitted, looking radiant. Her eyes shone, her graceful arms lying along her thighs. Walter was a babe regarding things feminine, but the long white dress, sheathing her from neck to toe, moulded her glorious figure superbly.

'D'you like it, father?' She swivelled on her heels to flaunt her shapely body. She bent over him, kissing his forehead.

'How much did the seamstress charge you, mother?' the tanner asked huskily.

'Never mind,' his wife answered. ' 'Tis my concern: a secret between Arlette and me.' She tweaked at the shoulder of the gown, smoothing out a fold.

'And you, brother?' Arlette asked softly, enveloping herself in a grey fur mantle, white on the inside. It was unlaced, revealing the swelling of her bosom and the whiteness of her neck.

He rose from the bench and put his arms around her. 'Robert's a lucky duke,' he said. 'He'd better look after you.' He turned, hearing a faint tapping on the outside door. Opening it, he bade the two men enter. Long cloaks hid their finery, but any townsman of Falaise could have recognized them: the duke's personal squire and the chamberlain. The knight spoke in low tones, ignoring the courtesies, his eyes on Arlette.

'The duke's waiting, my beauty,' he said, a smile twitching at the corners of his mouth. 'We've not been sighted. See, we've brought a woollen cape, so no one can recognize or mock you. Your neighbours will know nothing: before the lark rises at dawn, we'll escort you back here.'

In the awkward silence, Walter watched his father striding angrily towards the hooded men, but Arlette thrust herself between them. She stood defiant, magnificent, her eyes flashing:

'When my lord duke desires my love and my body,' she blazed at the chamberlain, 'I shall not go to him like a woman of the streets or a poor chambermaid. Tell the duke, if I go to him, it will be with the pride I feel, as the daughter of an honest tanner of Falaise, a wise, good man of integrity. I shall sleep with my lord tonight only to give honour and to win his love and respect.' She was livid, her cheeks flushed as she flung wide the door.

'Tell him, my masters, to understand this. I shall come to him honourably, without reproach or condescension from his people.' She called into the night after them: 'And I shall not climb to the castle on foot to share his bed. Fetch me a palfrey, so that I can ride to him in all dignity.' She slammed the door upon them and stood there, her bosom heaving inside its bodice. She had washed her hair this afternoon and it was falling about her shoulders, the firelight flickering in its golden strands. Mother had given Arlette the silver-braided snood which Arlette's trembling fingers were now juggling into position. She began to sob wretchedly. Father opened his arms and she stumbled into them, her head nestling on his shoulder to smother her weeping.

'*Mon Dieu!*' he muttered to himself. 'Duke of Normandy and all but eighteen. She ought to come running – the others did.' Robert the First, duke of Normandy, stood at the small window of his bed-chamber on the third floor of this castle which his grandfather had built from the trees of his surrounding forests. Robert preferred the friendliness of timber to the chill of this stone but, when eventually he would succeed to force unity upon his duchy, he would make this favourite town of his impregnable by continuing to rebuild the walls in stone . . . he could never forget the humiliation of watching his battlements splintering and shattering from his brother's catapults. But until better days dawned, he would content himself with these richly decorated, warm rooms tucked into the castle walls overlooking the Ante valley.

The new moon was hanging over the town and it was a clear night. Venus was sparkling low above the craggy hills they called Mount Myrrha – so named after Our Lord's agony, Robert's priest had told him. The after-glow of sunset still lingered to the westward but, at the duke's feet two hundred feet below, the orange pin-points of light from the town houses glimmered like glow-worms in the hedgerows . . . from here, alone at this window, he'd watched for Arlette's brief appearances on the path to the *lavoir* and the fountain during the five long days of negotiations. Thanks be to the Good Saviour that the waiting was almost finished: his wooing would have been simpler had he been born son of a townsman . . . but in a few minutes he and his small court would be welcoming her into the castle. He'd cross to the ramparts to see if he could glimpse her palfrey and her escorts.

She was certainly a spirited wench! Though he'd immediately agreed to his emissaries' demand for a suitable palfrey, he'd told them to enter by the postern gate: he'd still prefer discretion for his seduction of this luscious Arlette – and he smiled to himself at the memory of her glance at the fountain. He'd clumsily taken three girls already, but this was, he felt certain, his first experience of falling in love. His heart had never raced like this before – and merely at the thought of meeting her in a few minutes . . .

As he reached the ramparts, he heard voices raised by the postern gate, the words of his chamberlain floating upwards from the darkness: 'Don't be afraid, girl. Follow us inside; see, the keeper has lowered the gate for you. You won't be seen here.'

Robert recognized the whinnying of his best palfrey, heard the stamping of its hooves on the cobbles. Then Arlette's voice shrilled disdainfully, her words echoing from the walls beneath:

'When the duke sends for me, it's not fitting that he should keep the great gate of his castle closed to me. Open the main gate for me, or I'll return to my honest father. It's not by a secretive, postern gate that I'll enter: such a greeting dishonours my God and me. Open the great castle gate for me, my lords!' There was laughter from the escort as the angry gate-keeper cursed.

Robert grinned to himself when minutes later he heard the faint clatter of the iron-shod steeds at the main gate. He hastened back inside the castle to watch her from the battlements. She could not see him if he stood by the embrasure which overlooked the steps leading up to the massive door in the wall. He'd have time to gain the hall, to greet her suitably when she entered.

He felt his heart pounding beneath his deerskin jerkin as he peered through the slit of the embrasure. He'd long since ceased to care about the amused glances from his friends and the guards. He'd ordered his chamberlain to bedeck the chambers in their finest fashion and to command his court to be assembled in the Great Hall to greet her. He'd silently resented their snide whispers, their suppressed smiles – but he ignored them all.

Ah, there she was! The pale stuff of her gown was showing distinctly in the clear night as she rode towards the base of the steps. The palfrey was picking its way through the granite outcrop and servants were scurrying to take the reins. He watched her sliding from its back, tossing her shoulder-length hair, picking up her long gown. Unhurriedly she began to mount the stone steps. She was magnificent! Her head held high, looking neither to left nor right, she climbed upwards, her escort and the guards scrambling after her to rap on the massive portal. Robert ducked below the stone archway and hurried across to the Great Hall.

'I thought they'd never go,' Robert said, taking Arlette by the hand. He led her swiftly to the room in the outer wall adjoining his bed-chamber at the corner of the keep. Sweeping the curtains close behind them, he watched her hesitating at the two windows overlooking the fountain.

'We're at such a height up here,' she gasped. 'Look! There's father's house . . .'

Her eyes were everywhere, amazed by the opulence of the ducal apartments. The vaulted roof provided a rich setting for the gilded designs painted on the vermilion background of the oak panelling.

He spread wide his arms to the couch beneath the tapestry of the chase in St Andrew's wood. He watched her, a half-smile on his lips as she curled into the brocaded covers. Their eyes met and her arms reached out for him. 'It's past two o'clock,' she said softly. 'Only four hours till the lark rises.' Her blue eyes gleamed as she shook free her hair, golden like ripe corn. The light from the candle flames glinted in the heavy tresses curling about her soft, rounded shoulders. He bent over her and her arms encircled his neck. She pulled him down and lay still while his lips lingered over every feature of her face. Then his mouth found her parted, trembling lips.

The lick of desire swept through them, their pent-up passion liberated at last, shattering the constraint of the past three hours. He drew back swiftly.

'Do I not please you, my lord?'

He knew she was watching, as his eyes devoured the rounded loveliness so provocatively accentuated by her delicate white robe.

'Ah, my beauty,' he cried. 'I've wanted you for so long. You're the first I've really loved.' He watched her smiling inwardly to herself, sure of her dominance now, joyously hanging on his words. 'It's not that I want only your body, Arlette: I need your love too. All I have is yours, queen of my heart. You have only to ask.' He stood by the couch,

peering down at her to savour the delicious moment. 'I'll cherish you as
my wife, your family as my own.'

She lay supine, shy now; her slender arms, which showed through
the slits in the voluminous sleeves of her gown, lay still on her thighs.

'My lord,' she replied, 'you're filling my heart with gladness. And,
since I have your love, I'm overflowing with the joy of knowing that the
honour is mine alone to give you the pleasure you desire.' She reached
up and her long fingers traced the outline of his face, the tips finally
brushing his lips. 'I'm yours,' she breathed, 'to take as you wish. My
lord –' she added softly, the light dancing in her blue eyes as they held
his – 'I am your slave, sire: your companion, your friend, your lover.'
He could hardly hear her now: 'May God grant us joy and His
happiness.'

Robert gently pulled her to her feet. 'Wait, my lovely one,' he told
her, as he drew back the curtains. He strode the few paces to his
bed-chamber. He peeled off his clothes, let them fall on the rushes. He
flung himself on the great bed beneath the stone vaulting. He crossed
his arms behind his head. 'Come,' he called to her, his gaze riveted
upon the doorway.

The silken screens parted, flung wide. Arlette stood there motionless
in the candlelight. She advanced slowly towards him, her eyes holding
his. She halted, gazing down at him, a vision of unbelievable loveliness,
as she slipped the fur pelisse from her shoulders.

For a moment she waited, not moving, her haughty tall figure erect,
her chin held high, the corners of her wide mouth curling with pride.
He heard her swift intake of breath, sensed her watching him as his eyes
roamed the length of her sinuous body: rose-tinted flesh swelling
beneath the tracery of her low-cut gown; dark, violet shadows
accentuating her secret places, the rounded perfection of her body
outlined against the candle-flames. Her hands flickered upwards to her
chin. With a violent, swift movement, she tore the gown apart, ripping
it from neck-band to toe. Slipping free her arms, she parted the tracery
wide. She stood there, still, watching him.

Robert drew in his breath. 'My Arlette,' he asked softly, 'why've you
ruined your robe?'

And as his eyes devoured her again, she spoke proudly, with no false
modesty:

'My lord: I am daughter of neither king nor queen. The hem of my
new gown has dragged in the dust and the dirt. When you take me, and
should you tuck it upwards, I would not have it sully your count-

enance.' She leaned over him, towards his outstretched arms. He drew her down. 'Don't be afraid, my lovely,' he murmured. 'You're the most beautiful creature I've ever seen.'

He trembled as her long fingers slid across his back. Points of gold flickered in the tresses curling about her shoulders. 'Be gentle with me, my lord,' she whispered as she closed her eyes. 'No other have I loved before.'

Through her drowsiness she heard the cock crowing distantly, somewhere far below. Her half-closed eyes registered the pale, first lightening of dawn through the little slit of a window she had not noticed – and reassured by the warmth of the man in whose arms she lay encircled, she sighed with contentment. Turning from him, she felt him stirring, and allowed the delicious aftermath to envelop her again. She lapsed into a half-sleep, waiting once more for him if it was his pleasure. Then she fell into sleep, a slumber interrupted by a succession of wild, fantastic dreams . . .

Her body was writhing from a strange, delicious pain: her being was overflowing with a feeling of fulfilment, burgeoning with a total sense of fruition. A great tree, heavy with green leaf, was bursting from her body. The branches stretched outwards, ever outwards and upwards into the deepest of blue, blue skies. The tree's limbs grew and spread, becoming longer and thicker, stretching above her to cover the infinite firmament. It was so immense, so high this tree that the black shadows from its branches were stretching across all Normandy, across the sea to those mysterious islands shrouded in mist. Warriors battled there, fair-haired and long-bearded, with huge, blood-stained axes . . . with a scream, she awoke, dazed, groping for the man at her side.

'What is it, my sweet one?' He was enfolding her head against his chest and stroking her head. 'Come – tell me.'

She struggled with the words, afraid of his ridicule. 'It's a joyous dream, foreseeing the future.'

'Don't be afraid,' was all he said.

'When shall we be together again?' she whispered. 'I love you so.'

'You'll stay here with me. We'll be together often, whenever I can!'

She flung herself upon him and, while they loved fiercely once again, she heard the rapturous singing of the lark, high above the castle walls.

2

THE PENITENT

Osbern the Steward stood at the end of the balcony, apart from his peers. He needed to be alone with his thoughts on this most extraordinary of days, 25 December 1034. He disliked the crowds, the rabble, and, in truth, even the company of these talkative barons bustling around him to make sure they were noticed by the archbishop. Below in the palace courtyard the rows of benches had been erected, tier upon tier, for the privileged to witness this amazing event. He wondered what proportion of them knew the duke as 'the Magnificent', and how many, 'the Terrible'? The sobriquets depended upon which side a man had been during these traumatic seven years of Robert's reign – and Osbern, now forty-one, searched amongst the gay colours of the stands for his Emma: their son, fitz William, would be with her, her proud escort, now that he was fifteen and no longer in need of Walter Fulbert's training.

Osbern sighed: he'd grown to value Walter's loyalty to young Fitz. The retainer from Falaise had gone through a bad patch, apparently. At twenty-five, he'd been crossed in love with a merchant's daughter in Louviers. Even the Steward had registered the bewilderment on Fulbert's wan face one afternoon when he was putting Fitz through a bout of cross-sticks in the courtyard of Vaudreuil castle. So Osbern had been able to recommend Walter to the archbishop for the vital new task as the personal guard of the duke's son: he'd had ample experience with Fitz but, even so, Fulbert was fortunate to land on his feet as he had done, just as he was contemplating starting a new life as a fisherman working out of Trouville . . . and Osbern raised his hand in acknowledgement to Emma who was waving her yellow silk kerchief from the nobles' stand.

Dressed in the darkest of blue velvet, she was looking so serene compared to the others. Fitz looked up too, waved and looked away. The boy was getting through his adolescence without problems: a fine son, Osbern acknowledged to himself, if compared to those of some of his friends – and his eyes travelled slowly along the line of nobles adorning the stone balcony. Each had played his part during these past chaotic seven years. It was Duke Robert's remarkable achievement that at twenty-five he was now a self-assured and respected ruler both in Normandy and abroad. During these bloody years he had produced unity (cynics might aver, skin-deep) amongst his avaricious and violent nobility – and the Steward glanced with dispassionate interest at his fellow peers who shared the balcony with him, all summoned here by the archbishop.

The prelate sat heavily in his chair in the centre, the most powerful man in Normandy after Duke Robert. Archbishop of Rouen, he was also count of Evreux and a great land-owner. His seventy-one years were rapidly taking their toll but, though his massive frame was now bent, the mind of the old eagle was as sharp as ever, his intellect unimpaired. One arm was round the shoulders of a fresh-faced, well-built boy who was standing on long, sturdy legs by the side of the chair. Sixty-five years separated these two: Archbishop Robert, ruler of Normandy in all but name – and young William, Duke Robert I's bastard son and heir.

Remembering that afternoon seven and a half years ago in Falaise, Osbern was still secretly content with the part he had played in bringing the impetuous young duke to his senses. Though he loved his Arlette passionately and gave her another child, Adelaide, Robert had sensibly convinced the headstrong girl that he could never marry her. The Normans might accept a bastard as heir to the dukedom, but these dangerous and uncertain days required political marriages to prosper Normandy's fortunes. Arlette, always ambitious, settled for Robert's proposal that she should marry a good, solid fellow, and she had taken on Herluin whom Robert had made *vicomte* of Conteville. A happy solution obviously, for Osbern could identify Arlette in the front tier of the stands, proud and dignified, her six-year-old Adelaide at her side, while a nurse struggled with the irrepressible Odo, her three-and-a-half-year-old son by Herluin. She had caught Osbern's gaze and was inducing her little girl to wave towards him. Arlette was a lovely creature, twenty-four now, glorious as a ripe peach, but how was she accepting today's events? Robert had certainly shown his gratitude, but without her during those first three terrible years of his reign, he would have lost his reason, let alone his dukedom.

The little William, so named after his great, great-grandfather,

William Longsword, was born to Arlette and Robert on 19 June 1028. Osbern smiled to himself as he recalled the old-wives' tales of the infant boy's attributes – a unique child, even then, by all accounts. Arlette had initially brought him up in her parents' home until she moved into Falaise castle for safety. And when William was six, his first tutor, Turchetil, began teaching him to read and write: Osbern could see the clerk, tall and rangey, behind Emma's stand. He had found his pupil headstrong and strangely self-contained for his age, but the lad was intelligent. The schoolmaster too, had earned Robert's gratitude, in spite of the chaos following the bastard child's birth. The young duke's succession to the dukedom had immediately been challenged in 1028 and, ignoring the archbishop's conciliatory command, Robert had angrily squared up to the threat on his south-western borders.

Alan III, count of Brittany, was Robert's first-cousin. Alan's mother, Hawise, was Duke Richard I's daughter, who had been intelligently married off to the count of Brittany – and so in 1028 Alan, seeing a bastard as a possible successor to the dukedom, had angrily pressed his own claim by attacking the duchy from the west.

Robert, infuriated by his uncle's condemnations, had besieged Archbishop Robert at Evreux. The castle surrendered and on 2 December 1028 Robert impetuously banished his uncle and his sons from the duchy. From the safety of France, Archbishop Robert peremptorily excommunicated the whole of Normandy – the gravest punishment the prelate could impose – at the same time appealing to the pope. Robert I was to rue the interdiction: not only had he polarized resistance around the archbishop's second son, Ralph of Gacé, but the duchy errupted in rebellion. Alan III of Brittany began open warfare across Normandy's southern borders; Bishop Hugh of Bayeux rebelled from his castle at Ivry; and the disgusting monster, Talvas, began ravaging southern Normandy from his key fortress of Bellême.

Robert reacted with furious energy. But, during the next two frightful years, he had little chance to solace his young Arlette who bore him Adelaide in September of 1029, a rare moment of joy. First he subdued Hugh of Ivry, who fled to France to escape with his life. Then the duke, still mad with rage, overwhelmed Talvas of Bellême. Robert forced the cruel count to pay homage, his saddle across his shoulders, before fleeing to the refuge of France. And finally Robert turned on Brittany where the memory of his appalling cruelty would live for generations: the Breton corpses littered the fields, 'their throats slit like sheep at the slaughter,' they said . . . but the strife continued until the weary duke was forced to recall his uncle from banishment, the only man who could reconcile the adversaries and impose peace. The archbishop's first act, nearly four years ago, was to reconcile Robert with his cousin.

The archbishop had exacted his terms before lifting the interdict: his ecclesiastical possessions at Rouen were restored to him and during the next three years peace once again reigned throughout the duchy, a period when, through the prelate's influence, all nobles of goodwill rallied around their terrible duke.

Alan had been persuaded to lay down his arms. In November of 1030, at Mont-St-Michel he had bowed the knee before his duke and signed a treaty of peace confirming his vassaldom. He had loyally kept his bond, becoming a staunch friend of Osbern's. Gilbert too, count of Brionne, the key fortress in the fertile valley of the Risle in central Normandy; Humphrey of Beaumont, the duke's best friend; and even the old enemy, Tosny – they had all formed a loyal band supporting Robert, around which the dukedom had rallied. Tranquillity once more blessed the land; Duke Robert was renowned amongst monarchs far beyond his duchy's borders – and in particular across that turbulent strip of sea which was to become known as the English Channel. Robert had not been slow in exploiting the English political scene.

Robert's formidable aunt, Emma had married the English king, the feckless Ethelred II, in 1002. When the Danish king, Sweyn 'Forkbeard', finally and successfully invaded England in 1013, Ethelred dispatched Emma and their two sons, the athelings, Edward and Alfred, across the sea to the safety of the Norman duchy, 'the Unready' himself following in January of 1014. The succour which Robert's father had given to the Anglo-Saxon dynasty had consequently involved Norman politics with those of England. Forkbeard died in February 1014, whereupon Richard II backed Ethelred's return to England in his abortive attempt to recapture his kingdom from Forkbeard's son, Canute. Ethelred fled again to Normandy where he died in the same year in which Canute, already king of Denmark, became in July 1016, the king of England. A year later, the redoubtable Emma crossed the Channel to marry the great king: the fortunes of Normandy and England had been inextricably linked. And here they were, these Normans, congregated on this balcony to witness an incredible development . . .

Osbern glanced towards the gates of the courtyard, whence he heard the distant cheering of the crowds lining the narrow Rouen streets. So

26

the people *had* turned out, had they, to witness the procession? In a few moments, Robert the Magnificent would be entering the archbishop's palace to meet his assembled nobles . . . but who amongst them here on the balcony would have foreseen three years ago this extraordinary sequel, when Robert was at the summit of his popularity, both in the duchy and far beyond its borders?

In 1031, young Henry I, succeeding his father to the throne of France, was driven by his ambitious and cantankerous mother, Constance, to seek shelter in his Norman vassal's duchy. Robert, offering Henry refuge in Rouen, was largely responsible for restoring the French king to his throne; and now, Osbern realized thankfully, relations with Normandy's royal neighbours were better than they had ever been. Unhappily this was also the year when Robert's accord with King Canute's empire began to deteriorate – and the year when the duchy, as most of Europe, was decimated by the ravages of bubonic plague.

Appalled by the smouldering heaps of corpses, early in 1032 Robert hurriedly summoned his most trusted nobles to Rouen. Osbern thought back to the ceremony in 1033 when he, with Alan of Brittany, Gilbert of Brionne and Humphrey Beaumont solemnly vowed before the duke and the archbishop to accept the four-year-old William as Robert's lawful heir.

'I shall not leave you without a duke,' Robert said. 'By God's grace, my young William will grow into a wise ruler of integrity.' He thereupon appointed Alan of Brittany as regent of Normandy; Gilbert of Brionne as guardian; Turchetil, tutor; and Osbern, child William's seneschal.

This was the moment too, for prudence's sake, that a personal protector had been proposed for the child. Osbern's Fitz was then thirteen and well advanced with his martial education, so the Steward proposed that Walter Fulbert should transfer his allegiance to the heir, William: a particularly agreeable solution, because the child was the bastard son of Walter's sister. Fulbert had remained by the heir-apparent's side ever since that solemn gathering, an occasion when the visiting guest, count Baldwin IV of Flanders, had been present. Osbern heard it rumoured that the count had tentatively mooted a future political marriage between his own baby daughter and the four-year-old boy. To Osbern the suggestion seemed at the time premature, but undeniably the match could one day be good for both provinces: Baldwin IV had married Adela, daughter of the hen-pecked king of

France, Robert the Pious, and his shrewish wife, Constance, who had tried to drive Henry I from his throne. It was Adela who had presented Baldwin with his little daughter and so now Flanders was joined to France through the royal blood.

The cheering of the mob was growing closer and Osbern wondered what memories Archbishop Robert was recalling: possibly, like Osbern, last December's allegiance ceremony? And, watching the ageing prelate's arm slumping protectively around young William's shoulders, the Steward tried to suppress the anxiety he was feeling.

After Humphrey Beaumont had bent the knee to the infant bastard, Duke Robert had bade them all be seated – and Osbern was impressed by the sight of the duke standing in the centre, clad as was his custom at court, in his finest regalia: the badge of nobility, his rectangular, rich purple cloak held in place at the shoulder by its jewelled clasp; his emerald-green, silken tunic which descended to his feet, a further indication of royalty; his deerskin shoes. A majestic figure, not over-tall but sturdily built, his heavy face clean-shaven, unlike his bearded father. And then, last year Duke Robert had sprung his amazing decision upon them all.

To expiate his sins and to save his soul from damnation he was proposing immediately to embark upon the long pilgrimage to Jerusalem and the Holy Land. Should he not return to his duchy, his son, William, was to succeed him as duke of Normandy. For a full minute, the assembly had remained stunned, a silence eventually broken by the long-suffering archbishop:

'My lord duke, even if naught befalls you, the risk of rebellion during your absence is great: there are those, as you full well know, who still bitterly resent your designated heir. And should you not return . . .'

It was Alan who erupted, bursting with indignation:

'There'll be anarchy abroad in the land, sire.'

Beaumont added, 'You're jettisoning all we've achieved for you, my lord. We've fought long and paid dearly for the duke's peace.'

'And you, Steward?' Robert rasped. 'Do you quarrel too, with your duke?' And Osbern, true to himself, had replied quietly, 'I do not quarrel, sire. But you are putting at risk all your subjects have endured these years.'

The opposition, as they all sensed, was to no avail, in spite of worsening relations with England across the Channel: Robert, in an attempt to provide a legitimate heir, had reluctantly agreed to marry Canute's sister, Estrith; but after a year, he had repudiated her – and

Osbern still thought the cause of the rejection lay in Robert's continuing devotion to his Arlette . . . Canute was now estranged, his pride affronted and a powerful, potential enemy.

Duke Robert had dismissed his council, his eyes flashing with anger: 'I depart to Paris tomorrow,' he thundered as he swept from the chamber, 'to pay homage to the King of France.' A month later he was on his knee before Henry I at Poissy, and knighted as his vassal.

The roar of the crowd outside the gates snapped Osbern back to the present. The portals were swinging open, the guards holding back the press with the shafts of their spears to allow the first horsemen through. And as the audience in the stands rose to its feet, a silence more astonishing than the clamour descended upon the expectant spectators.

A broad figure, unmistakable even in his penitent's sackcloth and cowl, walked slowly through the gates, solitary, ten paces ahead of the silent file of pilgrims; all of them were like their leader enveloped in their black monkish habits, their heads shrouded in cowls, their hands thrust in their sleeves. Between them and their penitent duke another hooded figure walked, carrying a simple cross of two pieces of wood thonged together. As the duke reached the centre of the palace yard, he slipped back his cowl for all his court to recognize him. He raised his eyes towards the balcony and commanded in his hoarse, strong voice: 'Bring me my son.'

The press on the balcony shivered, like corn bending to a passing breeze, and the boy at the archbishop's shoulder hurried from the scene. The onlookers remained silently in their places as, a moment later, the sturdy child ran across the courtyard to his father. Even as William knelt, Osbern could see the child choking back his tears. Duke Robert placed his hands upon his head, stood motionless in prayer, then looked up towards Archbishop Robert. The prelate, one hand on the arm of his chair, raised his other in benison. With a last glance towards Arlette Herluin in the nobles' stand, the black-robed pilgrim hooded his head with the cowl of his habit. He turned his back, then slowly walked out through the gates. As the pilgrims made way for him, Osbern watched the mounted escort, laden with jewels and treasure for the journey, jockeying for position as they brought up the rear.

Osbern stood apart with his thoughts as the silence broke into a hubbub of excited talk. The balcony was emptying of all save the archbishop, who remained slumped forward in his chair, regarding the bustling courtyard below. Osbern moved to his side, shocked by the change in the great man: suddenly he was old and tears were trickling down the leathery cheeks.

'See, Steward,' he murmured. 'Our future duke's but a child,' and he nodded towards the nobles' stand below. William had run to his mother. His head was laid against her bodice and her arms went around him as she bent over him, trying to comfort her distraught son.

Osbern assisted the prelate to his feet. 'I hope I shall not live to see the outcome of this folly, Steward.' The ageing archbishop spoke softly. 'After all we've achieved . . . May our Good Saviour protect Normandy this day.'

He made the sign of the cross. Osbern stood aside and watched the hunched figure stumbling unsteadily to the open doorway at the rear of the balcony.

'Remain in the palace until two o'clock, Fulbert,' Osbern commanded. 'If the archbishop's council has not finished by then, start riding with Master William back to Vaudreuil. The days are drawing in and the squire wants you back before dark.'

'Let's do some more practice tilting, Walter,' the rosy-cheeked boy interrupted, tugging at the servant's arm. '*Please*, sir,' he said, his blue eyes pleading with Osbern. 'Master Turchetil's let me off this morning.'

'Why, William?' Osbern asked kindly, watching the excited seven-year-old. 'Why no lessons?'

'He's got a fever,' and the boy began pulling Walter towards the courtyard. 'Tilting's *fun*, sir. Please let me.'

'Off with you, then.'

The Steward watched them scurrying from the chamber, then slowly he began climbing the spiral stone stairway to the council chamber of the archbishop's palace.

Archbishop Robert was seated in the centre of the long table, whence he could watch through his windows the spacious courtyard below. It was cold in the council chamber and lords Alan and Gilbert had already occupied the chairs nearest the blazing fire. This weather was one of those hard, cold snaps which early October sometimes sprang: the third of the month, Osbern realized, but it didn't seem possible that a year had already swept by since the penitent duke had walked out through those gates. The assembled nobles parted for the Steward as he made his way to the vacant seat next to the prelate. The old man beckoned him to the chair. 'Be seated, Osbern,' he murmured wearily. 'I feared you'd not arrive in time.'

'How so, my lord? What brings the council together?'

The world-weary eyes met Osbern's momentarily; then, with a tired gesture, Archbishop Robert indicated the crowded chamber. 'I thought it meet to summon you. A messenger has ridden all yesterday from the knight Toustain.'

'The pilgrim, my lord?'

'The very same.'

'What news?'

'He sends no hint, seeks audience only of me.'

Osbern met the old man's troubled gaze: 'It bodes ill, Steward,' was all the prelate said. 'Toustain was riding at dawn. He's talked to no one since leaving the Holy Land, it seems.'

Osbern remained silent, trying to hide his concern, conscious that many in the chamber were watching. He sensed a deep unease, as he tried to thrust the inevitable fears from him, like a man in the night feeling his footsteps across the quicksands . . . there were, he knew well, vultures amongst this council here, hard-faced, ambitious men poised to swoop on the carrion – and, unobserved, Osbern traversed the crowded hall with his shrewd glance.

Grouped around the long tables were the inner members of the council, the real power behind the archbishop: Alan of Brittany shared a fleeting smile; and Gilbert who had galloped from Brionne, having joined with Humphrey on his ride from Beaumont. Most of the duchy's personages were here, it seemed; they had to be, if the highest in the court, those who ranked with the Steward, had heeded the prelate's summons. There was the Master Chamberlain, a man whom Osbern respected for his efficiency, but not for his carping pedantry. Responsible for the *camera*, the duke's treasury, he was proud of his new measures for collecting the ducal revenue fairly throughout the duchy. He had few friends when, in these violent days, strength and prowess at arms represented the manly virtues. Close to him stood the rotund figure of the Butler who was plagued by the minutiae of trying to run the duke's household. And, on the opposite side, Osbern picked out the Constable, his most trusted friend on the inner council. His office was responsible to the absent Robert for ensuring that ducal justice was not abused by the *vicomtes*, that new breed of somewhat over-inflated officials who, under the courts, kept the peace in the counties.

It was when Osbern was first called to office by Duke Richard II that the post of Constable had been instituted. The Steward had backed Richard's scheme vigorously, because he foresaw with stark reality the anarchy which would follow the ageing duke's death. And the violence had erupted so swiftly, with such tragic consequences when Richard III was poisoned – the reason, malicious men averred, for Duke Robert's insane and impulsive pilgrimage of penitence. The saving of a man's soul was paramount, Osbern was the first to agree; but Robert had left a void behind him, a power vacuum which if it continued much longer could lead only to chaos – and this was a grievous sin of omission in itself . . . Richard the Good would not have done such a thing, but then the failings of Robert's father were mostly carnal and generally accepted, unlike the mortal sin of murder by poison. The old duke Richard II (he had lived such a full life with his two wives, Judith, the Breton duchess; and with Papia from Envermeu who had previously been his devoted mistress) had selected Osbern to be his *dapifer*, his personal Steward at court. And for thirteen years, Osbern had held the Stewardship, conscientiously and patiently forging the office into the high status it now enjoyed.

He would always be indebted to the good Richard . . . and proud, too, of his own Norse ancestry, always aware that it was the traditions, the customs and the discipline of his forebears which had given him the qualities he was exploiting. It had helped, too, that his father, Herfast, was brother of Gunnor, Duke Richard I's vivacious concubine by whom he had his numerous bastard children – advancement these days depended on connections with the ducal family . . . The Steward's concentration was jerked back to the present by the press behind him as the assembly surged towards the windows: hooves clattered in the courtyard, grooms were yelling and then footsteps were echoing on the stairway.

The doors flung open. The crowded chamber divided and through the silent nobles a mud-spattered knight, his sword at his side, his helmet crooked in his arm, his squire out of breath at his heels, staggered towards the hunched figure in the archbishop's chair.

'Speak, Sir Toustain,' the prelate growled. 'We await your words.'

'My lord,' the knight rasped, between his gasping breaths. *'Our duke is dead.'*

No movement in the chamber, the rain slashing across the windows the only sound . . . And in that instant, Osbern noticed a younger man, Ralph of Gacé, the archbishop's son, edging forwards. There was a gleam in his eyes, Osbern was sure, a flicker of triumph, his lips curling contemptuously while he canted his grotesquely huge head to catch Toustain's words. With a sinking heart, Osbern turned away as

Toustain began recounting his news.

Dispensing largesse to the destitute throughout his amazing pilgrimage, Robert had cemented his sobriquet as 'the Magnificent'. In expiation of his sins, throughout his long journey to Jerusalem he set his pilgrims an example both of extreme piety and extravagance. Toustain was recovering his composure as he settled to his description of the unique voyage . . .

Late one night, footsore and exhausted during his journey through Burgundy, Robert knocked on the postern gate of a castle which had been organized for the pilgrims' sojourn. The churlish gate-keeper, seeing before him the cowled and limping figure, lambasted him and tried to send him packing. Robert's infuriated knights hurled themselves upon the man.

'Let him be,' Robert cried. 'I prefer his blows to the comfort of life in Rouen.' In Rome, the pope was waiting to commission the duke for a Norman crusade and to bless his pilgrim's staff. The Magnificent, to accentuate his homage and Norman pride, cast his splendid royal cloak across an adjacent nude statue of Constantine. At the gate of Constantinople, preparing for his meeting with the emperor, the Magnificent shod his and his knights' mules with golden shoes, deliberately using nails which were too short. When the shoes fell off in the city's streets, it was the beggars of Constantinople who recovered the gold. At the emperor's state banquet of welcome, before seating themselves in oriental fashion on the floor at the low tables, Robert and his knights swept off their ornamental cloaks to use them as cushions, leaving them where they were at the end of the feast. Allaying the emperor's astonishment, the Norman duke, with that deep, booming laugh of his, told his Byzantine host:

'You don't believe, do you, that we Normans carry our chairs on our shoulders?' Again, the Magnificent had emphasized that the dukes of Normandy and his knights were matchless in their grandeur. Osbern listened with the remainder of the silent assembly, as Toustain painstakingly followed the duke's pilgrimage.

When Robert arrived finally at Jerusalem, he found a crowd of impoverished Christians from all corners of the world encamped in misery outside the walls. They were waiting hopelessly for the promised besants due to them after their months of arduous travelling. The Magnificent bellowed, 'In you go, all of you, where the besant won't be missed.' And seizing the gold from the overawed pasha, he doled out the golden besants himself.

The silence was complete as all in the chamber sensed that Toustain was approaching the climax. The knight was speaking slowly, carefully choosing his words:

'Our duke returned through Asia Minor,' he continued. 'On the third of July in the province of Bythinia, at meat in the city of Nicaea, he complained of violent pains in his stomach.' Toustain was staring at the archbishop as he said, barely audibly:

'Duke Robert rendered up his spirit two hours later, my lord.'

The insinuation was all too evident, but even the archbishop dared not utter his suspicions as the knight continued:

'Poison, sire.'

'Who?' the old prelate asked softly.

'The knight Mowin, my lord, we suspect. When asked to escort the holy relics which Duke Robert was bringing back from Jerusalem, Mowin refused the honour. He disappeared from our company, but the relics are following me, borne by faithful men.'

Archbishop Robert nodded. 'Where lies our duke?'

'I left immediately, my lord. They intended to dig his tomb on the crest of a hill overlooking the pilgrims' way. From there, they said, our duke would continue to protect the penitent on their journey to the holy city.'

They made way for the exhausted Toustain, as Archbishop Robert climbed to his feet.

'You have the boy here, Steward? Have him brought before us.' He turned to the silent assembly:

'Before Duke Robert departed on his pilgrimage, you all swore to accept his son, William, as his successor. Duke Robert is dead. When William enters you will all make obeisance. Before God and before me, you will kneel and pay homage to your new duke. The official crowning will take place here in Rouen as soon as possible, before I ride to Paris to present him to our monarch, Henry of France.'

Osbern was watching the splendid old man, bowed and motionless, when a commotion broke out at the far end of the chamber: like autumn leaves fluttering downwards, the assembly began falling to its knees. And there, solemn and upright, dignified even with only his seven and a half years, young William strode slowly between his kneeling liegemen.

'Turn, sire,' the prelate commanded, taking the boy's hand. 'Accept the homage of your lords.' Raising his hand in benediction, Archbishop Robert's words rang through the chamber:

'William, duke of Normandy,' he pronounced, his voice firm and strong. 'My lords, do ye swear allegiance to our liege lord?'

As the roar of assent faded in the council chamber, Osbern rose to his feet. His gaze was fixed on Ralph of Gacé who was already upright. A crooked smile creased his dark face, an ugly grimace unconcealed by his shock of black hair. 'He's smelt the sweet scent of success,' Osbern murmured to himself. 'Mowin was one of his knights.'

Leading the child-duke by the hand, the old archbishop walked slowly from the chamber. Alone in the silent hall, the Steward watched the dark clouds sweeping across the roof-tops of Normandy's great city. 'This day, the ninth of October 1035,' he muttered to himself, 'is one which will long be remembered.'

PART II

THE CRUCIBLE

3

MARCH MORNING, 1040

'Ominous, don't you think, Gilbert?' the Steward remarked, nodding towards the palace yard outside their private chamber. 'Hatred's brew continues even with the young.'

The thirty-three-year-old count of Brionne, Osbern's junior by fourteen years, did not reply immediately. He too was of the dead duke's generation, was Robert's step-brother and loyal friend. Since the Magnificent's death, Gilbert had been trying to hold the duchy together by supporting the other three principals in the ducal party: Alan III of Brittany, young William's chief tutor and a wise, valiant man determined to save Normandy from the present turmoil; Turchetil, the able schoolmaster who had so much influence on the unhappy young duke; and, of course, the Steward realized, he, Osbern, himself. But without the French king's support, even at the price of vassaldom and being considered part of France, Normandy would have fallen into total anarchy.

Outside in the courtyard, the next generation was playing at war, absorbed in their mock tilting tournament.

'It's like watching two armies,' Gilbert observed. 'The good and the evil.' He nodded towards the huddle of older onlookers on the far side of the yard. 'It's not difficult to guess who's taking the part of the devil,' he added.

Osbern followed Gilbert's gaze: Ralph of Gacé, at forty-five, middle-aged, his huge head smothered with a mass of frizzled hair, stood in the centre of his satellites, most of them twenty years his junior.

'Donkey Head's still biding his time, Gilbert,' Osbern said. 'Gacé's not entirely sure of his minions yet.'

'He's wasted little time since his father died. He *blackmailed* us with the threat of rebellion into voting Mauger for the vacant archbishopric.'

'An appointment which is as great a disaster for Normandy, as

39

Robert's was a blessing.'

Gilbert nodded: 'Only three years since the old Archbishop Robert died . . . how right he was with his warnings!' He strolled to the window to regard the youngsters. Two ponies were being led into the yard; the boys were clustering around the grooms, but William stood apart, as usual. Osbern watched also in silence, absorbed by his thoughts.

The failing prelate, Robert, and his three counsellors had kept the peace in the duchy for the two years after Duke Robert's death, until the archbishop's soul departed this life in 1037. That calm had been vital because it had allowed Alan to take charge of the young duke. Walter Fulbert was appointed as William's guard and Osbern noted the thirty-one-year-old Falaisian leaning against a pillar: his arms folded, the short sword always at his belt, he, too, was watching the cadets apeing their seniors, as they balanced the practice lances, while they made their choice . . .

Within a month of Archbishop Robert's death, the storm broke upon the duchy, the anarchy, as always, worst in the rich valleys of the Ouche country. By the beginning of 1039, family feuding had descended to hideous depths.

No one, bishops, abbots, *vicomtes* (who continued to do their duty despite the anarchy), nor the inner council, could prevent the barons from tearing at each other's throats. Like ravening beasts in their greed to enlarge their possessions, they hurriedly built their motte and timber castles to protect themselves from their predatory neighbours. The most powerful lords in the land hurled themselves upon each other in their bloody, vengeful family wars. In the Risle valley, Hugh Montfort, 'the Beard', and Walkelin of Ferrières pursued their hate to the death, taking their unfortunate followers with them. In mortal battle, they finally killed each other at Plasnes, north of Bernay. But, for sheer ferocity and determination to unseat the boy-duke, no family could rival the hideous feuding carried on by the Tosnys.

Osbern swore to himself: this upstart family had originated too close to Vaudreuil for his liking. It was Roger Tosny who forced his prisoners to share with him the broth of chopped-up flesh hacked from his captives. He had set himself up as champion to oust the boy-duke. 'It's a disgrace to Normandy,' he proclaimed, 'if amongst us we can find no better successor than the illegitimate son of a tanner's daughter. I'll never accept the little bastard as duke.' Whereupon he immediately laid waste to the estates of those neighbours who were loyal to the child-duke William, Roger of Beaumont being the worst sufferer.

Roger had inherited his father's qualities and held the honour of Beaumont on the Risle, close to Vieilles, five miles south of the river junction with the Charentonne. Goaded beyond endurance by Tosny's pillaging and insults, Roger decided to avenge the upstart Tosny and to finish the feud finally, one way or the other. Tosny, aware of the decision, quickly gathered his troops around him and rode full tilt into Beaumont's domain to carry back the booty before Beaumont could organize his defences.

Roger, waiting impatiently for his impetuous and over-confident enemy, watched Tosny's mounted column forming up for the charge. Beaumont drew up his knights and taunted the marauders to do battle across the rich pastures bordering the silent, swift-flowing river. Tosny leading, his sons, Herbert and Elinant, on either side of him, thundered at full tilt towards Roger's force. The shock of the charge, they said, echoed through the valley, the sparks from the clashing swords lighting up the twilight. By nightfall the ditches were running with blood: Tosny would trouble the old count no more. He and his sons lay dead on the field. Robert of Grandmesnil lay slaughtered, his belly ripped open. And already the widows were frenziedly seeking new husbands . . .

For a space Roger of Beaumont's honour was vindicated. The young Roger, Osbern judged, though only six years older than his boy-duke, was serving his lord well, because peace had temporarily returned to the upper Risle valley – and the Steward turned as Gilbert signalled him towards the window:

'Young William is sturdier than any of 'em, Osbern. He's just as excited as the others, I'll warrant, but he's not showing it. Bastard he may be, but, by God, he's in control of himself. See, Osbern . . .'

William was waiting at the side, watching the first contestants battling on their ponies. Fitz, Osbern's son, and Robert Herluin, William's half-brother, stood on one side of William; Walter Fulbert on the other side, while the duke's opponent, Guy of Burgundy, was clumsily adjusting his child's shield-straps. William was already dressed, calmly assessing the contestants while they charged across the courtyard, their padded lances wavering as they lunged at each other's shields.

'He's already a man, compared to the others,' Osbern murmured. 'And he's not yet into adolescence.'

'Bastardy is a cruel thing for a child to endure, Osbern. While Walter brought him up amongst the peasants, he was safe. But at court . . .'

'Boys are merciless animals, Gilbert, you know that. They've given him a rough time, most of them: they've scarred him deeply.'

'If it hadn't been for your Fitz and Roger Beaumont, the boy could never have survived the baiting.'

'Fulbert's helped too: he's taught the boy never to lose control – whatever the provocation.'

Gilbert was propping himself against the wall, the better to watch the scene. 'Twelve and a half years: his is an old head on young shoulders. He's already thinking for himself; he doesn't make friends easily, but he chooses carefully. Like you, Osbern, I fear for the future: William's got too many ambitious, ruthless enemies among his own generation. Look at them, there, lined up like vultures waiting their chance after we've gone . . .'

'Ralph of Gacé,' Osbern murmured while he watched the dark clouds of a summer storm gathering across the hills to the westward. He could hear the distant thunder. 'Gacé manipulates them like marionettes.'

'He should know better: he's twenty-five years older than your Fitz.'

The Steward nodded. In Ralph of Gacé lay the menace to the duchy, he was convinced. If it wasn't for himself, Alan and Gilbert, Gacé (who was already being mooted to take command of the duchy's official defence force) would lead a planned rebellion to take over the duchy: only Alan's inner council stood in Gacé's path. Osbern was sure Ralph was in direct league with the wily new archbishop, Mauger; his brother, William of Talou had also been promoted two years ago to become count of Arques, supposedly to strengthen the interests of the ducal dynasty. Arques stood apart, talking earnestly with Gacé.

'They're a sinister lot, the opposition,' Gilbert murmured, reading Osbern's thoughts. 'Look at Guy, there, only ten, but already hooked to Gacé. A bumptious brat: they've pumped him full of his claim to the dukedom.'

'And egged on by his half-brother: Foulques is plain evil. What's he up to?'

'No good, for sure,' Gilbert grinned. 'Bad blood always leaves a stain.'

Walter was glancing up at the swirling clouds, while the sun darkened. But this last bout, William against his cousin, Guy, was to be fought out in spite of the heavy drops of rain already falling. Young Odo, only eight, was running for shelter towards his brother, Robert

Herluin.

The Steward had never liked Foulques, the dark-skinned youth of sixteen who was holding Guy's pony. He was the bastard of the ambitious duke of Burgundy who, through his wife, Alice (Richard II's daughter and sister of Robert, the Magnificent) could press claim to the dukedom. Foulques wore a perpetual sneer on his swarthy face; always pushing his younger brother forward, he never missed an opportunity to belittle William, a reaction, perhaps, to Foulques' own bastardy. It was Foulques who had organized this morning's contest – and Osbern could not but wonder why.

The youngsters were hauling their ponies round at opposite ends of the courtyard. Foulques stood in the centre, his arms raised. The boy contestants faced each other, ponies tightly reined, hooves stamping the dirt upon which the raindrops were splashing. The lances levelled, the shields, held firmly, raised . . . Foulques' arm dropped – as a violet streak of lightning sizzled in the sky, directly above them.

Guy of Burgundy was sitting his barrel-shaped pony splendidly, his child's body seeming part of the animal, his toes curled round the stirrups. Holding his unwieldy shield in front of him, he craned forward, his lance levelled . . . and as his steed broke into a gallop, a thunder clap crashed immediately above the palace.

'What's up with William?' Gilbert snapped.

The burst of thunder had occurred at the instant when William was hauling round his mount to face his opponent. The terrified animal was bucking and showing the whites of its eyes, as the boy used all his skill to remain in the saddle. To regain control, William had dropped his lance; retaining his shield in his left hand, he was gathering up the reins with the other. Walter was running towards his master, his hands raised towards Guy as he tried to halt the ten-year-old's charge.

'My God!' Osbern shouted. 'Guy's not pulling off.' The Steward felt his heart miss a beat as he watched the child's lance levelled unerringly at the struggling William. And as both older men stood transfixed at the window, they watched Foulques snatching up William's fallen lance. Feigning to offer the weapon back to its owner, he swung round to entwine the shaft between the terrified pony's hind legs. As Guy's lance was about to strike, William's pony reared again. Half-slithering from the saddle, the boy glimpsed his danger. Flinging up his shield at the last moment, he parried the lance impact squarely; twisting his wrist, he neatly deflected the shock. As Guy hurtled past, his balance unsettled, William allowed his shield to continue its swing, its edge

43

tapping Guy's right leg from its stirrup. Both youngsters were now unsaddled and lying in the soggy slough of the yard. Gacé and his admirers were laughing; Fitz was gesticulating with Foulques; Walter and Robert Herluin were running after the bewildered ponies.

'They're going to finish it with their claws,' Gilbert grinned. 'Like leopard cubs.'

Guy was pummelling his elder cousin, his puny fists beating William's chest. Stooping like a bull-calf, William lunged towards Guy and flung him into the dirt. For an instant the duke stood above his cousin, gazing down at him. Then he turned and, squaring his shoulders, without a word he limped across the courtyard towards his pony. Ignoring the jeers from Guy and Foulques, and the laughter of Gacé and William of Arques, he snatched the reins from Walter and led his quietened animal towards the stables.

'By the Holy Rood,' Gilbert chuckled. 'There's little love lost between the cousins. Come, Osbern, let's to the day's business.' He put his arm about the Steward's shoulders and together they strolled across the chamber. Osbern spoke softly:

'No good can come of this. Did you see the hate burning in Guy's eyes, Gilbert?'

'. . . Only apeing his elders. Kid's stuff: they'll all forget the incident tomorrow.'

But Osbern was troubled. He sensed an unease, a presentiment deep inside himself which he could not explain. The thunder storm raging above them outside seemed an ominous portent for the future: he must discuss his fears with the inner council because evil stalked among the highest in the land, he was now certain. His instinct had not failed him yet.

4

RED IN TOOTH AND CLAW

The peace of this soft December evening, with the mists floating imperceptibly across the gleaming ribbon of the river Eure below, belied the fears gnawing inside Steward Osbern. So shocked was he by the recent events that he had sent his wife with Fitz to Rouen for safety. He had never known Emma before to behave the way she had: Fitz had forcibly to prise his mother from Osbern's arms, before settling her on her mare. She loved this Vaudreuil he was building for her. They'd often stood here at their private window, saying nothing, seduced by the tranquil view of the river Eure winding through the Seine valley. Far below the castle battlements, the silver river, curving around the northern edge of the Louviers beech forest, flowed to its union with mother Seine at Pont-de-l'Arche. The great river then curled westwards before snaking north again to the capital city of Normandy which the Romans had first developed: Rouen had become Europe's most important link with the world beyond the seas. But now, watching a pair of hawks wheeling in the valley below him, Osbern, for the first time in his life, felt his years. Emma and Fitz were celebrating his forty-eighth birthday when his squire had burst in with the news from Rouen . . . and this, only six weeks after Alan of Brittany, virtually Normandy's regent, had on 3 October dropped dead at Vimoutiers as he stood drinking with Roger I of Montgomery, one of Gacé's senior supporters.

The traitors were daily growing in arrogance in their attempt either to take control of the bastard duke, or by murdering him to remove for ever the shame they considered was Normandy's. The poisoning of Alan had been the catalyst which had polarized this mortal struggle for control of the boy-duke and the duchy. If they killed William there were many alternative claimants: Mauger or his brother, William of Arques; the ten-year-old Guy of Burgundy; or any one of the grasping, power-crazed counts: Montgomery; Gacé; the Giroie twins at

Montreuil-l'Argille; Thurstan of Montfort on the Risle; and, the worst, the Talvas, further south at Bellême.

The fundamental error which the inner council had made was the bargain they struck with Ralph of Gacé: he was commissioned to take charge of the ducal army, that paid, small élite force created to enforce law and order, on condition that fitz Osbern should succeed his father as Steward of Normandy should Osbern die. So, when Alan, the lynch-pin of authority, was murdered, Osbern had acted swiftly to forestall any further *coups* by the suspected traitor. The Steward had insisted that his friend, Gilbert of Brionne, should become William's new guardian; and that the good and loyal Turchetil be elevated to the post of chief tutor.

But the dreadful slaughter continued: Turchetil was not to escape, being hacked to pieces on 10 November; Gilbert then insisted that William should be shared between himself and Osbern, with Walter always present as the personal body-guard. The ducal party was on the defensive, withdrawing inwards upon itself at Rouen and Vaudreuil, while the traitors closed in. Even then, Gilbert had considered himself and Osbern safe, so loyally were they being supported by the *vicomtes* who were desperately trying to maintain order . . .

'I can't believe it,' Osbern murmured to himself, alone now with William and Walter in the fastness of his castle which was guarded by his own trusted troops. 'I still can't believe it.' And as he watched the pink glow of sunset tinting the fleecy clouds drifting in from the west, he realized for the first time that he had lost the savour of living.

It was only eight days since Emma and he had dined with Gilbert in the palace at Rouen, the day before Gilbert returned to his castle at Brionne to prepare for Christmas . . . and only fourteen days after the foul murder of the mild, defenceless Turchetil. Gilbert had ridden over to Echauffray to meet his friend Jocelyn of Pont Herchenfret. The objective of the meeting was still unclear, but it seemed that one of the Giroie twins (the notorious Robert who had fallen in love with Thurstan's daughter when dining at Montfort) was accusing Gilbert and Jocelyn of malpractices in the affairs of the *comté*. The other twin, Foulques Giroie, had sided with Gilbert, and the combined meeting took place at Echauffray bridge, Foulques being late for the rendez-vous. Tricked thus to the assignation, without more ado the un-suspecting Gilbert was slaughtered by Robert Giroie and, when Foulques arrived on the scene, Robert felled his brother also.

Osbern still did not know whether Jocelyn had betrayed his friend,

Gilbert, but one fact was certain; the knight of Pont Herchenfret was one of Gacé's men . . . The waters of the Charentonne beneath the bridge ran dark with blood and the crime of Echauffray would never be forgotten . . . and bleak despair began to suffocate the Steward as in his solitude he watched his valley being shrouded slowly by the autumn mist. When, dear God, would this violence cease? How could he, the last survivor of the inner council, preserve much longer the existence of this pathetic little bastard, the boy-duke William, against the plottings of these hard-faced, evil men?

1035 had been a tragic year for Normandy and not only because of the Magnificent's death in July: four months later, the great Canute, king of England, Denmark and Norway, had also rendered up his soul. He left his sea-based empire to the son given to him by Emma: Harthacanute who was in Denmark when his father died. Taking advantage of Harthacanute's absence, his half-brother, Harold 'Hare-foot', rallied enough support to become joint-king of England. The widowed Queen Emma and the most powerful influence in England, Godwine, earl of Wessex, bitterly opposed the arrangement. The old English party, the anti-Scandinavian faction, began negotiations with the claimants of direct lineage to the throne: Edward and Alfred, the athelings who had been exiled in Normandy for so long.

Long befriended by Robert, particularly after his repudiation of Estrith, the athelings had been supported by the Norman dukes in this game of balance-of-power, while the Scandinavian empire had prospered so dramatically and dangerously. The issue of the English succession had been kept simmering, and William had often enjoyed the company of his cousins, Edward and Alfred, when they were present at his father's court.

Then, in Normandy in 1036, Alfred, prompted by the pro-English, anti-Godwine, anti-Danish faction, chose to cross the Channel to visit his mother – a highly sensitive decision and one which could be assumed as an attempt to rally support for an *English* solution to Canute's succession.

Godwine, earl of Wessex, a man of humble origin, and a former Sussex thegn, had trampled his way to advancement: with his wife, Gytha, and sons, Harold, Sweyn, Gyrth and Leofwine, his was the most influential family in England. Scenting the source of power, he soon made allegiance with Harold Harefoot: Alfred's visit to Emma could have been construed as a direct challenge, not only to Harefoot, but also to the house of Wessex – and the crime which followed, Osbern regretfully acknowledged, surpassed in horror even those now being perpetrated in Normandy.

Alfred and his retinue landed at Dover. On the road to join his mother, his company was halted by a force commanded by the earl of Wessex. After massacring the atheling's men, Godwine himself handed Alfred over to a section of Harold Harefoot's soldiers. Returning to Dover, they forced the atheling back on board a ship in the harbour; there, with horrible callousness, the conspirators gouged out his eyes before sailing with him through the Downs and up to the east coast. The wretched Alfred was taken secretly to Ely where mercifully he died from his dreadful mutilation. The crime had shocked all Europe, and now, even four years afterwards, the Norman support was strong for Edward, the surviving atheling who was still being succoured in the duchy.

Osbern was sick of it all, as he watched the sun dipping below the forest to set its blood-red seal upon another day, this eighteenth of December 1040, so close to the anniversary of the birth of the Prince of Peace . . . He sighed again bitterly; Harefoot having died suddenly this June, the earl of Wessex, it seemed, had once again switched horses and was now supporting the return of Harthacanute to claim the throne of the English. Steward Osbern turned from the beauty of the soft twilight, disgusted by the sickening machinations in the lust for power. He entered his chamber, barely noticing the fire lit by his servants flickering in the fire-place. He felt nauseated, needed no food tonight. The others would have already eaten. He crossed to the doorway and jerked the bell-cord. He'd check with his squire that the guards were set, then make for his bed-chamber. Fulbert would not object to an early night: he could bring William straight to bed and they could all get some rest.

'What hour, sire, in the morning?'

Walter Fulbert, standing in the doorway to the small annexe, found nothing untoward in being present while the Steward prepared for bed. For years, he had sometimes shared the same bed and often the same room with the boy-duke. But it was only during the last few weeks since Gilbert was murdered, that Steward Osbern insisted upon William always sleeping in the same bed-chamber – and that the duke's bodyguard should become the boy's shadow, never leaving him. So, even when Lady Emma shared her bed with her lord, Walter had become accustomed during this past month to sleeping in the adjoining annexe. And when the Lady Emma was absent, the Steward had often permitted Walter to pass these minutes before sleep to discuss their shared charge. William was the hope for the duchy's survival; dead, Normandy would return to the bestial anarchy of the dark ages. And watching the quiet reserved boy undressing for bed, Walter realized how swiftly the years were slipping past.

In a year or so William would be entering the difficult years of adolescence. Standing stripped there, the boy was already balanced upon the threshold of puberty. His long limbs made him tall for his age (he was already up to Walter's shoulders), but it was the breadth of his shoulders that differentiated him from his companions. He was beginning to fill out, but his voice had not yet broken. Walter smiled wistfully: in spite of the advantages of dukedom, paradoxically no child could have suffered such an appalling childhood, and the sooner William could reach manhood and be able to defend himself, the better for his chances of survival – and for peace in Normandy.

Walter shuddered as the memories of these terrible years flashed through his mind: that horrible night in the serf's cottage when a band of the opposition's assassins, their daggers drawn, were combing the village for their prey. It was only the resourcefulness – yes, and the courage – of the bondmen as they passed him from hovel to hovel that had saved William then – and so it had continued throughout these long years since his father's death . . .

'You're shivering, Fulbert,' Osbern's deep voice boomed from beneath the woollen shift into which he was slipping. 'Better take another blanket.' The grizzled head emerged, a sardonic smile on the kindly, but severe features. 'Yes, I'm determined to have a good night – undressing for once. I'm weary of it all, Walter: my brain's tired and I need rest. Call us at six o'clock.' He flicked back the coverlet and climbed into his side of the bed, but not before propping his scabbarded sword at the head. 'Ho, Will,' he chided, 'so you're waiting for me to warm up the bed first, are you, lad?'

'No story tonight, sir?' the child asked as he hopped into his side. 'Tell me of Roland again, *please* . . .' he wheedled, his blue eyes fixed on his new protector.

'I'm tired,' Osbern replied firmly. 'Tomorrow, I promise.' The grey head nodded towards the candles. 'Douse the lights, please.'

The lights in the iron sockets were made from the pith of rushes soaked in grease from the kitchens and as Walter doused the final one on the wall-bracket opposite the bed, he caught sight of the small russet head on the pillow beside the Steward. The bright eyes held Walter's for a moment, and as the spluttering flame died, the rancid fumes invaded the chamber.

'Good night, my lord. Sleep well, Master William.'

It was cold in the annexe, but the faint after-glow of the sunset permeated the bare chamber through the slit embrasure in the tower. Walter stood for a moment, peering through it to the darkened castle courtyard below. He could distinguish the loom of the battlements curving towards the keep and, just visible, the postern gate close to the base of the tower down which the small stone stairway from this annexe spiralled. Across the yard on the far side, he could make out the outline of the service buildings, the bakery, the forge, the chapel and, in the shadows across the gleaming water of the moat, the near-end of the stables.

Unbuckling his scabbard, he laid his short sword on the rushes alongside the right-hand side of his couch. Twice he withdrew the blade half-way, snicked it back fully into the scabbard, then, satisfied, but without removing his deerskin shoes, he dropped to the couch. He flung the woollen coverlet across him and lay still on his back, his eyes open, staring upwards into the darkness as his right hand closed habitually around the dagger beneath his jerkin. The roughness of the sharkskin handle, to provide a firm grip when slippery with blood, always gave him comforting reassurance . . .

His mind was restless tonight, troubled by his terrifying responsibilities. Sleep would elude him, he knew, until exhaustion finally overcame his tired brain – but through the open archway into the Steward's chamber, slept the boy for whom he would give his own life to protect. And, as each night passed, Walter offered up a prayer of thankfulness that another day was safely accomplished. But, how many more, dear God?

Judging by the rumours in the servants' hall this night where they had supped and drunk well, the duchy was riven with dissent: Lord Ralph of Gacé was gathering the ducal troops to take over Rouen and establish his own rule; Thurstan of Montfort would support him; Talvas of Bellême was marching north to join Gacé; vengeance for Lord Gilbert's death was being mounted by his sons from Brionne, but Gacé intended handing over the castle to that jackanapes, the little horror, Guy of Burgundy. Rumour, rumour – but the effects were tearing Normandy apart – and, if the traitors *did* succeed in snuffing the life of this unhappy boy sleeping in the next room, what was there for himself, Walter? He turned onto his left side, his eyes riveted upon the faint light from the bowmen's embrasure.

He was thirty-two now and must start thinking of himself: after his abortive wooing of Miriel, his mind had atrophied; he'd been content only with the present, serving the Steward as best he could. He should have realized that Miriel's mother would never accept him as suitable for her daughter's hand. He sighed bitterly, resentful at the sacrifices he'd made to win Miriel; but even the purchase last year of his own half-breed stallion had failed to shift her haughty mother . . . he'd never been back to Louviers, though it was only on the far side of the forest – Miriel had probably married one of her own sort by now, anyway.

Walter cursed softly in the darkness of his chamber, then heard the hooting of an owl from somewhere below the battlements; he liked its weird note, so solitary, floating across the valley, a sad cry in tune with his own loneliness. He felt disgusted with himself, wallowing in self-pity. It was time he got in touch again with his boyhood friend from Falaise days: Gaston had left home and found work among the fishermen on the Nacre coast. He was now part-owner of a yard servicing the fishing boats working out of the Touques estuary at Trouville – and the black mood began lifting from Walter's anxious brain, as his thoughts jostled into the future. As soon as he could (he might even take William with him to escape the maelstrom here) he'd work his passage in a boat sailing down the Seine from Rouen; he'd leave her at Honfleur and walk to Trouville . . . he then felt his senses blurring as drowsiness overcame him. The clean sea air would be good after all this miasma of horror . . .

Through his shallow sleep, Walter heard it, the distant hullaballoo of a hound barking somewhere outside the walls – irritating, for he'd never sleep again this night. And each time that the dog ceased, as Walter turned again on his side, the monotonous barking began again, on and on, echoing down the valley. Then, as Walter turned in desperation to lie on his back, there was a high-pitched yelp of terror. Silence, total stillness from the valley . . .

Walter crossed his arms behind his head and holding his breath, listened with all his concentration, his nerves taut, his senses alert.

Nothing . . . it was pitch-black outside now, the dark clouds masking the night sky, so that not even the reflected starlight showed in the slit of the embrasure. But what had aroused the dog, caused the yelp of terror? Strange . . . and then he heard it, the faint slam of a door across the courtyard. And suddenly Walter's nerves tingled, his instincts recognizing the scent of danger . . . slipping from the couch, he buckled on his belt, adjusted the scabbard and tip-toed to the embrasure.

He stared through the slit, his heart hammering against his ribs: he could almost feel the opaque blackness. His imagination, with all these recent happenings, was playing him up . . . the Steward would not thank him for waking him unnecessarily. He turned about and was unbuckling his sword-belt when he stopped half-way to the couch: a faint sound, like whispering, from the annexe stairway? Again, silence – but that faint pattering? And suddenly he was certain that his ears were not deceiving him.

'My lord . . .' he called softly. 'Wake, sire!' He stole softly towards the open archway, feeling his way through the darkness. He was about to call again when he froze, not certain of his senses. Was that dark rectangle which was the door to the bed-chamber growing lighter . . .? And as he tip-toed forwards, he realized suddenly that the chamber was filling with silent, crouching figures, their skin shoes whispering on the soft carpet as they crept towards the bed. A torch flared from outside the chamber. A group of cloaked men loomed about the far side of the bed, one of them crouching above the struggling figure beneath the coverlet.

The Steward was gurgling horribly as the strangler wrenched tight the knot. A tall, cloaked knight was raising his arm and striking again and again, plunging his poniard into the twitching bundle. The red blade glistened from the ghostly light and in that instant Walter recognized the twisted, grotesque face of William of Montgomery, the knight who had visited Vaudreuil last week.

'Strike, strike, you varlets!' the monster hissed, his arm not wearying of the butchery.

And then, from the dark shadows beneath the bed, Walter spied the small shape of the boy rolling from the coverlets, slithering out of sight towards the annexe. Crouching low, Walter slid towards him and, with all his strength, scooped him into his arms. He reached the annexe as they spotted him.

'The Bastard - kill the Bastard!' roared Montgomery. The shadowy assassins surged towards the small chamber, as Walter dropped the boy on to the upper steps of the spiral stairway.

'For your life, Master,' Walter hissed. 'Wait for me at the bottom,' and with slimy, slippery hands he jammed the door tight behind him, throwing the wooden beam across on the outside. Taking the steps two at a time, floundering down the narrow spiral, he reached the courtyard as he heard them battering upon the door above. William was cowering in the shadow of the wall, ugly dark stains disfiguring his night-shirt.

'*Murder! Foul murder!*' Walter yelled across the courtyard. 'Wake the guard!' He grabbed the terrified boy's arm and pushed him ahead towards the postern gate. As he reached it, three figures ran towards him; by the faint light shining from the tower, Walter saw the gleaming blades.

'Halt!'

And in that second, he recognized the voice as belonging to the Steward's provost, the doughty Bjoern.

'Fulbert, sir,' Walter gasped, wiping the wet blood on his hands across his jerkin. 'The duke's here, with me.'

'Flee, then, Walter,' Bjoern bellowed. 'We'll hold the varlets to give you time.' He nodded at the two men racing towards the main stairway.

'*On, master – to the postern . . .*'

And when they reached the gate where the drawbridge was already down, the boy fell headlong across the horizontal body of a man. The whites of the keeper's eyes stared sightless and the dark slash across his throat caused the boy to scream in the night.

'Shush, master! Run, run for your life.'

And overtaking the child, Walter grabbed him by the hand. 'To the forest, boy,' he panted. 'Run as you've never run before.'

Crouching and running by turns, stumbling down the rocky pathway and towards the dark mass of trees, Walter and his protégé finally reached the sanctuary of the silent forest.

'We'll cross to the other side,' Walter panted. 'We'll lie up for a bit, then make Louviers at dawn.'

Suddenly the dam burst: dry sobbing rasped William's shaking body and, as they collapsed into the hollow of a rotting beech stump, Walter Fulbert gently encircled him with his arms:

'You've the courage of a king, young master,' he murmured. 'The courage of a king. Rest, boy, awhile. I've friends in Louviers. They'll take care of us.'

The boy's head, its hair clotted with dried blood, slumped across his lap. The duke was suddenly asleep.

5

HUMILIATION AT TILLIÈRES
15 MAY 1043

Separated from the French king and his entourage, the new count of
Breteuil and lord of Vaudreuil castle, William fitz Osbern, stood apart
with the young duke, silently watching the culmination of this week's
dramatic events. From this field in the stillness of the warm May
evening, he could hear the creaking of the mechanism and the regular
clanking of the chains, as the massive drawbridge of Tillières castle
slowly began to lower.

'So it's come to this, William,' fitz Osbern said quietly. 'Norman
against Norman. I wish I had no part in it.' He felt sick inside himself
as he watched the French nobles disdainfully shoving back their
helmets to lean nonchalantly on the handles of their sheathed
swords.

'You're one of those in charge of our forces,' the young duke said,
his voice cracking. 'You must share the shame with me,
Fitz.'

Fitz Osbern, nine years older than his young duke who was
approaching his fifteenth birthday, grimaced sourly. Today's humiliation would fester in the duchy and he wished that he could rid himself
of part of the responsibility; but Ralph of Gacé, in command of the
ducal army, had remained in Rouen, preferring to delegate to Fitz and
Roger of Beaumont the loyal Norman contribution for the Tillières
débâcle. So here they were, supporting Henry I and his powerful
marauding force outside the walls of Tillières, this impregnable stone
castle which Thurstan Goz had perfected and then appropriated for
himself during the years of anarchy following the murder of Fitz's
father. The river Avre curled around the town to make the fortress
unassailable, this castle which since 1013 had been garrisoned by the

Normans to resist any invasion from the Chartres plain and the French monarchs.

'You can understand King Henry's anxieties,' Fitz said, speaking his thoughts aloud. 'Especially with today's anarchy inside our Normandy. Tillières is the key for the safety of his kingdom.'

'He needn't have been so brutal with his demands,' William said, slapping his sword scabbard. 'I didn't ask for his help. Surely, we can settle Thurstan on our own, Fitz?'

Osbern smiled at the youth whose blue eyes were smouldering with resentment. It seemed difficult to believe that only three years ago, the boy had stumbled into Rouen, blood-soaked and mud-spattered under the protection of the doughty Walter Fulbert. After two years in hiding, and always shielded by Walter from the daggers of William's would-be assassins, fitz Osbern and his companions had decided to re-establish the young duke. And now William was approaching manhood, his voice beginning to crack, a light down sprouting above his wide upper lip. He was filling out rapidly and already topping Fitz's height, his russet head on a level with the Steward's. And, Fitz realized, the young warrior was disappointed that he would, not, after all, be scenting battle. William had thrown his helmet (the cne they'd hammered especially for him, which was already large enough to fit the head of a full-grown knight) to the turf in disgust; he was peeling off his gloves, but his gaze was never far from his destrier which now would not be needed.

The rapid erection of Henry's catapults and siege platforms had polarized the choice which Henry was offering to the defenders who, if they had not been led by the doughty Crispin, would have surrendered days ago. But Gilbert Crispin was as loyal a sub-tenant to his murdered master, Gilbert of Brionne, as could be found. He had repeatedly refused to cede the castle to the investing French army. Ignoring the siege engines of the massed French troops, he had insisted that he and his loyal garrison would hold Tillières Castle to the death for his young duke. Gacé had vindictively filled the vacancy at Brionne by giving the honour and the key town of Vernon on the Seine to his ambitious and bumptious protégé, Guy of Burgundy. The thirteen-year-old Guy could now style himself count of Brionne, so even more salt had been rubbed into Gilbert Crispin's wounds. The brave Crispin's loyalty had proved a shameful embarrassment to the knights of the young duke and Fitz. No, neither Fitz nor Duke William could fairly blame the king of France . . .

After the murders of 1040, Ralph of Gacé, using the power he enjoyed as chief of the ducal army, immediately took control of the boy-duke. But William, loathing his forty-nine-year-old cousin, turned vehemently towards his protector who had for so long grown up with him almost as an older brother: Fitz, through his qualities of good-humour and natural leadership, had become at once the focus around which the supporters of the duke had rallied, a ducal party which served as the one counter-check against the rapacious Gacé. With Beaumont and many of the younger counts gathering round fitz Osbern, Gacé dared not jump again – not yet. Fitz had not resorted to vengeance against his father's murderers: the provost of Vaudreuil, Bjoern, outraged by the killing of his lord, had organized an execution squad for Montgomery. In secret, Bjoern and his men relentlessly tracked down the assassins and slaughtered them in Montgomery's own domain. An uneasy truce now existed between Gacé and Fitz, each being aware of the other's power. Fitz could find no proof against Gacé for the murders; Gacé dared not eliminate Fitz. And now Gacé, manipulating the adolescent duke, was virtually regent of Normandy – what need therefore to kill the bastard duke?

Both factions shared a common interest for a return to the rule of law in the duchy – as did also King Henry of France. After Tosny's rebellion, and a revolt led by Bishop Hugh of Bayeux at Ivry, it was the peasants' up-rising at Sées which had been the final straw for Henry: the cathedral town of Sées neighboured the Exmes district which, close also to Talvas of Bellême, was Thurstan Goz's territory. In the Sées region, the three brothers of the Sorreng family and their bandits ran berserk, pillaging, burning, looting and raping the terrified women-folk. After Sées cathedral was set ablaze, the priests under their bishop organized the people to defend themselves because of the failure of the *vicomte*, Thurstan Goz's deputy, to enforce order.

The infuriated peasants took the law into their own hands. A serf spied Richard Sorreng with a wench in a hut by a lake: driven out by pitch-forks, Sorreng's skull was split wide by a hatchet as he fled through the door. His brother, Robert, scuttling off with plunder, was hacked to pieces; Avesgot Sorreng, the last of the brothers, was skewered by an arrow whilst setting a house ablaze. And as the violence in the duchy closed in upon the duke, King Henry, for several reasons, decided that the time for action had arrived.

The growing anarchy in the Norman province neighbouring his French border was bound to threaten France if allowed to continue.

William's father had saved Henry's throne in 1030, so the French monarch, now twenty-three, was under an obligation to Robert's bastard son. The king felt responsible also for William's safety, because Henry had approved William as Robert the Magnificent's successor: Robert and William, both having paid homage at Paris, were therefore vassals and entitled to protection. Henry had even knighted the young duke at Poissy and promised Robert to become William's honorary tutor and guardian. The safety, status and prestige of the young bastard *had* to be preserved, because it was obvious that a deliberate and co-ordinated campaign was mounting for the annihilation of the duke.

Now that Alan III was dead, Brittany continued to be a potential threat from the west; and Baldwin V of Flanders, a close ally of the German emperor's, could not be trusted to remain loyal to France. Finally, the misery of the peasants at Sées had convinced Henry that he had no other option but to go to the aid of his young vassal.

Fitz Osbern turned as William read his thoughts:

'King Henry may have good reason, Fitz,' the youth muttered angrily. 'But I detest his arrogance.' The boy was facing the cluster of Frenchmen guffawing amongst themselves outside the king's tent. 'Look at them, Fitz, mocking us. They've good reason.'

'Henry's right, Will. He told you that you'd either have to vacate Tillières castle and leave it alone for four years or he'd demolish it himself.' Fitz smiled ruefully. 'But neither you nor Henry reckoned on Gilbert Crispin's loyalty.'

William said softly:

'It is I who have betrayed *him*. He's loyal and true: he could not believe we wanted him to hand over the castle.'

Noting the boy's scowl and the determined jaw, Fitz did not pursue the argument. At the joint parley with William and the French, Crispin had besought the emissaries with his impassioned words:

'I did not know, sire,' he raved angrily, his eyes fixed on William, 'that you would ever *command* me to surrender your castle to the enemy. You have come here armed, not to defend your castle but to persuade me to render it to these Frenchmen. I can see you're miserable about this, my lord: you're being tricked and you will rue this dreadful day. I can never give up this castle which you have entrusted to me. I'd prefer to be burnt or hang rather than surrender, so do you still insist, my duke?'

And Fitz recalled the dejection in the bewildered youngster's face as his barons pressed about him, persuading him to adhere to the shameful decision.

'If Sir Gilbert yields,' Beaumont added, 'he can leave the castle honourably. And the castle will not be destroyed when King Henry gives up the siege.' Beaumont turned on Crispin:

'It's your duke's command, noble knight.'

All eyes upon him, William had nodded dejectedly. 'Cede the castle, Sir Crispin. King Henry has promised not to attack if you hand it over intact . . . That is my wish and my command.'

The ageing knight, his eyes boring through the young duke, flung down his sword. 'I am your liege, sire, and I have no right therefore to hold your castle against your wishes.' And as he stomped from the silent gathering, he shouted furiously, 'I warn you, sire. The French are tricking you; Henry will never keep his word.'

Out here in the fields, the evening itself seemed to be holding its breath. The duke's troops were subdued, lounging on the grass, muttering amongst themselves; only the French were showing any enthusiasm for this business.

'Here they come, Fitz,' William blurted. 'Look at Sir Crispin: he's as proud as ever.' At the head of his men, the old knight sat erect in his saddle, his head held defiantly, his soldiers scurrying behind his charger as they apprehensively watched the French troops on the other side of the moat.

'Henry must keep his word,' Fitz muttered. 'He's *promised* peace, provided the castle is left empty and allowed to crumble. You put our case well, William. Henry respects you.'

'I don't trust him,' William croaked. 'I'll be glad to see him on his way back to Paris.'

'You don't like your king, do you, Will?' Fitz laughed. 'He fights well but he's no politician.' Fitz respected Henry who, at twenty-two, was three years his junior: he carried his crown with dignity. The Capet house of France ruled by divine right, his court acknowledging automatically his royal superiority in all that he did. It was a pity that the stubborn barons of Norse stock were not of the same mould, fitz Osbern thought, though their Viking traditions *were* holding the duchy together at this moment, the *vicomtes* still loyally attempting to maintain order.

Most of them regretted that the abbot of St-Vanne's plea to introduce the Truce of God had finally been rejected last year by the rebellious barons: to vow not to wage war from Friday to Sunday and on the Church's holy days, as most of Christian Europe had done, would curtail the aggrandizement of their power and their estates. Fitz Osbern knew Abbot Richard for a persistent cleric: his abbey at St-Vanne was one of the few untainted centres of learning of the Church. Of the others, only Fécamp still held out against the degeneration represented by Archbishop Mauger, his rapacious bishops and illiterate clerks. The evil of simony was rife: the simple faithful were being forced to pay even for absolution. 'Bishops', proposed by the greedy barons seeking their own preferment, were buying their mitres and cardinals' hats. The other unsullied community was the new monastery which had finally been established at Le Bec in the Risle valley, an oasis of holiness founded by the saintly knight Hellouin which was attracting the most brilliant scholars. Last year, a new teacher from northern Italy, who had recently been teaching in Avranches, a man called Lanfranc, entered the community of Le Bec in his search for serenity and sanctity: a genius, by all accounts, Lanfranc was attracting good men from all over Europe . . .

In July of that same year, 1042, the English had invited another pious man to be their king. On the death of Harthacanute, Edward, the atheling, had been invited from exile in Normandy to take the throne of England. Not only was Edward the strongest claimant through his famous Saxon ancestor Alfred the Great, but because of his long exile in Normandy, his leanings tended towards the duchy which for so long had befriended him.

Ralph of Gacé had decreed that every strong notable was needed in the duchy to quell this rebellion, so no great Norman had been able to accept the invitation to witness Edward's crowning on Easter Day, less than two months ago. A fortuitous coronation, Fitz ruminated, because at one stroke the threat from across the Channel had been removed at the moment when the divided duchy was at its weakest – and Fitz was dragged back to reality by the cry from William who was tugging at his arm:

'What are the Frenchmen up to, Fitz?'

The last of Crispin's escort was filing disconsolately across the moat, when a yell of triumph rang out from the knights grouped about the French monarch's pavilion. Leaping into their saddles, they were spurring their horses towards the drawbridge, their battle-cries urging on their troops to follow. The foot-soldiers were running after them and then Fitz saw the first of their torches flickering in the failing light. The Steward, with the white-faced boy at his side, watched helplessly as the attackers streamed across the moat to disappear into the silent castle above which the red banner of Normandy with its golden leopards still fluttered.

'My God,' fitz Osbern breathed softly, 'look at that, William, in the tower . . .'

From the lower slits in the wall, orange flames flickered, leaping upwards until a crimson glow began lighting up the interior. Smoke billowed upwards, as above the crackling of the fire, the shouts of the pillagers echoed across the moat.

'Treachery,' William shouted as he began running towards the tall figure standing motionless outside the royal tent. 'The vile traitor!' Fitz Osbern hurried after his duke, caught up with him as William halted in front of Henry. The boy's face was twisted with rage as he screamed abuse at the king.

Henry, a condescending smile twitching at the corners of his mouth, stood motionless watching the sacking of the castle.

'Take the boy away, Steward,' the king shouted above the roar of the flames. 'The castle will menace France no more: let this be a lesson to all my subjects in my province of Normandy.'

'Come, William,' Fitz called angrily. 'Put not your trust in kings.' And as he led the duke away, the boy's face ashen with humiliation, William yelled:

'My Normandy pays homage to France, sire. Let Tillières alone, as you have promised. Return to Paris and let my duchy live at peace.'

'Learn first to rule, boy,' Henry shouted, his gloved hands on his hips. 'Leave Tillières undefended or I shall return. Crush rebellion and I'll trouble you no more.' Contemptuously dismissing his vassal duke, Henry turned towards the tall figure of his seneschal:

'Dismantle the siege engines,' he commanded, 'and recall the troops. Strike camp, for tomorrow I return to Poissy.' He called after William:

'I need your Normans no longer, young duke,' he yelled above the roaring of the inferno. 'Return and restore order in your duchy.'

Controlling the rage boiling inside himself, Fitz led William away. The young duke had been spoiling for the fight, to win his spurs. But all he had tasted was bitter humiliation – and whatever the duke suffered, the duchy would suffer sevenfold . . .

Steward Osbern was loath to replace his forged helmet: the rivets aggravated his itching scalp, for it was one of those airless July evenings, sultry with the threat of thunder down here in the valley at the foot of Falaise castle. His head was sweating beneath the chain links of the headpiece completing the expensive coat of mail reaching below his knees. The nose-guard was also hindering his vision. And because he was a principal actor in this crucial struggle for control of the young duke – and therefore of Normandy – he, fitz Osbern, needed every scrap of information, required to hear every nuance, every inflexion in the traitor *vicomte's* voice, *if* Thurstan Goz was going to respond to this last chance being offered him by the marshal of the duchy's army: there was no ambiguity in Gacé's final ultimatum . . . and peering up again at the walls looming above him, Fitz replaced his helmet.

The loyal Normans had not recovered from the trickery of Tillières and never again would Henry I of France be trusted. There were French mercenaries behind those embrasures and bowmen's arrows from such a height pierced the toughest of leather shields. William also was a conspicuous target where he stood alongside Ralph of Gacé, probably just out of range but within a few paces of that overhang provided by the granite outcrop. Fitz Osbern could see movement behind the castellated tops of the corner tower: there were crossbow-men among the Frenchmen and a bolt loosed from a height of at least seventy metres could kill even a helmeted man.

This impregnable castle, the new stonework having been started by William's grandfather and almost completed by his father, Robert, not only commanded the heart of the Hiémois, but to loyal Normans represented the symbol of ducal power. The bastard Duke William was sired and born here, the reason, the Steward supposed, why the traitor *vicomte* of the Exmes, Thurstan Goz, had decided to launch his new rebellion from this focal point, so close also to Ralph's domains at Gacé . . . and a sardonic smile worked at the corners of fitz Osbern's firm mouth as he watched Gacé's grotesque figure crawling on to the spur of rock where he was trying to keep his balance. Cupping his hands to the hole in the centre of the black fuzz encompassing his grotesque head, Gacé bellowed upwards to the defenders gathered on the smaller, square tower at the western extremity of Falaise castle:

'Fetch . . . your . . . lord,' he roared, his words reverberating among the rocks to echo across the valley. He waited for the cawing of a disturbed bevy of rooks to subside, then went on:

'Duke William seeks to parley with Thurstan Goz before his loyal troops assault and retake his castle.'

Derisory jeers floated downwards, but Fitz spied several figures disappearing behind the battlements. Moments later, Thurstan's personal standard broke from the truck of the pole reaching high above the tower. The flag fluttered defiantly in the sultry evening breeze as Goz appeared fully clad in his chain-mail. He stood alone, tall and impressive, his unsheathed sword pointing downwards. His deep voice boomed from the battlements:

'Tell him to get back to his books!' he roared. 'I'll never bend the knee to the feeble little bastard.'

A roar of defiance echoed from the castle walls, as Gacé pushed William forwards. Laying his mailed fist on the boy's shoulder, Ralph bellowed:

'Pay homage to your duke, Thurstan Goz. This is your last chance. Lower your standard.'

Fitz shared the chagrin which the fifteen-year-old boy must be suffering. After the humiliation of Tillières, Henry had again gone back on his word: not only was he rebuilding the stronghold of Tillières and garrisoning it with French troops, but he had returned into the Hiémois as far as Argentan which he sacked before finally returning to Paris. And now, the final insult, the citadel of William's birthplace was occupied by a traitor backed by the French king: Goz was declaring publicly that he would supplant the duke and take over the duchy. Thurstan was yelling again from the battlements:

'And if I refuse to pay homage,' the warrior roared, 'what can the bastard do? This is my castle now. I have many good Normans here with me who'll govern the duchy with pride and honesty – we don't surrender our fortresses like you did at Tillières. I can hold out here for ever: the French king will return if I need him. What *can* you do, Gacé, heh?'

But it was the boy who shouted back, his voice cracking with the passion he was feeling, all eyes upon him:

'You'll not leave Falaise alive, Thurstan Goz. I'll kill you for the traitor you are. You'll suffer shameful execution, if you don't surrender.'

Fitz could see the huge man's body shaking with mirth:

'Come and get me, boy! Then how will you kill me, eh?'

Gacé was trying to push William from the rock but the boy, having none of it, was cupping his hands to his mouth:

'I'll split you wide, traitor Goz. My horses will see to it.'

Fitz watched William, the young face ugly with hate. There was no doubting his intention to order such a repugnant execution, a death reserved for only the most shameful of crimes – and even the hardened Steward felt sickened. Only once had he witnessed such an execution:

an arm and leg of the condemned man were tied to a horse on one side, the other arm and leg to a second animal. And when the executioners spurred their steeds, the wretch's body was torn asunder by the galloping horses. Even Goz's laughter ceased before he roared his reply:

'Come and get me then, you bastard!' Goz nodded to one of his knights and the standard jerked repeatedly to the top of the pole. A hail of stones rained down and suddenly, as Gacé pushed William from the spur, a shower of arrows whistled downwards. Fitz stepped back, holding his shield above him, as a goose-feathered, steel-tipped arrow thudded at his feet. From behind the granite outcrop, Gacé raised his sword, stretched wide his arms. Fitz Osbern heard the troops' roar of support as in the failing light they moved into their positions for the assault.

Fitz Osbern stood apart from the other knights, the pommel of his sword taking the weight of his crossed arms. At twenty-five, he was, he supposed, reaching the zenith of his prowess on the battlefield. But he was exhausted, as much from the lack of sleep as from the fighting, a fierce struggle which had continued throughout the whole of yesterday, the longest day in the year, 21 June 1043 – and two days after William's birthday. And now, at four o'clock on this early dawn of the 22nd, with the orange sun creeping up behind the jagged outline of the roof-tops in the town, an unearthly silence breathed upon the carnage both within and without the castle walls. With their knights grouped about them, William and Gacé waited on the granite mound inside the castle battlements, their eyes fixed on the heavy oaken portal in the keep through which William's mother had passed sixteen years ago to keep her troth with Robert.

But now the bailey inside the walls was filled with corpses, the rocks darkened by blood, the silence of dawn still pierced intermittently by groans from the dying. This was a strange climax, this unnerving silence after the clamour of yesterday's long and furious battle, a struggle which was to decide the existence or extinction of the youthful duke – and of Normandy itself. William had from the outset insisted upon being consulted by Gacé and his lieutenants, Beaumont and fitz Osbern; and it was William who had rallied to Gacé for this final onslaught to dislodge the ambitious traitor. It was William's rousing harangue just before the final assault which had been the turning-point.

During the last night, Gacé's troops had taken up their planned positions: Beaumont facing the unscaleable and sheer walls on the western side of the keep; and Beaumont's troops too, opposite the northern walls and the postern gate; Gacé, with the main body, was to attack the main gateway from the open space of the town's market-place. William, with fitz Osbern beside him, was to invest the southern wall and try to overwhelm the small gateway below the keep's great tower. Throughout the night the meticulous planning went on, the inevitable lack of sleep being the price. At dawn the horns blew from Gacé's sector and the assault began . . .

The heat was appalling. During the whole of that long morning, as the sun burned higher and higher above them, the furious charges continued against the weakest points in the walls. The catapults heaved their stones, the bare-chested soldiers toiling until, collapsing from the heat, they were replaced by men from the town – and all day long the carts continued to trundle their stone loads towards the piles beside the machines. The scaling ladders were replaced time and time again, until the attackers could reach the tops of the walls by scrambling up the mounting piles of dead. Gacé had insisted upon a swift outcome of the issue, victory through assault after slogging assault until the defenders were exhausted, a tactic which precluded the long-drawn-out tech-nique of mining under the walls. At ten-thirty, Gacé's horn blew again, the signal for Beaumont to attract to himself the main fury of the defenders.

Beaumont was successful. Thurstan was forced to concentrate along the western and northern walls, while William and Gacé's forces on their sides snatched at the lull to refresh themselves with food and drink. By twelve-fifteen, they were ready for the final effort, at the precise moment when Thurstan's men were exhausted and convinced that the attackers were also easing up for their midday breather in the baking heat. It was a moving moment when William stood alone by the southern gate, calling for the supreme effort seconds before the final assault.

He was magnificent in his duke's armour, holding his man's-sized shield, its gilded leopards emblazoned proudly across it, as in the other hand he lifted his sword, its Toledo blade still unbloodied. He was taller, stockier even at his age than most of the twenty-year-old knights around him. His years of being hunted by many such men, years in which he had been reared by the serfs and peasants who succoured him, were standing him in good stead now: disdainful always of his bookish contemporaries, his astonishing physical strength had been developed

64

when guiding the plough, chopping timber, heaving grain sacks into granaries, an education vastly different from that of his courtly-trained contemporaries.

Watching William then, thirsting for his first taste of blood, Fitz had felt misgivings for this abnormal youth who was so fierce, yet so icily in control under what must be an ordeal. Killing by the sword for the first time was always a traumatic test, but not normally demanded at the age of fifteen. William was already a competent swordsman, could handle the freshest of stallions and hurl his javelin as far as most seasoned warriors. And this youthful leader, splendid in his ducal battle-dress, had caught the imagination of the thousands watching him. When the horns had at last summoned them, they had hurled themselves with frenzied fanaticism upon the castle walls.

Thurstan Goz pulled his defenders back from the western battlements to deal with the ferocious and fresh attacks on his disengaged sides. Wave after wave of the ducal troops were repulsed, the scaling ladders time and time again heaved backwards at the last moment. The onslaught continued throughout the sweltering afternoon, Beaumont continuing only a token action while resting his main body. Then, blowing his horn at four o'clock, he led his men from the Risle valley in a furious rush for the postern gate. *'Dex aïe! Dex aïe!'* echoed Beaumont's battle cries. William's men took them up themselves, *'Dex aïe!'* redoubling their onslaughts now that Beaumont was again drawing off Thurstan's flagging troops.

It was then, at William's gate, that the first scaling ladder held. Seconds later the refreshed troops were scrambling over the outer wall to hack down their adversaries inside the bailey. The battering rams pounded even more furiously upon the gateway, when suddenly, helped by the gallant men inside, the oaken, iron-bound portal disintegrated under a ram carried by fifty doughty men of Falaise. William leading on his charger, his troops streamed through the pierced gate like a torrent. Once inside, Fitz was hard put to restrain the young warrior from being cut off, as his men battled towards the main gateway, so that Gacé's main force could burst through. The sight of the fifteen-year-old boy drawing his first blood shocked even the hardened Osbern.

William was in danger of being separated from his knights: with only his standard-bearer and Fitz with a few foot-soldiers fighting around him, the duke was being forced backwards towards a granite spur. Suddenly the fight became desperate as two of the enemy slipped inside

William's guard and began hacking at his horse. Though Fitz was hard put to it defending himself, he caught the look of intense concentration on the boy's face as he drove his blade for his first kill. No hate, no blood-lust, no frenzied yelling to bolster his own courage – just professional, ice-cold technique, as Walter had so often taught him: thrust home, twist, the swift withdrawal, the bloodied, dripping blade as he came on guard again, waiting for the expected blow from his other adversary, William's deft parry and then his lightning swing which sliced off the soldier's head. '*Dex aïe!*' he cried, his only sign of emotion as he slithered from his falling mount, its hamstrings severed by the foot-soldiers. His young face white beneath his helmet, he stood resolute, shield squarely held, stabbing, parrying, swinging his sword until he had scythed an empty circle around him again. His knights rushed in and the situation was saved.

The boy's courage seemed to inspire those around him to super-human efforts as they slowly drove back the enemy . . . and by four-thirty William and Fitz had forced the main gate from inside. Gacé streamed through with his force and an hour later all the outer defences had crumbled to the duke's army, Thurstan Goz having retreated inside the massive keep. In no time, faggots and timber were piled beneath the walls from which desultory arrows and stones still flew. And then, as twilight began to close in, Fitz had been the first to notice Thurstan's defiant banner creeping down its flagstaff.

'See, sire!' fitz Osbern called. 'The traitor's had enough.'

'Stay the fires!' William called, signalling his men to withdraw from below the walls. 'Let the traitor now pay homage to his duke!'

Gacé's stumpy figure was striding across the clearing from the higher side of the outer bailey. His shield and coat of mail were drenched in blood and his dark eyes burned from beneath his helmet:

'What are you waiting for, William?' he stormed. 'I told you to get the varlet – roasted, if you can't have him alive.' He turned towards the troops. 'Light the faggots!'

'Stay,' William commanded icily. He nodded at Fitz. 'I'll not burn my own castle. See to it, Steward,' and Fitz rushed forward to knock the torch from the soldier's hands.

And so all this night long, the parleying had continued with Thurstan. Gacé was for executing him this very morning, ripping him apart with horses in the market-place as an example to would-be traitors. But William, for the first time beginning to exert his youthful authority, had stood his ground, backed by Fitz and Beaumont, an achievement, against such a formidable man as Gacé. Yes, thought Fitz in the lightening twilight, at last William has won his spurs – and he's beginning to choose his own friends. And here, in this midsummer dawn, the Steward could sense all about him the change in attitudes of even the older knights. They recognized a leader when they saw one. Here on the trampled grass outside the main gate where they all waited, it was towards the duke that many glances turned, towards William's group that the senior knights nudged their horses. And in the market-place the townsfolk were already gathering, waiting to identify and collect their dead.

'Here comes the traitor!'

Down the great stone steps from the keep came a silent file of dishevelled knights and soldiers. Strictly observing the duke's terms, Thurstan Goz, wearing only his under garments, led his similarly clad remnants, knights and soldiers alike stripped of all honour. Walking barefoot through the rocky outcrops, he passed through the main gate to where Duke William on his battle-charger waited for him to make obeisance. With Gacé on his left, Beaumont and Fitz on his right, William remained silent as the traitor shamefully prostrated himself before his duke. For an interminable moment, the hushed crowd waited. Then Duke William spoke, his voice firm as he pronounced the retribution which Beaumont and fitz Osbern had advised. Using the final dishonour, William addressed the prostrated Thurstan Goz.

'Traitor Goz,' he pronounced. 'You and your family are banished from my domains. All your wealth, all your estates are forfeited to me.' Lifting his helmet, William turned towards the silent crowd. 'Begone, traitor!' He had not even unsheathed his sword.

The tall, half-naked figure on the ground slowly climbed to his feet. Backing from the motionless youth on the charger, he regained the dusty roadway. Then slowly he began stumbling towards the market place, his dishevelled supporters straggling shamefully after him. With the howls and insults from the crowd still echoing in his ears, Osbern turned towards William as, without a word, Ralph of Gacé stomped angrily from the mound.

'My mother shall have Goz's possessions,' the duke said. 'See to it, Steward.' And touching the belly of his horse with his spurs, William trotted towards the lower road leading to his grandparents' old house. The cheers were echoing from the narrow street as men, women and children surged forwards to greet their young duke.

'He's come far this day, Fitz,' Beaumont murmured. 'His vengeance for Tillières is complete.'

The Steward looked up, his sense of satisfaction blighted by the sight of Gacé's large force gathering on the far side of the market place for its journey back to Rouen.

'I've a feeling that today's only a beginning, Roger. The most dangerous man lies yonder, I warrant,' and he nodded towards the grotesque, stumpy figure swinging himself into his saddle.

'Gacé will never forgive us for today. But there's one great change in things, Fitz.'

Osbern raised his eyebrows.

'Our boy-duke's become a man,' Roger Beaumont replied.

6

VALOGNES
31 OCTOBER 1046

Fitz had exaggerated the risk, William was convinced, as he stared with half-closed eyes at his only remaining companion at the long table. William fitz Osbern was unashamedly asleep, his fair head lolling as he breathed stentoriously through his mouth. It was typical of his loyalty to accompany his duke on this possibly stupid and unnecessary incursion into these rebellious territories of the Cotentin and Bessin. But William had accepted the dare, as much to prove confidence in himself and his followers, as to display his contempt for the opposition – and pushing his half-empty goblet from him, Duke William leaned back in the only high-backed chair. Entwining his hands behind his head, he belched and allowed his thoughts to wander.

The chamberlain had produced a reasonable meal, though deliberately William had kept his visit to Valognes unannounced. His incursion into the heart of the Cotentin was intended as a challenge to the rebellious *vicomtes* of these two western provinces of Normandy.

The rebel Nigel II administered the Cotentin from Saint-Sauveur four leagues south-west of Valognes which Fitz had selected as suitably sited for William's thrust into unfriendly territory. To reach Valognes, a well-sheltered town nestling in a shallow valley, the duke and his small court had deliberately made their presence known as they rode westwards through the Bessin: the other rebel was Rannulf, *vicomte* of the Bessin, whose traitorous influence had turned Haimo's head to joining this treasonable new faction. Haimo 'Hawk Head', was the powerful lord of Torigny and Evrecy who also held the castle of Creully in the Bessin; he was an atheist and his influence was great among the other traitor *vicomtes*. The Bessin bordered central Normandy which, with Falaise and the up-and-coming town of Caen, still remained loyal.

William's grandfather had realized the strategic importance of those groups of hamlets in the rich plain where the Odon joined the Orne; and since Richard II's interest, the town of Caen, with its stone quarries and tidal outlets to the sea, had developed apace. But close to the south in the Cinglais, and to the south-west, lay the other rebel *vicomtes*, Ralph Tesson of Thury and his neighbouring rebel leader, Grimoald of Plessis. Under Grimoald, in open council at Bayeux, capital of the Bessin, these *vicomtes* were betraying the trust placed in them by their duke. They had recently declared publicly that they would supplant their bastard ruler by a more worthy and honourable duke: Guy of Burgundy, the young claimant through his mother, Alice, who had been Duke Robert the Magnificent's sister . . . and William slouched in his chair again as he contemplated the remnants of the evening meal scattered on the disordered table. Roger of Beaumont's goblet still lay where he'd knocked it over; the wine was staining the table and the damp wood glistened in the candle-light.

Norman tradition applied the Salic law when choosing a male successor, but the female line retained its law of heritage, and this was the argument which William's antagonists were using in fostering their pretender, the seventeen-year-old Guy of Burgundy – of course, he was spawned from the right side of the blanket . . . and William's fist crashed on the table to send the other goblets flying. Guy's grand-mother was Richard II's first wife, his Breton Judith, who had produced legitimately three sons and three daughters before she died. To William, this present blatant rebellion was as much an insult to his mother Arlette and her Herluin family as it was to him. *The Bastard* . . . He'd become used to the taunt. Now that he was becoming a force to be reckoned with, he was turning the affront to his own advantage. He'd even signed a charter, using the sobriquet.

Guy had never forgotten the boyish indignity he'd suffered at William's hands in the jousting yard six years ago. As Fitz had observed, the youth's jealousy for his cousin William was continually being inflamed by Ralph of Gacé and his opposition party. The culmination was this blatant challenge by the *vicomtes* led by Grimoald of Plessis – a revolt which was most certainly being fanned by Archbishop Mauger after his ecclesiastical council at Rouen six weeks ago. William grinned to himself as he pushed back his chair; he climbed to his feet and began pacing the chamber.

He had insisted upon being present at the council and the memory of the discomfiture of Mauger and his detestable brother, William of Arques, still gave William pleasure. But, by God, how Gacé had manipulated William when he'd been a boy! Now, better able to use his own judgement, William could see that he should have resisted Mauger's elevation to the highest ecclesiastical appointment in Normandy; nor should he have agreed to honouring Mauger's brother as count of Arques. The two brothers were now, with Gacé, the most powerful men in the duchy. Guy was their pawn, but they must have laid their plans years ago, when they gave him Brionne castle after murdering Count Gilbert so foully.

For all its hypocrisy, the ecclesiastical council in Rouen had certainly revealed how the lines were being drawn. Mauger, head of his degenerate Church, had made a surprising attack on the despicable practice of simony: the poor were being fleeced by being forced to pay for even the lowliest of Church benefits; but far worse was the dealing in Church appointments, a practice enthusiastically supported by the barons who were happy to finance the bishop of their choice in order to further their fortunes. Astonishing, too, was Mauger's insistence upon his clerks being better trained and able to read and write. Amazing to William, because from what he'd seen and learned, the despicable archbishop was an example of the basest of temporal failings and excesses which the new pope, Clement II, was condemning. Mauger's scandalous way of life was being commented upon by even the lowest in the duchy: his marriage and his womanizing, his greed for money and at table, his love of cock-fighting and of things occult, all these habits had reached the ears of the pope. Mauger refused to visit Rome, fearing that the pope might deny him the *pallium*, that coveted insignia of office.

At the council, the archbishop had remained silent when William told him bluntly that in a year and a half's time he would be twenty and reaching his majority. Mauger and those around him had heeded the inference . . . but now it was time for sleep. William halted beside his snoring friend at the end of the table.

'Rouse yourself, Fitz, and go to bed' he said, shaking the Steward's shoulder. 'Adeliza'll be after me, if you return home worn out.'

Fitz grunted, shook his head. To William's pleasure, Fitz had married Tosny's daughter two and a half years ago; she was a fine girl and the union had brought peace between the two families. Fitz's influence was such that now the Tosnys were firmly behind the ducal party. William followed his friend to the doorway, accompanied him into the courtyard, then dispatched him to his lodging. 'Sleep well, sire,' Fitz mumbled. 'It'll be a fine day for tomorrow's hunting.'

The night was crisp, the stars brilliant in the indigo sky. The moon was full and frost could not be far off. The duke strolled towards the stable, sucking in the cold air, clearing the fumes from his brain. Baldur, the beautiful dappled stallion given to him by the king of Spain, was a splendid animal. William cherished it almost as much as his beloved destrier Samson, also a Spanish gift, his battle-charger which awaited him in Rouen. Baldur whinnied softly, nuzzling against William's shoulder. William was gratified to see that his seneschal had already cleaned the harness and saddle ready for tomorrow's sport. Yawning, William returned slowly to the house and climbed the stairs to the bed-chamber the chamberlain had allotted him. Closing the door, he stood by the window to gaze down upon the shadowy cluster of humble houses stretching darkly into the fields.

It had been a rollicking evening, made so by his favourite jester whom he'd brought with him. Gollès was a hunchback, but full of fun; it was due to him that the lurking anxiety in everyone's mind this evening had been dispelled. The clown was a devoted servant. William was loath to turn him away on this crisp night but he'd be comfortable in the hay with the court's horses. Most certainly, this abandonment to the hunt was doing them all good: the worries of state were forgotten for a few days.

There *were* signs that things weren't all going the rebels' way: Henry, king of France, had assured Gacé that he would always support his Norman vassal, William, against those who were trying to use the minor for their own ends, or who planned to rid the duchy of their bastard duke. Count Baldwin v of Flanders was a more slippery ally: though he'd married Adela (daughter of Robert the Pious, Henry I's father) he was adept at playing off Henry against France's powerful neighbours.

There were signs of hope, too, inside the duchy. Since Falaise three years ago, a new spirit of reform was stirring, particularly from the movement in the Church which was opposed to Mauger's degeneracy: the purifying influence of the new foundation at Le Bec-Hellouin was beginning to be felt. William had met Lanfranc last year after the new prior's investiture in the serene valley of the Risle river: a fine man, but difficult to get to know. And across the Channel, influences friendly towards Normandy were also at work.

Edward (they were calling him the Confessor because of his piety) had been persuaded to marry the powerful earl of Wessex's daughter, Edith Godwine – a strange marriage, it was rumoured, but opportune now that King Magnus was threatening to invade England from Norway. King Edward of England, after his long exile in Normandy, was bolstering his court with his Norman friends, a move which was not meeting enthusiastic support from his Saxon barons. William liked the docile king, remembering his kindness when Edward and his brother, Alfred, used sometimes to be at Robert I's court.

Those were boyhood days, before Walter Fulbert became William's stalwart friend and guard, the man to whom William had become so devoted and with whom he felt safe. It was to Walter, William felt sure, that he owed his ability now of correctly assessing character: he had an instinct about people. He could sniff out treachery – and he wondered how Walter was getting on with his new life on the coast. The last William had heard of him was that he had married and was trying to settle down in his friend's boat-building enterprise at Bonneville-sur-Touques. Walter had always loved the sea: strange, the pull it had on a man, like the attraction of a woman . . . and smiling secretly to himself, William pulled the curtain across the window.

He undressed and (Walter's training had become routine) folded his clothes to place them in reverse order by the bed, ready for instant use. He laid his sword-belt across the foot of the couch. Lastly, he checked his sword was free in its scabbard. He had refused the offer of a fire, disdaining the comfort, but it was cold as he slipped naked under the eider-feathered coverlet. Now he could savour before sleep the image of the girl who was beginning to invade his secret thoughts.

The last time that Baldwin v had visited Rouen, he had brought his wife, Adela, with him. The pleasant visit had resulted in William's return visit to the count of Flanders' court at Lille. Baldwin, a hospitable, fair-haired man of the north, had done all he could to make the Norman duke's visit agreeable and he had been supported enthusiastically by his French wife. Adela was a vivacious, sallow-skinned lady of some wit. They had talked much of Baldwin's neighbour, Henry III, the youthful emperor who had been on the German throne for six years. His aggressive annexation of Burgundy and its extensions across the Alps to Italy was worrying Baldwin who had become used to the emperor's meek predecessor: Henry II's concern with things spiritual had been less of a menace to Flanders.

Henry II, like Robert the Pious of France, had been a victim of the new morality on marriage which the reforming Church was trying to introduce during these topsy-turvy years: the ritual of marriage was for procreation and not for pleasure. Unlike the worldly Frenchman, the

German Henry had made his childless eight-year marriage with Cunégonde a spiritual union only. On his death-bed he told his parents-in-law, 'I leave your daughter with you as you gave her to me, a virgin.' But in the rumbustious ex-Viking duchy of Normandy, Rome's new morality was making little impact: the Danish Custom still prevailed, and William's generation believed that marriage *was* to be enjoyed carnally, as well as providing the formula for political aggrandizement, and the procreation of suitable and strong successors for the family.

William felt sleep fast claiming him . . . but still the image of the Flemish girl drifted into his mind, the result, perhaps, of the germ implanted so long ago by Baldwin: a marriage between the families of the counts of Flanders and the dukes of Normandy could benefit both provinces. Such a union could buttress an alliance against France should its king become too demanding. All this had been very evident to William on his recent visit to Lille and he grinned in the darkness of his chamber: such a prospect might not be too disagreeable. Baldwin's daughter was entering her teens, and when he and Adela presented their diminutive Matilda to William at court, she seemed to him full of promise. Proud, but mischievous, she was not the simpering maid like so many of them at that stage. Quite the contrary, she vaunted her obvious physical attributes and teased him provocatively. She was still a dumpy, tiny girl-woman, dark-eyed with shining black tresses dangling across her white shoulders . . . four years younger than him, but she'd be a ravishing beauty very soon. Worth waiting for? Unlike his lusty friends, he'd resisted fornicating with every lass who came his way, as was expected of him. He'd determined to remain on his own this night, while they were making most of the opportunities offered them in the town . . . and, turning on his side, William allowed sleep to envelop him.

From somewhere far away in his muddled dream he heard it first, the distant banging. Then the shouting which, in his half-waking, he could not make out. The fellow was not drunk, only fuddled – and then William recognized the high-pitched, unmistakeable mouthings of his jester. The disorientated hunchback was making a devil of a din, rapping on the doors down the street. Then William caught the note of terror in Gollès' confused cries. As the duke clambered naked from his bed, the hammerings upon the door of the neighbouring house awoke the street. From the window William sighted the dishevelled Gollès, straw still sticking to his hair, clouting the unfortunate neighbour's door with his jester's double-ended stick: 'Awake, Duke William! Arise, flee for your life, my duke . . .' and as William leaned across the window, Gollès caught sight of his master.

'Flee, flee, my duke, or they'll cut you in pieces!' The pathetic, lunatic eyes rolled in their sockets. After his childhood, William could recognize terror when he saw it.

'Wait for nothing, my duke! I've seen 'em: Nigel, Grimoald, Haimo and Rannulf. They're armed and making for your chamber. Quick, Duke William, fly for your life!' He collapsed to the cobbles, mouthing and weeping, as William heard shouting further down the shadowy street.

Flinging his cape around him, William grabbed his belt and scabbarded sword. That overpowering feeling of terror he knew so well drove him from the chamber as, barefooted, he took the stone steps two at a time. The white-faced chamberlain was drawing back the door-bolts and William pushed past him to vault over Gollès' huddled figure. Fastening his sword-belt, he dashed across the yard to the stable. He flung open the wooden door, unhitched the drowsy Baldur. Lifting the saddle, bridle and harness from the pegs, he flung the saddle across his shoulder and silently led the horse to the mucking-out door at the far end of the stable. It creaked as he opened it and for a moment the stallion hesitated, its eyes rolling.

'Quiet, now, Baldur.'

He rubbed the animal's muzzle, murmuring soothingly to it – and then he had Baldur through the door and into the midden-yard. As he led the stallion towards the hedge, he heard horsemen dismounting in the street, the hiss of swords sweeping from their scabbards. He fitted the belly-band, tightened the final notch in the girth, hitched on the stirrup leathers. Whispering to the restless Baldur, he led him in the shadow of the hedge to the gate at the end of the paddock. And then, as William swung into the saddle, Baldur stamped the ground, whinnying with anticipation.

The clamour from the house died. William jabbed his bare heels into the horse's belly and as the stallion sprang forwards from the pressure of his master's knees, the silence was shattered by angry shouts from his would-be executioners. As Baldur broke into a gallop, William heard the clash of swords driving home into their scabbards, the clattering of hooves on the cobbles. Crouching low, he felt the mane brushing his cheek as he patted the stallion's neck:

'Go, my beauty!' he told him. 'Gallop as you've never done before:

it's your life as well as mine.' He felt the thoroughbred respond, saw its ears flat-a-back as it stormed south-west out of Valognes, to leave the startled cries from house-dwellers echoing after him. He'd gallop for as long as Baldur could stand the pace, then turn back eastwards. 'Give me time, Sweet Jesus, time to think . . .'

The murderers must have heard his flight, forced the terrified townsmen to divulge his route. Nigel knew that his quarry couldn't continue for long towards the south-west, straight into the *vicomte's* territory of Saint-Sauveur – and certainly, the duke would not ride north or west. Southwards was out of the question, too, so far from the heart of loyal Normandy. They knew he *must* turn east, to the south-eastward probably, to squeeze perhaps between the marshlands south of Beaupte and the key town of Carentan at the head of the estuary. But then he'd have to cross the Merderet and the numerous streams draining this part of the Cotentin. No, he *must* keep clear of the rivers, *must* stay this side, risk the spring tide . . . and he brought Baldur round to cross the track they'd followed into Valognes only the day before yesterday. He'd pick up St-Cyr and then follow the familiar road for the church of Sainte-Mère . . . he flicked and loosened the reins.

'Go, Baldur, you splendid beast!' and flattening himself across the animal's neck, his weight forwards, his legs stretched fully in his long stirrups, he stared ahead to recognize anything, any identifiable landmark to put him right on his road. The dark line of a stream leaped at him and under the brilliance of the moonlight he prayed as he gave Baldur his head. The stallion cleared the far bank in his stride. He stumbled momentarily when his hind hooves caught the bank; then recovering magnificently, he was opening his stride again. William gasped, the wind squeezed from his lungs.

A pulled muscle or injury now to Baldur would cost William his life. He reined the animal back gently as a lightning-sundered beech stood up starkly, its lifeless branches reaching towards the moon: they'd passed it two days ago when nearing Valognes. Seconds later, Baldur's irons were hammering on the hard track. William kept to it: not only would his pursuers be hard put following the hoof-marks, but he could be certain of picking up the fords crossing the tributaries of the Merderet. He'd avoid the hamlets if he could: the more his hunters wasted time in seeking directions, the more distance would he gain. A horseman travelled faster on his own, but if Baldur fell . . . William shivered, feeling the cold steel between his shoulders, hearing the swishing of blades as they hacked him to pieces . . .

'Ease up now, my beauty.'

He walked his steed across the ford at St-Cyr, heard a dog barking. The road the Romans had built clattered beneath him, a pale ribbon in the moonlight. He had gauged Baldur's rhythm now, cantering at a free-going pace, his breathing regular, as if he knew that both their lives depended on his stamina . . . but how far had they to go before they were safe into friendly territory? How far behind was Valognes? At what hour of the night had they bolted? Ecausseville next, not far off. Then straight down to Saint-Mère. He'd keep clear of the village because his hunters were bound to check there – and as he steadied down to the long slog, he forced himself to think logically.

He'd turned the hour-glass which had shown past midnight when he'd gone to bed. He must have slept for a couple of hours. If he'd fled Valognes at three o'clock, he'd have another hour at least of this moonlight before dawn broke. But the moon was sinking low already and casting black shadows across the pale track. Darkness would conceal Baldur's marks, but until then his enemies would have no difficulty in trailing him – and when dawn broke, where would he be then, if they had not overtaken?

In an hour his stallion could cover four leagues at this free-going canter: the safest route would be through Carentan, because there he could be sure of crossing the six rivers. Though at the most another three leagues would be added, he'd not have to risk floundering through the marshes south of Vierville. It was better to be recognized by the people of Carentan than to be overwhelmed by the shifting sands in the Douve estuary. He'd detour Carentan, then make up towards the ford at Les Veys on the Vire estuary. The Bessin was hostile so it would be best to make for the coast road, as far north of Bayeux as he dared – and then he saw the chapel roof of Saint-Mère black against the sky. He took Baldur south before rounding up again for the road.

Ten leagues from Valognes to the ford at Les Veys? Allowing for half an hour's lost time should he lose his way, would make it a dawn crossing. And then for the first time, despair turned to hope: he'd have enough light for the dangerous crossing of the wide estuary which barred his escape. Everything depended upon the state of the tide if he reached the Vire. Mercifully the autumn flooding had not yet swollen the rivers but, with this full moon, the spring tide would be at its fiercest. And while he prayed to his God, the realization came to him that there was only one town within Baldur's endurance: and from that instant he began longing for the staunch burghers of Falaise, those men and women who had nurtured him from his birth. Lying low across Baldur's back, he choked with emotion. He'd ride east of Bayeux then risking all, he'd scythe his way southwards before Haimo's men at Creully could cut him off. There was still a chance, if Baldur stayed the pace – and if the tide was right at Les Veys where he'd once long ago crossed the estuary. Murmuring softly to his snorting horse, he allowed the rhythmical pounding of the hooves to submerge the anxieties swirling in his tired brain.

7

HUMAN QUARRY

William counted them, the six rivers at Carentan: the Gourdon, Douve, Groult, Madeleine, the Taute and, finally, the Vire. He crossed them all safely, as the first silver streak imperceptibly lightened the dawn. It must have been an hour since the moon had set below the night clouds. He'd seen several lights in the town which he left half a league on his left, but he had not been prepared for the shock at the bridge: men were assembling sleepily and, under hectoring from two horsemen, were beginning to haul tree branches across the road. William galloped straight at the barrier. Baldur took it in his stride; several varlets made a half-hearted lunge to reach William, but were knocked spinning against the parapet as Baldur thundered onwards. Nigel must have dispatched a lone horseman ahead, for the Carentan people were evidently alerted to William's flight: his pursuers could not be far away. Refusing to glance behind him as the dawn came up, he heard the church bell of Carentan ringing its call to arms. Lights still burned in this half-twilight and at any moment the traitors would be on his trail again, gaining on the tiring Baldur, following his hoof-marks. 'Give me all you've got, my beauty,' he gasped. 'Don't drop now – we'll be safe soon.'

He forced the failing stallion back into the gallop: Catz next, then Les Veys where he'd know his fate. His existence depended on the tide, for Nigel's men must be warning Haimo's troops at Creully. If William did not cross the Vire soon, the enemy's messengers would be reaching Isigny to snap shut the trap. Mother of Christ, how much longer could his horse keep up this pace? He was becoming short-winded and, as the flat marshland of Catz stretched before William for the second time, he felt despair.

Another half-hour to the estuary, but already Baldur was blowing badly, blood flecking the froth from its nostrils. He eased the poor beast to a trot. The enemy was close behind him, he felt sure, but if

Baldur fell now . . . the gallant horse must be nursed, *must* reach the Vire, even if the estuary had to be crossed on foot, even swimming, if necessary. William allowed Baldur to recover his wind, then gently pushed him into the free-moving canter which he found so easeful . . . *Ah!* there was the hamlet, a huddle of cottages trickling along the grey streak of the river bank. He stood in his stirrups for his first glimpse of the state of the tide.

By the Holy Cross, the river was wide here! A grey expanse of calm water, with a mist curling over it . . . and as he halted Baldur to gauge the tide, he spotted movement in the village, men running about like chickens. And then he saw them, the horsemen – half a league at most.

He pulled his horse round, bent low and trotted for concealment behind the dyke. Following it northwards until a bend shielded him from the houses, he then forced Baldur to a slow gallop northwards down the estuary. He reached the marshes, stumbled across another dyke and made for a cluster of huts showing ahead. The stallion was blowing hard, as William bellowed at the serf who blinked at him from the opening in the rush-topped hovel.

'Can I cross the estuary further down, fellow?'

The shaggy head nodded slowly. An arm lifted beneath the bedraggled wolfskin.

'A league further down, lord: past the salt pans.' The whites of his eyes rolled in his startled face. 'Cross there. St-Clement's on the far side.'

'Is the tide low enough?'

The simpleton nodded slowly and as William forced Baldur into the gallop, he could hear the serf shouting unintelligibly after him. Squelching through the half-frosted mire of the marshes, William sighted the white, salt-encrusted field; he turned obliquely north-east towards the grey-green line of the sea stretching across the horizon ahead. He was half a league from the shore when he sighted the low roofs of a village on the far side of the estuary. Then, as Baldur struggled frothing and blowing through the soft ground, William's heart leapt – there, ahead, the marker. The dead tree, black and gaunt . . . He patted his stallion, whispered to him, forced him on . . . He spotted the cart-tracks converging towards the post and then he was certain, watching the running tide poppling across the shallows, that he'd found the ford. Reining in his gallant animal he rode it at a walk down the slope and into the cold waters.

Holding up Baldur's head, he forced the stallion forwards, step by step . . . deeper, deeper until the brine was swirling to the animal's breast. William loosened his sword-belt, preparing to fling it away if he had to swim. The tideway hissed against his right leg. The horse's eyes rolled in their sockets as it pricked its ears, feeling for each step, terrified by the unknown. The dark line of mud glistened on the opposite bank which was showing as the tide raced into its fierce, spring ebb; slowly, agonizingly slowly, the far shore-line grew nearer. His eyes ached from searching for the deep holes which could bring catastrophe – and then he realized that the water-line was dropping to Baldur's shoulder:

'*Steady . . . steady . . .*' The stallion was whinnying, aware also that the danger was almost behind them. He was trying to trot, stumbling in the boiling stream.

And then the rider and horse were splashing from the swirling waters, firm ground under them. As William turned in his saddle to scan upstream, even the hissing of the water failed to drown the sound of the bell tolling from somewhere behind him on the other side of the estuary. Tightening his sword-belt, he nudged his horse onwards, up through the waking hamlet of St-Clement and its square-towered church. Coaxing him again into a free-going pace, and praying that the cold immersion would not induce cramp, William kept Baldur going easily, his own heart heavy, knowing that he was killing his trusty, brave friend. He would make for the coast road and once clear of Bayeux, he'd start curving to the south. William was now in unknown territory, but once with Fitz he had ridden to the fishing port of the Bessin, returning to Caen through the coastal hamlets and the small town of Ryes. If he could find that road, even if Baldur dropped under him, he'd be within reach of help if he could find another mount . . . Fitz, Beaumont and the others would be storming after the assassins, to cut them off and to alert the Hiémois. He set his face to the north-east and, after another long hour, halted on high ground overlooking the Seine bay. That must be the Pointe du Hoc to his left, where the grey clouds were hanging across the high cliffs.

He'd lost all sense of time. The sun was above the eastern woods now and he must have been going for over two hours since the estuary . . . and then he recognized the valley curving down to the Bessin's chief fishing village. In half an hour he'd be north of Bayeux. Dared he hope yet that this nightmare ride could soon be over? Seconds later his dreams were shattered: Baldur was faltering, beginning to limp on his left hind leg. God's blood, there was no doubting it. His horse *must* not fail now, not here leagues from anywhere, on the only track which his pursuers were bound to follow once they sniffed out his trail from St-Clement. Too many hamlets had heard the lone horseman, glimpsed the exhausted rider galloping eastward, ever eastward. 'Steady, Baldur. One last effort. You can rest at Ryes.'

The vavasour of Ryes, Hubert, stood in the sunlight directly beneath the central stone archway of his farm which he had built with such pride. High enough, yet of ample width for the hay wains, to his eyes it was in perfect proportion to the two smaller doorways which balanced the main gateway. The sturdy, simple watch-tower which served as a pigeon loft, abutted the new gateway and certainly added distinction as well as defensive strength to the masterpiece which had cost so much. He'd carted the stone from Caen and his three sons never ceased chiding him for his extravagance; but even a minor vavasour, vassal to Haimo, the lord of Creully, needed prudence. Being able to trim one's sails to the wind was a necessary quality for survival during these violent years. Though Hubert could not support the *vicomte's* declared intention to unseat Normandy's bastard duke, he had no choice but to pay lip-service – much to his second son's disdain. Eudo stood strongly for the pro-ducal party.

'Are the boys coming to mass or aren't they, Marie?'

He glanced irritably at his wife waiting by his side. 'How often have you told me that Monsieur le curé, detests late-comers?'

'They're getting the bullocks in,' she answered shortly. 'They'll not have time to wash.' She took his arm and together they began the stroll he enjoyed so much these days. At sixty-one, he was finding tranquillity in these Saturday services at the little church tucked into the side of the hill skirting the road to the sea. He tried to attend the Mass daily, but this had been a difficult, wet summer. Marie was prattling on as she always did, happy to have him to herself for once. Their sons were now taking over the farm; this could have been the first autumn during which Marie and he could have eased up, had it not been for the unsettling local politics. Holding Ryes for *vicomte* Haimo was testing Hubert's loyalties to breaking-point, dividing his family. The three girls were all for tranquillity, seeing in Haimo's sons an opportunity not to be missed.

But the boys – ah, no! They were like him, secretly dedicated to Robert the Magnificent's young successor: a bastard William certainly was, but a fine down-to-earth fighter by all accounts. And often, in the solitude of the church, Hubert had praised his God for surrounding the young duke with such a nucleus of up-and-coming young men – Roger of Beaumont, Montfort, Tosny – and William fitz Osbern who had succeeded the old Steward. The leaves of the woods behind the long field were turning gold and it was good to feel part of this eternal rhythm in the scheme of things as the seasons came and went. Hubert had spent his life here in Ryes, building up the domain he'd inherited from his father. Nothing spectacular, but of his sons only Eudo showed ambition – and Hubert wondered how long his second son would remain at home before setting out to gain his fortune through the strength of his sword-arm.

'Someone's making haste,' his wife was complaining. 'Doesn't he know that's our calving field? Admonish him, Hubert.'

The vavasour watched his cattle scattering, saw the lone horseman growing larger as he rode wearily down the Ryes road. The rider seemed exhausted, was rolling drunkenly across his big limping horse which was itself about to drop. The animal was snorting, its muzzle smothered with crimson froth as its rider pulled it to a stop. Its flanks sweated through the slime of dirt and its rider was in no better state as he slid from the mud-spattered saddle: shod with neither shoes nor hose, Hubert saw that beneath the rich mantle, the heavily-built young man was naked. By the sword at his belt he was of noble birth.

'Is this Ryes?' the unshaven youth gasped. 'Ryes, in the *Vicomte* Creully's domain?'

'I am Hubert its vavasour. I hold the town for my lord Haimo.' Hubert stretched out his arm for the youth who was staggering and near collapse, when suddenly with astonishment he recognized to whom he was speaking.

'Sire,' he said, dropping to one knee, 'what brings my lord duke here in such dreadful state?'

Marie stood transfixed, fascinated by the mud-spattered figure. Then she too made obeisance. 'My lord,' she cried, 'accept the welcome of our simple home.' She rose and began hurrying homewards. 'Rest your weary limbs while I prepare you food. I have a guinea-fowl cleaned, ready for the spit.'

Hubert took the horse's bridle, started to lead the animal back towards the farmhouse. *'Sainte Marie!'* he exclaimed. 'Where are your knights, sire? What's befallen you to be in such sore distress? You can trust my house, for my family has served your father, yes, and your grandfather. Let me succour you, sire: I'd give my life for you, my duke.'

The broad-shouldered youth had pushed back the hood of his mantle. The russet hair, the low fringe across the wide brow; those ice-blue eyes which gave nothing away; that normally clean-cut face which was now splashed with mud, the strong chin shadowy with unshaven stubble: so this was their legendary bastard duke, son of the great Robert . . . even his short, broad aquiline nose and the cast of his widely spaced eyes bore a remarkable resemblance to his father . . . Duke William, recovering his breath as he began to walk towards the house, spoke jerkily:

'Worthy knight, trust you I do. I have need of help. Swiftly. And food. Above all a new mount.' The steady eyes bore into Hubert's. 'Your lord Haimo stands among the traitors, Sir Hubert. They're hunting me down like a brute animal, determined to butcher their duke. Would that I could explain more, but they are not far behind. Quick – a horse and put me on the track for Falaise.'

Marie had run on ahead and when Hubert ushered his duke through the fine gates, Eudo was running across the yard towards them. He bowed clumsily, sweeping his hand towards the stable. 'We're saddling the hunter, father,' he said. 'Give me my duke's horse: we'll see to it.'

Hubert poked his finger into his son's ribs:

'Quick, son! Fetch your brothers as soon as you've saddled up all your horses. The three of you are escorting our lord duke to Falaise. You know the route: get him there, even if you pay with your lives.'

Eudo's glance flickered across Duke William's face and was held momentarily. He nodded, began sprinting across the yard, scattering the squawking fowls, setting the hounds barking.

'Our humble home, sire,' Hubert said, pushing open the oaken door. 'Marie will give you hot water and towels.'

The big, red-tinged head shook in refusal. 'A bite of food, Sir Hubert. While I eat, show me the track to Falaise.'

Hubert crossed to the corner cupboard and extracted the worn map he had had fashioned for him when he'd been appointed vavasour. He spread it upon the table as William started gulping the hot broth which Marie always kept simmering in the *marmite:*

'I know the route, sire, but Eudo knows it better: he hunts in the autumn on the edge of the *vicomte* of Thury's honour.'

'Ralph Tesson's another traitor,' William snapped. 'He's with Haimo and Grimoald of Plessis at this moment, hard on my heels.'

'Eudo will keep clear of his men, sire. My boy knows the country well.' Hubert yelled across to the stables and seconds later his three sons were crouching across the table.

'The tunnel,' Gilles, the first-born suggested. 'Why doesn't our duke take it? It's large enough for horse and rider.'

Briefly Hubert explained the proposition, nodding towards a doorway at the rear of the house. 'The far end opens inside Creully castle: you're an idiot, Gilles.'

'Well, father, why don't we reverse the shoes on the horses? That could confuse the traitors, gain us time. . .'

William smiled briefly, but shook his head, silent as he gulped his steaming broth. His chair fell backwards as he stood up.

'Lady, my thanks,' he said. 'Stay I cannot, neither for clothes nor for your guinea-fowl.' He wiped his chin with the back of his hand, as Marie hurried across with a newly baked loaf. 'Take it, my lord duke: you can eat it from the saddle.'

Seconds later, with the duke's exhausted stallion safely concealed in the stable, Eudo was leading the horsemen through the gateway. The duke did not even glance backwards as the clatter of hooves echoed in the rectangular yard. Hubert watched them breaking into the gallop across the Long Field which opened to the track leading to Vienne and Martragny. The vavasour was feeling his years when his wife came up behind him to encircle his waist with her arm.

'Eudo'll get him there,' he murmured, half to himself. 'Even if they have to fight their way through.'

'But how will they cross the Orne?' Marie whispered.

'The old Roman ford, just up-river of the cliffs. I used it once before we married.'

'Bully Mill, on the Bretteville-Verson road?'

Hubert nodded his grizzled head. 'Percauville and Chinchamps are on the other side. They'll skirt north of the Cinglais forest and pick up the Falaise track at Potigny.'

'But if the Orne's in flood'

'They'll cross by the islands. They can swim if they have to . . .'

Marie's arm tightened.

'Horsemen,' she cried. 'Can't you hear them? From the church road.'

She loosed him, scurrying to the table, sweeping the remnants into her apron. Hubert hurried to the porch, picked up his scabbarded sword, clipped it to the belt beneath his sheepskin cloak. He hurried outside, closing the door behind him. His heart thumping with that irregularity he feared, he strolled deliberately towards his gateway. Standing squarely beneath its archway, he saw the first of a large party of knights galloping round the bend of the road. The leader hauled up his snorting mount, making it rear. There was no mistaking that hard-faced knight glaring down at him:

'You've seen our bastard duke, Sir Hubert?' Lord Haimo shouted, his red face darker than usual. 'Which road's he riding?' His free hand rested on the handle of his poniard, as the remainder of his band reined in around him, their steeds blowing and lathered in sweat. 'Which way's the traitor gone?'

'Hide nothing from us, sir knight,' another bellowed, a huge man whom Hubert recognized as Grimoald of Plessis. 'You know William's passed this way. Your life's forfeit if you lie, sir,' and the sword blade glinted in the morning sunlight.

'Of which William d'you speak, sir?' Hubert asked mildly, trying to contain the beating of his heart as his hand beneath the coat tightened on his sword handle.

'Fool! Our brutal, shameless duke: William, the Bastard.'

Hubert nodded enthusiastically. 'Yea, my lords – not long since. What's amiss?'

'Haste, old man. Don't quibble. Come, lead us the way and we'll talk while we ride. Hurry, sir knight, to horse.'

Hubert felt the frozen grin cracking his leathery skin. 'Willingly, my lords. Our Bastard's humiliated Normandy long enough.' Turning from them, he shouted over his shoulder, 'I'll fetch my horse and ride with you. Before I return home this night, we'll have a better duke on the throne, I pray,' and he stumbled towards the stable. As he fumbled with the harness he heard them shouting roughly from the road. How much longer could he delay, assuage their impatience? Then, leading his horse outside, he climbed stiffly into the saddle. He trotted the old cob across the yard, through the gateway and onto the road. The leaders opened for him and then he was breaking into a slow canter – down the road towards the centre of his little town. The party remained silent when they reached the cross-roads by the market place but without faltering he took the eastern track, leaving the stream on his right.

'He was in a hurry, was William,' he grunted to Haimo, who was beside him, on his right urging him on. 'He took this road past the forge, making for Crépon.' The horsemen followed, impatiently reining in to allow him the lead. At Pierre-Artus, down on the flat, he gained more time by asking the villagers if they'd seen a lone horseman. And on he led them, as far as the Provence river to the east of Crépon. It was *midi* when finally his escort reined in angrily.

'The Bastard will have crossed the Seulles,' Hubert told them, slumping in his saddle. 'My lords, I can ride at your pace no longer.'

'By St Peter's beard!' Grimoald roared. 'Leave the old man, Haimo,' and digging his heels into his animal's belly, the lord of Plessis took over the lead. Seconds later Hubert was on his own, watching the assassins galloping eastwards. With a slow smile he turned his old cob, felt the westerly breeze caressing his sweating face.

'Home now,' he murmured, stroking his horse's mane. 'Our Marie will be sick with worry.'

He touched the animal's belly with his heels:

'You can gallop now, my beauty,' he whispered. 'Show us how you can go, or we'll be late for supper.'

The vavasour of Ryes was watching his heifers being driven in from the Long Field. There was no necessity for him to be out in this dreary, chilly evening of the second day of November. André, his most experienced cowman, an unambitious, steady bondman who had served Hubert from boyhood knew his beasts better than his own children. But the first hard frosts were coming in now and the decision was imminent as to when to winter the cattle: this, the ageing Hubert felt, was excuse enough for the vavasour to be out here in the cold instead of by his log fire. The light was fading fast and a dank mist was hazily weaving across the wet meadows. Instinctively Hubert counted his beasts as they squelched through the muddy morass at the gateway.

The vavasour could endure no longer his wife's nagging anxiety over her three sons. It was a half-day's ride to Falaise, even when taking the short cut over Bully Ford. Allowing for a day's rest in the castle, the boys should have been back by noon today; and Hubert himself now felt disquiet. But, just as he was cursing himself for a fool, he noticed the hindmost heifers scattering in alarm in the darkness at the edge of the copse. Seconds later he saw them, the three horsemen cantering slowly up the muddy track, the dirt spattering behind them. Gilles was in the lead and a tired smile creased his face as he slid from the saddle.

'Our duke is safe, father, with the people of Falaise. He's already dispatched messengers to rally his friends round him.' He added nervously, 'We lost your gelding, father.'

'Crossing the Orne?'

'At Bully. It slipped on the weed. Eudo* grabbed the duke and got him to the far bank.'

'How'd you lose the horse?' Hubert asked testily.

'Swept away by the current,' Eudo interrupted. 'The river was very full, father. We skirmished with some of Tesson's men in Percauville, but after Cinglais forest we grabbed a mount in Bretteville for the duke.' And Hubert's second son concluded impatiently, 'We reached Falaise at dusk.'

Gilles explained, 'Eudo shared his horse, father, until Bretteville.'

'Come, my sons,' the vavasour of Ryes said, gripping Eudo's arm momentarily. 'Mother'll be waiting. You've earned your suppers.'

---

* Eudo was later rewarded by William who appointed him Sheriff of Essex, an appointment Eudo filled with renown. Many of the sheriff's tenants in Essex originated from Ryes.

Another of the vavasour's sons was also later appointed bishop of Sées, when finally the bishopric was taken from the notorious family of Bellême.

8

❦

VALLEY OF THE DUNES

William fitz Osbern, after these interminable weeks of preparation, could not believe his eyes: the shadowy fields encircling the dark, snug little town of Argences seemed to be stirring, like flies in a loft in spring-time.

The Steward of Normandy sat on his piebald destrier, his favourite battle-charger, apart from his squire and the contingent of guards. From this rise overlooking the fields which sloped gently to Argences, he could detect at once if the duke erred in direction because he was now most certainly leading his army at the head of his troops. William had faced up firmly to Gacé after the council at Rouen: in the inevitable battle which must materialize for William's survival, the duke would lead his own army. In three months he would be reaching twenty and his majority. Falaise had proved his qualities and skill in the art of war. Gacé had sulked, agreeing that he could with honour still play a role in the army: at fifty-three a soldier was well over the hill, but he insisted on bringing his own contingent, if only to demonstrate to King Henry that a spark of loyalty still smouldered in Ralph of Gacé's twisted make-up. Fitz suspected that the eighteen-year-old traitor and pretender to the dukedom, Guy of Burgundy, though flattered by his rebel *vicomte* sponsors throughout the duchy, now despised the ageing Gacé.

'See, sire,' the squire called. 'There's our duke!'

Fitz squinted towards the eastern hills, where the slice of new moon was swinging into the lightening twilight. It hung like an infidel's scimitar above the sleepy little town into which the duke's army had marched five days ago; it had bivouacked along the banks of the Laizon while William conferred for the last time with the French king at Les Forges. From the look-out post on the spur above Valmeraye, the rebel army had been sighted farther south than expected, along the escarpment on the western side of the plain. William's scouts confirmed the reports, so Henry moved south-west to the excellent

89

strategic position of Valmeraye whence he could block the rebel army's eastward advance to Rouen. Fitz, as the duke's personal emissary with Henry, had watched the French host taking up its positions on the 18th March. The French king had kept his promise to his vassal: his three thousand horsed knights were seasoned campaigners, magnificent in their ardour and bearing.

Henry, now an experienced warrior of twenty-six, was not boasting to Fitz when, from the crest of the pine-topped hill overlooking the sandy plain, he had spread his arms towards the base of the hill. A tented town was encamped there, each battalion grouped around its commander's pavilion where fluttered the lord's banner. A lance required at least four men and three horses to support the knight who carried it: counting the archers and servants, well over twelve thousand men and nine thousand horses must have been encamped on the downs overlooking the hamlets of Billy and Navarre.

Fitz and his party had risen early on this Monday morning to ride the league and a half to this ford between the villages of Vimont and Bellengreville. Bérenger Ford they called it, this shallow crossing of the Sémillon, the stream meandering through the plain from Billy to join the Muance south of Troarn. William would cross here to lead his army along the left bank of the Sémillon, until he met Henry's host which would be already on the move and following the stream down from Billy.

'The duke's horn, sire,' the squire announced.

'Answer it,' the Steward commanded. 'Sound three.'

William ought to hear the signal, with the westerly breeze: the fleecy clouds were scudding like ships across the western hills where the enemy host had been lurking for days, concealed in their commanding positions overlooking the plain. The night clouds were slowly collapsing below that long ridge bordering the right bank of the Orne as far as Caen. The third blast from the squire's horn drifted down-wind. There was an answering acknowledgement and then Fitz spotted the duke's contingent wheeling towards him.

They looked magnificent, those three hundred cavaliers trotting behind their standard, many of them Fitz's friends, young men who were casting their lives and their fortunes behind this impressive bastard youth trotting at the head of his army up the gentle rise towards Vimont. Fitz could hear the commands now, the jingling of harness and the laughter of the archers and foot-soldiers slogging uphill behind their knights. It was a measure of William's leadership that he had been able to recruit this motley collection in such a short time since his escape from Valognes.

'Ride down to welcome them, Gilles,' Fitz ordered his squire. 'Tell the lord Beaumont that the going's soft, once they cross the ford.'

The young squire galloped eagerly down the slope. For too long he and so many others had been waiting for this moment, and most sensed deep in their secret selves that this day could be their last. This must be the final reckoning for Normandy: before the sun set on this valley of the dunes, the sandy soil below the pine-topped ridges would be dark-soaked with blood. Guy of Burgundy or the Bastard? One or the other would be wearing the ducal crown tomorrow. William would lose his life if victory went to the rebel traitors; Guy had no duchy to lose, but his life and those of his supporters would also be forfeit. Vengeance was merciless in civil war . . . and the Steward shivered beneath his shirt of mail. The breeze had a touch of north in it; the buds on the trees were swelling, but the apple blossom, they said, might survive the winter's snow and ice.

William's energy had been remarkable after he'd safely reached Falaise with the vavasour of Ryes' sons. He had remained in the town he loved, ruling as best he could while his duchy collapsed around him. Rouen declined to pay its dues, refused homage; the *vicomtes*, spreading the rumour that the Bastard was dead, deliberately provoked terror and anarchy from east to west, north to south, whipping up support while they ravaged the duchy. William's energetic reaction was amazing, but in contrast to the little men who were suffering so grievously beneath the rebelling barons. The small men of the Hiémois were losing all they possessed, but once their duke was promised French support, volunteers streamed into William's army – from both sides of the Risle they came; from the Evreçin; from the Caux in the north, from the Exmes in the south; from Falaise and from the Auge, across the marshland which this scratch army had just traversed with such hardship. Only a fortnight after his escape from Valognes, William had reacted with astonishing speed. While his ungrateful and treacherous cousin, Guy, rampaged through the Ouche from Brionne, William rode with Fitz and a loyal band of supporters to Paris.

William found Henry at Poissy. Followed by the embarrassed Fitz, he had stormed into the royal court, mud on his boots, his clothing soiled. The king was holding audience, but William burst into the council chambers and threw himself at his sovereign's feet.

'Your vassal, sire,' he croaked in that deep, hoarse voice of his. 'Your vassal begs your support to save your duchy.'

There had been nothing undignified about the gesture, as the nineteen-year-old youth prostrated himself at the feet of his monarch, only seven years his senior.

'You fled to Normandy with only twelve men – a child, hounded from your heritage by your mother. Do not forget that my father put you back on the throne, sire. Remember your promise to him when he departed for the Holy Land.'

'Rise, Duke William,' the king said. 'I have not forgotten. For months I have been watching the anarchy in your duchy. With the count of Anjou threatening my authority at Blois and in the Loire valley, it is time to reassert my authority.'

And for the next two days Frenchmen and Normans listened to each other and planned. Never before had Fitz witnessed this side of William's character: smooth of tongue, calm, determined and sure of himself, he presented his case with remarkable persuasion.

If Guy and his open rebellion won the day, not only would Henry be threatened by a new, hostile duke and his over-bearing and triumphant Norman barons, but France would be menaced from the south-east by the expanding province of Burgundy which was friendly with the German emperor and which now stretched across the Alps. Geoffrey Martel, the count of Anjou, was also feeling his strength: he'd captured Blois and forced Count Eudes to swear fifteen times on the sliver of wood from St Symphorien's staff that he owed allegiance to the count of Anjou. So Martel was now controlling the Loire valley from Tours. France could be menaced from all sides for Baldwin v of Flanders still remained an unknown quantity on Henry's northern boundaries . . . William's argument could not be denied. If Normandy went under, France could be vanquished too when the vultures on her borders finally swooped.

So Henry was convinced: he promised to come immediately to his vassal's rescue, but whether he could muster a large enough army in time, before the Norman rebels struck, remained the vital question. William had returned to Falaise on 28 November. Ignoring Guy's machinations from Brionne, the duke devoted all December, and the January and February of the new year to riding through the loyal regions of his duchy to whip up support. The fifteen hundred troops now advancing towards the Steward were proof of his success . . . In a few moments the duke would be within hailing distance: Fitz drew his sword, preparing to salute his lord.

February had been spent in a frenzy of meetings co-ordinating the coming campaign. The duke's spies provided a mass of information: Guy had rallied most of the duchy behind him, urged on by the proud *vicomtes* whose army of twenty thousand men was concealed behind that western sky-line, in those woods now tinged rose by the growing dawn. Guy had been at Bayeux and intended to march on Rouen. He and his *vicomtes* had set out from the Bessin and the Cotentin, collecting support as they rode. Reports from William's spies had streamed in during this last week, all confirming that the rebel army had crossed the Orne by the old Roman ford at Bully, the mill by the huge weeping beech tree which William and his escort from Ryes knew so well. Then the river had not been swollen before the snow melted – but today, with the equinoctial tide having its effect as far up as Caen, the great river must be running fast and full . . .

On 5 March, Henry set out from Paris. Following the traditional route from the Chartrain, he sacked rebel-held Argentan a week later, then moved north to Falaise where he met William to finalize their plans. The duke then hurried back to the Auge to lead the motley army waiting for him under Beaumont's command. The Laizon camp on the 18th, then the linking with Henry at Les Forges, after the king moved north to Mézidon from Falaise – and here they were, the allied armies ready to fight to the death for survival, on this bright spring Monday, 23 March 1047.

'My lord duke!'

The Steward raised the cross of his sword-guard to his lips, holding the blade upright, then lowering it before his duke in homage. And at that instant, even his hardened spirit felt the surge of loyalty to his sovereign lord. This day, Fitz was offering his life in fealty to this young man with whom he had already shared so much – the terrible past, their close friendship, their intimate sharings of their personal lives: William was almost as delighted at the safe arrival of Fitz's second son four months ago, as was Adeliza. He had asked to be Roger's god-father, and after the christening William had opened his own heart to Fitz: beneath that iron exterior, William kept closely hidden the secrets of his personal life.

'Sheath your sword, Steward,' William shouted, reining in Samson, his favourite destrier. 'You'll be needing it anon.' He was already helmeted, but still carried his shield across his back, while his squires bore his lances. 'Where's the ford, Fitz?'

'Follow, sire.'

Minutes later, Fitz splashed across the Sémillon where it crossed the Caen–Lisieux road. William halted beside him, lifting his head to stare westwards, sniffing the fresh breeze.

'What's the going like, this side of the stream?'

'Soft, sire, especially through the peat higher up. Follow the stream.'

'Tell the king we've crossed. Where should he be by now?'

'Approaching Navarre, sire. You should meet him by eight o'clock.'

The Steward pulled down his helmet and, nodding to his squire, pricked his charger forwards. The soft ground squelched, the saddle leather creaked as his mount began picking its way through the boggy field. Behind him he heard the duke's knights crashing across the ford, then the frightened whinny from a young squire's mount. The inexperienced youth was showing off, not appreciating the danger which the stream presented: with its deep, steep banks, the stream was too wide for an armoured knight to jump, too narrow for a horse to manage both its fore and hind legs in the concave bottom. Then came the crash of the falling horse and its armoured rider, the sudden silence and then the horse's squeal of terror: it had broken its leg and the horrified youth was drawing his dagger. Fitz peered straight ahead, searching for the harder going beside the stream. Sensitivity was out of place these days. Before the sun set this evening, thousands of men would never again see another dawn – and Normandy, as he knew it, might cease to exist.

Steward Osbern did not encounter King Henry's host until above Navarre. The monarch was starting to ride down the slopes above Valmeraye, where he had slept the night in the priory, and Fitz met him by a clump of pines to the west of the chapel of St Brice. There in the square-towered little church, perched above the banks of the Muance, Henry attended Mass, to the pleasure of the clerks: never in their lifetime had they enjoyed such an offertory. The chapel stood by the edge of a deep track leading up to the crest of the down; from the top of its tower the plain could be seen stretching to the ridge of low-lying hills. The western boundary was formed by a succession of hump-backed hillocks originating behind Bellengreville. Curving like a horseshoe, the ridge reached its highest point at the village of Secqueville, which overlooked the plain to the eastward. The valley was almost a league wide, Fitz reckoned, and over a league in length; the eastern boundary was limited by the line of hills on which he stood and by the Sémillon stream, with its attendant bogs and marshes lower down and its source at Beneauville. The valley between these two boundaries sloped gently to the westward, up to the ridge of the flame-coloured, spring-budded woods which linked Conteville, Secqueville and Bellengreville.

'There, Steward Osbern!' the king shouted across to him from his destrier. 'To the right of the pine clump opposite Beneauville: see, their armour's glinting from the sun.'

Fitz watched as the lower edge of the far wood seemed to quiver where the enemy was drawing up his shock battalions. They were ready, then, to do battle, once Henry reached the plain. The sooner the Normans joined forces, the better . . .

'It's difficult to judge where the enemy will concentrate,' Henry bellowed. 'I'll deploy my battalions as soon as I meet Duke William.' He twitched his rein and, to the cheers of his eager troops, he set his charger's head down the slope, towards the two hamlets nestling at the foot of the downs. He carried no shield as yet, was without his helmet; he was wearing only his chain headpiece, but his knight had just clipped in place the vital straps which held in place the chestpiece. The king was wearing a double suit of chain-mail today, fashioned in Spain and beyond price, it was rumoured. The weight required a strong charger and a strong warrior – and to Fitz's eyes, the dark-eyed, stocky man of twenty-five with the sleepy, supercilious eyes, the broad nose and humorous mouth, looked the part he played. And evidently, as King Henry I of France trotted across the first field on the plain towards the track leading to Billy, his cheering battalions thought so too.

At Navarre, ten minutes later, the French scouts were galloping back on their tracks, turning in their saddles, pointing whence they came: the duke of Normandy was waiting by the well at the crossroads in the centre of Beneauville hamlet.

And a quarter of an hour later the Steward watched the meeting of these young leaders of two very different armies: William, the proud vassal; Henry, his liege monarch, remote, disdainfully confident. The duke, fully dressed for battle, lowered his blade in salute, then sheathed his sword. Behind him, encircling the stone wall of the well, Beaumont and his knights dipped the tips of their lances.

'Montfort's covering my right flank at the pine wood which stretches from the hill at the north end of Chicheboville,' William reported. 'The remainder of my troops are forming up now between Montfort's men and here, sire, at Beneauville. My left flank is ready to join your host.'

Henry nodded, as a squire approached with the king's helmet and shield. 'To the plain then, Duke William, where I can deploy my battalions southwards. Our enemies will have the sun in their eyes if we don't tarry.'

Fitz followed the two leaders as they rode together, making their final dispositions. After trotting across the village holdings, they reached the edge of the sandy plain sloping gently upwards to the ridge ahead, where already the enemy was blatantly manœuvring his cavalry. The rebel army stretched from the slope above Chicheboville southwards to the pine clumps above Conteville. Fitz could see them now, the standards, the gonfalons streaming in the breeze, the banners thickest at the highest point around the woods at Secqueville, where the church tower and the roof of a farmhouse poked through the trees.

'They're grouping as we thought, William,' Henry said, adjusting his helmet and feeling the balance of his shield, that royal shield which glinted in the brittle sunlight, its almond-shaped surface emblazoned with its golden eagle. 'Your scouts have got it right, after all.'

The two leaders were peering from below their conical helmets, their faces enveloped by the chain-mail of their head-pieces; only the slits of their mouths and their eyes flashing from either side of their nose-guards were visible.

'Won't be long now, sire,' William rasped, impatient to regain his troops. 'This'll give Beaumont and each baron time to identify his foe.'

'And who is yours, Duke William?' Fitz felt irritated by the patronizing tone of the king's query.

'Rannulf, sire. Rannulf of the Bessin.'

'Ah – I can see him and his knights.' Henry was squinting to his right, to where some three hundred horsemen were cavorting back and forth below Secqueville. 'He's impatient, I warrant. As you expected, there's your traitor *vicomte*, Grimoald of Plessis: on their left flank, opposite your lord Montfort. That's Grimoald, by the size of him and his destrier. He won't enjoy being under Rannulf's command: you've a trusty knight opposite Grimoald?'

'Beaumont, sire. I have no more valiant warrior than him.'

Henry swept his sword from its scabbard, accepted his lance from the squire. He circled his shield to the southward. 'Dispose my battalions,' he commanded. 'I'll leave Nigel of the Contentin to my lords. Lord Haimo is my adversary.'

And as the groups of warriors followed their commanders cantering south to take up their allotted positions, Fitz smiled grimly to himself:

Henry was renowned for his jealous pride. Haimo enjoyed a reputation for courage and skill at arms second to none – and Henry, though much younger, intended to enhance his own renown today. The young monarch was recklessly selecting the most redoubtable of adversaries, and Fitz did not miss the glances passing between the battle-hardened knights closing up behind their king. He should have been content with Nigel of Saint Sauveur, *vicomte* of the Cotentin who was commanding the enemy's southern group. This Nigel (the 'Falcon') was renowned as a valiant fighter: had he not hurled Ethelred's Saxons back into the sea at St-Vaast when Richard II was duke of Normandy?

Nigel had well chosen his disposition. With his rear against the high ridge running parallel to the Orne, and his left flank protected by the commanding height of Secqueville, the rebel *vicomtes* held a distinct advantage: the French host and its Norman ally were compelled to charge uphill and could never turn Nigel's and Grimoald's fronts. There was only one anxiety for the rebel army. It *had* to be victorious this day. If the French host was defeated, it could escape to the south and east; but the *vicomtes* could retreat only towards Caen whose inhabitants were holding for William. Admittedly, many of the Caennais were now fighting alongside the duke, but if Nigel and his barons were defeated, the remnants of the men of Caen could hold up the rebels long enough for Henry and William to overtake them. The *vicomtes*' only other escape route back to the Cotentin would be at Bully, over the ford which crossed the swollen Orne.

Fitz was watching the French battalions wheeling, reining in behind the barons of their respective noble houses, their gonfalons streaming from the lance heads. And as each contingent wheeled into position, its commander lifted in signal his sword over his head. The gold and silver from the shields of the richest lords glinted in the sunlight. The horses reared, snorting with anticipation, stamping their hooves, bred for generations to charge to their deaths.

'Duke William,' Henry asked abruptly, 'that knight there, prancing with his rich battalion between the lines. He's a Norman, but for whom is he declaring today? For the traitors or for his duke?'

William too had noticed the magnificently equipped lord and his large force of knights and archers. They were gathering between the rival armies, in front of Grimoald's battalion. A white banner fluttered from the lord's lance, the emblem repeated by the bannerets of his two hundred knights. They had been parleying amongst themselves, when abruptly the knight in the black helmet and glistening coat of mail, pulled his charger towards the duke's section. These were disciplined professionals, following stirrup to stirrup, close behind their commander – and then Fitz recognized the white streamers as wimples from their ladies at court.

'Duke William,' Henry rapped. 'Ally or foe?' The king slipped his helmet across his forehead, grasped his lance and nudged his charger forward. 'Whoever has this brave warrior on his side will gain this day.'

'Ralph of Thury, sire. He owns two-thirds of the Cinglais. They call him Tesson, the old word for 'badger'. Ralph Tesson is a noble lord, but why is he not with the traitors?'

'He turned his back on them,' Henry added, levelling his lance. Yelling the battle cry 'Thury', the black knight was now cantering directly towards William who drew his sword. Ralph Tesson reined in at the last moment, his charger rearing only paces in front of the duke. The knight's right hand swung upwards. Fitz heard the slap of leather across William's shoulder, as Tesson's gauntlet struck twice.

'*Par la splendeur de Dieu!*' William roared, lifting his sword as Ralph Tesson reared high, his deep laugh booming. His eyes flashed, but he kept his lance upright, his left hand far from the pommel of his sword.

'My duke,' Tesson rasped. 'Hear me!' He jerked his jead towards his knights waiting on their restless mounts behind him.

'Speak, lord of Thury.' William's face flushed beneath the helmet, but he had lowered his sword. 'Do you hold for or against your duke?'

The black knight growled:

'At Bayeux, Guy of Burgundy and his traitor barons tempted me to join them, with promises of more land. I confess, sire, that witnessing the anarchy in your duchy I fell. I promised on the saints that I would be the first to find you on the battlefield and the first to strike you. Riding down from Secqueville, I saw your crimson standard flying proudly above the others, with its cross of Normandy and its two golden leopards. The sight halted me: Sire, I remembered that day when I knelt in homage with the other barons at Rouen, swearing to your father that we would follow you to the death . . . and today, seeing this great French host stretching before us, brought me to my senses.

'There,' and he twisted in his saddle, 'there, between the armies, I sought the opinion of my knights and archers: to a man they told me that honour would remain with us for ever if we followed our duke; shame, if I broke my oath of allegiance to your father. Now that I have struck my duke twice, I am absolved from my oath at Bayeux. I crave pardon, sire, for striking you with my gauntlet, but my lances will speak for me and for the men of the Cinglais this day.' Ralph Tesson's eyes glinted from beneath his helmet:

'The lord of Thury holds for his duke.'

And as Tesson's steed reared on its hind legs, wrenched savagely round on its hind quarters, William snapped his sword back into its scabbard. Shouting his gratitude, he watched Ralph Tesson galloping back to his men. 'Form up on my left flank, Sir Ralph,' he called after him. 'Between King Henry and my true Normans.'

Fitz watched the knights wheeling into formation, with lances raised; Ralph Tesson of Thury then swung them into the gap, but slightly to the rear, between the allied armies.

'Take up your position, Duke William,' Henry called. 'When I hear your horn, I'll signal the charge.'

The duke slapped the top of his helmet, drew his shield into the battle position, dipped his lance in salute. 'Stay with the king, Steward,' he bade Fitz. 'I'll sound thrice should I need you and your knights.'

Fitz watched his duke galloping towards the centre of his army, barely a thousand paces distant. There, the lord Beaumont beside him, he reared Samson, the great horse pawing the air with its forelegs.

Facing his knights and raising his helmet, William harangued them briefly. His standard borne high behind him, the duke, resplendent in his new chain-mail, made an unforgettable impression. He balanced with precision his heavy shield; instinctive parry and feint in shield-work was as important a skill as swordplay or hurling the lance. His thonged leggings were covered by the chain-mail; his long legs were fully extended, with the balls of his feet in the stirrups, his toes clamped around the steel.

Unlike his French ally's, his Norman lance was lighter, shorter, of applewood, tipped with Castilian steel. William was deadly at lance-throwing, hurling the weapon javelin-like, then demolishing his adversary with a swift sword attack, the instant his throwing arm was free. He did not favour the axe and although he had used the mace at Falaise, he considered it a blunt and unwieldy weapon. For him, the sword: wide-bladed, ridged down the centre, narrowing to the rounded tip; its guard curving towards the point, the upper pommel-cross short, for in-fighting. The swift cut, the lightning thrust . . . He had decided to keep his archers in the rear today, having agreed with Henry that this was to be a battle by individual commanders fighting their battalions to the death and under their personal banners . . . and Fitz, glancing across at the lines of enemy cavalry prancing in the spring wheat less than a quarter of a league distant, saw that the opposition were adopting the same tactics. Their pack horses and the provision trains were well to the rear, hidden in the coppices.

The duke was turning to face the enemy: a splendid, awe-inspiring sight, this martial youth. They were cheering him, roars of loyalty from over two thousand Norman throats . . . Henry's destrier snorted. The king raised his shield arm. His standard bearer blew upon his horn, the signal being repeated down the thronged lines to the southern battalions.

The royal standard fluttered high. The young monarch was spurring his charger forward, his lance lowered to the charge position; and as he leaned low across his beast's mane, the plain filled with the fierce French war-cry: *Montjoie! Montjoie!* To Fitz's right, the challenge was taken up by William who was also starting his charge, *'Dex aïe, Dex aïe!'* and down came his lance. The Steward nodded to his seneschal who, like him, crossed himself. Then swinging his shield before him, fitz Osbern pressed his knees against his horse's ribs. Keeping close to the left side of the royal charger, he bent low, intent now on the business of killing.

Spurring to the charge was the instant, the only moment in his disciplined ordered life, when the Steward, son of Osbern, lost control. This searing, primordial instinct surged through him, overwhelming him with the lust to kill – and, yelling his battle cry, the frenzy sprang when his sword hissed from its scabbard, the sword for which his father had grabbed but never reached in time. *'Dex aïe! Dex aïe!'* And comprehending himself, peering at himself as if from outside, he knew that he was touched by this flash of madness – as were the thousands of warriors around him, the thousands who knew not, when the shock would reverberate around the valley in a few seconds' time, how many of them would fall, never to rise again . . . Swinging his sword about his head, the blade flashing in the early sunlight, Fitz leaned low across the mane of his charger. He knew he could kill and kill efficiently. For this he was trained. So far, eleven years after winning his spurs, he'd lived to see another dawn.

'Dex aïe!' And glaring from below the rim of his helmet, gripping the saddle cloth even more firmly between his knees, he spurred onwards, ever onwards, his eyes mere slits to avoid the dirt flying from the hooves pounding so close in front of him . . .

9

BATTLE FOR SURVIVAL

The first charge which opened the battle of Val-ès-Dunes began shortly before nine o'clock on 23 March 1047. On that crisp, spring morning the lonely, barren plain, with its solitary, isolated hamlets, suddenly burst into a clamour of war-cries from both sides of the valley: the frenzied yells were as important to bolster a young man's courage, as they were vital identification for keeping the battalions together, clad as the warriors were in their indistinguishable mail armour. Shields and standards, helmets and gonfalons all bore the distinguishing colours of the battalion's commander, the simpler the emblazonry, the higher the rank.

'*Montjoie! Montjoie!*' from the French was answered by '*Dex aïe!*', the roar being challenged at once by the rebel lords as they thundered across the plain to meet their foes. '*Saint Amant! Saint Amant!*' was the loudest cry of all from the deadly Haimo and his knights galloping with such precision, lances levelled, serried in lines of twenty destriers as they hurtled across the plain. '*Saint Sauveur!*' roared Nigel's knights from the Cotentin while, from the Chicheboville flank, Rannulf's battalion bellowed '*Saint Sever! Saint Sever!*' at the ducal force galloping in admirable formation up the gentle slope. The sun dimmed as the dust swirled upwards, the air trembling as the crescendo of thudding hooves rumbled into one overwhelming cacophony of sound.

The clash of the colliding armies sent a shock wave reverberating across the valley, the sound being heard in villages as far west as the Orne, as far north as the fishing ports on the coast. And then, in the instant of unnerving silence, fitz Osbern was swept back to sanity by the distant cawing of rooks seeking refuge in the hills. Until that moment the Steward had registered nothing in his mind.

Then, the squealing of horses, the screams of broken men, the crash of wooden-slatted shields; the grunts and animal cries as blades thrust home and withdrew to slash and cut again, biting through chain, reaching the cringing flesh; the hand-to-hand grappling to the death, face-to-face, hemmed in, no room to swing the sword: up with the shield, turn on the heel, open one's guard for an instant, chop upwards, punching outwards to catch your enemy in the face with the short, upper cross of your sword-pommel. The agonized surprise, the terror in your adversary's eyes as the blood pumped, blinding him, an eye torn . . . and then Fitz sensed the disengagement as Henry turned and galloped back from the line as a fresh troop thundered into the attack past them. Turn short, charge again, battering, hacking, slicing at those now forced to fight on foot, their horses hamstrung, bleeding to death on the dark-stained, golden soil.

And so, as the sun crept across the bloody plain, the battle raged, charge after charge, as the fresh horses trotted forwards from the rear, led by the trained grooms. Then back into the charge, wheeling, manœuvring to outflank the redoubtable, efficient enemy. Forming and reforming around the standards, the clash again of steel-tipped lances on twisting shields. Across the front which stretched for almost a league, the battle swung, the issue balanced on a dagger's point as the noon sun hovered overhead, then began to dip towards the west. And on his eleventh charge and his fourth mount, Fitz found himself once again on the edge of King Henry's battling core of knights. The ground was strewn with bodies and he found it hard to keep his balance, his horse terrified by the carnage, its hooves pounding into the human flesh beneath the immense weight of charger and knight.

The French were fighting furiously around their king and the golden eagle of his standard . . . *'Montjoie! Montjoie!'* As so often in the *mêlée* of battle, the Steward sensed the instant when the tide was beginning to turn. And, at the moment when he felt that this hard core of Haimo's men was beginning to waver, the incredible happened close to him.

'Saint Amant! Saint Amant!' A huge knight, his shield emblazoned with Haimo's colours was hacking a path through the king's personal bodyguards – even the gonfalons were dripping blood, while the warrior forged closer to the French standard. Lances shattered upon shields, the mounds of corpses piled even higher, to the accompaniment of screaming from the wounded as the hooves of the chargers pounded them to pulp. The huge knight was surging irresistibly forward like a battering ram for his prime target – when Henry suddenly realized that he was in mortal danger. This mysterious knight, his shield covering him, lance at the ready, was spurring his charger straight for the royal target.

Fitz saw the devastating blow which would have sundered Henry in two had he not been wearing his double hauberk. Half-stunned, the king jerked from the saddle and tumbled to the ground. The Cotentin warrior stared for an instant in disbelief at his success in unhorsing his royal adversary who lay squirming for breath on the sodden soil. The knight could have turned in that instant, galloped back to his battalion – but in that moment of hesitation, a French knight, his shield unrecognizable from the crimson blood upon it, hurled himself at the Cotentin warrior to topple him from the saddle.

Fitz heard the cries of fury around him from the rallying French guards as the enemy knight, his hand already on the pommel of his saddle, sprang to remount. He was swinging upwards when someone hacked at the horse's belly, scything the girth in two. The saddle was torn away. The knight fell. And seconds later his body was ground to pulp as scores of Henry's knights rode deliberately across the twitching corpse. Fitz turned away as they hoisted Henry back into the saddle.

The effect of the disgrace produced an immediate effect on Henry: hacking and lunging again, he was trying desperately to redress the demoralization his fall had caused, an advantage now being pressed home furiously by Haimo's battalion. The shame of his unhorsing was driving him mad, such was the blind rage with which he was now fighting, but still the enemy was gaining, forcing the Frenchmen backwards. His knights were forming a circle around him, trying to restrain their monarch: to lose him now would bring catastrophe – then Fitz, recognizing the moment of decision, disengaged from the *mêlée*. Spotting a gap in the wall of battling knights, he wheeled his charger clear, then jabbed it with his spurs. The destrier sprang forwards. Fitz crouched low across its slippery, blood-soaked mane and set its head northwards, to the clamour of battle raging furiously in the Norman section. This was the decisive moment in the battle which William must seize. He *must* spring at once to his royal master's succour, if the day was to be saved.

The battle was swinging back and forth, a vicious slogging match on the duke of Normandy's front. William, still in the van of his troops and encircled by his diminishing band of knights, was resting for a moment, watching his reserve battalions wheeling in their turns; the escarpment of the pine-wooded spur, the hillock which led to the Bourguébus–Bellengreville road, was protecting his right flank. For a brief moment, he rode Samson to the rise at the foot of the pines.

Standing in his stirrups he searched again for his declared enemy, Rannulf of the Bessin, who had so long eluded him. Where *was* he amongst the mass of warriors swaying first this way, then that as the merciless carnage continued?

The sun was already settling across the crests of the woods stretching to the south-west. The slopes rolling upwards to the woods were littered with the carnage of five and a half hours of battle. The French king's battalions seemed to be wavering, halted in their advance across the plain. A furious struggle was raging around the royal standard. *By the splendour of God!* This was the moment when Ralph Tesson should be hurling in his support . . . but, God in heaven, where *was* the lord of Thury?

'Sire, *there's* the count of the Bessin!'

William's weary eyes followed his standard-bearer's outstretched arm. *God's blood!* There he was at last, the tall, lean Rannulf and his diminishing band of knights.

'*Dex aïe!*' William yelled, '*Dex aïe!* We have him, my lords!'

Springing Samson to the gallop, he leaned forward into the attack, his lance levelled, the charge gathering momentum, straight for the surprised count of the Bessin. The distance shortening, Rannulf and his knights wrenched their chargers round, lowered their lances. Before Rannulf gained the gallop, the duke and his cavaliers swept upon the enemy like a swarm of hornets. William felt his heart pounding, saw the tip of his lance flickering between Rannulf's neck and chest, that vital, lethal point of aim . . . 'Steady Samson: *now* . . .'

But, a split second before the expected shock, William glimpsed the looming shadow of an enemy knight, bearing down steadily upon him. The pounding of hooves, the cry – and the duke swung from his target to counter the avenging knight. William swept up his shield to parry the lance, caught it squarely, felt the shock tingling through his arm. The enemy's lance shivered, splintering at the neck to leave the iron tip embedded in the duke's shield. And in the same instant William's lance levelled straight for his assailant's throat. The point drove clean, the aim true – and as William careered past his impaled enemy, he swung round, opening his lance arm to withdraw the steel, for otherwise, with a man so transfixed, William would have had his arm wrenched from its socket. But the iron tip had stuck fast in the stricken enemy and only the shaft came away in William's hand. '*Dex aïe!*' Hurling his shivered lance from him and sweeping free his sword from its scabbard, William charged straight for Rannulf, his astonished personal foe.

'My poor Hardie!' Rannulf roared. 'You brave man!'

Rooted to the spot by the horror, the count of the Bessin saw his sworn adversary almost upon him. William caught the flicker of recognition, the hatred in Rannulf's eyes. And the count, seeing his knight twitching and screaming on the blood-soaked soil, wrenched at his bridle. Digging deep his spurs, his chin in shame upon his breast, he sped in flight from the avenging duke who was galloping furiously after him. Full well might the traitor flee: death by the rope or disembowelling was assuredly his fate if captured.

And then William, coolly calculating the merits of continuing the chase, heard a horn blowing close on his left. There, brandishing his sword, was a knight bearing the colours of the Steward of Normandy. The duke hauled Samson round, bade his knights draw rein.

'My lord,' Fitz shouted, raising the pommel of his sword. 'The counts Nigel and Guy of Burgundy are driving the king from the field. Haste, sire! King Henry's knights are falling with exhaustion where they fight.' And wrenching his destrier back on its haunches, Fitz and his escort rode furiously back through the carnage, William galloping close on his heels.

The duke recognized the crimson-stained standard and its golden eagle, still held high but jerking and swaying in the furious _mêlée_. And as William reined in Samson to allow his knights to concentrate, fitz Osbern was turning in his saddle to shout above the clamour:

'They've just found the lord Haimo. He's dead, sire, lying on his shield. It was his brother, Guillezein, who unhorsed the king.'

So the valiant Haimo had perished too. And as William searched amidst the desperate hand-to-hand fighting where best to apply the pressure, he heard above the clash of steel the blood-curdling war-cry of the ancient Vikings:

'_Thor aïe! Thor aïe! Thury . . .!_'

A sardonic smile twitched at the corners of William's mouth; Ralph Tesson and his knights were trotting in impeccable formation towards him. As one, their lances lowered in salute; as one, lifted, then descended again for the charge. The black knight wheeled his two hundred fresh knights into line on William's right. The duke raised high his sword. Then the war-cries mingled, floating on the wind towards the exhausted combatants locked face-to-face in the gory mire around the king's standard.

'_Dex aïe!_'

'_Thury, Thury! Thor aïe!_'

And seeing this fresh, resplendent force, pennants streaming, armour gleaming, sweeping down upon them from the side, Guy's men wavered. Broke suddenly. Wrenched round their chargers as they saw their flank crumbling. The last to turn was Nigel of the Cotentin. Battling to the last, William saw him roaring to his knights to die where they stood. But, like poplars leaning to the breeze, the lines were disintegrating and even Nigel's stalwart band was fleeing.

Following the king of France, the allied armies, or what was left of them on the evening of that day, hacked their way westwards, riding down and putting to the sword every rebel they overtook. Knights threw away their mail, discarded their arms, ran like bolting rabbits as fast as their legs would carry them. Some, feigning death amongst the corpses, were ridden down by those of their own side who were frenziedly pushing their exhausted mounts to the gallop, away, away from the merciless avenger. Riderless horses galloped in terror across the bloody plain.

William closed his mind. This was the justice traitors understood. More importantly, those unconnected with the battle and those like Ralph Tesson, who were waiting to see which way the wind would be blowing tomorrow, those and all the uncommitted would know the fate awaiting treachery. So, with Fitz slicing and hacking beside him, William and his army, Henry with his host, pitilessly, relentlessly pursued the fleeing enemy. Over the western ridge from which Nigel had descended but ten hours ago, across the plateau south of Caen, and down the slope towards the Orne, the slaughter continued.

At last, sickened by it all but showing no pity, sparing no one, William reined in Samson. On the high cliff between St André and May, above the swiftly-flowing river, the duke sat silently on his blowing charger. With Fitz beside him, he watched Beaumont's troops chasing the enemy across the fields to the very edge of the cliffs. He could see Thury hounding the stragglers as they stampeded for the ford at Perceauville which crossed to Bully. He could hear the screams as the foot-soldiers and sergeants hurled their defenceless prey into the Orne. He could see the floundering, drowning knights, their horses threshing in the swift current below the alders. Corpses impeded the swimmers, many of whom sank where they flailed, dragged down by their arms. Others, grotesque in their nudity, had abandoned everything, to escape with their lives back to the Bessin and the Cotentin.

William raised his head, sniffed at the soft air of the westerly breeze. For an instant, he did not hear the screams, had no eyes for the massacre. The evening light glowed, the western sky darkening with the approach of the night clouds. The sky was slashed crimson. The setting sun had dipped, its reflection staining even darker the surface of the river of blood. Gulls flapped slowly inland for the night; a flight of peewits tumbled from the sky to settle in the distant field; and from the darkening wood the first owl hooted.

'God be thanked,' Fitz murmured softly, as he wearily pushed back his helmet, 'for the victory He's given us this day.' He crossed himself, his bloody gauntlet leaving a smear across his brow.

William too made the sign of the cross. Meeting his friend's eyes, he flipped his rein, and turned Samson away from the cliff. Slipping his forearm from the battle-straps, he buckled the carrying strap about his neck and swung the shield across his back. With his friend beside him, he rode in silence, back towards the valley of the dunes. As the light faded, he saw the sergeants picking over the dead, like shadowy vultures. Tomorrow the counting would begin, the booty gobbled up, the wounded collected, the graves dug.

For what purpose, this slaughter? The duke, a bloodied warrior now, stared eastwards across the silent plain where Death reigned. God had given him the victory. His twenty years of minority would be accomplished on his birthday in less than three months. Then he would rule on his own, knowing that at last a proportion of his hard-faced barons would bow to his authority: if they respected nothing else, they saluted valiancy on the battlefield.

'Your thoughts, William?' Fitz asked quietly. 'How to deal with the traitors?'

William shook his head. 'They've condemned themselves. Better they should return to their duke. I'll give 'em the chance.'

The silence descended again between them. Then Fitz said:

'Ralph of Gacé abandoned his battalion. He crossed to the enemy in the afternoon when Henry was unhorsed. If he crosses the Orne . . .' The Steward was glancing towards the eastern horizon. The clouds of night were building up, dark and ominous across the silent plain.

IO

⋘⋙

TEMPESTUOUS UNION

The Steward of Normandy was enjoying his few moments of tranquillity by the bridge in the centre of this turbulent town of Brionne. Using the eddy below the stone pier, a trout darted from the weaving strands of green weed. This serene river glided through the valley named after it, the Risle which had seen so much bloodshed, the Risle which had inspired the gentle knight Hellouin to found his simple brotherhood at Le Bec, on the little tributary running into the river a league further north from Brionne. His example of humility and spiritual simplicity had attracted its present abbot, the brilliant Italian theologian Lanfranc, whose teaching contrasted starkly with the bloody siege being waged in near-by Brionne, an investment now entering its second year.

Fitz Osbern lifted his eyes wearily to the massive sinister keep looming over the town of Brionne. Of solid stone, the great tower of the castle reared from the craggy cliffs to overlook the town which guarded the lush valley. The outer walls of the fortress ringed the perimeter of the rock, and from the castle battlements its defenders could spot the slightest movement for leagues across the valley. Mining beneath the walls was out of the question in this hard rock; reduction by fire impossible, even if the duke's men could reach the base of the battlements. Irritated, the Steward watched the Burgundian banner fluttering from the top of the keep; this sultry summer morning was the sixteenth of July, 1049 and the flag had been flying defiantly for over fourteen months.

Guy of Burgundy was wounded at Val-ès-Dunes, but succeeded in extricating his battalion by slipping south to St-Sylvain. Crossing the Laison at Maizières, he took the St-Pierre road to Orbec, then finally reached Brionne. From his secure bastion, he immediately proclaimed his defiance, hoping thereby to rally further resistance and, perhaps, save his skin: his cousin, William, might show mercy, as he had done with some of the other defeated rebels.

Though the battle of Val-ès-Dunes had saved William and the duchy, the victory had not guaranteed peace. The forces arrayed against him, particularly in the north of the duchy and its capital, Rouen, remained viciously hostile, so much so that Fitz and the others had entreated the duke to remain in southern Normandy. William, always the prudent realist, had agreed but taken an irrevocable decision: after his twentieth birthday on 19 June 1048, he assumed his majority and firmly took charge of his duchy – or that part of it where his authority was enforceable.

First, he developed Caen from a collection of villages into a growing, unifying town, as his grandfather had dreamed. The men of Caen had been loyal to him throughout and he felt at ease amongst its friendly citizens. Many of them had fought valiantly in the battle which had brought the destruction of the rebel army: long would be remembered the mills of Borbillon, their water-wheels blocked by the thousands of corpses being swept down-river by the Orne. Second, weighing correctly the massive opposition, he realized that clemency towards the defeated *vicomtes* would stabilize the duchy more effectively than continuing vengeance. William exiled Nigel to Brittany on the understanding that should the count demonstrate loyalty he would be reinstated as *vicomte* and his possessions restored to him. Though Rannulf was disgraced, William allowed him to pass on his *vicomté* to his son, Rannulf II. The valiant Haimo, a direct descendant of Roland, lord of Thorigny, of Maisy and of Evrecy, was buried with full honours by Henry I of France in front of the church of Notre Dame at Esquay, only a league on the western side of the Orne. But the duke dealt harshly with many of the traitors, as a warning for the future.

He razed all *chateaux adulterins* in the duchy to the ground. He then forced the insolent burghers of Rouen to render him homage and to pay all their dues owing to the ducal exchequer. Grimoald of Plessis was taken prisoner during flight from the battlefield and, having been accused of being the main conspirator at Valognes, was thrown into Rouen gaol. William, still surprisingly lenient, offered Grimoald trial by duel for his life. But, on the eve of the contest the traitor was found strangled in his cell. He was buried, still manacled in his chains; his honours and positions were given to Bayeux cathedral. Fitz would never understand William's leniency towards the arch-schemer, Ralph of Gacé, who had escaped with his life, after making his fatal decision. Beneath Archbishop Mauger's wing, he had suceeded in re-establishing himself out of reach of William in Rouen; but now, his influence being forced underground, the gall of an embittered ageing man was more pathetic than dangerous.

The Steward glanced towards the Rouen road winding upwards around the base of Guy's castle towards the plain which stretched to the forest of La Londe. He could pick out the duke on his morning rounds of the siege works, checking, bullying, leaving nothing to chance. He seemed to have gained an immeasurable inner strength since Val-ès-Dunes. His regard was less restless, his gaze steadier – he was more certain of his own competence. Fitz admired William for eschewing vengeance: the political objective had been achieved, the ducal crown saved for the time being – but the insolent defiance from the brooding castle was underlining the insecurity of the duke's position. As soon as Guy installed himself in Brionne, William had hastily tried to storm the stronghold by rush tactics. He was repulsed, and Fitz could still recall the contemptuous taunts hurled at him from the battlements.

William was in a dangerous dilemma: with the Pretender, Guy of Burgundy, astride the rich valley of the Risle and controlling the main road complex into central Normandy, the ducal authority was once more being challenged. The longer the defiance persisted, the more dangerous the situation became. Here in Brionne festered the germ of fresh rebellion; while Guy remained triumphant, William could never leave the region. Brionne represented an alternative duke: the fortress *had* to be reduced and taken.

Fitz had been astounded by the speed with which William had thrown up his siege works and catapults. Ringing the castle with high timber towers in which his besieging troops could be secure from the lightning forays of Guy's troops, he cut off the defenders from the world. Gone were the nights when the town's folk slipped food and water through the cordon; finished, the lightning raids from inside the castle. Since the siege had begun, two years earlier, nothing had infiltrated the lines – but still the enemy was holding out. Fitz could easily recognize the duke, massively built, head and shoulders above his troops and engineers, inspecting the latest catapult which they had set up yesterday. Incendiary arrows had been a dismal failure; but now that hunger was beginning to pinch inside the silent castle, morale and health would become critical factors. Dead cats and dogs were being shot over the walls at night; corpses, preferably those rotting with disease, were being catapulted across the battlements.

Guy had to surrender. Though William was becoming morose, his impatience remained remarkably controlled, as if some inner fire burned within him. And Fitz smiled secretively, waiting down here on the turf by the river. He could tarry for ever in these peaceful meadows where the king-cups glowed golden along the banks, but William must not waste time if he was to catch the abbot of Le Bec-Hellouin before he left his serene valley for the last time. Abbot Lanfranc was a man of his word . . . and Fitz could not prevent his thoughts from returning to the festering sore threatening Normandy's southern borders.

Geoffrey Martel, the rapacious count of Anjou, was not called 'the Hammer', *le Marteau*, for nothing. Cruel, hard, and unscrupulous, from the day he had thrown Bishop Gervais of Le Mans into prison, the Hammer had become master of the south and west, having already taken Tours, the key to the Loire valley. Martel was turning his eyes northwards towards Le Mans and Maine which, under the ailing Count Hugh IV, was in constant turmoil. Geoffrey Martel's threat northwards towards Normandy, a vassal province of the king of France, concerned Henry who was already sounding out William as to whether they should again join forces to dissuade the Hammer . . . and then the Steward turned towards the sound of William's horn echoing through the valley. The duke would be riding soon, up to Le Bec.

True, last year William had almost lost Rouen and upper Normandy, but he had displayed his resolution when compelling Archbishop Mauger to hold the ecclesiastical council at Caen, instead of at Rouen. Not only was Rouen unsafe, but William was sufficiently far-sighted to recognize the strategic and economic importance of Caen, his favourite town, as capital of Lower Normandy. The town had access to the sea via the Orne and the little ports of Ouistreham and Bénouville, and, in addition to the valuable stone quarries, its people showed remarkable loyalty and business enterprise. If he could make Caen capital of this half of the duchy, his dream of uniting Normandy might become reality. So, leaving Gacé in Rouen, the wily, worldly Mauger had reluctantly brought his bishops to Caen in October to discuss matters of vital consequence affecting the Church.

William insisted upon being present with his barons while the bishops discussed the adoption of the Truce of God by the duchy; the proposal was energetically backed by the papacy to reduce the European disease of internecine strife.

Five years earlier, the Truce had been rejected but now even the barons, most of whom had been on the losing side at Val-ès-Dunes, were satiated with strife. They were ready to accept the Truce, which would be administered and enforced by the Church from whose authority only the spiritual blessings and sanctions accrued.

The Truce of God was already working reasonably in parts of Europe where it was operated solely by the bishops. At the council at Caen its terms were adopted: from Wednesday night-fall until Monday morning, no Norman could make war upon his neighbour. The Truce applied to saints' days and also during Advent, Christmas, Lent, Easter and Pentecost. Infringement of the Truce brought the dire sanction of excommunication and the denial of all Church rites. Fitz remembered the solemn moment when he and the assembled lords swore upon the holy relics which the bishop of St-Ouen had brought with him from Rouen. A step towards peace had been taken, one which the peasantry throughout the duchy acclaimed with relief. But William, backed fervently by Beaumont and the others, had insisted upon one rider: the ducal army and that of the French king were to be excepted. Only thus, William argued, could the duke's peace be enforced.

This exception had been hotly contested by Mauger who for the first time was pitting his power against a duke who claimed to rule the duchy entirely through his own authority. In exercising his ducal power, William was copying his powerful northern neighbour, Baldwin v of Flanders, who had adopted the same exception in the Truce of God. And once again that secret smile twitched in the Steward's visage. There existed more between the Flemish family and Duke William than the Norman court realized.

Mauger and his ecclesiastical hierarchy returned to Rouen, their cause for the Truce of God successful, but their power weakened. The duke had proclaimed to his people that the Church's influence was dependent upon the secular power of the reigning duke, a factor which in the following months became vastly important. Across the Channel, King Edward the Confessor was able to relax his defences against the threatening invasion from Norway when King Magnus died suddenly. Though the lifting of tension was beneficial to Normandy, William's personal worries increased in proportion through another act of God: in November, Leo IX became pope, a strong Alsatian determined to promote the power of Rome.

Two turbulent years followed, and then came this new year of hope, 1049, with William consolidating his ducal house by surrounding himself with trusted friends from his own generation while he waited for Brionne to fall. He needed this relative period of tranquillity while wrestling with his personal desires and quandaries of the heart. And as Fitz watched the duke's horse trotting towards him, he knew well why William wished to encounter the abbot of Le Bec this morning.

'The new catapult's badly sited, Steward,' the duke called. 'I'll inspect it again next week when they've moved it.' He smiled at his friend, his glance of understanding softening the stern face. 'Come, Fitz, let's now to other affairs.' And turning his horse northwards, he waited for Fitz to ride alongside him. Leaving their squires behind, they rode on in silence. William was evidently loath to broach the subject again, the secret he had shared with no one except his friend. As Fitz waited patiently, accustomed to his role as William's sounding-board, the Steward's shrewd eye took in the lush valley through which the silver stream ran: it was not surprising that this rich terrain was contested so hotly by its barons. Fitz was jolted from his dreaming when the duke broke the long silence: 'You've never ploughed a furrow, Fitz?' William nodded to where a serf was wrestling with the new, fashionable plough and its iron-tipped shard. It was slicing the soil like butter, while his woman guided the oxen. 'It's easy here in this rich valley,' William brooded. 'Try it on stony, rocky land. Back-breaking.'

'Memories, sire?'

'Aye. Falaise ground's different. I used to lead the bullocks.'

Again that morose silence: Fitz recognized the symptoms. Even at twenty, William was already displaying a gift for diplomacy, exercising caution when uncertain of what course to steer. Secretive, guarding his thoughts and judgements, he could be violently moody, a disconcerting trait for those around him, not knowing which way he would jump. He could be brutal, as Fitz knew, after witnessing the massacre of the fleeing enemy at Val-ès-Dunes. Pitiless, but – if politics required it – magnanimous; fearless in battle, immensely strong and one of the finest horsemen in Normandy. The iron in his nature showed in his inherent authority, a cold, aloof dignity before which elder men quailed . . . but, at this instant, riding alone with him and out of earshot from the others, Fitz sensed William's longing for reassurance.

'Fitz . . .'

'Sire?'

'That abbot,' and the duke nodded towards the beech woods in the crook of the valley a league ahead. 'Lanfranc – you don't approve of my decision, do you?'

'Throwing him out of his abbey?' Fitz frowned. 'Stupid, unwise. He's brilliant. You need each other.'

Fitz waited for the outburst, but William remained cool: 'He's too dogmatic. Too close to Rome.'

'Nonsense, sire. If he'd spoken otherwise, you'd label him a hypocrite. He's repeating only what the pope decrees.'

'What's Lanfranc know of love, eh?' William thumped the pommel of his saddle. 'He's never had a woman.'

'You may be right about the abbot,' Fitz answered slowly. 'He's unlike most of our worldly prelates.'

'Mauger's no right to obstruct my marriage plans: his own palace is no more than a brothel.' William was staring at his friend. '*You* understand, Fitz?'

'The politics, if you wed Matilda? Good for Normandy.'

'No, my dense friend. That I *love* her.'

'*Love* your intended wife?' Fitz asked incredulously, staring straight at his duke. 'Not only a political wife, then?'

'That's incidental. Her father's the enthusiastic one.'

'Baldwin's borders will be guaranteed if you marry his daughter, the king of France's niece.'

'Baldwin's now hotter for France than Germany. He's afraid of the emperor, now that Henry III's joining across the Alps with Burgundy. Flanders, France and Normandy could become a formidable force against the emperor and his ally, the pope. *Sacré barbe!* The Church's objections are sheer hypocrisy. Rome's jealous of our power, that's all: Leo IX's using consanguinity as an excuse to prevent my marriage.'

'You can't deny Matilda's a cousin.'

'Fifth degree only,' William snapped. 'We're both descended from Rollo, the Viking.'

'A long time ago; what of the rumour that Matilda's grandfather married one of your grandfather's daughters?'

'Hearsay. If so, it was the Danish Custom.'

Only the horses' trotting disturbed the sultry morning, as both men remained silent. William's different from the others, thought Fitz. His bastardy, probably. He's never used women as did so many of his court.

'You need Lanfranc, sire. Give him time. He'll change his opinion.'

William grunted, unconvinced.

'The abbot's got a sense of humour. That's an asset for you.' Fitz stopped short. The duke was notably deficient in the quality.

'Bah! He may be a worthy theologian, but that's no commendation. I distrust intellectuals. What do they know of suffering?'

'Come, William,' Fitz chided. 'Don't cherish the chip on your shoulder.'

William's face lit with that rare grin of his, a smile illuminating that craggy, severe visage, with its stubborn protruding jaw beneath the wide mouth. 'You're right, Fitz. *You've* tasted real love. Adeliza's a good wife to you: how's your little Emma?'

'Just weaning. William and Roger worship their little sister, thanks be.' Fitz smiled openly, his thoughts on Vaudreuil. He added, following his train of thought, 'The lady Matilda's seventeen now?'

'Just.' William smiled broadly. 'Old enough, Fitz.'

'I've seen her only once, when she came to court. A lovely maid.'

Fitz saw the pleasure in the duke's face: 'I'll do all I can with Lanfranc, sire. But you must not undermine me.'

William seemed to ignore his friend as he led them towards the shady woods. Silent again, deep in thought, he rode onwards, impatient now to catch the abbot. Then, as they trotted round a bend in the hard track, they sighted a small band of horsemen wending between the grey boles of the leafy beeches. There was no mistaking that lean, dark figure in the centre, upright on his flea-bitten nag. William glanced at Fitz, reined in. 'Command the squires to wait, Steward,' he ordered softly. 'We'll parley alone with the good abbot.'

Blocking the shady track, the duke waited for Abbot Lanfranc and his red-eyed monks to halt before him. They stared at the despot who was banishing their leader from their serene monastery.

The reproach in their silence expressed more than words: the brotherhood they were creating by the stream which meandered into the Risle was being unjustly dragged into worldly politics.

'You're being damned slow in clearing out,' William rasped at the abbot. 'Can't you find anything better than your limping nag?'

No birds sang in the heat of noon, even beneath the leafy shade. His dark eyes flickering with amusement, the scrawny Italian from Turin faced the sturdy duke seated so arrogantly upon his resplendent destrier.

'The mare belongs to you, as does everything else,' Lanfranc answered softly. 'If you don't approve, you should give me a better one.'

Fitz waited in stunned astonishment for William to explode with anger at this fearless cleric whose gaze remained steadily upon his speechless duke. The quietness of the wood was then shattered by the laughter booming from the younger man. Vaulting from his horse, William strode across to the nag, took its bridle and helped the Italian to dismount.

'Come, worthy abbot, it's too hot a day to quarrel,' and taking Lanfranc's elbow, he dismissed the astonished monks. 'Return to your cloister,' he told them. 'You still have your abbot. He'll return to you later.'

And as Fitz watched the bemused cortège disappearing back through the glades, he took William's horse to tether it with his own by the side of the track. Then he rejoined the two men where they stood beneath the grey bole of a massive beech. They were already deep in discussion; Fitz knew that only Lanfranc and he shared this innermost secret of William's heart.

'Why do you persist in opposing my wish to marry her?' William growled, in control of himself, his tone reasonable as if confiding in a friend. 'You know I love Matilda; her father is keen for the match. And even *you* have admitted that the marriage would be good for Normandy.'

The elder man, twenty-one years older, replied with understanding:

'I know your love to be true, sire. But I, also, must be true to myself. His Holiness forbids your intended marriage.'

'You accept the new pope's edict that, being cousins of the fifth degree, we cannot wed?'

Lanfranc inclined his head, rubbed some beech-nuts between his palms. He watched the chaff trickling through his fingers, proffered the kernels towards William:

'If Pope Leo IX so ordains, it is God's will,' he said simply.

William was struggling with himself, angered by the enigmatic priest:

'There you go again,' he muttered. 'Defending your dogma. I've heard it so often, arguing your theme – as always, you're jealous of your old teacher, Berenger.'

Fitz watched the two men fencing with each other. Lanfranc's dispute with his first teacher was shaking the core of Europe's beliefs. Berenger was denying the infallibility of the pope, was attacking the sacrament of the Eucharist; he'd even visited the court while William was at Brionne to present his argument. The old man was attacking the ideas of baptism for the newly-born; and the view held by Rome that pleasure in the marriage bed was sinful. William had heard Berenger in silence while he preached in the church of St Martin in Brionne.

But Lanfranc was not being drawn: he listened to William, but even during the long silence his authority pervaded the discussion. Not only was he an outstanding theologian, but he was a counsellor with rock-like views, a man who tempered severity with humour. It was the Italian scepticism which he had inherited from his native Turin that provided his insight into the violent, impetuous character of the Norman; he was apart from secular affairs, yet part of them. He was, thought Fitz, the only intellectual whom William tolerated.

'The pope is objecting, only because he is alarmed by Flanders' growing power,' William declared. 'Now that Norway, even after King Magnus' death, has become Baldwin's ally against England, Flanders is a state to be reckoned with. And if I strengthen this alliance . . .'

'By marrying Matilda?'

William fixed his abbot with an obstinate glare. 'Flanders, Normandy and France – my future mother-in-law's French, don't forget – will be an alliance which Rome will have to heed.'

'Politics, politics,' Lanfranc breathed wearily. 'You're becoming a diplomat, William.'

Fitz was watching them both: besides the Steward, the abbot was the only man in the duchy who would dare to use the familiarity. But the duke was grinning, his face creased by that secret smile. 'I know what I want,' he said. 'When I know I'm right, nothing shall stop me.'

'Even the pope?'

'Even Leo the ninth.'

'And the maid? Supposing she will not have you?'

William laughed harshly. 'She'll do what her father wishes.'

'If she was moulded of such stuff,' Lanfranc said smoothly, 'you'd not take her to wife.' And in the dappled shade beneath the beeches both men chuckled.

'There *are* maids who would wish to marry the duke of Normandy,' William added lamely, his colour mounting. 'So my mother once told me.'

The smile lighting Lanfranc's face was gentle, the taunting glint in his dark eyes absent. 'A fine lady,' he added. 'Is the lady Arlette in better health now?'

The duke shook his head. 'I'm worried about her.' Then he murmured, 'She's the only other woman I've loved.'

'Don't be too sure of the lady Matilda, William. Though I'm opposing your desire to marry her,' the abbot said, rising to his feet, 'I shall pray for your happiness. You, of all people, must have a good partner, a consort whom our Church can approve. But the privilege of being duke carries also its duties.'

'Marry another? To beget children without love, to furnish the duchy with heirs the barons can approve?' William jumped to his feet. 'Never!' He glared at the silent abbot: 'Anyway, I've made up my mind.'

'I know it,' Lanfranc smiled with no hint of malice. 'When will you seek the lady's hand? When ask her yourself?'

William did not answer. Instead he led the abbot back to the tethered horses. He turned to Fitz:

'Tell my squire to give the abbot a respectable horse, Steward.' He grinned at the cleric. 'We may not agree, Lanfranc,' he said. 'But return to your abbey which needs its abbot. I thank and respect you for your counsel. I would have you as a friend, but not at all costs.'

Lanfranc nodded. 'I well understand that,' he said. 'Our ways may be different, but we're made of the same mettle. I thank you too, sire, for confiding in me.' His eyes were laughing as his thin mouth twitched at the corners:

'When will you be seeing the lady Matilda yourself?'

Again the duke refused to answer. He helped the abbot to mount the horse which Fitz had fetched, turned the animal towards Le Bec.

'I ride today,' he shouted after the receding, upright figure, 'to the court of Flanders.' Turning abruptly, the restless, blue eyes met the Steward's resigned gaze.

'You're coming with me, Fitz,' the duke commanded. 'Bring only my personal guard.' He leapt into the saddle and, as his horse sprang forwards, he yelled over his shoulder: 'The gifts are ready in Brionne. We'll pick 'em up and start at once for Lille.'

Fitz could not believe it. In secret, the duke had prepared his betrothal presents. The crafty fox . . .

'We'll eat tonight,' William called. 'The remounts are waiting in Rouen. See to your business, Steward.' And as the galloping rider opened the distance, his raucous laughter echoed through the wood.

'He could have chosen Vaudreuil,' Fitz sighed wearily. 'I could have seen my Adeliza.'

As the Steward waited for the squires to catch up, he wondered as he had so often, how much longer he'd be able to match his friend's frenzied energy.

'Our wine's not to your taste, Duke William?'

He felt the countess Adela's perceptive gaze upon him; he preferred the red.

'Three glasses is always my limit, lady.'

'This is the last of our Moselle,' his hostess added tactfully, on his left at the end of the table. 'The worst penalty for my lord's quarrel with the emperor. Henry III's Teutonic sanctions are barbaric: stopping our wine quota!'

'Henry of France would never stoop to that, lady.'

William regretted his words, but this cultured woman, perhaps his future mother-in-law, showed no resentment when she replied softly:

'Do I detect a trace of sarcasm, William? My uncle's been a good guardian to you.'

The duke coloured. He knew that his boorishness was out of place at this Flemish table overseen by the niece of the king of France. And Matilda, who had remained silent opposite him throughout the interminable midday banquet, allowed a hiss of contempt to escape her lips.

'Forgive me, lady. Normandy will never forget Val-ès-Dunes.'

The countess laughed pleasantly, turning the conversation to her husband at the far end of the table:

'Does the son of the earl of Wessex prefer his beer to our dilettante tastes, Baldwin?'

The middle-aged man with the blond curls turned to the guest on his left. 'You must always be honest, Tosti, if you wish my half-sister's hand in marriage,' and he smiled at the fair, buxom girl on his right. 'Judith's a perceptive lady. Come now, beer or Moselle, which is it?'

William allowed the laughter and the banter to ripple around him. After his three nights and two days in the saddle on the road to Lille, he was in no mood for courtly niceties. Fitz, next to Matilda, was failing to suppress his yawns. William had caught his glance as the Steward had manfully attempted to break the awkward silences by talking across the table to the woman of uncertain age on William's right: Eleanor was a brittle lady, Baldwin's step-mother and William's step-grandmother, Richard II of Normandy's second wife after grandmother Ogiva had died. Eleanor did not conceal her distaste at William's courtship and, William, having nothing in common with her, had barely spoken to her.

He pushed back his chair to ease the cramp in his legs for there was insufficient space beneath the table without the risk of touching his hostess' feet – or brushing those of the girl for whom he'd ridden seventy leagues to woo.

He and Fitz had received a reasonable welcome this morning and, after the servants had bathed them both, the best of Flemish apparel was handed them. William had shaved in the inn outside Lille, but Fitz was stubbornly sticking to his straw-coloured beard. The Steward's finely chiselled face was grey with tiredness and for a moment William felt a twinge of guilt for the treatment he was imposing on his friend. Before the banquet, William had presented the parents with their presents, sumptuous lace coverlets from Bayeux for Adela, a jewelled goblet from Spain for Baldwin. But the duke's betrothal gift for Matilda had not yet been presented: the gold, pearl-studded necklace was still in the squire's safe-keeping.

The messenger William had dispatched ahead ten days previously had forewarned the Flemish court – and Baldwin's chamberlain had excelled himself with the domestic arrangements. The only coolness came from this old cow on his right – and from Matilda herself. Baldwin had dropped many a hint that the courtship would challenge William's resourcefulness, but that he, her father, would insist on the marriage. And William swore softly to himself.

He was *not* going on bended knees to this girl. She might be of royal rank but, though he was illegitimate, was he not the duke of Normandy? He too had his dignity, by the splendour of God! William caught Baldwin's eye at the bottom of the table: thank God, this sticky ceremony was ending . . . the ladies were excusing themselves, but Matilda averted her eyes as William watched her following her mother and the old lady from the hall.

She bore herself haughtily, no longer the adolescent girl he'd first met. Proud, her graceful neck arched, her jet-black eyes restlessly flashing, she was strikingly beautiful with her curls of black hair framing her tiny head. For an instant, his eyes devoured her slim, exquisite form floating so gracefully across the rushes, the tips of her minute feet peeping beneath the hem of her silken gown, a flowing robe of the darkest green which accentuated rather than concealed the seductive shape of her figure. Minute she was, but like a miniature exquisitely fashioned in proportion and detail. Her plaited tresses swung across her shoulders, the ends reaching the crimson jewelled girdle encircling her waist. Unlike the older ladies, whose hair was enclosed within the lacery of their veils, Matilda's elf-like, pale face bloomed like an arum lily, thrusting from its sheath of green. And William felt his blood quickening as his eyes lingered upon her bodice: a red band encircled her beneath the bosom, thrusting upwards the delicious roundness of her form . . .

'Come, William,' Baldwin was booming. 'We'll let Judith and Tosti off the leash. Our Saxon friend's journeyed from afar and he's rejoining his father tomorrow. A cup of mead will do us no harm in the cool of my chamber.'

The servants poured the mead then withdrew, leaving the count of Flanders and the duke of Normandy seated in the oaken chairs, at last alone. William watched the fair, curly-topped man with the heavy, rounded face, as he meticulously arranged his silken cloak. His renowned foppery belied the skilled diplomatist concealed beneath the dilettante façade. He'd rebuilt his castle, including these beautiful chambers with their overhanging, finely-carved minstrel galleries.

'There's no doubt you love her, our Mahault,' the count smiled. 'I thank you for the gifts you bear.'

'I'm asking you for her hand,' William replied brusquely, ignoring the proprieties. 'I want her to wife.' He peered straight into the depths of Baldwin's blue eyes. 'I love her – and there are advantages for both our provinces.'

The count of Flanders' red lips curled: 'And what can the marriage do for Normandy?'

William sensed that the astute Baldwin was appraising him as his prospective son-in-law. He picked his words:

'In spite of my bishops' hostility to the marriage,' William said, 'I mean to marry. If you, sire, are in agreement, not even the pope will stop me. The duke rules in Normandy, not the Church. My barons are supporting me, as is Henry, the king of France.' He hesitated, not wishing to disclose his own secret desire to prove his rank: a wife of royal blood would demolish the stigma of his bastardy once and for all. The marriage would be a political triumph, at the moment when William was still not fully in control of his own duchy. He continued forcefully:

'Such an alliance between my duchy and the powerful count of Flanders can but advance Normandy's influence throughout Europe.'

Baldwin settled himself more comfortably, hugging the compliment to himself. William went on:

'And as for Flanders, what benefits, sire? Your relations with England are strained, are they not?'

Baldwin sipped his mead:

'Adela turns me towards France, so any state friendly to Henry is a natural ally of Flanders. I need friends at the moment: my neighbour in upper Lorraine is suffering from that insatiable prig, Henry III, who is doing his best to gobble us up. He's a lackey of the pope, so Rome is solidly behind him to form an alliance aligning Leo IX and the emperor against France, myself and –' Baldwin's face creased into that charming smile which had made him as many enemies as friends, '– and Normandy if you become my son-in-law. We must exploit the Confessor's difficulties in England, while Godwine is so hot to usurp him. The earl of Wessex has never forgiven Edward, you know that?'

'I've heard rumours. Personally, I have happy childhood memories of Edward. He wouldn't hurt a fly but he's very Norman in his habits.'

Baldwin laughed coarsely:

'But not in his appetites, eh? He's refused to bed Edith from the night of the marriage. Revenge, they say, for Godwine's abominable murder of Edward's brother.'

'I liked Alfred, too,' William said quietly. 'A foul deed.'

'Edward's brand of cruelty is different: Edith is Godwine's daughter and the poor girl has her pride. She's in a convent – the Queen of England, a nun!'

'Tosti isn't with you only to woo Judith, then?'

The slow smile broke again across the heavy, pale face.

'Godwine is using his sons as ambassadors to seek support in Europe for the day he strikes for the English throne. Gyrth's in Norway, Harold and Leofwine in Denmark, but Sweyn's stayed with his father. They tell me Edward's fitting out his navy to raid my coast.' Then the count of Flanders ended softly, 'So you understand, William, why I need allies.'

'What makes you think I'll make a good husband for your daughter?'

'Even her father can see that you're hot for her. You need heirs for Normandy, but you love her too.'

The smooth tongue, the blatant politics: Baldwin was noted for getting his way. The blue eyes were averted when William blurted out:

'By God's blood, yes, I love her.' He asked, his voice grating, 'Why else have I ridden across Europe to win her? But does she love me? Will she take me for a husband?' He jumped to his feet, towering over the reclining man grinning up at him from the chair. Baldwin glanced upwards towards the gallery:

'You should ask her yourself, noble duke.'

William had not seen her. For how long had she been listening silently on the gallery above them? Had she overheard his declarations? He felt the blood mounting in his face as he turned towards the slim, imperious maid who, arms spread-eagled along the rail, was glaring down at him, her bosom heaving with anger:

'Come, sire,' she cried, her high, musical voice echoing through the chamber. 'Have you not the courage to ask me yourself?'

William swung towards the staircase, then checked himself:

'My lady,' he called to her. 'I want you to wife.' He felt the fury raging inside him at the humiliation she was deliberately causing him. He yelled at her, reckless, as he watched Baldwin crossing to the foot of the stairway:

'Will you marry the duke of Normandy?' William thundered.

Matilda was white with anger, her slender arms trembling where she gripped the oak rail. Her strident voice shrilled:

'I'd as lief take the veil,' she screamed at him, stamping her foot, 'as give myself to a bastard.'

Her terrible words rang through the chamber. For an instant William stood transfixed, watching the passion flickering in her flashing eyes. He felt his rage boiling within him, as if his head would split. His self-control broke. Roaring with rage, he thrust Baldwin from the bottom of the stairway, flinging him against the wall. Taking the stone steps two at a time, he bounded up to the gallery, oblivious of the count's shouts of protests.

He heard the swish of her gown, glimpsed her dark shadow swerving at the end of the broad passageway. Charging after her, he overtook her as she slammed the door of her chamber in his face. He burst into her private quarters and saw her on the far side, trembling with fury, her slim body splayed against the tapestry. For an instant his madness overwhelmed him: he'd take her across her bed. Roaring with rage, he leaped across the silken coverlet and with one sweep gathered her in his arms. Shrieking and kicking, her teeth sank deep into his wrist. He dropped her and, grabbing her tresses, dragged her from the bed:

'*You bastard!*' she shrilled.

She fell to her knees on the rushes. He kicked her backside, grabbed her again by the hair and dragged her, threshing and flailing down the passageway and back to the gallery. Leaving her sobbing hysterically, he vaulted down the stairway to yell at her astonished father:

'That, sire, is how the duke of Normandy deals with insults. He'll marry no shrew.'

He strode across the room, reached the banqueting room and bellowed for his steward. Then he saw Fitz hurrying anxiously towards him:

'To horse, Steward,' he bawled. 'Back to my Normandy.'

Without looking behind him, he stormed from the hall and into the courtyard. Minutes later, he was in the saddle and galloping furiously westwards. 'Find your own way home, Steward,' he yelled over his shoulder.

'And you, sire?' Fitz shouted after him.

'I ride by myself,' William roared. 'I'll take the coastal road.'

Then, the wind whistling past his ears as he galloped, the frenzy gradually eased, the passion spent. He'd traverse the Caux country and cross the Seine for Pont-Audemer to avoid Rouen. He needed the one true companion of his childhood, the uncomplicated Walter Fulbert. *He* would understand and would listen without giving counsel. Walter was a seaman now; at Honfleur the seafarers would surely know of his whereabouts.

11
❧

LAND OF PRINCES:
EU, 21 JUNE 1051

It was two years, less one month, since the Steward had been overtaken by Baldwin's horsemen during that traumatic afternoon at Lille. Fitz had been persuaded by the count of Flanders to return to the Flemish court for the night, before setting out on his return journey to Normandy. But the misery of that embarrassing and sullen evening had been shattered by the final shock. Matilda had burst into the banqueting hall to confront her father. And now Fitz, sitting in the front pew of this simple church on the edge of the great forest of Eu, smiled secretly to himself at the memory of the words which had burst from the tempestuous girl's lips.

'That duke must be a proud one,' she'd cried, 'if he rides so far to thrash his beloved before her father's eyes and in her parents' home.' She'd swung fiercely on her heels to face Fitz:

'Tell your duke I shall become his wife when he chooses.'

And here they all were, the principal actors in the drama, assembling on this twenty-first day of June in the little town of Eu on the count of Flanders' border. The simple church was bursting its walls, while the townsfolk thronged outside, singing and cheering as they waited for Baldwin to arrive with his daughter. The bell rang joyously while the priests, led by the bishop of Lille, sorted themselves and the excited choir at the entrance to the chancel. Fitz turned solemnly to watch the proceedings as, once again, he felt surreptitiously in his pouch to touch the gold ring: it still lay safely there for him to produce for the impatient bridegroom. And the Steward felt satisfaction that William had chosen him for this honour: he could have nominated his half-brother, the burly Odo, now twenty years old, whom William had consecrated bishop of Bayeux after the shock of Arlette's death in June last year. The duke had taken the tragedy grievously, but today for consolation was the presence of his sister, Adeliza, here among the guests. She was between her betrothed, Enguerrand, the present count of this Ponthieu region, and his brother, Guy – an ambitious land-grabbing pair, volatile, playing off Flanders against Normandy whenever they could, but William hoped that his sister's union to Ponthieu might cool the broth a little.

The countess of Flanders, William's prospective mother-in-law, had organized the seating: she had adopted the Norse custom of separating the guests by families, instead of herding the ladies on one side of the church, the knights on the other. In the second pew on the right-hand side of the aisle were Robert, the count of Eu, and his mother, the formidable countess, Lesceline. Behind them was Adeliza, her flaming red hair peeping from her veil. The third pew was taken up by the count of Arques' family: William of Arques with his son and his wife, Enguerrand's sister – an isolated trio; the count of Arques' brother, Archbishop Mauger, had not been invited to officiate. The duke had bade him prepare for the official coronation of his duchess in Rouen. The ceremony was to take place as soon as possible after today's marriage and was to be as magnificent as Mauger could organize. The respect for tradition and dignity, this love of ceremonials, was a trait which William had inherited from his father. With his own natural gift of leadership, William knew that an awe-inspiring presence, a display of splendour enhanced his own position, even amongst the highest. And, from the corner of his eye, Fitz watched the impressive figure of William, duke of Normandy, presenting himself before the noblest in the land who were gathered to witness his marriage before God to Matilda, daughter of the count of Flanders.

He stood half-facing the western door, supremely confident, caring not a jot for the unspoken criticism from sections of the congregation: among them were Abbot Lanfranc, who had travelled from Le Bec, and the many priests; and the more pious of the barons who were putting Rome before the interests of the duchy.

There were plenty of such men here who remembered that first week of October two years ago, in 1049, when the ecclesiastical council met at Rheims. Led by Mauger, William's plea of secrecy had been ignored by a majority of the bishops: so Pope Leo IX's condemnation and his threat to place Normandy under interdiction if the marriage went ahead became public knowledge. That William and Matilda were distant cousins could not be denied. But however vehemently Rome objected to the marriage on the grounds of consanguinity within the proscribed degrees; however bitterly the archbishop of Rouen and his bishops ranted, Duke William had been past rational argument, even when Leo IX placed the duchy under interdiction. William was in love – there could be no doubting it as he waited for his bride while the choir broke into its paeon of praise, the melodious singing floating to the rafters.

William was wearing the massive gold coronet of Normandy, but the crown did not detract from the strength of his heavy, determined face. His vivid blue eyes flickered, his glance reaching the farthest recesses to identify those present. His russet hair was shorter than fashionable, shaped in a line about the nape of his neck, fringed straight across his wide forehead. As always when at court, he was clean-shaven, which accentuated his short, broad nose and stubborn, protruding chin. The full lips of his wide mouth were already turned down at the corners and this accounted for the humourless, stern appearance he presented – an impression he used to effect when it suited him. In all, thought Fitz, a unique young man of twenty-three, in control of himself; a youth who had suffered more hardship than most older men; a leader who could be ruthless to achieve his objectives.

Today William was wearing his finest state apparel: the heavy cloak of royalty, of deepest indigo, heavily embroidered with gold thread and fastened at the right shoulder by a priceless, ruby-studded circular clasp. His bull-like neck was enclosed by the collar of his vivid, emerald-green silken robe which extended in royal style almost to his deer-skin shoes. His deep gold tunic, overlaid upon the robe, contrasted richly, making the colours sing. He did not bear a sceptre, but wore his scabbarded sword, even in the house of God, a detail which no one had missed: the symbol of his ducal authority backed by strength – for this man excelled as a warrior, as he had proved.

As at his coronation in the cathedral at Rouen, when he had taken the three Norman oaths – to keep the Church's peace, to dispense justice without fear or favour, and to eradicate rapine and plundering – it was upon the sword of state he had sworn. And now, after the silence at the end of the anthem, the choir was soaring into William's favourite hymn, *'Christus vincit . . .'* There's no doubt, thought Fitz, under whose banner the leader of this assembly rules. And as the words floated upwards, the priests took up the refrain, their words echoing through the church, *'Feliciter . . .'* It was an impressive moment, as the horns began sounding in unison outside; the congregation was turning towards the western door.

She looked so fragile, this minute girl on her father's arm. Baldwin was as richly apparelled as the duke, but whereas William exuded strength, the count of Flanders, despite the dignity of age, gave an impression of foppishness, of pretentiousness – and the closer he approached the massive man waiting at the chancel, the greater seemed the disparity. Matilda, sheathed in white and heavily veiled, seemed to float towards her duke, her dark eyes flickering with excitement – and then, as they came abreast, the Steward stepped from his pew to take up his position behind the bridal pair. Was that a gleam of triumph he caught in Baldwin's fleeting smile?

Fitz Osbern was a religious man and, like his duke, attended his daily Mass, morning and evening if he could. But he preferred the simple, unadorned occasion when he could attempt to share in the mystical spirituality of the Lord's Supper; for him, these three-hour ceremonies detracted from the beauty of the communion. The bishop, resplendent in his regalia and surrounded by his cowled priests, was proceeding with measured dignity, intoning sonorously the time-honoured words of the marriage service:

> *Gloria in excelsis Deo,*
> *Et in terra pax hominibus bonæ voluntati.*
> *Laudamus te . . .*

And as the Mass began, Fitz wondered for how long this young couple standing before the altar, the groom dwarfing his proud, spirited Matilda, could remain in harmony. As long as she provided Normandy with a stabilizing heir, she would have fulfilled her function. But this union, the Steward realized, was no mundane political alliance: like his own marriage to his lovely Adeliza, the flame of love blazed between them.

> *Credo in unum Deum . . .*

It was in the bitter February of last year that Guy of Burgundy finally surrendered Brionne, his defenders starved and decimated by disease. From that day the duke was able to exert his authority, move freely through his duchy. Only three weeks later, he had installed himself in the hostile Rouen he distrusted, the Frankish Rouen which was nevertheless the capital of his duchy, the city run by Archbishop Mauger and his cronies. But not for the first time, William exhibited unusual leniency: he allowed his humiliated cousin, Guy of Burgundy, to flee the duchy for his native Burgundy. The duke had even allowed those who had surrendered and who were prepared to pay homage, to

re-establish themselves in the duchy. Even Guy's half-brother, Foulques the Black, had been granted this privilege; within six months he
was already inveigling his way back to court. An error, thought Fitz,
but at the time William had affairs of the heart to concern him, affairs as
unsettling as events boiling up outside Normandy's borders . . .

. . . . *Crucifixus etiam pro nobis: sub Pontio Pilato passus, et sepultus*
est.
Et resurrexit tertia die . . .

The threat came from the Hammer in the south, Geoffrey Martel,
count of Anjou. When Count Hugh IV of Maine died in February, the
count of Anjou marched north and accepted Le Mans from its
inhabitants. He thereupon exiled the widow, Bertha, with her son and
daughter, at the same time releasing the imprisoned Bishop, Gervais, in
order to control the Loire valley. The bishop, after ceding Château-
du-Loir in payment for his liberty, sped to William's court and after
weeks of pressure finally persuaded the duke to act against the menace
on Normandy's southern borders.

Henry of France, affected by the same threat, joined forces again
with his vassal duke. In April 1051, William joined his king in the siege
of the Hammer's stronghold at Mouliherne to the east of Angers but,
when William was invited across the Channel by the English king,
Geoffrey Martel, sure now of Le Mans, moved swiftly north to threaten
Normandy's border. He captured and installed his forces in Domfront
and Alençon, the fortress towns controlling the invasion routes from
the east and south . . . and Fitz's thoughts reverted to the present.

The bishop was starting the Consecration, soon the heart of the
service would be reached – and Fitz was wondering what was passing
through William's mind at this moment, this turning-point in his
turbulent life. This year of our Lord, 1051, the first in the second half of
the century, was certainly a landmark. William's mysterious trip to
Winchester only six weeks ago was a secret he had disclosed only to his
closest associates, but the confidence which Edward the Confessor had
shared with the duke was strengthening the king's hand in the difficult
decisions Edward was having to take.

The Confessor had at last faced up to the earl of Wessex and his
formidable family. Godwine had emerged triumphant from his bloody
struggle for ascendancy with the other two English earls, Edward
playing off north against south: both Leofric of Mercia and Siward, the
Northumbrian, had retired back to their bleak fastnesses. The earl of

Wessex was lord of southern England from Land's End to London and the North Foreland; his sons, Sweyn and Harold, were masters of the southern Midlands and East Anglia.

Edward's reaction was to gather Norman support: surrounding himself with immigrants from across the Channel, he appointed them to key positions in an effort to counter Godwine's power. The son of the count of Vexin was made earl of Hereford, having married Edward's sister. And in the Church, the Confessor appointed his Norman friends to the bishoprics. He made the abbot of Jumièges bishop of London and then elevated him to the archbishopric of Canterbury early in the year, filling the London vacancy with a clerk of the court. The inevitable clash was sparked by the disgraceful incident at Dover last month . . .

Sanctus, sanctus, sanctus Dominus Deus Sabaoth . . .

Edward *is* a feeble monarch, Fitz mused. Why couldn't he himself have punished the citizens of Dover? They had beaten up his brother-in-law, Eustace of Boulogne (he, too, had a legal claim to the throne), on his return journey to France after visiting Edward. The Confessor had weakly commanded Godwine to chastise the offenders, but the earl of Wessex, infuriated by the appointment of a Norman to the see of Canterbury, refused the king's order. Instead, he roused the Londoners and, with his own army and those of his sons, confronted the king. Edward, now backed by Mercia and Northumbria, had waited at Gloucester for Godwine to attack the royalist army . . .

. . . *Benedictus qui venit in nomine Domini;*
Hosanna in excelcis.

The bishop would soon be inviting the couple before the table. The clinking of the censers was the only sound as the incense drifted through the nave, the pervasive scent reaching to the farthest corners of the church . . .

Though the rival armies never clashed at Gloucester, Godwine refused to defend himself and his sons before a judicial court in London. Banished from England, Godwine was at this moment sheltering under Baldwin's protection in Flanders. His sons, Leofwine and Harold, were in Ireland, busily preparing for a co-ordinated seaborne invasion along the south-eastern coast, where the men of Sussex, Kent and London were waiting impatiently for their strong, revolutionary leaders . . . Fitz *must* pull his thoughts together: the marriage service was entering its most solemn moment.

Uxor tua sicut vitis abundans in lateribus domus tuæ.
Filii tui sicut novellæ olivarum in circuitu mensæ tuæ . . .

If Godwine and his sons were to succeed, an event over which northern Europe was gloating in anticipation, it was certain that Edward would be compelled to rid himself of his Norman friends; it was hinted that Godwine would again be forcing the king to cohabit with his wife, Edith, the earl of Wessex's humiliated daughter. So, it was not surprising that Edward was concerned for a strong successor to his throne: Archbishop Robert of Canterbury, voyaging to Rome to receive his *pallium*, was commissioned to open the delicate discussions with the duke of Normandy. The two men had been alone together and William had not even confided in Fitz – and this meeting had taken place only six weeks ago.

Et videas filios filiorum tuorum: pax super Israel.

The church rustled as the congregation made the sign of the cross. The bishop was well into the epistle:

. . . for this cause shall a man leave his father and mother and shall be joined unto his wife; and they two shall be one flesh. This is a great mystery . . . those whom God hath joined together let no man put asunder . . .

and Fitz, fumbling for the ring in his pouch, smiled to himself as the memories flooded back . . .
The elfin girl was glancing up into her husband's face as a hush descended upon the throng of witnesses:

In te speravi, Domine, dixi: tu es Deus meus, in manibus tuis tempora mea.

The Steward handed the ring to the bishop and, man and wife, the royal couple moved to the Lord's table. Watching them, kneeling to share the bread and wine, Fitz offered his own prayer. So young they seemed to face the dangerous future . . .
William had moved swiftly after the archbishop of Canterbury's visit. He'd returned from England only just in time for the wedding.

Agnus Dei, qui tollis peccata mundi, dona nobis pacem.

The blessing, and then the glorious lifting of the choir's voices as the royal couple turned to face the congregation . . . Matilda's hand rested lightly on her husband's arm as they majestically made their way back to the nave. Following at a distance, Baldwin and the Steward began their procession down the aisle, Fitz behind the tall warrior who was wearing his crown with such natural dignity. Erect and glancing neither to left nor right, there was an aura about him which must have impressed most souls in that packed church, whether hostile or not – and then the duke and his duchess were outside in the bright sunlight, to the clamour of the bells and the cheering from the people of the town of Eu.

'I shall remember this day all my life, my lord.'

He closed his hand about her entwining fingers; he nodded towards the sea as he filled his lungs with the soft air.

'I thought the banquet would never end,' William said.

They were alone at last here at the bottom of the castle garden which bordered the river. The town of Eu was huddled into the final bend and bordered the left bank of the sluggish Bresle before the river joined the sea. The castle, the home of the counts of Eu, faced the church on one side, the coast on the other.

'It's kind of your uncle to let us use his home like this.'

William smiled, watching the finely chiselled face of his bride outlined against the failing light. She was exquisite, so unused to the self-interest of all those even remotely connected to the ducal house. The crimson orb of the sun hung momentarily, its lower rim touching the rose-tinged edge of night clouds building along the western horizon. He slipped his arm about her waist, while in silence they watched the pulsing sun bowing itself from their wedding-day.

'A long twenty-four hours,' he said, not looking at her but turning her towards the castle.

'The start to our life,' she murmured. 'I've felt frightened sometimes – but not now, not this evening,' and he felt the pressure of her fingers. 'I've prayed we'll always keep separate our personal lives from your affairs of state.'

'We'll start as I mean to continue, Mahault,' he said, using her father's pet name for her. 'My mother managed to keep private her life with my father.'

He was watching her intently, the subject of his bastardy no longer an embarrassment between them. The ladies had dressed her in this dark green gown; she had let down her tresses which, sweeping across her shoulders and down her slender back, were touched gold by the last rays of the setting sun.

'Their life must have been very different,' she said softly. 'I wish I'd known her.' Her smile flashed up at him. 'D'you think she'd have approved of me?'

He stooped to kiss her hard upon the mouth. They were nearing the western gate and he untwined her hand.

'Oylard's servants will be watching for us,' he murmured. 'The lady Lesceline is behind the count's kindness, I'm certain.'

William smiled inwardly. The old lady was a saintly soul, devoted to her ailing husband, William, the count of Eu. It could not be long before Robert, their eldest and William's uncle, succeeded to the *vicomté*. Robert had insisted that he and his parents should move to the large house at Mesnil-Val for the night. The kindness should stand him in good stead with his duke for the future. Only Matilda's parents and Oylard, the old lady's *fidelis*, her liegeman, remained tonight in the castle to oversee the servants and to supervise the ducal nuptials. Yes, William thought, this family deserves to prosper. Our marriage ceremony has been a family affair and Baldwin's choice of venue has been a happy one. Not only was Eu on the border between Flanders and Normandy, but its count was part of the ducal family. And William groaned audibly as he thought of tomorrow.

'What's troubling you, my lord?'

'Our ride tomorrow,' he told her. 'Six hours to Rouen and there's the pomp on our arrival: too much for you in one day.' He grinned at her as Oylard approached across the courtyard which, in spite of the hard ground, was a rich green carpet of freshly-cut beech branches. 'My duchess must be looking her best when I present her to the citizens of Rouen and its archbishop.'

He caught the glint in her dark eyes as she swept ahead of him through the door and into the hall. Her mother, Adela, the lady of the bed-chamber and the girls fluttered about her, chattering and laughing as they shepherded her towards the bath-house abutting the western wall of the castle. Oylard straightened from his obeisance, his face lined with anxiety behind his grizzled beard: 'They have carried up the water, sire,' he croaked. 'Is there aught I can do?'

'See that I am left in peace.' He nodded at the *fidelis*. 'Is Roger comfortable? Pray make certain that all is prepared for our ride to Rouen tomorrow.'

Oylard nodded, a twisted smile creasing his weather-beaten face:

Roger, the duke's liegeman, had drunk unwisely during the wedding feast, a failing to which he succumbed too often. But being the son of Humphrey, the best friend of William's father, Roger's loyalty compensated for his lapses.

'He's sleeping in my chamber, sire.' The older man smiled. 'When do the duke and duchess intend to set forth: morning or afternoon tomorrow?'

William countered the bland question: an early start would fly in the face of convention.

'I'll take the journey in two stages,' he said. 'Tell Roger we'll ride after midday.'

He strode between the bowing servants, climbed briskly up the oaken stairway which was garlanded with flowers wilting from the heat. He heard Oylard padding after him, the servants' whispers and chuckling behind him. The chamberlain met him on the gallery and strode ahead to the portal framed with lilies, their scent sickly in the airless passageway.

'The count and countess' bed-chamber,' the man announced, throwing wide the door: 'The guards await their summons should my duke require aught else.'

'Send them hence,' William growled. 'The duke needs no protection in the castle of the count of Eu.'

'Sire . . .' A fleeting reproach flickered in the old man's eyes as he slowly closed the door: 'The duchess' private chamber adjoins the far passage.'

William swore softly, relieved at being alone at last in this candlelit chamber. He had flaunted custom, determined to dispense with the ceremonial nuptials: not for him the crowded chamber, simpering and giggling women, coarse-tongued fathers and uncles, as they proffered advice and their well-wishes to the bedded couple. True, it was not long since that a wedding night had traditionally to be witnessed by an appreciative and instructive audience: the union was for the benefit of all and an efficient coupling was what mattered if an heir was to be engendered. He'd discussed the matter awkwardly with Matilda but she had been surprised by his reticence.

For her (she'd told him when she'd known him better) loving a man meant marriage and giving her husband pleasure within that union, whatever the Church was now teaching. And she had laughingly agreed to tonight's procedure, to the disappointment of her mother and the old countess Lesceline. Grinning to himself, he peeled off his clothes. He'd take the tub, scrape his face and be ready for his Mahault. He had planned for so long, prevailed his will over Mauger's opposition, waited for nearly two years for this night. Would she laugh at him, he wondered, if he told her she was his first woman?

After tonight, she could bath him herself, as the other noble ladies did – tonight he had refused the ministrations of the ladies of the bed-chamber and would take care of himself. The water was almost scalding on this sultry evening. And stretched in the tub luxuriantly, his thoughts as always turned towards the future . . .

The friendliness during today's roisterings was ephemeral, he knew: there *was* treachery still in the air. Though Gacé's influence was now negligible, the opposition engendered by the ducal marriage had proved that Normandy was still seething with unrest. How many traitors lurked, waiting to tear him apart should Geoffrey Martel succeed in exploiting his acquisition of Le Mans on Normandy's border? From Maine and from Anjou the Hammer threatened; King Henry was demanding why his vassal duke was again reluctant to act against the rebels. Perhaps Henry had never loved as hotly as William?

This passion seething within him for his Mahault had swept everything else aside. Even his visit to England had been one of frustration; he could not return swiftly enough to prepare for their wedding. He had risked leaving the duchy at the moment when the Hammer was consolidating his capture of Domfront and Alençon. And six leagues east of Alençon, the nauseating Talvas family of Bellême was biding its time, waiting to exploit the result of the contest, whichever way it went. William Talvas, the Young, was in exile now, a disgusting old man ravaged by disease, they said, the result of his dissolute life; but his daughter, Mabel, was proving as capable in terrorizing their domains – the family had built thirty-five castles since the original Talvas had taken Bellême.

William climbed from the tub, rubbed himself dry as he peered through the narrow slit of the window. It was almost dark, but he could just distinguish the gulls flapping inland for the night. And with that lick of desire flickering again inside him, he donned the silken gown they'd left conveniently for him at the entrance to the chamber. He was not a minute too soon: he could hear them crossing from the lady Lesceline's chamber – hushed voices, a girl's laugh which was immediately suppressed. The duke of Normandy hitched at the cord about his robe, smoothed the fringe across his forehead; he snuffed the candles, save the two in the wall brackets by the bed. His heart hammering, he waited in the centre of the chamber for his duchess.

She had always been a light sleeper. It was the pale shaft of twilight in the slit-window which first awoke Matilda. And lying with her head across his chest, she did not stir, watching through half-opened lids the imperceptible lightening of this new dawn, this first day of her new life as the wife of the duke of Normandy.

She did not know when they had finally drifted into sleep, but the hour now could not be later than four o'clock, for this was the day after the solstice. And without waking him, she gently clasped her arm more tightly about her man. Her mother had been right: to expect pleasure from the first time was naïve. The more ardent a virgin husband, she had advised, the more the certitude of a bungled first coupling. Adela assumed and hoped that William had practised what was expected of him and had enjoyed the Danish Custom, because only through experience could a man pleasure his new wife. As for Matilda, her happiness would lie solely in *giving* – the *taking* of the man she loved would come later. And last night, only four hours ago, their loving had been exactly thus for both of them. To her surprise, this had been the first time for him too. He had dropped immediately into slumber, his arm encircling her, her head where it was now, in delicious intimacy, her lips brushing his nipple.

So she was his duchess, not only in name but, at long last, in flesh – they had waited for so long, fought so fiercely against what had often seemed overwhelming opposition. If she had hesitated, however briefly, to support him she wondered whether he would have per-severed as he had – and she smiled to herself as the light of dawn stole through the chamber. She was wife to the most masculine of men she had met in her nineteen years – and she was thankful that theirs was no arranged match of childhood. For these times, they were relatively mature; he was already twenty-three and a man who made up his own mind.

Her duke was a strange paradox: tough, ruthless and secretive, often enforcing his will upon those older than him; already worldly in experience, he seemed years older than his age. She had never dreamed how totally a man, even one such as he, could be a slave to the woman he loved. He was a child in her arms, unconscious in his passion of the physical process she had to endure this first time. The moment had been miraculous for her, knowing that her man loved her – and now she could give him her body as he wished, lead him onwards as her mother had taught. She felt the excitement welling deep inside her womb, recognizing the mounting longing for him and for the part she was now to play in his life. Theirs was no mundane union – and her fingers began feeling for him as her lips found his mouth.

'My Mahault,' he murmured, his hands closing about her flanks. 'Have you done this before?'

'You should know, beloved,' she whispered. 'If I had, it would have been easier for you.'

His arms were bands of steel about her. She cried out as he crushed her breasts against him.

'Did I hurt you last night? You're so tiny.'

She did not answer. Instead she led him onwards wordlessly until she knew he could hold back no longer.

'You're so strong.'

And lying there listening to the birds waking the new day, she sensed suddenly that perhaps this moment could be the zenith of their life's happiness:

'My lord . . .' she whispered, when at last he lay stretched again at her side.

'My Mahault?'

'The next duke of Normandy,' she whispered. 'He's safe now.'

Those massive arms clenched again. He pulled her upwards across his chest and clasped her face between his hands:

'You're not frightened?' he asked, stroking her tresses.

'I don't care what anyone thinks or says.'

'Even the pope? He's excommunicating us.'

'Even the pope.'

He brushed her forehead with his lips: 'They'll make it difficult for us, you know that.' His hands were rhythmically caressing again, stroking her flanks, again rousing her desire.

'Did it hurt this time?'

'It was wonderful.'

'I can be cruel, Mahault. To my enemies. They're all around us.'

'But not to your wife,' she whispered. 'Oh, William, my lord . . .' She was hot for him again, as her mother had said would happen to her. She lay stretched before him, pushing up her small breasts for him, watching his devouring eyes, listening to his words while she waited. 'Some Normans are worse than others,' she whispered.

'So many are brutal to their wives,' he said softly. Then he told her of the atrocious barbarities being practised in his duchy. And, as she listened to the horrors, she realized for the first time that he was treating her as his equal, as his confidant and companion.

Caressing her the while, he told her of William Talvas of Bellême, known as the Hare because even his sons could not induce him to stand and fight; of the Hare's monstrous treatment of his pious wife, Hildeburg, whom he had strangled in the market-place on her way to Mass.

'That's horrible,' Matilda whispered, as she slid across her husband. 'And what became of Talvas?'

'He married his mistress immediately,' William said and, without embarrassment, continued to tell how the Hare had invited all his neighbours to the wedding, in particular the Giroie brothers who had previously murdered Gilbert of Brionne. But even they, disgusted by Talvas's conduct, refused the invitation. To show their repugnance, they sent instead to represent them at the jollifications, the unfortunate William of Montreuil, a slight which the Hare took as a personal insult.

'What'd Talvas do?' Matilda murmured, her caresses rhythmical with the cadence of desire.

'Slit Montreuil's nostrils, cut off his ears and . . .'

She waited for him to continue but sensed his reticence when she met the blue eyes appraising her, evaluating her sensitivity. 'You can't shock me,' she smiled. 'Flanders has been warring for years against the emperor.'

'They cut off his balls.'

She gave a little cry, held him tightly. 'He's a monster,' she whispered.

'The Giroies chased him from castle to castle but he always escaped, refusing to fight. Finally, his own son, Arnulf, truly of the Talvas mould, trapped him and sent him into exile where he is waiting to die.'

'D'you get used to these horrors?' she asked softly. 'Does the cruelty brutalize you too?'

He did not reply directly but continued his monologue, as if talking to himself. He told her of how Arnulf, who had inherited the Talvas fortunes, robbed a poor nun of her piglet; of how, that same night, after an orgy of over-eating the black pudding sausage provided by the piglet, Arnulf was strangled in his bed by his brother.

'Is he the last of the Talvas?' Matilda whispered, sickened by the awful cruelties.

'The daughter's ruling now – Mabel's as repulsive as the others.

Poison's her *forte*.' He was glancing up at her, his stern gaze unfathomable. 'She has an eye on Roger of Montgomery: good for Normandy, because he's loyal to me now.' She felt him stirring again but did not interrupt: it was good to listen to him unburdening himself. As his duchess, she must adapt herself to his Norman way of life. It was no more brutish than the Flemish and in an undefined fashion was less rigid, less ruthless.

'Roger's an outstanding man,' he was saying. 'I met Mabel Talvas once at Falaise: short, fat and coarse. Roger's putting his family before his own happiness, I fear.' The corners of his broad mouth curled with disdain: 'But a union of the two families should bring peace to this turbulent region of our duchy.'

She lay still as his hands harmonized with the rhythm of her caresses – so it was 'our' duchy? She knew now that however terrible the future she was inextricably tied to his ambition, to his beloved Normandy, part of him like the woof to the warp in a parcel of cloth.

'So you see, my little Mahault, why I have to leave you after you are crowned as my duchess in Rouen? I must retake Domfront and Alençon, or Bellême will join the Hammer.' His deep chest heaved as he sighed. 'The treachery will start all over again. They'll be at my throat, like hounds at the kill.'

She tried to hide the welling tears. To find this heaven and to lose it so swiftly, perhaps for ever, while he went to war . . .

'My sweet,' he murmured. 'You'll have to accustom yourself to these separations. It's because you're strong – that's one reason – that I've taken you as my duchess. When you're older, you'll rule in my absence.' His eyes were solemn as he rolled on top of her to gaze into her face. 'D'you think you can rule, Mahault? My truest friends will be at your side to guide you.'

'Oh, my lord – ' She gave a little cry as she took him to her. 'I will do my utmost to be worthy of your trust, our Good Lord so helping me.' She watched the strong face so close to hers, his eyes shut so tightly. 'Hush, now . . .'

And this time their loving was as God meant it to be, she felt certain, while afterwards she lay close to him, listening to the castle awaking to the fresh day. Hens were clucking, fluttering in the courtyard; dogs barked; there was the solid sound of horses being groomed and the clink of harness. The ray of sunlight piercing the embrasure carried the heat of summer with it.

'Mahault?'

'My lord . . .?'

He lay totally relaxed by her side, his blue eyes steadily holding hers.

'Can you keep a secret, Mahault?'

She smiled at him. 'I'm a woman – but your duchess also.'

'Would you wish to be my queen?'

She shook her head, uncomprehending. He chuckled while he threaded her long hair through his fingers. 'The crown would look well on your dark head.'

'What crown, my lord?'

'The queen of England's.'

She jerked to one elbow, peered solemnly at him:

'Do not mock me,' she whispered. 'I have been your duchess but a few hours.'

And then in his low voice, he told her of his recent visit to Winchester. When Edward died he would be childless. He was the son of Emma who had been twice queen of England, first as the wife of Ethelred and then of Canute the Great. Emma was the duke Richard II of Normandy's sister, and William's great-aunt. Duke William was therefore Edward's blood cousin, with a claim to the English throne stronger than most. At all costs, the English king was determined to prevent his crown passing to the family of Godwine who had so foully butchered his brother Alfred.

'I've waited long to tell you,' her husband ended, twisting her towards him. 'You'll have time to learn your apprenticeship.'

He kissed her gently and threw back the silken sheets. She watched him striding to the closet, her huge man with the long, sturdy legs; his large head, the russet hair cut short at the nape of his neck, was set proudly on the short-bull-neck which thrust from the massive shoulders of his barrel-like chest. She would give him all she had, her life if need be. And then, warm though it was in the chamber, she shivered involuntarily: the future was closing already about her, dark and menacing. She shrugged off the inexplicable unease and slipped from the bed. Tomorrow would take care of itself. Today, she would be worthy of him; for months he had dreamed of presenting his wife to the citizens of Rouen for her coronation as duchess of Normandy.

And the future? Within her she bore his seed, the seed which through their love, must burgeon into their son: the next duke of Normandy; and, pray God, monarch of those mist-shrouded islands across the Channel, the king of England.

12

WALLS OF SHAME:
ALENÇON, 10 FEBRUARY 1052

Aside from the frozen tents, the Steward of Normandy and his *fidelis* were standing on the rise which overlooked the river Sarthe and the battlements of the fortress of Alençon. Above their heads the bare branches of the trees rattled in the wind, white with frost; a flight of duck winged overhead, circling the castle walls. The battlements were perched above the moat formed by the stream, a tributary of the Briante which joined the Sarthe downstream. The banks were laced with icicles; a freezing wind whistled through the duke's encamped army, an east wind which scythed from across the Chartrain plain.

'Thank God, Gilbert,' fitz Osbern muttered, 'dawn at last!' He glanced towards the rose-tinted sky lightening imperceptibly behind the desolate wood. 'What about something hot inside us?'

Fitz watched the nineteen-year-old boy, *Vicomte* Erchembald's son, scrunching towards the bivouacs where the first sparks from the morning fires were shooting skywards. The duke must have decided that with daylight surprise would anyway be compromised – and in these hard conditions no man could fight on an empty stomach. 'I'm too old for this,' Fitz grumbled to himself. 'Dear God, let things settle down soon,' and he swung his arms about him, trying to restore the circulation in his numbed fingers. He was thirty-two, an old man amongst these warriors, but the duke still needed him, even after the drama of his marriage. It was, Fitz suspected, William's separation from Matilda and his wish to be with her when their first-born was due at the end of next month, which had prompted his spontaneous change of plans. This frenzied night ride from Domfront, seventeen leagues in six and a half hours, had been trial enough for the horsemen, but hell for the foot-soldiers: the stragglers were still drifting in, their feet frozen, to sleep where they collapsed around the fires before the onslaught began on the town.

The Steward stamped his feet, then strode to the clearing in the wood over which a cloud of vapour spiralled. The grooms were still rubbing down, watering and feeding the horses. He'd check for himself that nothing was being overlooked. The cavalry would not be used today after the first reconnaissance, and the animals needed a quiet day after this long night – there was enough time for the Steward to stretch his legs before the duke's horn sounded for the final council of war. All was bustle but the banter was absent amongst the grooms and squires this morning: every man from knight to cadet, from sergeant to bowman and foot-soldier sensed that today was to be a bloody assault. Geoffrey Martel's soldiers, with those of his Norman supporters as represented by the Giroies, were as battle-hardened and as tough troops as could be found in Europe today. Fitz stood on the iron-hard bank to survey the scene.

In spite of having written to the pope, Geoffrey Martel still remained excommunicated by Rome. As a result of Henry's request and Bishop Gervais' repeated prods, William spent the two months after his duchess' coronation in raising his army. With Roger of Montgomery, Montfort, and Fitz, the duke moved south to Falaise in October and then into Bellême territory from where he could assess the Hammer's strength.

When William reached this wild region he decided to attack immediately, but his first storming of Domfront, despite his personal valour and leadership, was repulsed. The Hammer proposed a personal duel between himself and the duke but, after Fitz's protracted negotiations, the challenge was repudiated. The Hammer slipped out of Domfront as soon as he saw William's siege works being mounted: four timber towers identical to those which had reduced Brionne, sprang from the base of the rocky escarpment. The defenders inside Domfront castle settled down to a protracted siege as the last leaves of November fluttered from the bare trees. Those were days and nights of drenching rain, of soul-destroying cold, as Roger Montgomery persisted with his daily assaults; but the siege of attrition against the keep and the impregnable walls of the gaunt castle, which had been built thirty years earlier by William of Bellême, was approaching stalemate. The massive keep reared two hundred feet above the Varenne which cut through the gorge and then scythed through the only gap in the hills guarding Normandy's southern border from Maine. Fitz had sympathized with the duke's frustration as, clad in his distinguishable armour and with his standard bearer at his side, he pranced on his charger below the castle walls. He was reluctantly settling down to the siege when two incidents brought near-disaster, two days before he celebrated Christmas Mass in the Roman chapel of Notre-Dame on the bank of the river. His insatiable greed had almost cost him his life.

One of the besieged Norman knights contrived to meet the duke outside the castle walls: there the traitor disclosed that he had acquired an immense booty of gold and jewels which he was prepared to exchange for the duke's pardon. Against Fitz's and Montgomery's advice, William rode with only fifty knights and seventy archers to the rendezvous. Opening a concealed postern gate on the far side of the battlements, three hundred Norman conspirator warriors with seven hundred professional troops stealthily followed the duke's tracks in order to cut him off from his own army. But, wheeling upon the traitors as they were about to pounce, William charged at them furiously. Thrown off balance, the leaders doubled back to flee for the postern gate. Their flight and the fury of William's counter-attack caused panic among the remainder who broke and ran. Before they reached the sanctuary of the castle walls, William snatched at the bridle of one of the rearguard, capturing him and forcing him back to Montgomery's camp. Treachery had once again almost claimed the duke's life.

But what had depressed William's spirit most was the disgraceful desertion of William, the count of Arques and Talou, and brother of Archbishop Mauger, who had abandoned the duke's army two days later. This powerful baron of the ducal house whom William had himself created count, quit overnight, taking his whole force with him: rumour had it that he was returning north, back to the fortress he had built at Arques. The effect on the morale of William's besieging troops, bored and dispirited already by the wretched conditions of the oncoming winter, was disturbing. The duke had called his council of war and decided to alter his plan of campaign.

William refused to be trapped again by an interminable siege, such as had materialized at Brionne. Instead, he would leave Roger of Montgomery to reduce Domfront by attrition and starvation, having thrown up the siege towers and sited the catapults. Then, taking Montfort and Fitz with him, he would strike swiftly at Alençon: he would reduce it ruthlessly, trusting that the news of the harsh treatment meted out to its defenders would filter swiftly back to the defenders of Domfront. Terror could be as compulsive a weapon as catapults, mining and the siege tower . . . And here they were, forming up outside the walls of Alençon on this bitterly cold February dawn.

The duke had set a terrible pace during the forced march of the long night. Passing through Méhoudin and St-Samson, he crossed the Sarthe by the icy ford at Condé; then he followed the left bank of the river until reaching the bridge which led into the town through the small fort guarding the Boulevard, the main approach to the castle. He had thus evaded the watchtowers of the castle and avoided falling into the trap of having the river at his back. Poised to strike from the direction which the defenders least expected, the duke would be attacking very soon, storming the Boulevard fort in order to probe the strength of his enemies and to gain information – Ah! The horn was sounding . . . Fitz must collect Gilbert and muster his own knights: the Steward's presence was vital at the council because his troops were providing the reserve back-up for the attack on the fort.

The storming of the fort had been undertaken with precision. Wave after wave of the duke's assault troops hurled themselves upon the timber tower and by eleven o'clock, as the feeble sun momentarily broke through the February haze, the last defender had been put to the sword. The standard of Normandy was flapping proudly, red and gold, from the fort's pointed roof. Fitz watched the seasoned soldiers taking up their siege positions just beyond arrow range from the timber stockade encircling the massive keep of the castle. The bridge now safely in his hands, William made a striking figure on his battle-charger, his armour gleaming, his shield spattered with blood from the hand-to-hand fighting. He had learned from his prisoners all he needed to know: the Giroies and the traitor Normans would fight to the death, confident of victory within the security of their impregnable castle.

The spiked timber stockade which encircled the castle was inter-spaced with watchtowers whence the concealed archers were method-ically picking off any of the duke's men rash enough to expose themselves. The square keep, its new stone fresh and pale yellow in the pallid sunlight, reared defiantly from the central mound, so that any movement from without was immediately detected. The silhouettes of the defenders flickered in the slits of the embrasures as they took up their firing positions on the battlements inside the walls; some were arrogantly defiant as they yelled down from their vantage-points above the moat which was crusted over with ice where the stream ran less swiftly.

Fitz's fears were confirmed. The castle could hold out for months.

The vast complex inside the walls comprised all the necessary impedimenta to support the defending troops for a long time: the houses which were built into the walls sloped down towards the bridge connecting the hamlet of Montsort to the town. Their roofs were visible above the spiked stockade, as were the two castellated forts, the one just captured and the other, with its drawbridge, on the northern side which protected the Argentan road into Normandy.

The keep appeared impregnable. Rearing from its motte, that sloping mound constructed through the sweat of the citizens of Alençon, the great tower surveyed the countryside through all points of the compass. Its drawbridge across the inner moat provided the keep's defenders with access to the service buildings crowding the area between the inner moat and the outer walls: the chapel, the bakeries, the shops, the forges for the arrow-heads. And Fitz, staring at that massive keep, felt a gnawing fear: was William accepting a challenge which could only humiliate his present prestige? He needed to suffer only one reverse and once again his existence would be at stake. Did not those insolent defenders bunching there along the walls confirm the truth of Fitz's anxiety? What *were* they up to, waving and holloaing towards the duke's party grouped outside the gate, where William was disposing his assault troops?

Then, at a pre-arranged signal, a raucous uproar erupted on the walls opposite the duke. William turned his horse, pushed back his helmet the better to hear . . . and as he did so, a loud clattering and flapping began echoing along the crests of the outer battlements. Scores of soldiers were hanging animal hides from the pointed stakes: Fitz could smell the stinking pelts from where he stood. As the defenders slapped and banged the hides in unison, they were yelling in chorus across the ice-streaked water of the outer moat:

'The skins! The hides,' they yelled contemptuously, taunting with crude laughter. 'See, your tanner's skins – get back to your tannery, you bastard tanner! The skins . . . every man to his trade!'

Again and again the insults were hurled from the battlements, while the defenders began beating the hides in unison. Fitz watched William's troops grinning nervously behind their shields, one eye on the enemy archers, the other on their duke while they waited for his expected reaction. Even from here, Fitz caught William's roar of rage. He was wrenching his charger round, making it rear as it pawed the air with its front hooves:

'*By the splendour of God!*' he roared upwards at the battlements.

'You'll pay dearly, you varlets! You'll not leave your town again on your feet. Never again will you use your fists, your hands . . . Never will you see again, neither close nor far, after I've finished with you . . .' He twisted in his saddle, his visage white, ugly with hate. 'Steward!' he shouted. 'My lords, hither. Join me . . .' He pounded the pommel of his saddle. 'Haste here, my lords!' There was a disturbing wildness, a detectable hint of agony in his summons.

Never had Fitz seen William so furious. Minutes later he was shouting his orders, dividing his assault force into sections: a hundred foot-soldiers to each knight. Within the hour, his preparations were complete, his archers aiming at any head rash enough to show itself on the battlements. Led by the example of their maddened duke, the assault troops hurled themselves upon the stockade. Filling the outer moat with hacked branches and earth, they attacked again and again until the first breach was made. The first roof of the nearest house within the wall was gained, held and dismantled. Then the next house, until the rafters and laths from the roofs were heaped high at the base of the outer walls.

The torches flickered, the flames leaped. And then the fires were blazing upwards, licking along the stockades. William hacked furiously through the breach as the defenders retreated before the raging inferno which was being fanned by the icy wind from the east. 'Dex aïe!' Surrounded by his knights, William was scrambling on his long legs across the crumbling defences.

His duty being to cover the assault, Fitz watched the attackers streaming through the gaps; heard the screams, registered the regular thumping of the catapults and then the crashing of the boulders as they smashed into the hellish inferno. Inexorably gathering momentum, the avengers reached the inner moat, where they were halted by the updrawn bridge. The duke could advance no further. He halted, his huge chest heaving as he called off his men; he stood back, his hard stare fixed on the hundreds of stunned prisoners being kicked into rows by the sergeants. Some were openly weeping, others grovelling on their knees. There was not a man who was not suffering, horribly burned or bleeding from his wounds. William barked, his voice hard, pitiless:

'Identify those who insulted me from the battlements,' he roared at the sergeants. 'Give me their names.' And as he waited, wiping his dripping sword, he yelled for his constable. 'Set up the execution block,' he rasped at the hard-faced baron. 'Here, on this mound where all can see.' His eyes flashed as he sheathed his sword and swung his shield behind him, being now out of arrow range.

Fitz noticed the glances being exchanged between the lords clustering around their duke. Most remained horsed, but some of the older
knights were wearily slipping from their saddles, handing their arms to
their squires and pushing back their helmets. As the Steward watched
the constable setting up the execution platform, a makeshift affair
made up of stones, boughs and shields lashed together, he un-
obtrusively nudged his mount alongside that of his friend:

'Sire . . .'

But William was not to be interrupted. Squinting with one eye, he
was lining up the execution block to the embrasures pierced high in the
walls of the dungeon tower:

'That's it, constable. See to it, exactly there.' He turned and sidled
his mount away from the busy soldiers. 'What is it, Steward?'

William was playing his official role, keeping his friend at arm's
length.

'Are you certain you're right, sire?' Fitz murmured, out of ear-shot
from the others. 'Justice isn't always vengeance; mercy, as you've
shown before, can produce better results.'

Fitz had never before seen his friend so utterly a slave of hatred, but
William's voice was flat, without feeling:

'Not today, Steward Osbern. My mind's determined. From now
onwards, traitors can know what to expect: I've erred too much by
leniency.' His glance was contemptuous as he stared deeply into Fitz's
eyes. 'By the pope's beard, no one shall forget today.' He slapped the
pommel of his saddle, in that characteristic gesture of his: 'You don't
think my decision's just a whim, do you?'

'I understand your anger, sire; not the calculated cruelty.'

William's laugh was ugly: 'That's the difference between us, Fitz.
You can't kill in cold blood. My people expect me to kill to keep the
peace. I have to, on their behalf.'

'So that's how you excuse it,' Fitz whispered, not bothering to
conceal the disgust he was feeling.

William flushed with anger at his friend's strictures.

'You're presuming too far, Fitz,' he hissed. 'There's reason behind
this, you'll see. If I terrorize Alençon by making an example of only a
few, not only will the town surrender, but news of the punishment
won't take long to reach Domfront.'

'You seem very sure of yourself: perhaps you'll only stiffen their
resolve? Domfront might prefer death to mutilation.'

'Not if the terror strikes deeply.'

'You're going to make certain of that?'

'I am.'

Fitz stood his ground as William pricked his own mount forwards again, towards the constable and his waiting executioners. The half-circle of knights drawn up behind their duke waited in silence, the only sound in the misty afternoon being the faint hissing and the dying crackling of distant flames.

'How many, constable?'

'Thirty-two, sire, who've confessed to yelling the insults. I have the names.'

The duke nodded, reined back his charger. He bellowed across the moat to the keep where a motley of heads was bunched behind the castellated walls.

'See,' he roared, 'what becomes of those who insult their duke. Heed well, for unless you surrender I'll spare no man, woman or child. Worse will befall those we capture tonight. Watch well the executioners . . .'

He nodded at the constable and sat back impassively in his broad saddle to witness the punishment. Not a muscle twitched in his face, Fitz noted; no hint of compassion softened those hard, ice-blue eyes as they recorded every ghastly detail. Fitz averted his gaze, unable to stomach this blatant cruelty, however inured his contemporaries had become to what was commonplace these days.

The first of the thirty-two terrified wretches was hauled kicking and grovelling on to the platform. Four burly foot-soldiers pinioned him steady, while another extended the prisoner's forearm on the wooden block. The executioner lifted high his sword, the blade glinting in the feeble sun. A hiss and the moment of shocked silence when the blade embedded itself into the wood; the scream; and then scuffling as the soldiers smacked on the tourniquets while the second arm was laid flat out on the block. Another agonized cry and the man was tumbling from the platform while the next wretch was hauled upwards.

'Two wrists at a time,' William snapped. 'Speed things up.'

Fitz vomited when they reached the thirteenth man, the first of the next batch to have their feet lopped off. Wrists and hands were being collected into separate leathern buckets, feet into others. And when the twenty-fifth man reached the platform, Fitz nudged his steed away from the scaffold. He never could stomach the punishment of blinding, however much the offender merited the punishment. These last thirteen were having their eyes gouged out – ammunition for the last bucket.

Waiting by the gate, Fitz counted the screams, until finally the thirty-second man had been blinded. White-faced, Fitz silently regained the rise as they winched back the catapult. He watched the first bucket soaring high, curving downwards to plummet behind the castle walls.

The duke was standing in his stirrups, a dreadful figure of vengeance as he bellowed upwards to the defenders:

'If your standard has not been hauled down before the sun sinks behind your castle wall,' he roared, 'I shall start the assault.' He nodded to his knights. 'Set the faggots.'

The Steward remained motionless, watching the soldiers dispersing to their assault positions. After this grisly episode, he could hope only that his ruthless duke's calculations would achieve the success for which he had planned. Failure now at Alençon would bring disaster to his winter campaign here, on the southern borders of Normandy. Domfront could hold out for ever and Mabel Talvas at Bellême would not be slow to draw her own conclusions.

William's cruelty, if Normandy erupted into flames again, would bring its own terrible retribution.

Fitz leaned with his forearms on the pommel of his saddle, his shield still unslung, his sword sheathed as once again he stared up at the gaunt fortress of Domfront. Only four nights ago (it could have been another lifetime) the duke had left here for the forced march to Alençon. But on this morning, snow-filled clouds were sweeping across the bare beech tops, the ice-bound branches clattering in the gusts. The duke stood conspicuously before the drawbridge, his lords around him, the archers with their bows drawn and sighted. William was taking no chances.

There had been no surprise when the duke's army arrived again at Domfront to join Roger of Montgomery's encircling troops. The drawbridge was hoisted. But when the duke's burly figure was recognized before the gate, erect on his charger, his gold and red standard fluttering behind him, the huge flag of Anjou which flapped from the keep's battlements slid half-way down its pole. The duke, Fitz acknowledged, had been right. News travelled faster than armies.

Roger of Montgomery had worked tirelessly, attacking night and day, allowing the defenders no sleep, and cutting off all food and contact with the town. The besieged had sought to parley with him, to probe his intentions, even before the arrival of William. The duke sat next to Roger who was also impressively tall in his black armour and gleaming chain-mail. William seemed well pleased and the camp was full of laughter now that hot food was having its effect.

'So I was right, Fitz,' William bawled at him. 'Admit it.'

Roger was grinning when the Steward shouted, 'They haven't surrendered yet, sire. Their bridge's got to lower.' But he laughed too when his horse shied to the clanking chain. And then down came the drawbridge, link by link – Fitz could see the brilliant colours of the knights clustering on the far side, waiting to surrender and preparing to pay homage. Terror spreads fast, thought Fitz. The duke had promised pardon if Domfront yielded immediately and, though Geoffrey Martel had fled back to Le Mans, there should be some big fish amongst the catch . . .

'*Veni, vidi, vici,*' the duke was muttering to himself. No false modesty, thought Fitz. Wherever William has struck, the walls have fallen: Alençon capitulated only two hours after the butchery; Bellême will join him now . . . and, as Fitz pondered silently, he heard William issuing his orders:

'Same as Alençon, Roger,' he rasped. 'Garrison Domfront, then raze the castle to the ground. I'll deal with Geoffrey of Mayenne at Ambrières and that should clear out the last of the rats. Leave another garrison there, Roger. Return north when you're happy.'

'And you, sire?'

'Back to Rouen.' The hard face softened: 'Our first-born's due any day. When you marry Mabel, you'll have the same worries, Roger.' He grinned at his steward. 'Eh, Fitz?' He laughed as he frisked his reins. 'Come on, Steward, home for both of us. But there's bloody work still to be done.'

They were both steeling themselves for the wearisome struggle which still lay ahead. Mauger's crafty brother had to be neutralized and Fitz wondered how William would tackle the rebel. Had not William, the count of Arques and Talou, already installed himself in his impregnable new castle at Arques? From the Talou he and his archbishop brother at Rouen could control Upper Normandy. If the French king exploited the situation, the threat to William's existence could be as dangerous as it had ever been.

'Dear God,' the Steward prayed as he wheeled his horse, 'before the blood starts spilling again, lift the burden for a few moments. My Adeliza has waited so long; and give William the joy of being with

Matilda for their first-born – perhaps the future duke of Normandy.'

He nudged his steed forwards. William was already picking his way down to the river; the tail of his white charger was flicking upwards, blown by the icy wind.

13

❧❀❧

THE SOLDIER:
VARAVILLE, 22 SEPTEMBER 1057

It was the bird-song which woke William fitz Osbern. Immediately awake, he was stiff and cold after the damp night beneath the dripping branches of the Bavent beechwoods. The duke had insisted on silence, when yesterday evening his seven hundred knights and the motley collection of peasants from the Hiémois and the Caen districts bivouacked for the night. The trees were effectively concealing this bloodthirsty rabble which, with pitchforks, bill-hooks and staves, waited vengefully for the armies of Henry and the Hammer to appear. Spies reported that the enemy was starting to march at dawn and was following the right bank of the Orne, towards the sea.

Fitz yawned, nodded at his squire: something hot and he'd be able to face another day of battle. He was thirty-seven now, a seasoned, battle-hardened warrior, his hair greying: a knight was over the hill at forty – and he had seen the hardest of campaigns. Val-ès-Dunes seemed long ago and, by an extraordinary coincidence, its field of battle lay only half an hour's ride distant, along the track to the south, through Troarn to Argences.

But, God, how things had changed in these few years since the duke's sacking of Domfront and Alençon! Three years ago – and Fitz rubbed the stubble of his chin. Adeliza detested him returning to Vaudreuil with too much beard: she had riled at her grizzled husband on the last occasion. 'You're getting old . . .'

Fitz could hear the soldiers moving, the squires checking their knights' horses and trying to quieten them. He strolled once again to the edge of the wood where, for the sixth time during the past twelve hours, he gazed down upon the river Dives winding through the marshes towards its mouth. From here, where the river skirted the small island of Robehomme half a league to the east of Bavent woods, the marshland and its osiers stretched eastwards across to the backbone of hills running inland from the coast behind the port of Dives. The hamlet of Bavent crowned the hill below the edge of the wood; the ridge sloped down to the plain where the right bank of the silver Dives carved into the islet of Robehomme, upon which was perched its tiny chapel less than a league from the sea.

The Dives then snaked towards its estuary where, after thousands of years, its silt had formed a kidney-shaped, sandy island off the mouth of the river: this natural breakwater provided a lee and sheltered water between it and the mouth of the river, a harbour and anchorage which shipbuilders and fishermen used to their advantage.

Across the flats at the northern edge of the islet of Robehomme ran the old Roman road linking Caen to Touques; and it was along this that the enemy armies would soon be marching, after swinging east from the Orne. The advance parties had already been sighted by the duke's outposts at Colombelles – the vast host with which the French king had invaded via the Hiémois.

The situation was now very different from that of Val-ès-Dunes, when Henry I had gone to the aid of his Norman vassal. Relations started to deteriorate between the French king and the duke after Domfront, when the count of Arques and Talou had blatantly deserted William during the siege.

The joy that the Norman court shared with its duke and duchess at Rouen, when Robert was born in March, 1052, had been swiftly overshadowed by continuous spy reports that Geoffrey Martel, having been frustrated in Maine by the fall of Domfront and Alençon, and the consequent alliance of Bellême to the ducal cause, was angling for *rapprochement* with the French king. Rumour became fact when William learned that the Hammer had been invited to Henry's court at Orleans on 15 August.

The potential threat to Normandy's southern border was obvious, so the determined young duke, then twenty-four, hastened to meet his monarch at Vitry-aux-Loges on 20 September. He pleaded with Henry but failed to change his mind: the king refused to continue dissipating France's energies over an inconclusive war between William and Geoffrey Martel. The duke had departed from Vitry a thoughtful and disillusioned man. From that moment onwards, Henry, with his powerful kingdom behind him and allied to the Hammer, was an implacable enemy. With the support of his slippery brother in Rouen, the count of Talou had rebelled openly in June from his castle at

Arques. Caught between the jaws from north and south, an organized rebellion within Normandy could have totally destroyed William and his ducal party.

Fitz turned as he heard the movement of troops in the wood behind him. Silently threading between the bare trunks of the beeches, Montfort was leading his knights and his infantry across to the right flank. The duke's guard was barely a hundred paces distant, where Ralph Tesson in his black chain-mail was silently unfolding the duke's standard. The squires waited impatiently, bridles in hand, for their master's beckoning. But William was biding his time, determined to stick to his plan which he had presented to them last night at his tented supper. He was proving as cunning a tactician as he was a skilled warrior and diplomatist.

When the news of the count of Talou's rebellion at Arques reached William in June of 1052, he was at Coutances in the Cotentin, near the Atlantic coast. Without a moment's indecision, William, accompanied by Fitz and six of his most trusted knights, forthwith galloped off on that incredible marathon ride: day and night the duke rode, picking up reinforcements at Rouen on his way north; gathering support from loyal men who had already been stopping supplies from getting through to the stone castle at Arques which the count had completed in 1043. Sixty-five leagues in thirty hours they rode, through those sun-baked, narrow dusty tracks which were no wider than the length of a lance. This animal intuition in moments of mortal peril was an instinct which William had heeded more than once during his tempestuous, young life – and in hindsight Fitz realized now that this arduous ride had saved the duchy. William *had* to prevent the count of Talou from launching his attack from the north, before Henry and the Hammer invaded from the south.

Richard of Hugleville, close south of Arques, with the two sons of the good Turchetil, the murdered former tutor of the duke, bravely determined to resist the marauding forays made from the fortress of Arques. They resisted valiantly from the fortified tower which Richard had built close to Hugleville at St-Aubin. In a skirmish with Arques' troops at Esclavelles, one of the sons and his followers had been killed. When the duke, weary and hungry after his epic ride, arrived outside the castle walls, he surprised an enemy force and immediately chased them back within their castle drawbridge.

The massive castle at Arques, so proudly and arrogantly built by William of Arques to withstand any attack, reared from its mound, looming above the flat, surrounding countryside; it controlled the strategic valley where the three rivers met, the Bethune, the Varenne and the Arques. Realizing that frontal assault was out of the question, the duke had at once set up those traditional siege works which had met with such success at Brionne and Domfront. The huge timber tower which soon reared to menace the defenders was left in charge of Walter Giffard, count of Longueville, while the duke rode south again to intercept the expected help from Henry and Geoffrey Martel for which the count of Talou was anxiously awaiting . . . and Steward fitz Osbern turned when behind him he heard footsteps in the damp undergrowth. Gilbert, his *fidelis*, was holding a steaming wooden beaker for him:

'They've heated up the soup without making smoke,' he grinned. 'A cunning lot, the Caennais.'

'When's the duke holding his final council?' Fitz nodded, sipping the broth.

'Twenty minutes, sire. He's working now on the final details with my lords Montgomery, Tesson and Montfort.'

'Get my battle gear together, Gilbert. Tell the squires to alert my knights: no lances today. The cutting edge of the sword, if the duke sticks to his plan.'

Fitz watched his liegeman returning to the Vaudreuil contingent gathering in the clearing by the lightning-struck beech. The last of the scouts had just reported: the French host was strung out and crawling along the old Roman road from Caen to Touques. In twenty minutes, their advance guard would be nearing the hamlet of Hérouvillette; they would then climb towards Arbre Martin before curling round the foot of the hill below Bavent. At their snail's pace, it would take a couple of hours before they reached Varaville; there the ford crossed the Dives river which snaked towards the white combers of the Channel, in the estuary opposite the port of Dives-sur-Mer.

William's plan was bold, but typically intricate: success depended upon timing and, therefore, upon the discipline each of his commanders imposed upon their battalions. Though Fitz was now middle-aged, he knew he was respected and obeyed to the letter, partly because of his close friendship with the duke who now stood in such high esteem as a soldier but who also understood the ways of the sea. Did he not use the destructive power of the flooded Orne to destroy his enemies after Val-ès-Dunes? Was it his Viking blood which turned him instinctively to using the sea instead of combating it? And, the beaker slowly cooling in Fitz's hands, the Steward moved to the northern edge of the trees to gauge the state of the tide, now that the sun was climbing above the Auge hills.

When in August of 1052, five years ago, the duke had moved south to confront the French and Angevin menace, across the Channel English politics were in the melting-pot. The exiled Godwine, earl of Wessex, having bid adieu to Baldwin in Flanders, conducted a brilliantly co-ordinated rendezvous in the Narrow Seas with his sons Harold and Leofwine who had sailed from Ireland. Their flotilla then overwhelmed Edward's fleet and, the south-east of England and London rallying to Godwine's triumphant return, the Confessor was forced to re-establish his powerful earl. The Godwine family was given back its lands and honours but, even more humiliating for the king, was the earl's insistence that the hated Normans should be expelled from Edward's court and deprived of their power. Robert of Jumièges was replaced, against the pope's wishes, as archbishop of Canterbury by Godwine's nominee, the disreputable Stigand, bishop of Winchester. The dismissal of Robert was a direct challenge to the authority of Rome; the pope excommunicated Stigand and the house of Wessex also came under extreme papal displeasure.

Fitz had admired William's astute reaction when the influential Norman colonials returned to their homeland. Despite the ecclesiastical cloud under which he and Matilda lived, William exploited the situation, emphasizing to Rome where his sympathies lay. Normandy supported the Church's reforming crusade; supported the English king against the ambitious earl of Wessex and his house; sympathized with the Confessor at the most bitter humiliation of all – Godwine had again compelled the king to co-habit with his queen, Edith, the earl's sister, who was languishing within her convent. Godwine and his family were firmly established as the real power in England.

The anti-Norman feelings had spawned an alternative choice for the Confessor's successor. The influential Witan, the Anglo-Saxon parliament, was inviting the son of Edmund Ironsides, Edward the atheling, who all his life had been in exile in Hungary, to pay a state visit to the king's court; the invitation was presumed to be a prelude to offering the throne to this descendant of the old Saxon house which stretched back to the great Alfred. Edward (he was known as the Illustrious) would be landing at Dover at any moment with his wife and family, the occasion being marked by great enthusiasm, particularly in Europe . . .

The duke's seneschal was rounding up the council for the final battle briefing. Fitz began striding up the slope to the duke's tent. Gilbert would have to dress him after the meeting. Storm clouds were building up from the west and rain could be on the way. It was vital that the ground should not be greasy underfoot if the duke's plan was to succeed . . .

While events had deteriorated in England, William had needed that year in which to organize his forces. He raised two armies, one under his own command in the south; the other, drawn from loyal knights in the north who were determined to protect their own estates from the ravages of the count of Arques and Talou. William gave the command of this second army to his old friend, Robert, the count of Eu. The duke's half-brother, Robert, now the count of Mortain, Montfort and Hugh of Gournay-en-Bray became his lieutenants, while Walter Giffard remained besieging Arques. Inside the castle walls, the plight of its garrison was deteriorating rapidly. The count and his wife were trapped within, cut off from all supplies. The count's ambition to become master of Upper Normandy was fading daily. The relief of Arques depended upon a swift response by the French king to the count's desperate appeal for help. From his mighty tower overlooking the castle, Walter Giffard had isolated the fortress from the world.

During October of 1053, while the Hammer was gathering rebellious Norman barons for his joint French–Angevin attack into Normandy, Henry I marched north from Paris. Synchronizing the attack from the east, Enguerrand II, the count of Ponthieu, entered the Scie valley to relieve the beleaguered castle of Arques. Duke William had still refused to fight his king face-to-face, and had consigned the ambushing of Henry's force to his northern lords.

On 25 October 1053, the French contingent, falling into the trap of a feint-retreat, was hacked to pieces at St-Aubin-sur-Scie, close to the castle walls of Arques. In despair, the count of Arques heard the death cries of his wife's brother, floating upwards from the bloody field of St-Aubin, as Henry's men turned and ran. Walter Giffard turned the screw even harder and soon the demoralized, famished and diseased defenders were in no mood to continue their resistance.

Henry returned to the Vexin where he coolly reorganized his armies for his intended campaign in which he would eliminate permanently the threat from his Norman vassal. At Mantes he began gathering his southern army: the Hammer with his Angevins and the Norman rebels; contingents from Guy-William of Aquitaine; men from Blois, Tour-raine, Sens and Berri. In the north-east, poised to spring the trap,

Henry's brother, Odo, was mustering the northern army: Guy of Ponthieu was thirsting to avenge the death of Enguerrand, his brother; and Rainald, the count of Clermont – all were eagerly gathering to ravage the rich towns and lush fields of Upper Normandy. But, while they were mustering their battalions, in December the duke succeeded in reducing the castle of Arques.

In exchange for the castle, William of Arques and his wife were dispossessed for ever, but the duke allowed them to flee to the hospitality of Eustace of Boulogne. Once again, the duke had displayed mercy: perhaps Adelaide, his sister who had married Enguerrand and was now widowed, had influenced William towards his uncle who had hated him for so long . . .?

'Sire?'

'Yes, Gilbert,' Fitz acknowledged impatiently "Tis time, I know. Deploy my battalion: I'll dress myself.'

Minutes later, battle-clad and shield in hand, he mounted his favourite charger, the white stallion, Coromandel, which William had given him. The sun was breaking through the gaps in the dark, iron-blue clouds sweeping in from the Atlantic, those warrior clouds which were like outriders wheeling into battle. Scats of rain shivered in curtains across the marshes, sweeping towards the hills behind Dives. It was almost 10.30 and Montfort should now be in position on the other side of the estuary, ready to ambush from the hamlet of Brucourt. The estuary was golden, its expanse of sand sliced by the silver thread of the ebbing river which snaked into the white breakers of the sea.

Fitz could identify the ford at the hamlet of Varaville. The Dives was a trickle now, at this spring tide's low water, but he could see already at the river mouth, where the fresh water mixed with the sea, that the flood was beginning. The anchored boats had already swung, their prows facing seawards. In minutes the stream would be swirling inland, streaming up-river in its relentless surge. Fitz nudged Coromandel towards the edge of the beeches. William was on his right, erect in his saddle, silently watching the French army as its levies and advance wagons lined up to cross the ford, less than a league below the heights of Bavent . . . All eyes were on the duke, waiting for his signal, but Fitz sensed there was a long wait yet . . . William had iron control of himself and his troops, as he had shown with such ferocity three years ago when Henry had finally marched north from Mantes.

The French king had brilliantly synchronized the attacks of his two armies: during the first week of February 1054 he moved north from the Evreçin with his southern army, led by Geoffrey Martel, raping, pillaging and looting as they marched. William retreated before them, destroying as he went, leaving nothing for the enemy, tempting him onwards. Beguiled by the ease of its advance, Henry's southern army became a marauding mob panting after its elusive prey which, unknown to the French king, was concealed in the woods on the far side of the Seine.

Simultaneously, Henry's northern army under Odo was ravaging westwards to Neufchâtel-en-Bray, through the Eaulne valley from Aumale. Satiated with rapine and pillage, Odo's army encamped that night of 13 February 1054, in the town of Mortemer.

The troops were totally undisciplined and encouraged to debauchery by Odo and his barons, and no woman or maid escaped undefiled that night in Mortemer. Lying befuddled by drink and naked with their captive women, they did not hear the crackling of the flames until it was too late. At dawn twilight the count of Eu and his Normans had set ablaze the wooden houses. As the occupants emerged naked, dazed and half-asleep, they were hacked down where they stood. Fitz had seen the result of the massacre afterwards: horrible, no mercy given, the roar of the flames still loud in his memory, the screams of the trapped, unfortunate women . . . The slaughter continued all the morning, did not cease until the light began to fade in the evening. Odo and Rainald barely escaped the avenging swords of Robert of Eu, Walter Giffard, William of Warenne and the others; but they slipped like thieves from the town to fly back to their lands, only Guy, the count of Ponthieu, being taken prisoner. Two-thirds of those forty thousand men were slaughtered during that terrible day. Fitz still recalled the light of triumph in the duke's eyes when Robert of Eu's messengers brought him the news, where he waited on the far side of the Seine, opposite the French king.

It had been a misty, damp night, with the chill of the flooded fields eating through men's bones. Fitz had been with William, when the duke had tried to shock Henry into withdrawal: William made Ralph Tesson climb a tall oak, and from its branches his sepulchral voice boomed across the swollen river:

'It is I, Ralph Tesson of Thury, who fought you at Val-ès-Dunes. Harken to me, king of France: it is I who bring you these awful tidings.' Tesson's words echoed through the trees like the voice of doom: 'King Henry: dispatch your death-carts to collect your corpses. Tens of thousands lie massacred. Rouse yourselves, Frenchmen, to bury your dead.'

The resonant, sinister pronouncement produced the required shock – and once again William had extricated himself from personally fighting his king. Henry broke camp and marched back to Poissy, leaving twenty-six thousand cadavers in the smouldering embers of Mortemer. I'd have thought, Fitz mused as he reined in his horse at the edge of the wood, that Henry would have accepted his defeat at Mortemer as final . . . The Steward glanced to his right: what was the duke waiting for?

Ralph Tesson was unfurling the duke's standard. It flapped in the breeze, beat against the bare trunks of the beeches. William sat motionless in his saddle, watching the French army streaming across the estuary which was already filling with the flooding tide. The silver ribbon had widened to a gleaming blue lake: wavelets poppled where the current bored round the curves in the river bed. The water was now up to the knees of the infantry splashing their way across . . . and in Bavent woods all eyes were upon the duke, as they waited for him to jerk down his helmet, the guard across his nose. Fitz felt his own heart pumping: ridiculous after so many years of campaigning . . .

And even after the appalling massacre of Mortemer, the French king still refused to face the realities of defeat: his northern army decimated; William the count of Talou exiled for ever; the last of the rebel Norman barons paying homage to their duke, their castles razed to the ground; the Hammer's armies quitting Normandy as swiftly as horses would take them. Even after these disastrous reverses, Henry still wriggled over the protracted negotiations with William which resulted finally in the agreement of November 1055: the duke of Normandy would re-establish Norman occupation of Tillières which had been lost so long ago; and in exchange for the return of prisoners taken by William at Mortemer, the duke of Normandy would repossess in perpetuity the lands of Maine which he had wrested from the Hammer. Nevertheless, Henry had still burned with resentment at the power of his Norman neighbour.

Immediately after Mortemer, the duke had commissioned Fitz to fortify and garrison Breteuil in support of Tillières, a task which Fitz had carried out swiftly. Adeliza had not been well and seemed to be wasting at Vaudreuil. Though she had improved and put on weight again after little Emma had recovered from the scarlet fever, Fitz was still worried about her; the physicians were mystified by her condition however much they tried to hoodwink him.

While Fitz dealt with Breteuil, William had consolidated his new-found prestige. The respect which the young duke instilled in those who had opposed him was enhanced by the swift decisiveness he brought to eradicate the rot within his duchy. Perhaps also Matilda, and his ruthless and formidable half-brother, Odo, the bishop of Bayeux, had been behind his cleaning out of the Augean stables? So, only two months after the battle of Mortemer, William arraigned his forty-one-year-old uncle, the detestable Archbishop Mauger and brother of the exiled count of Arques, before an ecclesiastical court at Lisieux. There, before a great concourse of bishops presided over by the bishop of Sitten, the pope's representative, Mauger was formally dismissed and exiled to Guernsey . . .

Mauger was a colourful personality. Banished by the duke, the rogue ex-archbishop enjoyed a riotous exile in Guernsey where his mode of living and his extravagant table became notorious. At his exuberant banquets, guests were regaled not only with the delights of Mauger's women, but by the amusement of watching cock-fighting, the birds being especially imported from the mainland.

Delighting in ignoring and taunting papal authority, Mauger had never sought to claim his *pallium*. He renounced his Christian faith in favour of his 'little devil', Toret, (a lesser Thor, the Viking devil), and dabbled in the occult. He took his favourite son, Michel de Baynes, and his women with him to Guernsey, but often visited the Cotentin. It was there on the west coast that on a hot summer's day, fuddled by drink and half-naked, he was drowned, ensnared by his braces which had become entangled about his knees. His body, trapped between two rocks, was recovered and buried ingloriously at Cherbourg. The manner of his going underlined the fact that, providentially perhaps, he was the last of the secular archbishops.

William replaced Mauger by the fifty-year-old Maurilius, a saintly priest from Rheims who had been educated in Germany. Now an austere, holy man, after a turbulent early career he became abbot of Fécamp whence William made him his new archbishop of Rouen. The appointment shocked the worldly ecclesiastics of Normandy, but William had been adamant, realizing perhaps that his own background lacked the finer intellectual and spiritual qualities which Maurilius' long life represented.

Fitz felt certain that Lanfranc had influenced the duke's choice. With the saintly monk from beyond Normandy's borders as his new archbishop, William consciously began to use his own power to influence Church affairs. From Le Bec, his friend Lanfranc had already pleaded with Rome to lift the ban on the duke's marriage. By combining the influence of both these great clerics, the duke rapidly began to draw the bishops and the monasteries together, much to the benefit of the duchy. Now, in 1057, a fresh, religious zeal was sweeping through Normandy. From now onwards, the duke – and only he – would appoint his bishops.

The victory at Mortemer, Fitz realized, had been just as important as Val-ès-Dunes: the opposition against the duke had been overwhelming – it was his resolute ride from Coutances to Arques which had, in the end, saved him and his duchy. If he had not recaptured Arques castle in that December, Henry must have destroyed his younger vassal. But then, the Hammer's reaction to William's repossession of the Angevin castles had not been as difficult to predict as they had all expected. Geoffrey Martel, once he had regained the safety of his domains, at once supported Geoffrey of Mayenne who, with Guy-William of Aquitane and Eudo of Brittany in support, was marching to Ambrières. The duke drove them off and re-fortified the garrison, but the Hammer remained in full control of Maine.

Last year, the Hammer was once more angling for Henry's favours, while William was involving himself diplomatically with regaining Maine. After the death of his father, the young count of Maine, Herbert, had been exiled by Geoffrey Martel from Le Mans. Realizing that the Hammer was now on the defensive, Herbert pleaded with William to help reinstate him in Le Mans. The duke turned the request to his own advantage: he would fight the Hammer in support of Herbert's cause, providing that the count of Maine promised eventually to marry one of William's daughters, for in February of 1053, Matilda had presented him with Agatha, and a year later, a fortnight after Mortemer, their second daughter, Adeliza. To seal Normandy's absorption of Maine, the duke also insisted that, should Herbert die childless, the province should become part of Normandy and should adopt Robert, William's heir, as its count.

By the turn of this present year, Henry could no longer contain his impatience to avenge Mortemer. After conferring again with the Hammer at Angers, the French and Angevin armies marched into Normandy through the Hiémois, bypassing William who remained on the defensive at Falaise; William was still mobilizing his 'host' in which his vassal barons and their troops were forced to serve for forty days. The duke looked on helplessly while his seven hundred knights and their levies, armed with staves, billhooks and pitchforks, poured in from the Caen and Falaise countryside. Halting at St-Pierre-sur-Dives to allow his ravaging armies to plunder the great plain of Caen, Henry then marched west with the Hammer into the Bessin, pillaging, burning and raping wherever they went.

William then marched north from Falaise and, fully forewarned by his spies, decided to lie in wait for the enemy at this strategic focal point, here in the woods of Bavent. With such a puny untrained and ill-equipped force, he was relying upon his only weapons: local knowledge, surprise and the hatred of his troops for the invader. The wide marshes of the Dives estuary were lethal for the stranger, the plain criss-crossed by the innumerable dykes and swamps running like fingers on each side of the old Roman road to Touques.

Once again, William could not countenance defeat: the future of Normandy, his life and those of all his loyal men depended upon the outcome of the battle. Fitz nudged his charger closer to the red and gold standard fluttering in the clearing at the edge of the wood. The duke's eyes were flickering with excitement as he turned towards his Steward:

'See, them, Fitz? The bulk of Henry's army is halted there at the foot of Robehomme. See them, where their armour's glinting there, in the fields next the road and the dyke.'

'Must be over half of them,' Fitz answered. 'Just in time, with the tide flooding so fast: it'll be up to the island soon.' The whole estuary was shining, an expanse of silvery blue, from Dives westward to the shore line of Varaville, where the remainder of Henry's army was trundling towards the rickety bridge. Loaded high with loot, the wagons were jockeying for position, barging each other in their panic to cross the Dives before the spring flood cut them off. On the flanks of this booty train, several squadrons of cavalry wove unceasingly to spur the rear-guard onwards.

'Whose banner is that, sire?' Fitz asked, screwing up his eyes against the glare of the September sun.

'The count of Blois,' Ralph Tesson boomed from the duke's right where, an impressive figure in his black armour, he was holding high the duke's standard.

The flood was swirling around the rickety supports of the bridge. The outriders were splashing in the shingle, searching for the shallows of the ford. The sea was already spreading across the marsh to the east of the river; the lower fields below the island were swirling with water.

The duke pulled down his helmet.

'You know your orders, my lords.' He drew his sword, held it high. 'Sound the charge!' he cried. *'Par le splendeur de Dieu!'*

His charger sprang forwards. Tesson planted the heel of the standard in the saddle pocket. As the duke and his knights burst from the wood the cry was taken up along the hillside: *'Dex Aïe!'*

As Fitz led his own battalion down towards the troops clustering like ants at the bridge of Varaville, he could see the crimson standard streaming before him. Down, down the field they galloped, the thunder of hundreds of hooves deafening his ears.

So often had Fitz revelled in this exultation, this animal wildness surging within him, knowing that within minutes would come the shock, the clash of arms as the cavalry met – a few more seconds, perhaps, of life. But today, his task was to prevent the enemy from breaking clear, up the left bank of the river, so he would not be in the hottest part of the fray – and, as he pressed his right knee against his horse's belly, he glimpsed his own knights, wheeling behind him, following off to the right, towards the bank across which the river was already spilling fast . . .

Montfort must have heard the charge; his troops would be lowering their lances for the attack. And then Fitz saw Henry's army, cut off on the far side of the ford, a restless mass, the chain-mail glinting in the sun. The king and his warriors were clearly identifiable below the blue and white standard, apart from the mass and on the rise at the foot of the island of Robehomme.

Fitz reined in his battalion along the bank of the Dives to divide them into sections of forty knights, ready for the enemy if he broke this way. He turned his charger tightly, the animal whinnying as it smelt blood – from here Fitz could pick out every detail of the fight as William hurled himself upon the enemy.

The duke and his standard-bearer, stirrup to stirrup with their knights, swords flashing before them, galloped a few strides ahead of their warriors. The thunder of hooves rolled across the fields, the clamour of the battle-cries ringing in the cold morning. Blois and his surprised cavalry were wheeling tightly, trying to cover the rear-guard. But the duke was already plunging into the yelling throng of outriders, slashing at the horses between the shafts of the wagons. Whips cracked as the drivers panicked, their terror infecting their horses. A wagon and a cart had become wedged, wheel-hub to wheel-hub at the entrance to the bridge. Those behind them were piling into the blockage, as they tried to force their way through to the bridge. The work-horses were rearing and plunging, crashing into the chaos as the wagons disintegrated beneath their threshing hooves. And now William and his warriors were right in amongst them.

The glint of sword blades, the upstretched, protective arms; the brave bowman on the flank trying to sight his arrows; the snorting of the maddened horses, the grunts of the battle-seasoned knights as their sword-arms rose and fell to scythe a path through the struggling mass; and then the cavalry were through to the far side, wheeling again for another charge on the other flank. And as Blois turned, desperately trying to cover his rear-guard, Fitz froze in his saddle . . . the rickety bridge was swaying, wobbling where the *mêlée* thickened, as wagon after bursting wagon piled in, one upon the other. The flooding tidal stream was almost to the level of the timber bearers; swirling in from seawards like quicksilver, a white froth was seething beneath the bridge supports, as the irresistible mass of water boiled up the estuary and into the river. The bridge was keeling over, holding for a second, then suddenly, to the screams of animals and men, toppling over sideways.

The waters became a maelstrom of flailing men and drowning, terrified horses; the sinking wagons, bubbling below the surface, were being whirled against the collapsing legs of the bridge to block the river still further. Blois was driving his men into the estuary to search for the shallows of the ford. His wretched troops had the choice of standing to fight with the water up to their chests; or of trying to cross the flooding estuary to join their king on the far side. Their cries wailed above the tumult to where Fitz and his knights were watching from their saddles.

The Steward saw Blois' standard; it fluttered briefly, then disappeared as the duke's butchers closed in . . . and then, to the eastwards Fitz sighted Montfort's battalions streaming along the dyke from Brucourt, their battle-cries mingling with the cacophony from the ford at Varaville. Watching the slaughter from below Robehomme, King Henry and his sullen army were powerless to help. However desperately the French king wished to succour his rear-guard, it seemed that Henry's knights were dissuading him from suicide in the swirling waters of the Dives estuary.

There was no need for Fitz's battalion to join in the slaughter: his seventy knights and their vengeful peasants would only confuse matters more. The waters swirling up-stream towards Bures were stained dark but the screams were lessening as the afternoon sun began dimming behind the film of cirrus now covering the autumnal sky. William had withdrawn his personal guard and was leaving the final butchery to his minor knights. He was joining his Steward to witness Henry's army streaming southwards, behind the far side of Robehomme.

'We could have cut them up,' Tesson growled, 'if we hadn't sent Montfort down to Brucourt. No man could have escaped, sire – even the king.'

William stared at his standard-bearer; his blue eyes were ice-cold and he spoke without emotion:

'I shall never battle personally against my sovereign, my lord Tesson.' He was turning Baldur gently, his favourite charger now spattered with gore and flecked with froth; as he set its head towards the road leading back to Colombelles and Caen, he said softly, so that only Fitz and those closest to him could hear:

'My duchy needs peace, time to stabilize. King Henry and the count of Anjou will never again set foot in Normandy.' He added quietly to his Steward, 'As you alone know, Fitz, I must have tranquillity in the duchy for the plans I have in mind.'

He smiled bleakly. As Fitz watched him pushing back his helmet to sniff the breeze, he caught William's gaze focusing on the horizon above the restless sea. The duke snapped his sword back into its scabbard. He pushed his shield across his back. He twitched at his reins. 'Dreams, Fitz,' he murmured. 'Just dreams.'

Fitz nodded as he urged his steed forwards. He did not reply. He was eight years older than his friend, and maturity brought prudence. There was much to do yet, before his ambitious duke could indulge in day-dreaming – and that heaving, storm-tossed Channel was a barrier which even William, with his Viking blood, must treat with the utmost respect.

PART III

AMBITIOUS SUBSTANCE . . .

14

NOBLE FLOTSAM

The Steward of Normandy stood with the inner council on the raised platform at the end of the great hall of Bonneville castle. Montfort, Beaumont, Montgomery, Vernon, Tosny, all were here today, 4 September 1064, to welcome the august assembly which had been summoned from across Europe. Few had not yet arrived of all those who had accepted the duke's invitation, a success which was due to his insistence that the assembly should not be too far from Rouen. Every day's ride counted though it was a splendid summer, but some of the distinguished guests had travelled far: the emperor's plenipotentiary had ridden from Aix-la-Chapelle, but the grey-faced apostolic nuncio's voyage had been even longer.

William had always liked this castle of his overlooking the river Touques and the restless sea: 'My good town' he'd called it and so it had been Bonneville ever since. Bayeux had been the popular choice (the accommodation was better) but, as Fitz had been appointed by the duke to set up this ceremony, the Steward had settled for Bonneville – and there were Archbishop Maurilius' wishes to be considered too. He had been very co-operative. The old man had remained in Rouen because Odo was here, as vital and decisive as ever. The tall, powerful figure in the bishop's travelling-cloak was approaching Fitz across the raised platform.

'Well, my lord,' he boomed at Fitz. 'I've had a hard ride from Dives this morning. Most of 'em are here, aren't they? I shall be seated.' The announcement was a command, peremptory for a younger man to his senior: Fitz was now forty-four, ten years older than Odo. The bishop, without further ado, sat down in the centre of the row of high chairs drawn up in a half-circle below the raised dais upon which stood the throne. The ducal throne had been carried from Rouen with the two symbols of state which, covered by white cloths, stood on the left of the throne. William was a stickler for the traditional dignity of the court and Fitz had had to keep a close eye on things while organizing this complicated gathering. He had regretted being unable to accompany William on his foray into Brittany, but now that they were all returned, the Steward knew that he could not have possibly left the organization of this important event to his deputies.

'Be seated, my lords,' Fitz announced as he noted the guests seeking the customary gestures of politeness. The seneschals began leading the most important of the personages to the front rows of the hall which faced the rostrums. The nuncio and the German plenipotentiary were taking their seats in the centre. Fitz remained standing at the end of the raised dais: the duke and his illustrious guest should not be too long now, for William also insisted on punctuality. Fitz would wait a few more minutes before summoning them from the duke's personal quarters.

Even Baldwin V of Flanders had managed to come. He was chatting amicably with his belligerent German neighbour's plenipotentiary. William got on well with his father-in-law, but Matilda had been unable to come: she was suffering sickness with her seventh pregnancy. One of the proofs of the growing stability throughout the duchy during these few years since Varaville was William's and his duchess' preoccupation with providing the duchy with heirs. Their fourth child, Richard, was born in December 1055; a second boy, he made almost certain a successor to the ducal house. Adela arrived in July of 1057, an event which was celebrated with rejoicing in the relaxed atmosphere after the battle of Varaville; and the last child, the red-headed little monster, William, was already five years old . . . time was slipping past in these days of relative tranquillity.

Fitz could not credit that it was seven years since that final battle of Varaville, the fight which put an end to Henry's aggressive ambitions. As the months passed, no longer was it the duchy's internal strife which preoccupied the duke's thoughts. After the interminable trouble in Maine had at last been crushed, it was the developments across the Channel which were now fanning William's secret ambitions. Using his Steward as his personal confidant, he was trying, through diplomacy and military force, to cut a way through the tangled web of intrigue surrounding the pressing problem of succession to the English throne.

Fitz was now convinced that William had made his decision through the influence of his high-born wife, the duchess of whom he was inordinately proud. The childless Edward had offered William the English crown three years ago. William was determined to seize the opportunity, despite the many other contenders.

There were several claimants of royal blood. The Confessor's sister, Goda, had married twice, her first husband being the count of Dreux and the Vexin. After his death, their son, Ralph, the 'Timid', had been made earl of Hereford by Edward but he had died shortly after Varaville. His brother, Walter, was now count of the Vexin, and had therefore a direct claim. Goda's second husband was the count of Boulogne, the unfortunate Eustace who had been attacked years ago by the townsmen of Dover. As Edward's brother-in-law (and with Baldwin of Flanders' support), Eustace too was staking his claim. But there were stronger contenders, ambitious men who would fight for the English crown, though no royal blood coursed through their veins . . .

First, there was the great earl of Wessex's house, the family which represented the real power in England. Godwine had died in 1053. His son, Sweyn, had already in 1046 brought shame upon the earl of Wessex's house by seducing the abbess of Leominster when returning from a Welsh expedition. Forced to quit the country, he spent several years in Denmark before returning to England in order to reclaim the land from which he had been dispossessed. Once again, he attracted the hatred of the English when he had his cousin Bjorn, brother of the king of Denmark, foully murdered on board ship. Banished again, he took refuge with the hospitable Baldwin of Flanders, William's father-in-law, before departing on a pilgrimage to Jerusalem whence he never returned.

Harold Godwineson, Godwine's second son, was a strong character, a leader who carried much of England with him in his constant challenge to the feeble Confessor. So when the atheling, Edward the Illustrious, was removed from the scene under sinister circumstances during the year of Varaville, it was Harold who benefited most from the suspected poisoning. From that moment, Harold Godwineson, whose father was of Sussex farmer's stock, had decided to aspire for the highest prize. But Harold's ambition was resented by an equally determined contender who, from his Norwegian fjord of Bergen, was planning to invade England when the moment was ripe.

This was Harold Hardraada, king of Norway, who argued his claim through an agreement reputedly made between King Harthacanute and Magnus, the previous king of Norway. Harold Hardraada had reacted swiftly to Harold Godwineson's obvious challenge and, a year after the atheling's mysterious death, Hardraada dispatched his own son to conquer the English islands. The Scots from the outer isles and the Irish from the south joined him with their ships, but the invasion came to nought. So Hardraada bided his time while patiently gathering together another invasion force and while rallying support from within the northern provinces of England. And it was there that Harold Godwineson suffered his first reverse.

When the Danish earl of Northumbria, Siward, died in 1055, Harold Godwineson attempted to bring peace to the hostile north of England by creating his younger brother, Tosti, the new earl of Northumberland. Though Tosti encouraged friendship with Malcolm, king of Scotland, his Northumbrian people remained as hostile as ever, largely because of Tosti's frequent absences from the earldom to harass the Welsh.

During the autumn of 1063, while Tosti was hunting with King Edward in southern England, three hundred of his most influential thegns rebelled and occupied York, after slaughtering Tosti's Danish and English supporters. Electing Morcar as their new earl, they marched south under his leadership to Oxford. King Edward prudently ordered Harold Godwineson to negotiate with the rebels. Morcar refused and, to avoid civil war, Harold advised the Confessor to accept Morcar as the new earl of Northumbria.

Enraged by his brother's perfidy and accusing Harold of having instigated the northern rebellion, Tosti accepted his banishment from the kingdom with alacrity. Now a mortal enemy of Harold's, Tosti took his wife, Judith, and their children across the Channel to the welcoming court of his father-in-law, Baldwin of Flanders. The vengeful Tosti, failing to gain Baldwin's support for an armed return to England, turned to the Norwegian king, Harold Hardraada, who readily accepted Tosti's help in the forthcoming invasion of England. There was only one event for which all claimants to the throne of England waited: the departure of the ailing king's soul from this mortal world.

Harold Godwineson now controlled most of England: he had joined Herefordshire to his own earldom of Wessex, while his brother, Gyrth, ruled all East Anglia; his other brother, Leofwine, was earl of the rich lands stretching from Kent to Oxford.

In 1064, the earl of Wessex was commanded by King Edward to visit the duke of Normandy. Acting as the royal ambassador, Harold was ordered to confirm publicly Edward's negotiations of 1051 with William that the duke of Normandy should succeed the Confessor to the English throne.

Repugnant though these orders were to Harold, he nevertheless sailed to Normandy from Bosham on 20 June, believing that he could thus best assure his own position for the future. His ship became becalmed and fog-bound in mid-Channel. The spring tides and twelve hours of fog caused the captain anxiety for the vessel's position; a strong south-westerly then blew up and drove the vessel to leeward. When daylight broke on the second morning, land was sighted on the starboard bow; the captain, after considering anchoring, opted to run his ship at low water on to the sandy beach, with the object of checking his position. Unhappily for the earl, the ship had made a landfall on the wrong side of the Norman border. Watchers ashore had been following the course of the ship and, in the Somme estuary, the famous passenger was taken prisoner as he stepped ashore. Realizing the high ransom value of his distinguished prisoner, Guy, the count of Ponthieu, who had been freed by William after Mortemer, incarcerated Harold in the dungeon of Beaurain castle.

Though Guy was under an obligation to the duke of Normandy, he nevertheless dispatched his emissaries to the Norman court to demand ransom for his illustrious prisoner. Forewarned by a soldier from the ship who had evaded capture, the duke himself rode up to Eu to pay the ransom – the gift of a castle and its lands on the Ponthieu border – and from that moment, Harold, the earl of Wessex, became in the eyes of the world beholden to the bastard duke of Normandy.

In January of '58, William, knowing that his duchy was at last safe from the French king, had moved south to retake Tillières, the town which he had surrendered so ignominiously so many years ago. Marching on to Thirmert which controlled the roads into the Bellême country, he captured and garrisoned the castle. Henry of France thereupon laid siege to the fortress, a siege which lasted for three years. It was then that Herbert II of Maine had agreed with the duke that, should Herbert die childless, William's heir, Robert, should succeed as count of Maine and Le Mans.

The seven and a half year old Robert remained under the tutorship of the lord of Mézidon where the monks of the monastery endured the hopeless task of trying to instil some intellectual discipline into their wayward and volatile pupil. Robert was proving a difficult child, but his father was determined that the inheritor to the ducal crown should be equipped at least with the elementary disciplines. An unattractive child, Robert was proving a disappointment to his parents: of stumpy appearance with broad shoulders and short legs, he was already known as 'Shorty' amongst the more polite members of the court – 'Short-arse' by the less respectful.

At Le Bec, Abbot Lanfranc had begun to evaluate his duke better, and was recognizing the dynamic energy which simmered beneath William's urbane exterior. By the end of the year, Lanfranc had begun to use his influence with Maurilius for a joint representation to Rome for the lifting of the interdiction on the ducal marriage. During these last seven years, relations between the Norman Church and the duke had developed into a cohesive force; compared to the rest of Europe, it was the prime factor in the upsurge of the duchy's progress to stability.

When men like Hellouin cut free from the secular evils to create their own simple spiritual centres of learning, a cleansing flame was kindled, to be fanned by men such as Lanfranc and his nominated successor, the holy and gentle Anselm, the son of a Lombard seigneur. Then, at the synod of Melfi in 1059, Lanfranc and Maurilius had persuaded the new pope to lift the papal interdiction.

As Lanfranc respectfully pointed out, if the pope refused and insisted on Matilda returning like a used glove to her father, the insult would cause war between Flanders and the Vatican. So Pope Nicholas II had agreed to lift the interdiction on one condition: the sinners must expiate their sin of disobedience by each building hospices for the poor at Bayeux, Cherbourg, Caen and Rouen. They were also to provide abbeys at Caen, one for women and one for men.

Matilda would complete hers in 1067, the Abbaye-aux-Dames rearing from the hill overlooking William's favourite town of Caen. She had appointed a remarkable woman, her namesake, as its first abbess. William had laid the foundations of his Abbaye-aux-Hommes, and in 1064 the walls of St-Etienne were sprouting from their sandstone footings in the heart of Caen. Here would stand his memorial for all time, his magnificent church and its monastery which his architects had designed, under his personal supervision, using all the skills and enterprise of which the masons and workmen of the city were capable. Lanfranc had been promised its supervision as soon as he could hand over the abbey at Le Bec to his successor. The Caennais, drawing upon the genius of the Italian and Spanish artists, engineers and masons, were contributing their own artistic pride. The massive strength of the Romans would combine with Gothic sensitivity as the yellow stone reared heavenwards – and the duke had been rightly proud: those two abbeys would emphasize that his favourite town was the second capital of Normandy and thus upper and lower Normandy would be drawn together. Of stone, his monuments to God should last for all time, free from the devastation of fire which ravaged so many fine buildings. Then, within a few months of each other, occurred the two remarkable acts of God which had set William firmly upon his ambitious course.

At Dreux, on 4 August 1060, the ailing Henry I of France died. A year earlier, he had consecrated his eight-year-old son, Philip, as his successor, his Russian widow, Anne, acting as regent. She had immediately consented to meet the duke and together they agreed to cease warfare. The siege of Thimert *ended; and two months later, Queen Anne married Ralph of Crépi and disappeared from the scene. The feeble Philip remained in the hands of his tutor, Philip's aunt's husband, Baldwin v of Flanders: for the foreseeable future the king of France was unlikely to threaten Normandy.*

The Hammer, seeing that his own life was drawing to its end and being frustrated of his Maine ambitions by William, decided to make peace with his own soul. Like so many of his generation, after a life of rapacious brutality the grand old warrior entered a monastery. Shortly afterwards, he was carried in agony into the cathedral of St Nicholas in Angers where, clad in his monk's habit, the last rites were pronounced. In less than four months, the main threats to William's duchy had been removed. By the end of that fateful year, 1060, Duke William's prestige stood high within and without Normandy's borders.

The duke had demonstrated to the world that his bastardy, far from shaming him, had given him the grit which others lacked. He had buried his mother with all the pomp which befitted the funeral of a queen: her tomb lay in the chancel of Grestain abbey, close to the estuary port of Honfleur.

This hard-won stability in the duchy was due as much to the support of the new nobility which William was creating around him, as to the example of the reformed Church. The political alliance of the two influences in supporting their duke was uniting the province. William, by giving power to his vicomtes *so that his duchy could be administered firmly and justly, had fashioned a new system unknown to Europe. He selected his* vicomtes *himself, fully aware of the danger which they could represent: he could never forget Valognes and Val-ès-Dunes. His inner council consisted of his trusted friends, the new men who had risked all for him.*

By judicious use of stick and carrot, William placed the men he wanted in the administrative positions and centres of power, thus stemming the flow of emigrant knights departing to fight in Italy. He distributed the lesser honours to those who were loyal and competent, but forbade the building of any castle. This ducal fief carried the obligation of servitium debitum: *the fief-holder had to supply his quota of knights and troops to serve the ducal army, but for no longer than forty days in the year. This duty was sworn on oath when the honoured knight paid homage as the duke's vassal, and each barony, monastery and bishopric had to produce its requisite quota. Failure to provide the* servitium debitum *was punished by the immediate seizure of the offender's fief. The other stick was the punishment of crime by the confiscation of the fief-holder's goods, lands and dwellings.*

Owning the majority of forests and the hundreds of towns in the duchy, the duke produced capital by selling them off to bishops and magnates. He augmented his income by imposing taxes on the new spirit of enterprise which was sweeping through the duchy: sturgeon fishing in the Seine, the saltings in the marshes; the barge trade, river ferries; road tolls, town dues; and taxes upon all flotsam and jetsam washed up on the shores, a harvest which included the many valuable whales. Anyone finding precious metals, ivory and furs, was forced to make payment into the ducal coffers. At Bayeux and Rouen William minted his own money . . . a monopoly he guarded jealously. He was immensely rich and his greed seemed limitless. He reflected his hard-won prestige through the magnificence of his court.

William, with his duchess beside him, was summoning his ecclesiastical court three times a year, at Easter, Pentecost and Christmas. Detesting being tied to one place, he would ride on ahead; the court followed, almost a thousand strong, counting the women and children. The horses, the baggage trains, the waggons and their occupants, the cattle and the palfreys – it was a noisy and smelly assembly which would gather for the night at one of his castles. The evening meal would be prepared swiftly on the trestle tables while the outdoor kitchens cooked the food in the iron tureens, heated the water and turned the spits. And on the following day justice would be dispersed, the cases being judged by the local bishop, baron or, if the duke ordained, by a council of local worthies. Life for the ordinary serf had certainly changed since that final contest at Varaville.

Before that decisive battle of 1057, internecine warfare had become unbearably expensive. A lord then needed twenty villages to support his castle, so the timber castles were spaced four leagues apart, a fact which led to eternal squabbling over boundaries. The more the barons fought amongst themselves, the more miserable became the plight of the peasants who were forced to provide for their lord's warfare. In return for their taxes in kind (hay and oats for the knights' horses and enforced military service to guard the castle walls) the lord assured his people's safety, provided he was a competent warrior. Not only did the baron enforce his own rough justice (the gibbet stood bleakly outside each castle wall) but it was he who supervised his serfs' fields to prevent cheating and the evasion of taxes; he who fixed the quotas; when to harvest, when to make the cider, mill the flour, bake the huge quantities of bread – all these banalités the lord took upon himself.

The wretched bondman had suffered atrociously in those days. Though he was not called upon to give military service outside his lord's domain and was debarred from standing witness in the hall of justice, it was the sergeants and provosts who benefited by their lord's sucesses. This peasant aristocracy exploited its leased farm holdings: these 'freedmen' lived in another world from their wretched 'bondmen', the serfs. It had not been surprising that the servus, *who comprised a fifth of the population, welcomed wholeheartedly the new Truce of God. It was the mounting cost of warfare which almost ruined even rich Normandy.*

A knight's steel helmet cost as much as one tenant's holding. To equip himself adequately, a knight required the equivalent of thirty tenants' incomes or the yield produced by one hundred and fifty hectares (360 acres). William's new army was raised by distributing fiefs de haubert *to those knights considered worthy. This fee absolved the privileged warrior from serving forty days' military service.*

Upon the shoulders of the serfs also weighed the cost of arming the baron's sons and relations who had proved their valour and who intended to adventure abroad to gain their honour and fortunes. The Norman warriors had won and forged a reputation abroad where their disciplined cavalry, the new military weapon, was proving irresistible. The chevalier *and his disciplined band of comrades fighting beneath their own house standard, now ranked at the top of the social class. The armoured cavalry were masters of the battlefield, but the cost was proving desperately expensive for those who had to pay through their toil. It was no wonder that the wretched peasantry had turned towards the reforming churchmen, like those living out their serene lives at Le Bec.*

Since the retreat of the eastern ordes, the population throughout Europe had increased rapidly with the result that, with the swift improvement in farming techniques through the development of agricultural tools, the forests were being pushed back; and, with fewer plagues decimating the population, more land was coming under the plough. A spirit of hope had spread throughout the duchy, the longing for freedom surging from below. Local industries were thriving; when the clergy were re-educated, schools opened in the towns; and above all, under the Steward's direction, a new class of Norman, the civil administrator, had brought order out of chaos.

Normandy was becoming an example for Europe, when the established order began to stabilize: the world was divided by God, as all men knew, into three classes: priests, knights and peasants. A stable structure was being created by monasteries and abbeys such as Le Bec, provided they could free themselves from secular interference: only through the Church and through its discipline could that brutal world be reformed. The scent of progress was in the air when William was able to begin enforcing law.

Even the bondman could then appeal to the ducal court for redress against baronial injustice . . . the duke's Chancellor had drafted a new legal system which at the same time preserved Normandy's age-old Viking traditions.

After Varaville, it was the settled conditions and the agricultural

*improvements imported from Europe which had so rapidly transformed the
duchy. Though these pressures were at first resisted by the barons, it was the
demand from the serfs and bondmen which had started clearing the forests.
Acting as entrepreneurs for the enrichment of their monasteries, the clergy's
influence soon convinced the barons of the advantage in exploiting the
newly-won lands. Rents increased, businesses started up and, for the first
time, investments were made for the sole purpose of bringing in an income:
the tide, wind and water-mills for grinding the flour; dyeing; the saltings –
through all these enterprises the profits accrued.*

*In the clearings, communal storage barns would spring up; the first signs of
a hamlet were the pigsties, and then a cottage would appear, then another
until eventually the growing community would call for its chapel. Finally,
the new village was given its charter, the written obligation between the
peasants and their landlord knight. By 1064, there were twelve hundred such
villages throughout the duchy wherein an ordered life existed, guaranteed by
law.*

*Once a village had grown in importance, by agreement with the lord or the
duke, it could gain the status of a* bourg, *when its taxes would be reduced
and its land obligations eased. Through this inducement, these isolated
communities attracted the skills which could improve the people's lot. At
Breteuil, Steward fitz Osbern had been one of the first to institute this*
bourgage *where, for the services rendered by the* bourg, *the lord was
beholden to the duke to keep the peace and to protect its* bourgeois
*inhabitants. Due to this revolutionary development, with fewer internecine
killings and more births, the population of Normandy exploded. For the first
time, stocks of grain, of salt, of timber were on sale against a bad winter. But
when Henry I and the Hammer died, this joyful progress was suddenly
threatened by the interminable warring which broke out once more in Maine.*

*When Herbert II of Le Mans died in 1062, the barons of Maine refused to
accept Robert, the duke of Normandy's ten-year-old son, as their new count
as had been agreed. It took the duke of Normandy over two years to crush the
resulting rebellion in Maine and the Vexin. At the beginning of 1064, peace
was restored, Robert being installed as count of Le Mans and Maine; and,
taking no risks, William eliminated brutally all potentially dangerous
opponents. He set in motion the building of the Grand and Petit Mont
Barbet castles at Le Mans and garrisoned Mayenne. The repulsive Mabel of
Bellême was now married to Montgomery and so William's southern and
eastern borders were secure for the foreseeable future. There remained one
last threat to Normandy if William were to leave his duchy to realize his
overseas ambition.*

Brittany was rebelling under the leadership of its count, Conan *II*, the great Alan *III*'s son, but his authority depended upon the support of the Breton nobility which was not unanimous in its enthusiasm for the rebel count. One of these was Riwallon of Dol who, loyal to his duke, was besieged in Dol by Conan. Riwallon appealed to William for help and the duke seized his chance to eliminate this last remaining threat to his duchy: having armed his beholden guest, he invited Harold to accompany him on his expedition to crush the Breton rebels.

After rescuing Harold at Eu, William had accompanied him with great pomp to Rouen. Showered with gifts and hospitality from William and Matilda, Harold Godwineson was encouraged to unwind after his ordeal at the hands of Guy of Ponthieu. Hunting with his falcons in the duke's wood to the north of the city by day, Harold spent the evenings in the privacy of William's family. And in the palace, at ease and relaxed with Matilda, Harold began to realize how, step by step, he had become beholden to the arch-diplomat, the duke of Normandy. During these long evenings the young Agatha, now approaching her thirteenth birthday, fell beneath the charm of the handsome, blond warrior of forty-two who had crossed the Channel to see her father. Harold's gaiety and sense of fun had broken many hearts (did he not live, Danish fashion, with the beautiful Edith, the Swan-neck, who had given him at least three children?). And when the family had retired, the duke and Harold Godwineson continued to talk into the airless, summer night descending upon the palace of Rouen, there in its hollow, bounded by the loop of the Seine. After a fortnight had slipped past, Harold had agreed in principle to the gist of William's proposals.

First, Godwineson accepted that King Edward had, in the spring of 1051, invited his cousin, William, the duke of Normandy, to be the lawful successor to the English crown. Harold remained silent on the rights and wrongs of the Confessor's decision, but had agreed to support William's claim when the time came. He would also act as the duke's personal representative in England and would garrison Dover castle with loyal Norman troops as surety for William's eventual crossing to claim the throne. As guarantee of his sincerity, he had summoned his youngest sister, Aelfgifu, a comely and lively maid by all accounts, across to Normandy. He would give her for wife to the son of any of the duke's vassals whom William would select. Aelfgifu duly arrived at court where her involvement with a frustrated young cleric very soon, with her Danish fervour, caused a scandal and cynical amusement.

For his part, the duke promised that when he became king of England, the earl of Wessex would retain his lands and status. The duke would also give

Agatha to Harold for wife when in a few years she would be old enough, Herbert of Maine now being dead. And, finally, William would release to Harold the two hostages who had been held as 'guests' in Normandy since Edward's promise to William thirteen years ago: Harold's youngest brother, Wulfnot, and his young nephew, Haakon. The sensitive, unwritten agreement being complete, the duke invited Harold to accompany him on his punitive expedition into Brittany to quell the rumbustious Conan II.

The duke's force departed westwards on 2 August. Conan rashly challenged William to a personal duel to decide the issue but, to catch Conan unawares, William ignored the bait and made a forced march across the Couesnon river in the estuary of Mont-St-Michel. There Harold displayed courage when rescuing personally two soldiers who had fallen into the quicksands. During the sacking of Dol he was impressed by the discipline of the duke's troops: no looting, no barbarities as had been expressly ordered by William.

Riwallon was saved and Dol retaken, the keys of the city being delivered by Conan on the end of a lance and similarly received by the duke. The symbolic gesture was not lost upon Harold: neither adversary had personally taken up arms against the other. During the assault, William was magnificently attired for battle in full chain-mail, from helm to heel, the only warrior so armoured. Not until Dol had been sacked, nor until Conan had been forced to flee, had Harold been considered tested in battle, and thus he had not been equipped as befitted a knight in the duke's army. But after Dol, the Saxon having proved himself, William had tied the penultimate knot.

The Steward sensed, as his eyes wandered round the room, that his friend had come a long journey since those appalling days of his childhood . . . and for an instant Fitz's eyes lit on a swarthy, sallow face at the back of the assembly, a face he recognized but to which he could not put a name. Then the weasel features clicked the mechanism of the Steward's memory: those close-set eyes, the pinched nostrils and thin red lips belonged to Foulques the Black, the cheat of William's boyhood and the half-brother of the banished Guy of Burgundy. William kept Foulques under surveillance by exploiting his doubtful qualities: he was an efficient spy and, through his upbringing, was acceptable throughout the courts of Europe. The duke had made him responsible for reporting on English affairs and Foulques had arrived only yesterday to report on developments in London. He was efficient at his dubious calling, but Fitz did not have to like the slimy creature. But William was not often wrong in choosing his agents and friends:

this gift was largely responsible for his success.

William had honoured his childhood guardian and his mother's brother by creating Walter Fulbert the baron of Calonne, that region which the Calonne river encompassed east of Pont l'Eveque, close to the sea and Honfleur where Fulbert had settled for his seafarer's life. Walter had been invited to today's court, but, as a senior shipmaster on this coast – he was now a sturdy man of fifty-six - he could not be present: he was in Cherbourg supervising the plans for the new quay.

At Bayeux, three days ago, at a ceremony witnessed by his army, William gave Harold a fine suit of chain of the latest design where, though the sword scabbard was enclosed inside the mail, the sword handle protruded free. Then, clad in his new battle-dress, Harold, kneeling before William, was knighted as his vassal, as his sworn 'man' to serve and protect his duke. And last night, the candles had burned late in the duke's chamber at Bonneville castle, as he and Godwineson talked alone for the last time before Harold sailed back to England.

After this morning's ceremony, accompanied by the papal nuncio and the highest of the dignitaries, together they would ride down the hill to the port of Touques: there the people would be waiting to cheer the distinguished Saxon earl, when at high-water he boarded his ship waiting at the quay in the river. William had told Fitz also to organize the handsome gifts from Rouen, the furs, the silks, the plates of gold – and the parchments for King Edward . . . but now the two principal actors were approaching, the burly duke leading, the taller, lithe Harold following his host, the two of them striding across the forecourt of Bonneville castle, their squires and seneschals at their heels. A horn sounded and as the Steward turned towards the hall, the assembly rose to its feet, all eyes on the wide, arched doorway.

The duke was making an impressive entrance. Inclining his uncovered head towards his nobles on the platform, then towards the packed hall, he half-turned, stretching out his hand for his guest. Leading Harold to the platform, he showed him to the oaken chair to the left of the throne. Waiting for the seneschals to find their places behind the two tables, William strode slowly across to the ducal throne which he had commanded from Rouen. The pages arranged the folds of his mantle of state, a bejewelled, indigo cloak, gleaming from the sunlight streaming through the narrow windows. Fitz, who was standing behind the duke's right shoulder, was able to compare the two men, one cool and confident, the other so wary of the proceedings.

A silence pervaded the hall. The duke sat motionless, waiting to speak. Resting on the ledges of the tiered footstool, his stockinged feet in their deerskin shoes protruded from the beige tunic which was richly bordered, in the royal manner, by a wide carmine border. Fitz handed the duke the sword of state, which William, accepting it in his right hand, laid point-up across his right shoulder.

By contrast, Harold seemed indifferent to this symbolic pedantry. He was already seated, waiting in his chair, a lean, tall figure, his long, fair moustaches neatly trimmed, his chin shaved, his longer, blond hair curling at the nape of his neck. He did not look ten years older than his host, perhaps because of his more austere apparel: the shorter, dark green tunic extended only to his knees; the less ornate cloak was clasped at the throat instead of the shoulder. The most striking contrast was the touch of humour in his face, his amused, blue eyes flashing as he glanced, almost disdainfully, at the vast assembly below the dais. He bore himself, Fitz thought, with immense dignity in this embarrassing situation, but with a majesty touched with contempt: as a man trapped by circumstances, a puppet in a prearranged play. And, symbolically, he wore no sword . . . The duke was speaking from the throne, his guttural voice reaching to the far corners of the silent chamber.

He was thanking the assembly for coming so far – and he turned to repeat the compliment for his distinguished guest. Harold inclined his head, smiled, and looked straight ahead – and then, with no more ado, William came straight to the nexus of the whole, complicated visit.

'My lords,' he growled, 'our noble guest, Earl Harold of Wessex, has visited us on behalf of the English king. He bears the message that your duke will, when the time comes, succeed King Edward to the English throne.' During the long pause, not a sound rustled in the great hall.

'My lords, I have accepted this formal invitation.' William added coolly, without expression: 'Thus will the duchy of Normandy be joined to the English kingdom.'

All eyes were riveted upon the impassive face of the Saxon. William half-turned to his companion on the dais:

'The earl of Wessex has pledged to me that he will support your duke against all other claimants to the throne of England, my lords. In return, he need have no fear for the future – and I have promised him in marriage our daughter, Agatha. My lord Harold is now an honoured knight of Normandy, has sworn his fealty to me.' William cleared his husky throat, fixed Harold with his eye. 'My lords, I am now asking the earl of Wessex, Harold Godwineson, to stand before you all, here on the dais. I invite him to witness his troth publicly, to swear on oath that he will keep his pledge when God finally calls King Edward's soul to His kingdom.' The duke nodded and with his left hand indicated to Harold that he should rise and complete the second half of the ritual. With a smile hovering at the corners of his wide mouth, the earl strode briskly behind the tables, then took his place between them in the centre of the dais. He said nothing but, by his attitude, it seemed that the English were unused to the pomp of state.

'My lord,' William demanded, 'do you, Harold Godwineson of the English earldom of Wessex, swear before this assembled company that you, as my vassal, will serve me, William, duke of Normandy, as your future king of England? Raise your hands and swear solemnly before this great congregation here assembled.'

Fitz could hear his own heart pumping in the silence. But, just as Harold was about to lift his hands, his seneschal pushed forwards from behind, his red face scowling as he muttered inaudibly to his Saxon lord. He was brandishing the lance in his left hand, but Harold pushed him back. Standing in the centre between the two tables, he raised his hands.

'I do swear it.' He spoke flatly, without conviction. He glanced at William, uncertain of what was expected next of him. He was muttering, 'I've already given my word.'

The duke had risen from his throne, his heavy face flushing with anger. With the tip of his sword he flicked the cloths from the tables; Fitz registered the gasp from the crowded hall as the sacred reliquaries from Rouen cathedral, the two most venerated relics in Normandy, were recognized. The one on the left still bore its travelling handles.

'Earl Harold,' the duke boomed. 'You have sworn on the holy relics of Rouen – the sacred bones of two English missionary saints who, while sheltering in France, suffered martyrdom for their faith.' William swung on his heel to face the assembly.

'Let every man here remember the noble earl's oath,' he thundered, raising the sword of state above his head. 'Harold Godwineson can never forget it.' He turned again to face his Saxon rival, but Harold had staggered backwards, appalled by the trick which had been played upon him. But ruse or not, no one in that hall was doubting the efficacy of the holy relics: an oath broken upon such sacred objects would carry terrible consequences.

The rangey Saxon, his colour returning to his cheeks, was recovering his poise. He stared long at William then, preceding him from the dais, strode down the steps and out of the great chamber. As the assembly rose for the departure of its duke, Fitz was watching Odo. Harold's momentary display of defiance had not been unobserved by the worldly bishop; and by many in the hall who had travelled across Europe to witness this climax to the events of the last two or three months.

With a heavy heart, Steward William fitz Osbern slowly preceded the procession from the dais. His friend had not heeded the Steward's warning: promises made under duress – and perhaps, some might say, through deviousness – were not necessarily durable. Duke William would need all his powers of diplomacy throughout the coming months to convince Europe and Pope Alexander II of the justness of his claim. But already the Steward was sensing two certainties: William possessed the necessary energy and powers of persuasion; but his devious methods were also bound to provoke animosity and doubts amongst even the most loyal of his potential allies.

15

WESTMINSTER

There must be over three hundred souls here, Foulques the Black ruminated as he sat, his back to the panelling at the end of the Great Hall in the royal palace of Westminster. Though he and the subdued assembly had been congregated in here for three days, Foulques had continued to keep himself apart: as head of Duke William's spy network in England, the less he talked at this moment with these magnates of London the better. His role as aide to Normandy's representative at the dying king's court gave adequate cover for Foulques' information gathering. He knew that he had a flair for sifting essentials from the chaff of rumour; the innumerable spies waiting upon his orders in the brothels and taverns of London bore testimony to the considerable organization which Foulques operated. It was, he realized, his nasty, suspicious mind which had hoisted him to William's notice. The duke gave the highest priority to accurate spy reports: how else could he have been victorious at Mortemer and Varaville?

Foulques exploited his way with women to the furtherance of his work. For the past fifteen months he had wormed his way into the Confessor's court; when the queen returned to London six weeks previously to be near her sickening husband, Foulques had not been slow to see where his chance lay: Martha was the twenty-two-year-old daughter of the queen's lady-in-waiting; she and three other maids waited upon the queen as her personal attendants. Queen Edith demanded little after her long years in the nunnery.

Martha was not only privy to the gossip, but she had also gained the royal ear. Queen Edith was passing on to Martha all that the king wished his Norman cousin across the Channel to know. And, for what Martha lacked in female beauty, she compensated for in ardour. Foulques enjoyed this twist to his work, but was surprised by the vehemence with which the queen distrusted her brother Harold, as disclosed in Martha's pillow-talk.

Queen Edith's long and chaste separation from her pious husband was accepted by the nation as another example of the Confessor's rectitude. There were already calls to canonize him as a saint; but the queen had recently confided to Martha's mother that the unconsummated marriage was not due to saintly restraint. Edith had meekly accepted her life of chastity in a nunnery because what court gossip had for so long hinted was true: Edward was impotent. The barren royal marriage was mirrored in his ineffectual rule. While Europe was bursting from the dark ages into cultural activity, the traditionally virile and rumbustious English creativity, particularly in art and literature, had degenerated into sterility during his long, childless reign.

Had Edward been normal, there would not have been this crisis of succession and now, as everyone in this Great Hall knew, the king was dying.

Queen Edith had been seen hurrying back to the king's chamber on the floor above, where the archbishops were already gathered: Aldred of York and the despicable Stigand of Canterbury, who had insisted on pronouncing the last rites himself two days ago, when they carried the king to his new church of St Peter, just outside the western walls of the city.

Only eight days ago, they had consecrated the abbey, the fruit of the king's dreams; but Edward had even then been too sick to witness the culmination of his life-long work. And now, with the dark January nights closed in, it was clammy cold in this draughty hall, while they waited for the final, inevitable announcement.

Foulques drew his black cloak closely around him, wishing that he had Martha inside its folds. This was the fourth night he'd endured, waiting for the old monarch to die . . . but Foulques had been shaken when Martha had earlier passed close to him, on her way up to the royal bed-chamber: 'Earl Harold's got everything organized,' she'd whispered. 'The queen's furious with her brother – the way he's manipulating the old king. They won't even let him die in peace,' she'd ended, her fingers feeling for him beneath his cloak. That had been two hours ago, and the night was freezing in this gloomy English hall, in spite of the flickering flames. Foulques was beginning to hate this dank English climate and longed for the softness of the Normandy springtime which he had briefly experienced last year.

The new year of 1065 had begun joyously for the duke when in February his duchess presented him with Cecily, their fourth daughter. But while William was energetically sounding European reaction to his overseas adventure, the Witan convened in the autumn of 1065 to expunge the name of the boy atheling from the list of claimants: Edgar was too young when strong leadership would be essential for the nation's future stability. So there remained William's two principal competitors: King Harold Hardraada, the redoubtable warrior poised in Bergen fjord who was aided by the vengeful Tosti; and Harold Godwineson whose prestige outside Wessex had slumped.

Foulques looked up as a commotion broke out on the balcony leading to the king's room. He could see the weeping women and hear the sonorous chanting of the clergy. A sombre figure stepped from beneath the flickering shadows; both arms stretched across the rail, he called down to the expectant, upturned faces:

'The king is dead. God rest his soul.'

The brief moment of silence and then the murmurs and rustling as men crossed themselves in the shadows – that was all, as Foulques rose to his feet. He freed himself from the press and slipped out into the bitter night where the sleet was slashing the churned-up mud. He'd contact his agent, Barnaby, then return for Martha. She'd be helping to lay out the corpse, but had promised to meet him when she'd finished. It was twenty minutes to midnight: he could be waiting long for her, judging by the bustling stream of the cloaked, shadowy figures of the barons entering and leaving the Great Hall.

Martha kept her word. At half-past six the following morning, when Foulques in exasperation returned to Westminster, the grey-faced girl had stumbled down the staircase with the others, after the bier had been shouldered from the Hall. Together they'd watched the subdued, smooth organization as the funeral party bore the bier into the darkness of the bitter morning: eight burly bearers, the staves across their shoulders, their breath like white balloons in the glacial air as they slithered on the ice after the night's rain. The corpse was carried head first, the two crosses surmounting the richly ornamented bier. Foulques felt a twinge of pity for this pathetic, shrouded bundle being hurried furtively through the darkness, on its final journey towards the uncompleted church of St Peter, before the citizens of London were awake.

Behind the bier walked the clergy, led by the archbishop of Canterbury with that sardonic smirk upon his face. The ice crackled, the priests intoned to the chanting of the sleepy choir boys as they preceded the dismal procession. The only concession to the late king's preference for things Norman was the funereal tintinnabulation of the handbells which the two leading choir boys were ringing. Drowsy heads poked through half-opened doors, that was all. Thus did the Confessor make his last journey: the authorities buried him beneath the earth of his new church before the noon bell sounded.

Martha had been allowed that hour's escape from her duties and Foulques had waited all afternoon for her. When the murky evening was shutting in again, she stumbled upstairs to his room to unburden herself of these strange events. Before dropping into exhausted sleep she'd understood that he must carry the news himself, instead of entrusting it to his agents. He'd left her in peace, saddled his horse and set off down the Kent road.

Another two hours of this bitter night and he'd have to lie up. Five leagues perhaps – could he make Rochester? Even with his groom, it would be dangerous to ride too late. He could certainly make Dover tomorrow – and he settled down to the canter, the wind mercifully at his back . . .

What an incredible day this Eve of Epiphany had been – Friday, 6 January 1066. Martha had been right: the slick proceedings in the palace of Westminster smacked of indecency. Earl Harold had things organized with military precision. The Witan, he said, must confirm the succession with speed, before the people had time to ponder the developments. Act first, ask afterwards, was always a leader's maxim . . .

Last night, in that room of death, they had supported the king into a sitting position while he approached his end in agony. His wife was weeping softly at the foot of his bed when, whispering that he should wear the crown of England, he beckoned Earl Harold to his side. Bidding Godwineson to care for Queen Edith, his words then became inaudible. Harold bent low over the expiring monarch, but no one heard those last whispered words, no one except the tall, stooping Saxon. When the king had croaked his last breath, Harold closed the lids over the tired, jaundiced eyes. The earl straightened himself, then turned to repeat softly the dying king's last command:

'Take my crown of England . . .' – and that was all.

Earl Harold was not to be gainsaid as the ensuing ritual proceeded mechanically. Even before Edward was beneath the soil, those magnates of the Witan who had hurried to London were meeting the city's leaders to invite the earl of Wessex to wear the crown offered by the king: by tradition the last words of a dying king always held the force of law.

During that same afternoon Harold was enthroned in the royal robes. Holding the sceptre in his right hand, the orb in his left, it was Archbishop Aldred of York, the pope's man, who placed the crown on Harold's head. The crowning was thus impeccably correct, but Stigand's ill-concealed satisfaction had not passed unnoticed when both prelates pronounced the blessing. While Edith wept silently at the rear of the uncompleted chancel, Harold was pronounced king of England.

The Northern earls would have preferred a claimant with royal blood and remained luke-warm over Harold's accession, though they accepted that a strong leader was needed at this critical moment: England was facing two inevitable invasions. Harold Godwineson was therefore the obvious choice, a warrior, a leader who could unite the kingdom to repel the invader. During that same evening of his coronation day, Harold was promising that he would forthwith be abolishing unjust laws, redressing injustices and cracking down on violent crimes; he intended to support the Church and to lead the nation by the example of his own piety – a difficult task, reflected Foulques. How long could the impetuous, ambitious man of action sustain the façade? As soon as the duke of Normandy heard the news, William would inevitably arraign Europe against the oath-breaker; how would Harold defend himself against the charge? Foulques bent low in the saddle, crouching against a scat of sleet. He'd persevere to Rochester where his groom knew of a warm tavern: then on at dawn tomorrow for Dover . . .

There were disquieting reports that the duke of Normandy was very ill. It was rumoured that prayers were being said in the churches for him. If Foulques could find a ship and the wind permitted, he could be in Rouen on the evening of Monday, the ninth. The agent averted his face from the snow now stinging his cheeks; he felt a satisfaction, a pride in his role as messenger and informant. The news he carried in his head was as momentous for the future of Normandy as could be imagined – and he, Foulques the Black, the despised bastard of Burgundy, was the principal actor for this brief moment, on the stage of history.

16

CONFRONTATION

On 8 February, after the traumatic assembly at Lillebonne castle, Walter Fulbert left his comfortable manor overlooking the river Chaussey which ran serenely into the Touques above Pont l'Eveque. His wife, accustomed to his seafaring life, had with cheerful resignation accompanied him to their temporary house in the port of Dives. Their daughters were off their hands: Matilda had married Ralph Tesson, so there was no worry there; and Clara was happy in her convent at Montilliers. So Walter Fulbert, Fleet Shipmaster of Honfleur, was able to give his all to the gargantuan task entrusted to him by the duke: the supervision of the building of an invasion fleet in six months, before the autumn weather set in.

The tall, rugged-faced man carried his fifty-seven years well. His broad shoulders were as yet unbowed as, cloakless, he stood alone on the main quay at Dives on this soft September forenoon. His keen eyes absorbed every detail of this fleet over which he had worried himself sick during these last five months. It was nine already, one of those September mornings when the first rays of the soft sunshine washed the freshly-stained ships: the diversely coloured planks contrasted one against the other, as they were meant to do in these clinker-built vessels. It was pleasing to his seaman's eyes, to see the wash-strakes pierced with their oar-holes, the planks dyed red, blue, green and yellow in the hundreds of ships. The differing colours of the planks had helped the master shipwrights, standing centrally at the stern-posts, to judge by eye the hull lines as the planks were clenched from the hog upwards, edge upon edge to the frames.

The forests for leagues inland around Dives had been scoured for the suitably shaped timbers with which to fashion stems, forefeet, frames' knees and stern-posts. Though Dives was the main assembly port for the Cotentin and Lower Normandy, the remainder of the fleet was congregating in the Flemish ports – and, for the hundredth time during this second week in September, the fleet shipmaster wished devoutly that the duke would heed his plea: this cumbersome fleet, which was cluttering up the crowded port of Dives, must clear the harbour before the equinoctial gales struck. He, Fleet Shipmaster Fulbert, would again try to persuade his one-time charge, the stubborn, prudent Duke William, to sail at once for the mouth of the Somme where the rest of the fleet was waiting – tomorrow if need be. The weather would not hold much longer and the army was restless, impatient; for over a month it had been restricted to the camps spread around the banks of the Dives.

The duke was on his way from Bonneville and should be here with his staff within the hour. And, through habit, Fulbert began his daily tour of the harbour, checking the warps, questioning the crews where the ships were moored stern-on to the piles, their bows aground on the muddy banks. But his thoughts were elsewhere, churning over the options he'd been given after the news of the English king's death five months ago – what a catastrophic tragedy if, after all this effort, the invasion fleet was to be wrecked by the inevitable equinoctial gales . . .

At Christmas, the duke had been so ill that even as far as Metz prayers had been offered for his recovery. He had been convalescing at Rouen and enjoying his first days of falconry in the Rouvray forest when they escorted that unpleasant Foulques to him, with the news that Harold Godwineson had broken the oath he had sworn two years ago. Unsurprised and without a word, the duke had taken his Steward with him, pulled the skiff himself across the Seine, and ridden straight to the palace. With only fitz Osbern with him in the chamber, William, still pale and shivering from the fever, had pulled his cloak about him. For an hour he had brooded silently, wrestling with his decision. From that moment, events had rolled with remorseless pressure towards the state of readiness which the invasion force now enjoyed.

Confident that from no quarter could Normandy now be attacked, the duke summoned his barons from the farthest corners of his duchy. At the same time, he made his last bid for gaining the English crown by peaceful means, an effort he knew to be fruitless. But the attempt in itself was proof to Europe that he was dealing with a devious rival, a man who had broken an oath sworn upon the sacred relics of Normandy. Twice William dispatched his ambassadors across the Channel to remind Harold of his promise and allegiance, to emphasize that Harold was the duke's vassal and a trusted comrade: had not the duke himself dubbed him a knight of Normandy, sealed the honour by showering him with gifts? And why had Harold not sent his sister, Aelfgifu, across the Channel to marry the Norman baron, as Harold had pledged?

'She's dead,' was Harold's rebuff. 'If the duke wants her as she is, I'll send her body.' He added in his reply that he had given his oath under duress; and that the English Witanegot refused to accept a foreigner as their king. 'In consequence, I cannot marry your daughter, Agatha,' Harold concluded.

When William sent his ambassador back the second time to England for his last attempt at compromise, he must have known that Harold could never accept the suggested terms: the duke would renounce his claim, providing Harold married Agatha and thereby joined England to Normandy. Once again, Harold's answer – but by deed this time – was as insulting as his first ambassadorial reply.

Immediately after his coronation, Harold marched north to allay the fears of his suspicious earls, Edwin and Morcar. Meeting them at York, he was forced to buy peace by agreeing to marry their sister: Edith had recently been widowed from her Welsh prince, Griffith, who had been murdered by his own Welshmen when attacking Hereford. She was a proud lady: her grandmother, Godiva, had earned eternal recognition at Coventry some years earlier.

For many years, Harold had been living, 'Danish Custom', with his devoted concubine, Edith the Swan-neck; she had given him three sons, but he renounced her to marry Edith, the Welsh prince's widow, as his queen of England. In answer to Duke William's conciliatory suggestions Harold blandly sent the news of his marriage to Rouen. The insult brought its immediate and expected reaction.

The alerted Norman barons were invited to attend the duke's emergency court at Lillebonne. There on the banks of the Seine, at an unforgettable banquet in Julius Caesar's (Juliobonna) ancient castle from which the Roman fleet invaded England, the highest nobles of the duchy debated acrimoniously William's project to invade England in order to seize his rightful crown. Walter Fulbert, who had been invited to act as the duke's nautical adviser, would remember that day as long as he lived.

The ageing barons were wearying of warfare: they were tired and wished to enjoy the spoils they had gained at such cost. Legally, they were bound to provide only forty days' service a year. They were not compelled to serve overseas: the proposed invasion was a potentially suicidal expedition which might last for years; an adventure which in a few hours could destroy all they had won in a lifetime's warring.

But the traditional hostility of the Rouen bourgeoisie evaporated at the promise of untold profits from the enterprise. The citizens of Rouen immediately proposed to make a generous contribution. They were demonstrating their support for their duke – and Walter Fulbert, alone on the quay again, smiled to himself as he recalled the greed and hypocrisy of those merchant land-lubbers . . .

Bishop Odo of Bayeux, the duke's forceful and ruthless half-brother, guided the proceedings as the arguments rumbled through the Great Hall of Lillebonne castle. Hugh, the son of the ageing count of Eu and the venerable countess, Lesceline, was vital to the expedition, because he controlled the Ponthieu and Flanders ports. And as soon as William promised the churches that they would benefit from the spoils, the bishops were also won over; they promised large contributions from the sale of their monastic lands.

It had been fascinating to watch them, as each was forced to declare himself: Archbishop Maurilius was present with the bishops of Evreux and of Coustances and the jovial old Yves, still bishop of Sées and head of Mabel's family at Bellême. Once the Church had pronounced for William, the leading barons soon joined them: William's other half-brother, Robert, now count of Mortain; Ralph of Conches, Roger Tosny's son; Hugh of Grandmesnil; the splendid Roger of Beaumont and his brother, Richard of Orbec; Henry of Vieilles – and even Mabel's husband, the fighting Montgomery.

But the argument became confused and unpleasant. The barons were already paying huge dues to the duke's exchequer and failure of the invasion would bring ruin – forget this ambitious, foolhardy project: let Normandy consolidate the peace for which it had struggled so long at such cost . . .

The Steward of Normandy had not spoken but as the assembly was dissolving in uproar, the dignified fitz Osbern rose slowly to his feet. Such was the man's presence, such the respect in which he was held, that the cacophony of strident voices stilled. Walter Fulbert remembered well the solemn, reasoned argument which the great Steward offered his duke in support.

Through paying their dues, the barons of Normandy had the right to voice their independent opinions, the Steward conceded, but had they considered the benefits to be won when the invasion of England succeeded? He concluded his reasoning by assuring the duke that the great majority of his vassal lords were solidly behind him . . .

Uproar broke out: 'Not so! Not so!' the bellowed indignation thundered through the Great Hall. 'What guarantee do we have,' the barons clamoured, 'that our support will not be used as a precedent for any of the duke's impetuous adventures in the future? We refuse to put our sons' heritage in thrall . . .' In this moment of crisis the duke showed his genius, his skill at bending obstinate men to his will. He thereupon dissolved the assembly, suggesting that everyone needed two hours of reflection. The distraught barons broke up in disorder, each to his own like-minded group – and during that breathing-space, William worked hard. Summoning the most influential of his lords, he talked to each individually, strolling with them beneath the castle walls in the cold February sunshine.

Blackmail was not an inaccurate description of the duke's persuasion: was this baron, so respected and trusted by his peers and by the duke himself, *really* refusing his loyalty, while his neighbour was contributing so richly, in funds and overseas service, knowing that there was such booty, such wealth to be won? Those who gave most would naturally be rewarded proportionally with English lands, with positions of rank and authority. Could the baron repudiate this opportunity, while so many of his friends were volunteering so loyally? It was unthinkable that the duke would tax those who stayed behind more heavily than those who volunteered . . . Naturally, the duke would be happy to furnish a sealed bond guaranteeing that the baron's contribution would never be used for future tax: this was a once-for-all contribution. The baron had to be made of granite to resist this persuasion, face-to-face with the thirty-eight-year-old duke to whom allegiance and the lord's fief were due . . .

William had waited for the Great Hall to be filled again before remaking his entrance . . . and Walter recalled the roar of acclamation that greeted their valiant duke: the hostility evaporated, and when the proudest men of Normandy jostled forwards to pledge their support, the lesser knights soon joined the queue. In the flush of enthusiasm, the duke immediately called upon them to build the fleet which must carry the armies across that turbulent stretch of sea. The assembly divided into organizing groups, then dissolved, the duke's final words etched into their minds: 'The scarcity of ships will not hinder us, because soon we shall have enough. Wars aren't won by numbers, but by courage.' They were standing when he departed, the rafters echoing to the roars of acclaim from the remotest corners of the Great Hall. And the next few months were the most hectic in Walter Fulbert's and many others' lives . . .

The duke's diplomatic offensive upon Europe flung the court into a frenzy of activity. A week after the Lillebonne conference, Lanfranc was indispensable at the duke's right hand; Archbishop Maurilius was too old, too saintly, so Gilbert, bishop of Lisieux departed for Rome, while William's ambassadors rode to all Normandy's eastern neighbours. First, Henry IV of the Germanic Empire was swayed by subtle argument: he would support the Norman duke's Christian crusade against the treacherous oath-breaker, against the ambitious earl who tricked his way to the English throne. Then, at Rome, the influential archdeacon, Hildebrand, the man expected eventually to become pope, was impressed by Bishop Gilbert's presentation of William's case and lost no time in rallying support.

The merits and demerits of the two adversaries were easy to cite. Harold, the usurper king, was not only a sacrilegious breaker of solemn religious oaths, but a sinner. A fierce, violent man, he lived by the Danish Custom which was anathema to the Church of Rome – although when a new opportunity presented, he was not slow to ditch the woman he'd loved. Edward the Confessor, a saintly monarch, had for long resisted the ambitious house of Wessex; he had even invited his cousin, William, duke of Normandy, to succeed him. It was only on his death-bed that the king, a dying man in the direst agony, *might* have designated the persuasive Harold to succeed him. Judging by the reaction in England, especially from the North, Harold's crowning was not universally accepted.

But he failed most in his relations with Mother Church. He and his independent Church refused to pay their dues, the deniers of St Peter, and neither did they present their traditional gifts to Rome – but even Edward had been dilatory in this respect. Harold employed no personal chaplain; on the contrary, he insisted on retaining the loathsome Stigand as his archbishop of Canterbury, the false prelate to whom three consecutive popes, Leo IX, Victor II and Etienne IX had refused the *pallium* of recognition. Alexander II, the present pope since 1061, not only interdicted Stigand but excommunicated him. Such was the man who had solemnly assisted in the coronation of Harold: it was this last offence which finally turned Rome against King Harold – and towards the duke of Normandy who more exactly obeyed the Holy Father.

Were not William and his duchess, in expiation of their admitted sin of disobedience, building a hospital, churches and the most prestigious monasteries in Europe? The duchess was hoping soon to be consecrating her magnificent Abbaye-aux-Dames at Caen, and the illustrious Lanfranc was the abbot-designate for St-Etienne, when finally the Abbaye-aux-Hommes was completed. Were not the Norman warriors, led by William Giroie, chief of the Holy Company, displaying remarkable courage and success against the infidel? And had not the duke promised total loyalty to Rome should he succeed in his adventure? He had even dispatched his personal envoys to the Holy City with the sacred taxes. The choice was not difficult for Pope Alexander II when he adjudicated in favour of the Norman duke.

William was nominated as the pope's ambasador and commissioned to punish the sacrilegious Harold. The duke's English expedition became a First Crusade and, to demonstrate his approval, Alexander blessed his personal banner and dispatched it by envoy for the duke to fly from his lance. By another envoy was sent a hair and a tooth of Saint Peter for William to wear about his neck as he went into battle. A papal bull of excommunication for use against Harold was also sent to the duke for use at his discretion. Alexander thereupon excommunicated Harold from the Church of Rome. Duke William, having won the diplomatic battle, then considered the mercurial and unreliable Tosti. In May, with Hardraada's support, Tosti tried to regain his rights in England by raiding the Isle of Wight from the sanctuary of the Flemish ports. He then sailed up-Channel to invest Sandwich, where Kentish seamen joined him to swell his fleet to sixty ships. He moved to the east coast where he ravaged the Humber estuary. Edwin, the earl of Mercia, reacting more in defence of his own territory than in defence of the king of England, crossed the Trent and hacked Tosti's mercenaries to shreds. With only twelve ships remaining, Tosti sailed north to the protection of Malcolm, the Scottish king with whom he had earlier allied himself, through the ancient rite of mingling blood. Harold Hardraada, who controlled the Orkneys, dispatched seventeen ships from the islands to help his demented ally. Tosti Godwineson then bided his time for the coming Norwegian invasion.

King Harold of England, convinced that the duke of Normandy was behind Tosti's foray, decided that the principal danger lay from across the Channel, a threat, incidentally, which most directly menaced his own Wessex. Leaving the east coast defended by only the dubious Northern earls, King Harold in June moved his *fyrd* to the south coast which he proceeded to fortify.

A curious phenonemon startled the European world during the night of 24 April. Trailed by its glowing tail, a brilliant comet moved slowly across the dome of the universe; it was visible for the whole of that week. Walter Fulbert, the seafarer, had felt the awe as keenly as anyone, while his fleet began to take shape. He was not the only thinking person to link this heavenly sign with that which had appeared over Bethlehem a thousand years ago: the coming crisis over England's succession would also affect the known world.

By the end of May 1066, the first ships were mooring up to the stakes in the mud of the Dives. On the fourteenth of June, the duke assembled his barons at his favourite castle of Bonneville. There he presented his duchess as Normandy's regent while he was absent overseas, the wise Beaumont remaining at her side to advise and help. He also declared Robert, his fourteen-year-old son, as his successor. To him the assembly swore allegiance, knowing that Robert would be travelling to Poissy to receive the approval of the young French king, Philip. On the next day, the duke passed through Dives to inspect the growing fleet and to check the arrangements being made for the arrival of the armies which were converging on the port from across Europe. On 16 June, he and Duchess Matilda were in Caen for the consecration of her Abbaye-aux-Dames; and for the announcement of Lanfranc's appointment as the first abbot of the church of St-Etienne, when William's Abbaye-aux-Hommes was completed. From then onwards, the pace for Fleet Shipmaster Fulbert had become hectic, as the ship quotas swiftly became reality.

Each baron, each monastery, abbey and priory were committed to building a contribution of ships. Boat-builders from every creek and haven, from every port and harbour along the Normandy and Flemish coasts, from the Couesnon to the Scheldt were committed to building and fitting out this amazing fleet. One thousand seven hundred major ships were being built from the green wood of the forests behind the ports; when the transports, barges, victualling boats and auxiliaries were counted, the total must be more than two thousand five hundred vessels . . . The Shipmaster sighed and pushed back his grizzled hair when he heard behind him the sound of hooves pounding upon the sun-baked road behind the quays.

Steward Osbern felt as exhilarated as evidently did his duke, while the ducal party cantered down the combe towards the sea shore. Below him, Fitz sighted the sea and the strand of sand over which the white crests of waves were breaking at the mouth of the Dives. The clouds were sweeping in from the Atlantic: it was time to sail, Fitz was sure, time to heed the fleet shipmaster's advice. The army camps stretched across the plain along either side of the river, the tents sheltered for leagues among the dunes. The soldiers were ready, their equipment dry. It was time to sail, which was why William was riding over from Bonneville this morning. And Fitz's spirits lifted at the realization that perhaps tomorrow the Dives estuary would once again be empty, devoid of the miscellany of troops from all over Europe. Ah! There were the ships, looking like beetles from up here, the serried lines of tents, the corrals where the destriers, the duke's formidable weapon, were tethered in their thousands.

The army had been encamped here for a month, some battalions for much longer. It was a measure of the discipline which the duke imposed through his commanders that his strict orders had been obeyed. The army had to live off its own rations and the local people were to be treated with respect. A peasant could go about his business without fear of attack, of losing his fowls, his pigs; his wife and daughters went unmolested. This happy state of affairs had obtained since Saturday 12 August, when Fulbert had reported that the fleet was in all respects ready for sea, an amazing achievement in only six months since February.

But this morning's report from one of Harold's captured spies told a different story from the other side of the Channel. Did this explain William's exuberance?

Last Friday, 8 September, Harold decided to return to London, having disbanded his *fyrd* along the south coast. The bored and hungry troops had ravaged the coast, had stripped the countryside bare and infuriated the peasants. His fleet, too, was quitting the Solent and sailing up-Channel to London before the equinoctial gales struck. And at last, on this side, the slant of the wind was raising the duke's hopes: if Fulbert agreed, he'd lead the fleet up to the mouth of the Somme, there to assemble for the final sailing across the Channel . . . the duke's party was at the bottom of the combe and swerving into the track which followed parallel with the beach.

It was a stirring sight, this fleet, ship to ship in trots of six, strung out along both banks of the river as far as Fitz could see, reaching far above the bridge. The smiling colours of the planks, red, yellow, blue and green; the shining masts in the gleaming sunlight; the pendants flapping from their trucks, vaunting the colours of their owner-lords; a sail drying in the breeze, ballooning in its brails and bright with colour, was reminiscent of the summer scene, instead of representing the lethal business of war. And there was Fleet Shipmaster Fulbert, unmistakable, four-square on the quay. He was raising his hand to his forehead in salute, while the gulls screeched and battled overhead.

'Greetings, Walter!' boomed William. 'My troops are ready to embark, so my lord Montgomery tells me.' He turned to the rider on his right, the dark, beetle-browed Roger, already greying at the temples, who was commanding the Franco-Flemish division. The lord of Bellême nodded. He spoke through half-opened lips: 'I await only your command, sire.'

'Take me round the fleet, Walter,' the duke said, vaulting from his palfrey. 'We can talk while I inspect my ships.'

It was good to watch those two together, the middle-aged seafarer who had worked harmoniously with his duke for so long during these six months: William had never forgotten the debt he owed his former guardian. The horses were left with the squires and the ducal party set out on its final inspection. Fitz dropped behind, leaving the fleet shipmaster and the army's commander to parley with their duke.

Among the dunes were encamped fifty thousand men, archers, foot-soldiers, slingers, the grooms, the victuallers and the miscellaneous trades which held such a host together: the organization, which included William's brain-child, his prefabricated timber forts, was vast. Every scrap of gear, from water skins to spare arrow-heads, from war-chargers to kitchen spits, had to be carried across that surging sea. On average, forty soldiers and its crew complemented each seventy-foot troopship, the longer, ninety-foot vessels taking the knights and their chargers. The horse transports were ugly, blunt barges ninety feet long and, with a beam of twenty-five feet, displaced forty tons when loaded. With five animals packed against each other in five separated compartments on either side of the fore-and-aft line, the transport carried fifty horses with their grooms and the loading ramps.

The troopships drew five and a half feet and carried two anchors, one with a stock and fitted with a tripping line for anchoring offshore while deciding where to land: the other, stockless, to be waded ashore for driving its flukes into the beach. The shrouds of the removeable mast were fitted above the wooden traveller which bore the long yard with its braces and coloured, panelled sails. Following the custom of their ancestors, the duke's ships were fitted at stemhead and sternpost with removeable figureheads, beloved by sailors to ward off the unpredict-able, evil powers at sea: grotesque dragon heads with long, lolling tongues; fierce eagle heads plumed with butting feathers – the more fearsome, the more efficacious – in Viking style, as, indeed, the Scandinavian *drakkars* were ancestors to these Norman ships.

Striding up the right bank, the duke spoke with the crews who were slapping on the last coats of stain, rubbing down the undersides, checking the anchor cables – the myriad details which made all the difference between a taut and a slack, dangerous ship. Sailors were bending on the sails to the yard of a late-comer who had been run on to the mud below the bridge, in the hope that she would catch the expedition. The duke's party paused to take count and Fitz was able to marvel once again at the functional beauty of these slender vessels.

This ship rearing from the river-grass close to him was one of the ninety-footers, of finer lines than the ordinary troopship. She was wide in the beam and drew five and a half feet when loaded; her fine lines swept from her pointed, canoe stern to the high stem; her savage figurehead lay above the tideline in the sea lavender, ready for final fitting. The reversed sheer below the forefoot made her sea-kindly, her bows cleaving the seas with an elegance difficult for a landsman like Fitz to appreciate. A beautiful, living creature, built in less than three months from the Bavent woods behind Dives. The shipwrights were hanging the steering sweep, a shorter, wider type of board than those oars, double banked and fifteen on each side, which were shipped in holes along the wash-strake. A short tiller was fitted to the head of the sweep which itself pivoted on a thole-pin, right aft of the steer-board quarter from where the helmsman steered.

The hull was almond-shaped and broad in the beam; inboard, the floors were laid over the carefully selected oaken frames. Unlike the Vikings, who used whale gut or the sinuous roots of fir trees with which to fix the clinker planks one upon the other, these Norman shipbuilders now used iron fastenings; though William's ships were less supple in a seaway, they leaked less than their forebears between the planks and the frames. Also, unlike the Vikings who overlaid their round shields outboard of the wash-strake in order to increase the freeboard, the Norman shields which were longer and narrower, were interleaved inboard along the gunwale. There were no thwarts and the oarsmen pulled standing and facing aft. To make the ship drier, a canvas dodger was lashed in the eyes of the ship, behind which the for'd look-out sheltered. To Fitz, who acknowledged that seafaring was a total mystery to him, and to whom being at sea meant nothing but nausea and fright, the skill used to fashion these floating shells was always astounding. The shipbuilder's art had developed through the mists of time and experience . . .

The mast, for instance, was stepped halfway along the hull to reduce the strain on the frames, because the ship could only run or reach before a following wind – another reason, too, for the canoe stern and the high stern post. The sail, bent to its yard which was hoisted to the hounds, was the same width as the mast height; billowing ahead of the mast, the sail exerted its centre of effort forward; because the sheets were slack much of the time, less strain was imposed upon the steering sweep. Control became more positive and the fear of broaching-to was lessened. To reduce canvas in bad weather, the sail was either brailed up or the yard lowered to bend on a storm sail. The varied and gaily coloured sail panels rendered the ships things of beauty and once at sea they became part of the element for which they were designed.

For Fitz, nothing fashioned by the hand of man could compare with the grace of *Mora*, the duke's own ship which had been given to him by his wife. *Mora*, who would lead the ships, was lying alongside the quay at Touques, ready for sea below the castle at Bonneville where the duke was always in residence when inspecting his invasion force.

The command of the fleet had been given to Fleet Shipmaster Fulbert, to reward him for the successful completion of the ships on time. Fulbert was rightly proud of *Mora*, built at Barfleur, of seasoned oak planks on oaken frames: she was one hundred and twenty feet long and, with her complement of fifty of the duke's most valiant warriors, she displaced forty tons. Fitz was thankful to be accompanying William in her: so large a ship might corkscrew less in the quartering seas. She was commanded by Etienne Erard, a doughty Barfleurais.

The three most important men of the moment were deep in thought –the final decision was being made, Fitz was convinced. At last, the long wait was over, the ships loaded and requiring only the embarkation of the army. The armour was loaded: the suits of chain-mail each weighed over fifty pounds and were carried on board by pairs of men, staves being rove through the sleeves and the ends of the batons borne on the shoulders; the swords and the helmets; but the shields, as also the horses, would be loaded at the last moment. Lances, maces and swords were already stowed, each in the knight's respective ship – the whole operation was a gigantic feat of organization. The foot-soldiers, slingers and archers were detailed to their transport; the men-at-arms, with their chain-shirts and iron helmets, their hatchets, broadswords, daggers and spears to separate ships.

Then there were the oats for the horses during the crossing; the wine in the especially built casks, hauled by the train of four-wheeled carts; the water skins waiting to be topped up at the last moment; the farriers with their portable forges; and, in twenty purpose-built ships, the pre-constructed sections of the two timber towers which could be swiftly erected. Everything had to be carried; even the food, because the harvest was not yet in and the southern fields of England would be bare now that Harold had been forced to leave from lack of food.

Walter Fulbert was sniffing the salt-laden breeze, shaking his greying head, when Fitz rejoined them. The halyards of the hundreds of boats were slatting against the stepped masts: an impatient summons rattling across the river from one bank to the other, for a league above the bridge. The shipmaster stood feet astride, solid as a rock, arguing with his master:

'The weather's breaking up, sire. Why ask me, if you won't take my advice?' His was the voice of the older man, confident in his calling, counselling as a father to his son. 'If you don't sail now, you could be storm-bound for weeks.'

'How long for the passage to the Somme?'

'Eighteen hours – depends upon the speed of the slowest ship. If we sail on the afternoon ebb tomorrow, Monday, with this wind we should make St-Valéry at eleven the next morning, the twelfth. Then there'll be only a crossing of sixty miles to England, instead of the ninety from here – a night's passage, that's all.'

William was grinning ruefully: 'I doubt whether my thousands of mercenaries will agree with you.'

'The shorter the passage the better,' Fulbert growled. 'Never know at sea.'

'When d'you want *Mora* to rendezvous with the fleet?'

'I'll join you during the late forenoon: I'll see the main body safely on its way. The fleet can start north across the bay and we'll meet it in *Mora,* off Cape de la Hève. Can you be ready, sire, to sail from Touques on the afternoon tide?'

'Four o'clock?'

'I'd prefer three. Twilight's closing in now. If the wind gets up, I'd like to pick up the fleet before dark.'

William nodded: 'Meet you on the quay.' As he strode towards his squires, he turned abruptly: 'And don't be late, Walter,' he grinned. 'There's no turning back now.'

She could hear them in the valley below the castle, threshing with their batons up in the granaries. She loved the beating rhythm, the sound which brought her the feeling of permanence for which she so longed. The thumping noise took her back to the golden cornfields of her Flanders youth: there was something eternal about the harvest, the gathering of the grain, the winnowing in the wind. And Matilda knew, as she curled against her husband, perhaps for the last time, that it was his fear of running out of food, of the collapse of the discipline he imposed on his army which worried him most.

It had been incredible how, through his unbending will, he had controlled that amorphous host encamped around the little port of Dives. For over six weeks most of them had been there, foreigners, mercenaries, buccaneers in the hope of plunder, yet there had been few incidents. Her William had carefully selected his team of barons to execute his orders. Like father, like son, they were saying in the taverns: Robert the Magnificent's inflexible discipline remained a memory among the older warriors.

Matilda loved Bonneville, loved its massive castle begun by Charlemagne. She had her William to herself here: this was their one home where they could be alone and were always happy, able to be natural. At Bonneville, William forbade court officialdom and procedure. Only their closest friends were invited; only in this smiling castle was William not surrounded by the hordes of hangers-on who followed him perpetually.

From their private chambers, in the upper storey of the manor house built inside its court, she could lie here across his chest, her arms clasped about him while he slept; the reflected light of dawn was washing golden the leaves of the oak woods on the rolling hills which led towards Dives and from which he had returned late last night with Fitz and the others.

Only she knew how close to desperation he had been driven during these weeks. And, stroking that dear, russet head between her hands, caressing his face which at an instant could take on its cruel mask – yet be so gentle – she tried to hold back the tears . . . Dear God, how she loved her duke. For so long she had dreaded this sailing day: in the deepest recesses of her being she feared that nothing but disaster could come from this complicated, insane expedition which was, even now, beginning to disintegrate.

For the past three weeks, William had been sleeping in his tent at the camp at Dives, to be among his knights and soldiers. It was only through his inflexible leadership, she was certain, by his example to the other barons, and particularly to Montgomery, that at last this momentous dawn of departure had arrived. For weeks he had been cajoling, wheedling them with promises of spoil across the sea, threatening the deserters with harsh, summary punishment, for after this long wait, soldiers were slipping away to their homes for the harvest. How he had prevented the hot-heads (and there were many in this mercenary army) from cracking skulls in the taverns had been beyond comprehension. No wind – there had been no wind for as long as she could remember, all through that blisteringly hot August.

It had been sultry, wretchedly, stewingly hot in the mosquito-ridden estuary. Victuals were running out, and yet he insisted on rationing rather than foraging on the peasants' farms. Of course, there had been accidents – the horses had seen to that – and many crushings with the heavy gear and the haste. By burying the dead secretly in the hills, he had tried to conceal the cost of waiting. And, when at last September came, the gales blew for days on end, churning the seas at the mouth of the Dives estuary into a foaming cauldron.

It was then that the desertions began to disturb him . . . it was not surprising that yesterday when the wind veered for those few hours that he and Walter decided to embark the host. He had spared no effort: in the church at Touques he had forced the priests to their knees, to pray for hours on end for a favourable wind . . . and as she heard the gusts whistling round the tower, she knew that at last the wind was blowing from the right quarter. Her man would be gone in a few hours. Afterwards, when she returned from the quay to the castle, she knew there could be no weakness – regents did not weep. She had even left Cecily at Rouen with the wet nurse so that she could give her duke every second of her time, her deepest, total love.

'You're awake,' he murmured. 'I knew you would be.'

He swivelled her like a child, watching her, trying to register her features in his mind. 'I want to remember you just like this,' he said. 'You've a difficult face to recall.'

'You're always saying that,' she said. 'Why can't I come to St-Valéry?' she wheedled softly. 'I'd be a comfort to you.'

'No, Mahault.'

That was all he said. She recognized the tone. From now on, his mind for every waking, every dreaming moment, would be concentrated on his objective. And now that he'd learned the details of the damage to Harold's fleet on its way round to the Thames, William was like a huntsman after the boar. That side of him she had never really understood – the ruthless soldier with only one object in view: the destruction of his enemy. But in his spirit he had already left her.

She slipped from him, lay still at his side, waiting – dear God, just one more time . . . Here, in this, their favourite haven where they had loved so often, conceived their children more than once – oh, God . . . She reached for him, but instead his chin scraped her face, his lips touching her cheek. Then he was out of bed and striding across the room towards the alcove. She watched him in silence, her huge, naked man, thickening already about the waist. He was thirty-eight, at the summit of his power and physical strength. He was as putty in her hands if she willed it, but now he needed her strength, required her unemotional dignity.

Nothing mattered more to him than that he could leave without anxiety the duchy in her hands. She sighed, contentment mixed with sadness. They'd come a long way together, found a tranquillity which was denied to many of their friends. She slipped from the bed, feeling the chill of the September dawn, as she wrapped her silk gown about her. Before ringing for her lady of the bed-chamber she'd snatch a moment at the window, whence she could just make out the masthead of *Mora*.

Matilda stretched on her toes for a better look at her ship. Her mast was distinguishable from the others by the cross of Saint Peter above the iron lantern, which Walter had fixed. The upper panel of the sail was richly decorated horizontally with golden orbs and diagonal green bars; vertically, the crimson canvas was divided centrally by a deep ochre panel. He'd chided her for her choice, but she'd told him the colours were to remind him of her. *Mora* was longer than the others, had a tall prow and her hull gleamed with its reds and blues and greens. William's coffers were running low. He was worrying about how to pay his army and she smiled ruefully: he knew he could take her last denier if he asked her – and she sensed him tip-toeing behind her. She caught her breath and remained rigid – and then his hands were encircling her. He nuzzled his stubbly chin into the nape of her neck:

'Mahault,' he whispered, 'my Mahault.'

She felt him stirring, even now. Pressing his hands against her, she leaned her head backwards across his chest, her eyes closed.

'My lord,' she whispered. 'Come back to me.'

He stood still. His arms were bands of steel, the muscles of his forearms knotting against her breasts as, looking down upon the quays of Touques, he said softly:

'If Harold should win, Mahault, you must rule yourself with the help of Beaumont.' He added without rancour, 'He's the only one I trust in the duchy who's stayed behind.'

She closed her eyes, trying to obliterate the nightmare of a future without her lord, a life of intrigue and strife to the end of her days – and without his rocklike steadfastness to sustain her. No, it could never be . . .

'Is it to be a fight to the death, then, my lord?' she whispered, crushing his hands to her bosom. 'You or Harold?'

He was kissing the crown of her black tresses where not a strand of grey yet showed:

'There is not space enough for both in the island,' he said quietly. 'But I shall come back to my Normandy and to you.' He spun her round to face him. Those vivid, sky-blue eyes were boring into her to the very depths.

'To fetch my queen. D'you not remember?'

The years rolled away, fifteen of them, to their wedding night when she thought he had been taunting her. She nodded and whispered:

'Queen of England.'

'And I your king.'

He kissed her roughly and swept from the chamber to dress for the day. She straightened her shoulders then pulled the bell-cord by the doorway. A busy morning lay before her, if she was not to forget the details of his last-moment demands. He had entrusted the pope's holy relics to her: she would fetch them now, hang the chain about his neck. When he sailed she would need all the strength of a duchess. She was becoming used to farewells, but this would be a fateful moment for them both on the quay.

17

DESPAIR: ST-VALÉRY-SUR-SOMME

The duke was losing his *sang-froid*. The Steward had never before seen him so tense, been so glad to have him to himself for a moment, though Fitz could have wished for a drier place: the ceaseless rain was continuing to beat across the battlements of Guy's castle. The proceedings during the afternoon had been a success, Fitz supposed, but he had wondered what had been going through the minds of those thousands of sodden soldiers as they plodded in the mud round the outskirts of St-Valéry. Led by the duke himself, mantled against the cutting north-easter which had rampaged across the bay for the past thirteen days, the whole army had marched behind the holy reliquary of St-Valéry's patron saint. The duke and his commanders entered the church of St Martin, while outside in the bitter wind the soldiers fell to their knees, the whole host humbly beseeching Almighty God to send the longed-for southerly wind. William and his war council then returned to the relative comfort of the castle and their requisitioned houses, but the troops were now grovelling into their sodden bivouacs along the banks of the Somme.

The duke was standing four-square to the gusts buffeting against the castle battlements, a wind which was sweeping across the wide estuary and whipping the shallows into a flurry of curling breakers. At the moment when the invasion fleet arrived on the twelfth of September, the wind veered round to the north and had blown from that quarter ever since: the length of this Picardy and Ponthieu coast was now a dangerous lee shore.

In silence, Fitz regarded his friend: the set of William's jaw was grim, his facial muscles taut in his cheeks. He was staring down upon the tower in which Guy of Ponthieu had imprisoned Harold. On the right, the spire of St Martin's scraped the base of the racing clouds; at its top was the jerking weather-cock to which William's eyes had been drawn throughout these miserably frustrating days. The point of

Hourdel curved like a fish-hook along the southern shore of the estuary; on the far side, the blue line of Crécy forest stretched to the east. And in the sea-lavender of the marshes along the river, the ships of the fleet lay scattered like water-beetles. The damaged craft were now all repaired after the battering they had suffered on the passage from Dives: the fleet was ready, waiting to sail the instant the wind veered.

'What did the sooth-sayer predict this morning, sire?'

'No change,' William snapped.

'But the priest,' Fitz reminded his friend. 'The clerk who came to see you – do you not take comfort in his prophecy?'

'He's not such a fool as the sooth-sayer. At least, he professes to be a man of God.' Then William asked softly, 'Fitz, is God really on our side? The troops are restless, as you know. Desertion spreads like an epidemic and my coffers aren't bottomless.'

'The clerk said you'd cross safely and land on the foreign shore without battle. "You'll be victorious", he said. Take comfort in that.'

The Steward knew he was wasting his breath. Though the duke controlled the seaboard from the Scheldt to Brest, the invasion was still a colossal gamble, if only because of the weather: this was the most dangerous fortnight in the year in which to cross those turbulent, tide-ripped waters. Against a contrary wind, no power on earth could sail those thousands of craft across those tantalizing sixty miles. The depressed and sodden troops were not idiots: in spite of the duke's daily tour of his army, encouraging, persuading, taunting, demonstrating his own confidence in this gigantic operation, those seething, grey waters struck fear into the bravest foot-soldier.

'You should have brought Matilda up here,' Fitz murmured. 'She'd have eased your burden.' He smiled ruefully, adding, 'My Adeliza's ill with worry: my going's bad enough, she reckons, without taking our two boys.'

'You've got Roger and William in separate ships?'

Fitz nodded. 'In the assault flotilla, with Montgomery.' Pulling his cloak around him Fitz asked:

'D'you trust the spy's reports, sire?'

William rubbed his upper lip where the red moustache was beginning to sprout – the beard he always grew during campaigns:

'Foulques' best agent: Hardraada must have sailed. This wretched northerly will have blown his three hundred warships straight across.'

The spy had reported that Hardraada had put out from Bergen on the fifteenth, then was joined off the Tyne by Tosti from Scotland. Six days later they sailed into the Humber, then rowed up the Yorkshire Ouse to Riccall where they left their ships. They sacked York but on quitting the city they were barred by Edwin and Morcar who hurled them back into the North Sea.

'One rival less, sire,' Fitz said.

'On the contrary,' William replied smoothly. 'Hardraada cut 'em into bits at Fulford Gate, four days ago.' The Northern earls had fled; Hardraada had regained his ships at Riccall and was ready to swoop on London by land and sea.

'And Harold Godwineson?' Fitz asked. 'How will he react?'

William grinned for the first time this day:

'Harold heard the news in London two days ago: Friday, the twenty-second. He's had a tricky decision to make. He knows I'm waiting for a wind.' The duke glanced at Fitz: 'He's a decisive character – a soldier who calculates the risk.'

Foulques had reported that Harold marched north from London that same night, with his *fyrd* and his housecarls. It was one hundred and ninety miles from London to York, so he could be meeting Hardraada that day or the next. The duke cried out suddenly, his words carried away in the wind: '*God*, give me a wind!' He beat the stone coping with both his fists. 'This is my one chance – *Give me a favourable wind!*'

For a rare moment, Fitz was penetrating his friend's self-imposed aloofness: the soul was exposed, raw, naked, with all its ambition, its greed – but the fanatical religious conviction of his crusade still burned through. The Bastard's two sides were complementary, one to the other: the means justified the end, if the end was to fight for God's cause. Fitz noticed that the precious necklace, as always, was strung beneath the open-necked jerkin; and the papal banner was safely in the fleet shipmaster's possession for hoisting at *Mora*'s masthead, if ever the fleet should put to sea. Both Walter Fulbert and *Mora*'s captain, Etienne Erard, had quarters in the castle: their health was vital, for the decision to sail lay solely in their judgement.

For the first time too, Fitz was realizing the appalling load which William was carrying, a burden he had supported entirely alone since that day last January when he'd learned of Edward's death. Bullying, wheedling; bribing, blackmailing; charming, inspiring, it had been solely his personality and dogged perseverance which had inspired and united his reluctant barons to this desperately chancy adventure. Even now, the final climax depended upon the vagaries of the weather. Even if this wind changed, argued the seafarers, was this not the one fortnight in the year when prudent seamen remained in port? This was the week when the highest tides combined with the first autumnal gales to lash those narrow seas into a white fury. Even if the northerly veered today, who could guarantee that the wind would moderate and remain southerly for the vital twelve hours of the crossing? In these unsettled conditions the gales could spring up again in mid-Channel, when the straggling fleet of small boats was at its most vulnerable . . . even if the wind stayed southerly, a terrible catastrophe could occur if it increased to gale force: the ships, many packed with stamping horses, maddened by terror, would be driven straight onto the lee shores of Sussex . . . the nightmare was too possible for those who knew the sea. 'Call it off', many were advising – and was the duke *certain* that Harold's fleet *was* sheltering in London river? There were too many adverse unknowns – the gigantic operation was a monstrous gamble to enhance the bastard duke's reputation; at stake were the lives of forty thousand men.

'The decision's mine,' William said wearily. 'Even you and Odo can't help me now.' He turned and grasped his friend's arm. As he led Fitz from the parapet, his eyes turned towards the dancing weathercock. Fitz shook his head.

'No, sire,' said the Steward, placing his hand on William's shoulder. 'The vane hasn't shifted. Courage, sire,' he added gently. 'We're all with you, those that matter, to the end.'

18

By Log and Lodestar

'Sound the trumpet!'

Standing aft in the sternsheets of *Mora*, Fleet Shipmaster Walter Fulbert de Chaussey breathed a long sigh of relief as the command for which he had waited so long rang from the lips of the commander-in-chief. Standing next to the grim-faced duke, Walter remained silent as Captain Etienne Erard took charge of his ship.

'Let go stern rope . . . bear off for'd. Ship bow oars. Give way port . . . Up together.'

The rope splashed into the water, was hauled in to the cheers of the townsfolk of St-Valéry – plaudits of relief as well as of well-wishing, because the army had been encamped long enough. The citizens could now clean up their town and resume normal living. It was three in the afternoon, just past high water and the ebb was beginning to run in the river. As *Mora's* bow swung into the stream, Erard shipped both banks of oars:

'. . . 'way together.'

The oars began dipping rhythmically. As *Mora* swung into the tideway, behind him Fulbert heard the trumpets, the horns, the answering cheers from the fleet echoing against the castle walls as the ships pushed out into the stream. Captain Erard lay back on his tiller to force the rudder sweep over to port. *Mora* was heading downstream towards Cape Hornu half a league ahead, the ebb swirling under her, the water brown and muddy from the interminable rain. The oars creaked, the water began chuckling at the stem and above them, from the truck of the bare mast, the pope's pendant began flapping when the wind caught the ship as she cleared the lee of the waterside.

'Steer for Le Hourdel, Captain,' the duke commanded. He was grinning while they watched Roger of Montgomery's ship trying to extricate herself from being pinned against the mark off the town quay.

Fleet Shipmaster Fulbert loosened the neck of his heavy jersey: the unaccustomed, stuffy warmth from the southerly breeze made warm clothing unnecessary, but it would be different outside.

Walter Fulbert had been woken by the duke's personal servant at five-thirty this morning. Half-dressed, he had stumbled to the parapet where the duke was leaning across the coping, his eyes fixed on St Martin's weather-cock, an inane smile on his face. The sooth-sayer was summoned, and after Walter and Etienne Erard had sniffed the air and walked around the battlements, together they made the momentous decision. Seconds later, the trumpets were clarioning from the castle keep; then the signal was taken up, horn after horn echoing through the town until the scurrying figures along the quays and in the ships convinced the watching duke and his gathering nobles that the embarkation was under way.

It had been a hectic, frenzied day, Wednesday 27 September. Sensible men kept clear of their masters, and particularly of the duke. He was everywhere, his massive, lithe figure popping up along the quays, in the ships, haranguing, whipping the dilatory into action; watching the loading of the cavalry, the last-moment stores, the fresh water. It had been hellish for those in command, for he was determined to catch the ebb; all the ships could never have cleared the harbour against the flood before dark. And for those hours Walter had kept an eye on that cursed weather-cock, spinning from the top of St Martin's spire.

Mora swirled downstream. Harold's tower disappeared behind Cape Hornu: the oarsmen were keeping good time, pulling easily, the ebb working for them as Captain Erard steered the ship close to the marshes, before altering to the northward again for the dunes and the hook of Le Hourdel. By four o'clock the cape was abeam to port; the tops of the withy marks were shivering in the estuary channel as one after the other they swished past the gleaming strakes of the duke's great ship.

Just after five, the true wind hit them, the moment for which Walter had been apprehensively waiting. He stood up, facing aft, his glance momentarily meeting Erard's: steady, not gusting; a firm breeze from the south-south-west which should bowl them along at two leagues to the hour. Astern, the leaders were swilling out into the estuary and soon the cluster of ships would be spreading across the southern horizon; the success of this crossing lay in communications, in keeping the fleet together. The town was becoming a distant jumble of roofs and towers, a mauve blur fading below the horizon.

'*Oars* . . .'

Captain Erard was taking the way off her, the seamen laying on their oars.

'We'll be reaching the edge of the shallows in five minutes, sire,' he said, facing the duke. 'I suggest we wait here, before we feel the swell.'

They unshipped their oars and secured them for the passage. Erard's officers checked the halyards, reported that the great sail was ready for hoisting. *Mora* lay rolling beam to wind in the confused waters, where the ebb from the Somme mingled with the floodstream sweeping north-eastwards up-Channel. As they watched the orange orb sinking below Pointe d'Ailly, the boisterous conversation died away. To the east, night was settling as the tideway carried them up-Channel. The larger ships were forming up now, their pendants distinguishable in the gathering twilight: the duke had insisted that his divisional commanders should be in separate ships, in case of disaster to any one of them. Roger of Montgomery, who had the Franco-Flemish battalions, was wallowing off the port quarter; Alan of Brittany, to starboard, commanded the larger division of Bretons. In *Mora* were the duke's two half-brothers, Bishop Odo and Count Robert of Mortain, who would share the largest division, the Normans, with the commander-in-chief, Duke William. The inevitable rivalries which had developed during these weeks were thus contained. Fulbert could see in the failing light that the amorphous fleet, which spread for two leagues across the darkening horizon, was now assembled, each to his own divisional commander.

The fleet shipmaster had planned to the last detail: he was determined not to set off too early, in case the wind freshened again to drive them too fast across to the enemy coast. What situation could be worse than making a landfall on a lee shore in darkness? To heave-to by furling sails and lowering masts in mid-Channel would be hazardous in the extreme, loaded to the gunwales as were the transports. But Walter Fulbert kept these fears to himself when, at six o'clock, he sighted the torches flaring from the rear whippers-up: the fleet was assembled, lying-to astern of their leader, *Mora*.

'Sire,' he reported, touching his forehead. 'The fleet's ready.'

'Make sail.'

No haste, no questioning. William knew that he could not return now against the wind. Did he share this apprehension churning in Walter's stomach? The wind had backed a point, was now from due south. Care would be needed to prevent broaching-to if it freshened.

The great enterprise was committed.

'Light the lantern, Captain,' Fulbert ordered Erard. 'Stand-by to set sail.'

As the seaman climbed up the mast, another handed him the flaming torch. Seconds later, the iron door of the lantern clanged shut, the flame flickering from behind its glass. The aureate glow shone upon the papal banner flapping lazily downwind, gilded the lower edges of the cross at the truck above the lantern.

'Ready to hoist, sire,' Erard reported.

The duke met Walter's eye, then nodded:

'Set sail, Captain,' Fulbert ordered. 'Boy, sound the horn.'

The youngster shinned up the stern figure-head, put the horn to his lips as the halyards began to squeal in the dead eye at the hounds. Traversing his head slowly across the horizon behind him, the boy blew upon his horn, time and time again. The call was taken up from ship to ship and as the call blared across the water, the ocean around *Mora* was fluttering suddenly with the dark outlines of sail: hundreds of them billowing, swooping, many sails out of control, others already being sheeted home.

'Secure for the night,' Captain Erard ordered his crew. 'Set night watches.'

The seamen were in charge now, the noble barons silent, watching the work. The huge sail was settling down, the rolling easing as the captain took control of the sheets. The stays were set up and adjusted for the course which the fleet shipmaster had ordered his captains before leaving harbour: If visibility permitted, set the polestar five fistful of knuckles off the starboard bow; if the cloud covered the stars, captains must set their courses by lodestone, having checked on *Mora* before nightfall. Fulbert would keep this sea broad on *Mora's* port quarter, providing there was no wind-shift: the expected landfall was to be the coast between the unmistakable cliff of what the English called Beachy Head and the low-lying spit of Dungeness. Captain Erard had sailed this coast before, during King Edward's reign when relations were friendlier.

The war council had demanded two overall priorities: a suitable beach on which to land cavalry; and a landing-place close to a good road to London. Etienne Erard knew that the beaches were of fine shingle the length of this thirty miles of coast, a foreshore backed by interspersed, low-lying marshland. The main concern was the cavalry, those horses crowding the giant transports wallowing astern on either quarter. *Mora* was already drawing away from the slower ships; her extra length and fine lines, though pleasing to a seaman's eye, were giving her excessive speed in this fresh breeze. The divisional leaders were maintaining position on the quarters; but in the gathering darkness the smaller vessels were losing bearing already, rolling out their guts in the quartering sea.

'Ease the sheets,' Walter commanded. 'We're driving too fast.'

The seaman checked the port sheet; the yard creaked, the sail ballooned over to starboard, starting a roll. The barons chuckled at Fulbert's feet, but already he could see the pallor of nausea showing on the Steward's sweating brow. What would the troop transports soon be like, packed with landsmen from the continent of Europe?

The apprehension which Walter Fulbert habitually felt on clearing port was evaporating, as he ran his seaman's eye over this splendid ship: the mast was well set-up, bearing an even strain, even when the sail ballooned. The log had been streamed and recovered, its half-moon, weighted wood giving just over two leagues an hour, as Fulbert had estimated. It was already half-past eight and soon they would be approaching the banks.

The night sky was largely covered with scudding cloud, the five-day-old moon already astern of them and giving no light. Between the gaps, the polestar glimmered fitfully as it raced in and out between the clouds – enough to steer by, but even the burly duke, who had insisted on taking the tiller, was having to work hard to hold the course. The ship was carrying considerable weather helm, the sail driving *Mora* up to port as she lurched towards a broach. It was heady stuff, the sea breaking in the darkness, boiling astern in the phosphorescent wake as the ship sped north-westwards. Bishop Odo, for once, had little to say and the other knights were silently enfolding their cloaks about them, trying to find a corner in which to wedge themselves for fitful sleep.

'Sire,' Fulbert urged gently, 'let the seamen steer now. They'll share the watches of the night. You must be fresh for whatever comes.'

'Another hour, Walter. Then I'll obey you,' the deep voice boomed above the music of the sea: the hissing along the sides, the creaking yard, the exploding of the canvas as the wind caught it on the crests of the waves; sliding down the far side of the swell, dipping into the troughs, the wind spilling, the sail flopping uselessly, then filling again as *Mora* swooped upwards. Even the divisional leaders were losing bearing on her quarters, but the lantern remained alight, its yellow beacon reflecting against the streaky bowls of the troughs. A gull, startled by the light, squawked as it took off, wheeling against the yard, weirdly beautiful in the desolate waste. The motion was changing, the seas steeper.

'The Bassure de Baas,' Erard reported. 'Six fathoms only. See, even at night you can see the colour change in the water, sire.'

So it was nine o'clock already – time for Walter to get his head down too. He had to be alert at dawn. Etienne and he were dividing the watches for the passage; both would be up for the landfall. The longer they could persuade their duke to sleep, the better for all concerned. He remained coolly remote but buoyant, now that the adventure was under way: it was the discipline he had instilled in his commanders which allowed him soon to sleep, curled snugly in his thick field-cloak. The ship remained dry, mercifully, the shields interlocking inboard of the wash-strake, keeping out the worst of the spray. William's eyes were closed, his face serene, the ends of his moustache fluttering above his lip, the russet hairs of his bare head wisping in the following breeze. The chatter in the ship had hushed, the eyes of most men on their leader, the man whose indomitable will had brought them to this incredible adventure. And, his memory flicking back in time some twenty-five years, Walter Fulbert saw, not this stern-faced, rugged leader of men, but a silent boy, terrified while hunters ferreted after him through the bracken with their long daggers . . . and, pulling his mantle about him, the fleet shipmaster fell into the half-sleep of the sailor . . .

'Master Fulbert,' a voice he recognized as Etienne's murmured in his ear. ''Tis midnight.'

Walter was immediately alert. It was very dark. A line of breakers curled ahead. The ship was bowling along, the motion more uncomfortable. She was plunging now, the seas steeper.

'Bassurelle?'

'On the south-western tip,' Erard said quietly. 'A league ahead of our reckoning, sir.'

'I've got her,' Walter said. 'The duke's sleeping?'

'They all are,' Erard said. 'Most have been sick.'

Walter needed no telling: the stench was wafting from the bilges. It was imperative that these barons, upon whom the future battles would depend, landed in good order. The darkness was tangible, the cloud lower, blacking out the stars. The lantern flickered, casting its glow eerily upon the base of the scudding cloud. The helmsman was a burly seaman, but he was leaning his whole weight against the sweep to prevent her from broaching.

'Where are the others?' Fulbert asked.

'Lost them an hour ago. I didn't shake you, for I can't reduce sail any further.'

'Maybe they'll catch up,' Walter said. 'We must stick to our course.'

Erard nodded and turned, taking Walter's vacant corner on the port quarter whence he could keep an eye on things when he was not sleeping. And then Fulbert was busy, as *Mora* plunged through the short seas of the Bassurelle. It was an uncomfortable hour, barons puking where they lay, rank forgotten, all men equal in their misery. Walter remained silent, alone with his thoughts as the ship swooped onwards. The waves were bigger, their crests beginning to foam around the ship. She was sheering continually up to windward, so must make their landfall to the westward, if the tidal stream cancelled itself out. Then they were out of the confused sea, the motion easing; the passengers stirred, trying to find sleep as they longed for the day. The sole, apparently unaffected member was the duke, who was snoring loudly, warm in his leather deerskin jerkin, woollen jersey and wrapped about with his battle-cloak. At three o'clock the wind fell away . . .

The ship wallowed, almost stopped; the great sail was re-hoisted and flapped uselessly, a situation even more trying to the landsmen than the earlier corkscrewing. The effect was immediate, most of the knights drooping across the gunwales, so that Walter had to even them out equally on each side to avoid dangerous listing. Erard was standing beside him now, confirming Fulbert's thoughts:

'We've crossed the twenty-fathom line, I'm sure, sir – more likely ten fathoms. I'm sure we're well ahead of reckoning.'

'By the mark eight!'

The leadsman's call awoke the duke. His heavy face was close to Walter, his breath stale, as he peered into the darkness:

'Where are we?'

'Nearing land, sire. Water's shallowing.'

'What time's first light?'

'Half-five, sire. Sunrise is at six.'

William was alert, peering into the darkness.

'Seen anyone since you last woke me?'

'No one, sire. It's been a dark night.'

Just before five o'clock, Walter sensed that his instinctive warning system was alerting him. 'Something's ahead, Erard.' He spoke softly, peered long over the port bow. A massive, darker shadow loomed there, he was certain. 'See anything?'

'*By the mark twelve*,' called the leadsman.

Deeper water again. Erard checked the sheets fully; the sail flapped in the light airs. First light was streaking to the eastward as all eyes stared into the darkness of the northern horizon.

'Send a man aloft, Etienne.'

The same seaman clambered to the masthead. By the time he had installed himself, the loom to the northward took on a shape, a massive, chalky-grey cliff towering above them. From so close, Beachy Head was an awe-inspiring sight, towering down on them from the sky above, the breakers curling white at the base of the gigantic cliff. There was no headland along the coast of Normandy or Brittany to compare in grandeur with this . . .

'That's Beachy, sire,' Fulbert reported. 'Three miles, I'd say.'

Daylight began stealing in, the horizon retreating. Walter estimated that visibility was five miles to the east; Beachy Head three, to the north; two miles westward, and to the southward? Four, five miles?

'Can you see anyone, sailor?' the duke bellowed. 'Where's my fleet?'

The barons were on their feet and staring aft. The masthead look-out was taking his time. With a voice in which fear and disbelief mingled he yelled from aloft:

'Nothing in sight, *capitaine*. Nothing – nowhere . . .'

The silence was broken by murmurings amongst the crew and the shocked knights: here was *Mora*, alone and cut off from the fleet. An observer ashore had only to report the strange ship and, if any of Harold's navy *were* in the offing, the commander-in-chief of the invasion fleet and all his staff would be at the bottom of the sea in minutes. Walter sensed the panic catching hold.

'What depth have you, Master Fulbert?' the duke asked.

'Nine fathoms, sire.'

'Anchor then. Brail up the sail and we'll have breakfast.' William grinned at them all. 'Buck up,' he bawled at Erard. 'Get your cook jumping! I'm hungry – and wine!'

The instant's bewilderment evaporated. Broaching the stores and wine swiftly restored confidence – and then the nobility were crouching on their haunches around their makeshift table of shields. Fulbert watched them slicing the hunks of cold roast pig, tearing at the damp bread, swilling down the dark fortifying wine of Burgundy. And as

Walter munched, feeling his strength returning, once again he was amazed by William's rugged leadership: his reaction to potential catastrophe was to call for a meal in mid-ocean . . .

'Sail to the southward, *mon capitaine!*' the look-out hailed from the masthead. '. . . *and four masts!*'

The ship's company had leaped to its feet, rolling the ship to its beam-ends.

'A forest of masts, *capitaine!*'

The look-out was pointing to the southward, his bearded face split wide with its grin. And minutes later the first sail, then another and another hove above the horizon.

'Weigh!' the duke commanded. 'Lower the sail. We'll pull out to meet 'em, then move up the coast for a suitable beach.'

The laughter of relief; the shouts of anticipation while the squires prepared their knights' chain-mail; the unlashing and shipping of the oars: all was bustle again, boredom and despair turning into excitement, as was the pattern of war.

'Weigh,' the fleet shipmaster commanded. 'Bring her round to starboard, Captain.'

The haze of a misty dawn was floating mazily from the eastern shoreline when *Mora* turned seawards, to the shanty of the oarsmen, double-banked now and irrespective of rank. Within a quarter of an hour the first ships came sweeping towards them, bones in their teeth, oars flashing, sails tumbling. The hails of identification, the ribaldry sang across the water between the sailors. The fleet had crossed and was together – and *there* were the notorious cliffs of England . . .

Walter caught the duke's glance, shared his glint of anxiety. Standing aft by the sweep, Fulbert felt naked as the coast slid past: *Mora* and the van of the fleet were horribly vulnerable should the enemy be lurking behind those beaches over which the early morning mists were curling. 'Bring her round!' the duke commanded. 'Steer east and close the land, Master Fulbert.'

Mora swung to port, the oars splashing rhythmically, the sailors singing in time. It was still dawn, miraculously calm; the swell undulated beneath them and while the ship headed towards the beaches, the silver mists began to burn away as the sun climbed above the blue outline of woods inland. By seven-thirty, the low-lying beach emerged from the last evaporating wisps two miles from their port bow – the strand of golden shingle fell steeply into the sea curling lazily the length of the open bay which stretched into the distance.

Walter Fulbert kept a mile off-shore, sounding continually, look-outs aloft and in the eyes of the ship, as they watched the waves breaking on the rocks close off-shore. The first rays of the sun were slanting upon the translucent grey-green surface of the sea: yellow shingle and pebbles were now clearly visible on the bottom.

'We're ready, William,' Bishop Odo growled, clenching his massive stave.

'Anchor ready for letting go, sir,' Captain Erard reported. 'Depth three fathoms.'

They were waving in the ship ahead and pointing to port. *Mora*'s masthead look-out yelled:

'There's a break in the shore-line, *capitaine* – fine on the port bow.' The man's voice quavered: 'There's a town inshore: a castle tower and fishermen's huts. A lagoon's opening out inside – looks like marshes.'

'That's Pevensey, sire,' Erard said quietly. 'A busy port.'

'*Par la splendeur de Dieu!*' the duke shouted, grinning at Fulbert. 'You've found my first choice! Anchor off the entrance. Time of high water?'

'Just after ten, sire: in an hour and a half.'

William was nodding, as excited as a schoolboy at the way things were going. Steward fitz Osbern was on his feet, the colour returning to his lined, good-natured face:

'There's not a murmur from ashore, sire,' fitz Osbern said. 'No-one in sight – seems too quiet.'

The silence was unnerving: only the inquisitive gulls and the lapping of the waves on the shingle disturbed the peace of the morning.

'Send in the reconnaissance ships, Master Fulbert,' the duke commanded. The cleft in the beach was opening up and through the gap the low-lying marshes were coming into view.

'*Oars* – ' the captain ordered. The main flood stream was under the ship, and as the seamen laid on their oars she drifted towards the opening in the coast. The ships astern were overhauling rapidly and Roger of Montgomery slid by, saluting and waving, acknowledging the duke's orders to proceed inside the lagoon with his supporting ships and to report back: Roger was to disembark and hold a beach-head inside the lagoon, as they had exercised so often during these weeks. His pendant fluttering proudly at his masthead, the long ship slid by, the hanging shields at her prow now taken inboard, as the oarsmen silently laid back on their looms. Another ship, then another passed the drifting *Mora* until, a quarter of a mile from the entrance, Captain

Erard let go the stockless anchor.

The great ship swung to the flood and pointed west as she came to her cable. Duke William moved forward to where he stood in the eyes of the ship for all his fleet to see him. And as ship after ship swept past, lowering their masts and preparing their ramps, the cheers rang across the sea. There was a popple off the entrance and, as the flood swilled through into the lagoon, there was breeze enough to produce a flurry of white horses.

'Thank God,' whispered Walter Fulbert to his master. 'A miracle, sire. Better get the transports inside or beached, before the wind and weather turn nasty.' He pointed where the horizon was bespeckled with coloured sails.

'I don't like this silence, Walter,' the duke answered quietly. 'The English must have been watching us since dawn. Once my assault troops are safe on their beaches, then I'll disembark.'

'But Harold's up north with his *fyrd*, sire,' Walter said, 'dealing with Hardraada and Tosti after the battle at Fulford Gate. He's unlikely to have mobilized the *fyrd* in the south and west.'

William laid his hand upon the shoulders of his stalwart friend:

'Can you tell me, Walter,' he asked softly, 'which Harold I'll have to fight? The Norwegian or the Saxon?'

19

❦

MICHAELMAS EVE: 28 SEPTEMBER 1066

The sense of relief felt by Steward fitz Osbern in *Mora* was difficult to conceal. Roger of Montgomery had sent a messenger back to the beach to yell his message from ship to ship: local resistance had been quelled, the town of Pevensey and its fort were under Montgomery's control.

At 10.20, with the wind increasing and hundreds of ships beginning to drag their anchors, the duke made his decision:

'We'll lead the fleet inside the entrance, Master Fulbert. Tell the van to follow me in, the remainder to beach on either side of the entrance.'

'And the cavalry transports, sire?' Fleet Shipmaster Fulbert asked. 'The first should be arriving within two hours.'

'Anchor off shore, if they can,' the duke ordered. 'Lie off and wait for further orders. I must see for myself.' He nodded at Captain Erard: 'Take me in before the ebb starts running.'

The stockless anchor came home, the oarsmen gave way and ten minutes later *Mora* was sliding through the entrance which opened into the haven of Pevensey. They lowered the sail and unshipped the mast, the leadsman sounding up the channel winding towards the town, a league on their port hand.

It was now high water: an expanse of sea opened inside the entrance, a wide lagoon three leagues across from west to east. At high tide this inland sea, half-moon shaped, was studded with islets. Sheep and cattle were grazing on the green pasture of these isolated islands which stretched towards the line of blue, wooded hills to the north. Peering eastwards, Fitz could see the ridge behind which must lie the port of Hastings, the harbour upon which William had set great store. And as Fitz glanced round the expanse of water, his eyes lit upon the long peninsula poking from the western rim of this basin into the inland sea. In the crook where this long spit joined dry land, the stone walls of the Roman fortified tower of Anderita showed above the roofs of houses.

William was watching silently in the stern, as *Mora* pulled onwards,

222

the only sound being the rhythmical splashing of the sweeps. Then Fitz saw the haven opening up behind the long arm of the peninsula: the turfed roofs of a fishing colony close above the tide-line; the mud and timber cottages of a hamlet and the rare house with its tiled roof; and then two wharves appeared, emerging from the rushes, at the edge of the town. Roger's ships were moored there, in trots, sentries at their sterns.

When *Mora* was a hundred paces from the jetty, William had told Erard to stand off. She had been anchored here close to the wharf since high water, while Fulbert directed the ships to their berths. Fitz Osbern had waited by his duke's side while order was slowly restored from chaos. By two o'clock, the contours of the harbour began to emerge as the ebb sluiced out through the entrance. The islets were joined by stone causeways which wove between the mud and these muddy rivulets streaming into the main channel. Before the water went, *Mora* hauled over to the wharf and moored alongside the berth which had been vacated for her. By three o'clock, the area inside the entrance was littered with grounded ships, like water-dragons in their bright colours.

The eastern arm of the entrance shelved steeply below half-water line, a feature which Fulbert had immediately exploited: over forty cavalry transports had managed to force their blunt bows onto this natural landing-place. They were unloading the horses more easily than hoped: half, at least, were able to clamber over the gunwales, which left the ramps for the remainder. By three o'clock, Montfort had two hundred destriers ashore on that eastern spit. When the flood began again, their knights would be ferried over with their armour and harness to mount them. Some of the squires were already ashore there; but William refused to take the symbolic step onto the soil of England until he was certain that his eastern flank was secure.

'Thanks be to God,' Fitz murmured. 'But do we land the main bulk of cavalry on the eastern or the western side?'

'You must decide swiftly, sire,' Fulbert said. 'The wind's getting up: the transports outside are on a lee shore.'

'It's easier to get 'em ashore on the western beach at high water, on the wharves here and along the town slipways. But if we decide on Hastings, can we get the cavalry around the northern edge of these marshes?'

'Better see for yourself,' Odo growled. 'It's time you stood on English soil.'

'You're right, brother,' the duke agreed. He turned to Fitz: 'Accompany me, Steward. Grab two dozen soldiers and we'll reconnoitre for ourselves.' He strapped up his chain-mail, reached for his sword and climbed on to the gunwale. For a long moment, he balanced there, gazing round the horizon at the land he must conquer or perish in the attempt. With the cheers of his soldiers ringing in his ears, he was about to leap from the ship when he lost his balance, slipped and fell prostrate into the strands of seaweed, sand and mud. As Fitz jumped down to help the duke to his feet, the cheers turned to gasps of dismay: was this a presage of disaster, an omen of doom . . .? But, roaring with laughter, William boomed with delight as he crunched the sandy dirt in his mailed fists:

'*Par la splendeur de Dieu!* Look well on this soil I've seized in my hands. Look well, all of you . . .' and he squeezed the sand between his fingers, to watch it trickling to the ground. 'No man will ever wrest it from us again!' And as he strode up the beach, his shield on his left, his sword in his right hand, William spoke to the crowd of soldiers gathering around him:

'Because you're a superstitious lot, let's ask the sooth-sayer his opinion . . .' He searched among the sea of faces. 'Where's the divine?'

A voice called out from the press:

'He fell overboard and drowned on the way across, sire.'

The duke shrugged his shoulders:

'He's no great loss,' he said, tapping the crown of his helmet, centralizing the nose-guard, 'if he couldn't forecast his own death.' William was in exuberant form, though he'd just learned that one ship had not arrived. He strode towards the castle, talking and questioning as he went. The townsfolk were cowering behind their doors, the Normans beating them back with the flats of their swords, the butts of their lances.

A young knight ran forwards, a fistful of turf held out to his duke:

'Here, sire, take this, your England!' As William accepted the symbolic gesture, a cheer rang out from the pressing crowd of soldiers.

The reconnaissance through the boggy marsh was the toughest challenge which Fitz had experienced for years. William had set a punishing pace and, for the first time in his forty-six years, Fitz could not keep up.

Turning back from the impossible track, William laughingly laid Fitz's chain-mail across his own shoulders and led the sortie back to

Pevensey and *Mora*. Wadard, the quartermaster general, had rigged the kitchens, having sent foragers into the countryside. Sufficient oxen, sheep and pigs were rounded up from the fields to provide the first meal on foreign soil.

The duke summoned his council to eat with him and they had broken another tun of wine to celebrate. Roger was there; Montfort had been carried across from the eastern spit; Odo and Robert of Mortain sat in the centre with Fitz and the others from the assault division. The aroma of roasting meat wafted on the breeze as for the first time since the crossing the sound of ribaldry and laughter was heard rippling amongst the troops. *Mora* lay under the lee of the castle walls and a dangerous feeling of false security was abroad.

'Are you still considering marching on Winchester, brother?' Bishop Odo asked, wiping the grease from his stubble with the back of his hand. 'You haven't forgotten our prime objective?'

William shook his russet head, snatched another hunk of mutton, sliced it with his dagger. Between tearing at the meat with his teeth and pausing for breath, he grunted:

'We've got to win a decisive, total victory whichever Harold we meet – we're all agreed on that. We've got to heed Foulques' opinion of the English: they accept strong leadership. The people will submit, if there's no doubt who's king.'

The grunts from the sternsheets of *Mora* were of unanimous approval, Fitz knew. Opinion was only divided on how best to achieve a decisive victory; the invasion force had only a precarious toe-hold on the south coast, with the bulk of the fleet still drawn up on the shingle on each side of the Pevensey entrance.

'Taking Winchester would give us the West,' Robert of Mortain told his brother. 'We could go on from there.'

'But not the quick, decisive victory, Robert,' Odo growled. 'How often . . .'

Fitz interrupted firmly, sensing the habitual discord between the blood-brothers:

''Twere best to wait for news from Foulques on the issue in the North. Godwineson and Hardraada will react in their own way, to an enticement to battle.' Fitz held out his wooden goblet for more wine: he could feel the stuff coursing through his veins, his strength returning. 'What say you, Roger?'

The dark, beetle-browed Montgomery spread his arms, leaned back against the gunwale:

'We're precariously placed, can be hurled back into our ships if the enemy, whoever he is, falls upon us now. We must stick to our original plan. Mortain is wrong: forget Winchester. London is our goal as the duke and the bishop suggest. Take the port of Hastings. Make it our base so that our fleet is safe.' Leaning across, he supported his shield upon his own and Fitz's knees.

Foulques' battered map was spread upon the makeshift table.

'Here,' Roger persisted. 'Inside Hastings' harbour, in the crook of the peninsula our fleet can lie safely. There's water, too, at all states of the tide, so should the worst happen, we can still evacuate by sea.' His finger traced a line to the north of Hastings: 'These hills and the Weald will protect us and give us warning of any enemy advance.'

'I'm convinced our strategy's right,' William interrupted. 'We've got to defeat the enemy before we march on London. If our foe is Godwineson, I'm sure we can lure him down here.'

'I won't forget the quicksands of Couesnon, sire,' Montfort said. 'He's a brave man.'

The duke nodded. 'These are his lands. He knows the country well, having set up his coastal defences during these months. He won't like seeing his estates in Sussex and Kent ravaged, his farms burned.' William was poring over the parchment. 'He'll come running to save his lands, to protect his people.'

'You'll pillage this bit of England?' Odo asked. 'That'll lure Harold down here, but not Hardraada.'

'We'll soon know,' Roger said impatiently. 'We must secure a base at Hastings, as swiftly as we can.' Montgomery slapped his thigh. 'What say you, sire?'

William, studying the roads and trackways leading from the port of Hastings, did not answer Montgomery directly. Instead, he glanced at his half-brother: 'What do you say, Odo? Do we take the London road through Maidstone and on to Rochester, where we'll pick up Watling Street into the capital?' His finger was tracing the route west to Caldbec Hill, on to Sedlescombe where the river was still tidal but could be forded; north to the bridge at Bodiam which crossed the Rother. 'Or march up the ancient trackway which starts on the coast at Fairlight?' His finger moved up to Ore, then to Baldeslow and on to Caldbec Hill – but then traced north-west to Netherfield, up to the Uckfield–Rye Ridgeway and on to Maresfield, where the track joined the Lewes–London Road.

'We're blocked by the marshes, bounded by the Brede river to the east, by the Pevensey levels to the west,' Odo replied. 'There's only one common road northwards from Hastings for either of the London roads: through Baldeslow, Telham Hill to Caldbec Hill: for either of the London roads, we're forced to pass through Caldbec Hill.'

Robert of Beaumont grunted, as impatient as his old father was prudent and serene:

'Because we can't skirt round to the north of this *sacré* marsh, sire, the only way to join our cavalry on the eastern spit is to do so by boat, as soon as the tide floods again . . .'

'Another two hours,' Fitz murmured, watching the stream beginning again to trickle up the muddy channels. 'It'll be dark for the horses.'

'We've talked enough,' William announced. 'Tomorrow I move against Hastings. You, Roger, with your two hundred cavalry, are to be off the town by dawn. Sail the ships at first light: they can pull under oars and lie off Hastings harbour until Montgomery signals the harbour is safe in his hands. Any of the horses which haven't disembarked by tonight can be put ashore at Hastings.' The duke turned to Montfort: 'You, Hugh, as soon as you've fortified this castle,' and he nodded towards the crumbling walls of the Roman castle of Anderita behind them, 'leave a garrison, then lead your battalion along the track inside the shingle beach to Hastings.' The duke rose to his feet, glanced at the tidal stream flooding again under *Mora*'s keel. 'Fold up the map,' he rapped. 'We've work to do.'

Fitz watched his companions striding back to their ships. Twilight stole across the marshes, the light faded, darkness fell; and as the invasion host tried to find sleep during its first night in England, a horseman galloped in from the Pevensey levels: the messenger came from a wealthy Norman, Robert of Wimarc, who for years had been established in England and who, as a token of welcome and loyalty, was dispatching a willing and noble lady for the duke's pleasure. From this emissary, William learned the news for which they had all been waiting.

Harold Hardraada and Tosti were dead, slain by Harold at the battle of Stamford Bridge on Wednesday 25 September. King Harold was recuperating and re-forming his exhausted *fyrd* at York. He would be marching south again, the instant he was ready, to defend the Channel coast against the expected Norman invader.

'So it's Harold Godwineson,' Odo growled, making the sign of the cross as he pulled his cloak about him. The bottom boards of *Mora* were dank, greasy and hard for a bishop's bed. 'God be praised.'

Fitz raised his eyebrows: 'It's Friday tomorrow, Odo, the twenty-ninth,' he murmured. 'Harold can't learn of our landing for at least two days.'

From the shadows in the sternsheets, Duke William spoke softly:

'The prophetic priest at St-Valéry was right, my lords. I'm content that Harold Godwineson is my adversary.' His yawn interrupted his final comment, before silence fell upon the exhausted knights:

'I understand Harold. He'll be hastening to do battle with me – down here on the coast – before I've finished with him.'

Fitz pulled his cloak to his chin, stared up at the fitful stars. There were moments when he detested this facet of his friend's character: from the tone of William's words, the next few days promised to display that cruelty which in the past had brought the duke such success. Alençon was a nightmare from which the Steward would suffer for the remainder of his days.

❧✖❧

20

SANGUELAC: 14 OCTOBER 1066

Steward fitz Osbern enjoyed these suppers in the duke's field tent –
which was more than he could say for the lavish affairs, such as the
thanksgiving feast, which William had laid on after the Pevensey
landing. William, who rarely drank more than three goblets of wine,
did not tolerate drunkenness: those huge feasts often ended in some
disgraceful scene, embarrassing to all and provoking the duke to his
customary rage. But tonight, Thursday 12 October 1066, was a sober,
quiet affair with William enjoying the company of his most trusted
commanders while they finalized their plans.

The duke sat between his two half-brothers: the decisive, beefy
bishop Odo on his right, at thirty-six two years younger than William;
the prudent, younger Robert, count of Mortain, on his left. Opposite
the duke sat Roger of Montgomery and Eustace, brother-in-law of the
dead Confessor, the oldest among them and count of Boulogne.
Because of Eustace's English connection and his understanding of the
unique Anglo-Saxon mind, the duke had appointed him chief aide.
Eustace, who had never forgotten his humiliation at the hands of the
citizens of Dover, did not get on well with the last member, Alan
Fergant, count of Brittany, the forceful and opinionated commander of
the Breton division. Alan sat opposite Odo, with Steward Osbern on his
left at the end of the table.

The meal was coming to an end and Fitz was beginning to crave
sleep. Though he was as competent as ever on the battlefield, he could
not share the zest for the coming fight which his companions displayed.
Forty-six now, Fitz felt he could best serve by governing rather than
soldiering, an opinion not shared by the duke who had asked him to
double with Eustace as his chief aide in the coming battle. As the
conversation murmured back and forth over the dark Cahors wine, Fitz
participated little, his mind recalling the events of this past, hectic
fortnight.

It was fourteen days since the duke had moved on the day after the
Pevensey landing, to take Hastings. Once his prefabricated timber forts

were erected, the invasion force was secure in its base: but though the Norman ships were safe inside Hastings harbour, the English fleet was reported to have sailed from the Thames. It was passing through the Downs, intent on attacking the Norman ships should they try to evacuate the invasion army encamped in the rain-sodden fields to the west of the castle. And though the rain had lashed down for the past fortnight, the duke had used these vital days to his advantage. He defeated boredom by exercising his troops; he pillaged the Sussex folk and burnt their villages in his deliberate attempt to lure Harold Godwineson southwards, thereby shortening the Norman lines of communication; he thoroughly reconnoitred the countryside northwards to the Wealden forests; he topped up his ammunition stocks of arrows; he acclimatized and restored the fettle of the destriers which had suffered during the sea-crossing. It had been a rushed fortnight, but a vital respite in which the duke sifted the reports flooding into his headquarters from the local communities.

Fitz had been surprised by the co-operation from the Anglo-Normans who generally seemed opposed to Harold. One such, a Sussex farmer, had vehemently insisted that Duke William must not give battle to the English king: was not King Harold invincible, having just decimated the ferocious Norwegians at Stamford Bridge?

During the evening of 1 October Harold was banqueting at York to celebrate his victory when a horseman had burst in to report the Norman landing at Pevensey. Harold, his housecarls and the *fyrd* were 190 miles from London but in five days the king had marched his battle-weary army south again to reach the capital on 6 October. Mobilizing more of his *fyrd* as he marched, and alerting the sheriffs of Tadcaster, Huntingdon, Ely and Lincoln, he waited for his troops in London while he discussed strategy with his advisers. According to Foulques, he had been involved in argument with his family, his mother, Githa, blaming him bitterly for the death of his brother Tosti at Stamford Bridge. His other brothers, Gyrth and Leofwine, were adamant that the inevitable battle with the Norman duke William should be conducted by themselves and not Harold: *they* had not perjured a sacred oath and Gyrth, the elder, could lead the English army with a clear conscience.

Siding with their mother, they counselled that Harold should devastate Sussex and Kent so that William's army would be starved to defeat during the coming winter. Having just learnt of further devastations by William's troops, Harold kicked them from his chamber: Gyrth's plans would bring terrible suffering upon the English people of whom Harold was king. And during those five days, the final attempts for a peaceful resolution of the quarrel took place between the two adversaries. Harold made the first move, while at the same time mobilizing his *fyrd* from the south-west and the Midlands, a force which included large contingents of priests.

The king's envoy, a cleric, presented himself at the Norman camp in Hastings. He was met by William who, to gain time for reflection on Harold's proposals, pretended to be one of the duke's personal seneschals. The priest intimated that Duke William would be generously indemnified financially if he would quit the Sussex soil and sail back peacefully whence he had come: the English crown belonged to Harold because, by English law, a death-bed bequest was legally binding.

At table on the day following, when the duke's identity was disclosed to the astounded monk, William emphasized that Harold's argument was spurious. Why had the Confessor dispatched the two hostages to Normandy in 1051 if he had not meant William to succeed him? In addition, had not Harold placed his hands on William's to swear his acknowledgement of Edward's wish? The bemused cleric returned to London. He was followed promptly by the duke's emissary, Hugh Margot, a Fécamp monk of repute.

Margot confronted King Harold for this final effort at conciliation: Duke William would accept the decision of a papal arbitration court. If Harold refused this suggestion, in order to avoid terrible loss of life, William was prepared to fight Harold in a judicial personal duel, the winner taking the crown; and, should both these offers be refused, Margot was commissioned to deliver to Harold the papal bull of excommunication which the monk had brought with him from Duke William. Harold was stupefied by this final twist:

'I shall march . . . we shall march to battle,' he replied. He seemed stunned, lifting his eyes skywards as he muttered to Margot, 'May God decide who is right between William and me.' The monk, driven by Harold from the room, had hastened straight back to Hastings with the news of the collapse of negotiations. Margot had reported to William yesterday, Wednesday 11 October, the morning during which the wind began to back to the south-east and the rain to let up . . .

'. . . Fitz,' Odo was booming across the supper table. 'Are you happy to leave your battalion to Hugh, while you support the duke in his command post?'

The Steward pulled himself together. They'd covered this ground so often recently: Montfort was a competent commander.

'Of course, Bishop,' Fitz nodded. 'Hugh can send for me if he needs help. Erchembald's a seasoned soldier now. He's a reliable second-in-command. My men respect him.' Fitz still thought of his ex-*fidelis* as 'young Gilbert' but the *vicomte*'s son was now thirty-three and a doughty fighter.

'Harold's advance patrols should be arriving tomorrow night,' Roger of Montgomery growled, 'if he maintains the pace he set from the north – one hundred and ninety miles in five days.'

'Good going,' Eustace grunted, 'even if the housecarls are mounted. It's another sixty miles from London to here: two hundred and fifty miles in seven days in this weather is demanding much of his troops.'

'Even when they're fresh,' Hugh of Montfort added. 'But those Englishmen have just fought at Stamford Bridge – even though the housecarls are the best professionals in Europe, they're bound to be weary.'

A brief silence descended. Fitz watched his companions, these commanders upon whom the future depended, as they brooded upon the battle prowess of their adversaries, those notorious housecarls: the king's royal bodyguard of 3,000 warriors, instituted by Canute. They were professional fighters paid by the king, and were superbly trained. Unlike the continental knights, they were mounted men-at-arms, using their ponies and horses only for transport.

Arriving on the battlefield, their custom was to dismount and to form a solid phalanx around their sovereign. They wore their hair long, their flaxen locks protruding beneath their conical steel caps. From these helmets hung tough leather flaps to protect the shoulders. The fierce, blue eyes of the Saxons, flashing from behind the nose-guard above the curling, blond moustaches, were an awesome sight when the hand-to-hand started. They fought with the Danish axe: a single blow from one of these long-handled battle-axes could fell an armoured rider and his horse. The housecarl carried a heavy round shield made of limewood but, because of the ponderous nature of his axe-swing, he had to be backed up by other swordsmen, javelin-throwing troops and slingers. Disciplined superbly, the housecarls were used by the king to provide backbone for the conscripted *fyrd* . . .

The duke was speaking, his first utterance for some time:

'Foulques estimates that after Stamford Bridge Harold can't have more than two thousand housecarls with him.' William glanced at each of his commanders in turn:

'But we must assume he's mobilized most of his *fyrd:* some will have joined during his march south, and others will have marched from Wessex. Foulques is right: they'll be concentrating where the tracks meet at the Old Hoar Apple Tree near Caldbec Hill.'

'The spy we captured yesterday confirms it,' Robert of Mortain muttered. 'The obvious rendezvous.'

'The *fyrd*'s a rabble,' Odo added. 'They're carrying only small shields and few have chain-shirts – leather jerkins and caps for the majority.'

'Stone-slings and spears,' Roger of Montfort said disdainfully. 'Scythes and bill-hooks, judging by the scouts and troops captured.'

'Don't despise their javelins,' Eustace of Boulogne added, 'and their short axes.'

'Most effective,' Alan Fergant sneered. Fitz disliked the count of Brittany's habitual sarcasm. There was little love lost between these two men and William intervened at once:

'Don't underestimate a man who's defending his homeland,' he reminded them. 'The English can fight like lions when they're well led.'

Fitz was relieved to hear the duke's admonition. The *fyrd* had originally been instituted by Alfred the Great: the workers of each five hides of land were compelled to support one soldier who was forced to serve for two months each year. Though the organization theoretically provided a force of 50,000 men, only 12,500 could be mobilized at any one time: if the man was forced to serve longer than two months, by law the kingdom had to raise Danegeld to pay for his extended service. The resulting force was a permanent standing army of two thousand men, the maximum the nation could provide without resorting to Danegeld.

'Odo,' the duke was asking his half-brother, 'what's your estimate of Harold's force?'

'Nine thousand,' the bishop snapped. 'Fighting troops.'

'Against our eight thousand,' Hugh said. 'But we've more auxiliaries, counting the army's train.'

'And support for our cavalry,' Fitz added.

'Harold's coming to us,' William mused. 'As I hoped.'

'Hit him hard, William,' Odo growled. 'Before his rabble's sorted itself out.'

William rose from the table. He faced them squarely before leaving the banqueting tent:

'Harold's banking on surprising us, confident that he can repeat his lightning tactics of Stamford Bridge.' The duke spoke firmly, his decision made as he glanced at his commanders:

'When Harold reaches the Hoar Apple his army will be in no state to fight – and *that's* when I'll strike, my lords.' As the servants parted the curtains to the entrance of the tent, William commanded brusquely:

'Get you to bed, my lords. Tomorrow night, I warrant, you'll have little sleep.'

On the crest of the hill outside Baldeslow village, Steward fitz Osbern reined in his war-horse. Leaving the duke and his staff to march onwards towards the enemy, William fitz Osbern needed his moment of reflection, possibly the last in his forty-six years of life: today's contest would decide the fate of every knight, man-at-arms and foot soldier who had crossed the Channel to seek his fortune in this mist-enshrouded island.

Unlike his companions, Fitz was experiencing more a tranquillity of spirit than the exultation enjoyed by the youngsters as they rode to battle. He inhaled a deep draught of the sharp air cutting across the hill from the east. Beyond the flat marshland above Fairlight cove, he watched the surging sea, blue and grey from the light of the fresh day. The sun was lifting above the distant blue line of the north Downs of Kent: the pulsing orb was shrouded by mist, a blood-red disc hanging above friend and foe alike. Would he see it sinking below the western horizon tonight? He sighed, touched his forehead and breast with the sign of the cross. He swivelled in his saddle to watch the army winding through the village of Baldeslow and up the hill towards him.

Today was Saturday 14 October. Yesterday had been a hectic day of comings and goings while the scouts' reports streamed in: Harold's army was hacking its way south through the Wealden forest; by the afternoon it was obvious that he had designated the Old Hoar Oak at the track junction on Caldbec Hill as the rendezvous for his *fyrd* converging from all over England. With his commanders' enthusiastic concurrence, at dusk yesterday William made his decision: the Norman army would strike during the early hours of this very morn, before Harold's exhausted troops were deployed. The duke intended to turn the weapon of surprise upon Harold himself . . .

Since quitting Pevensey a fortnight ago, the rain had fallen incessantly, but yesterday, Friday, the deluge had ceased. The drying east wind and the sun had dispersed the misery of the impatient troops. After the evening mass attended by the whole army, a mass celebrated

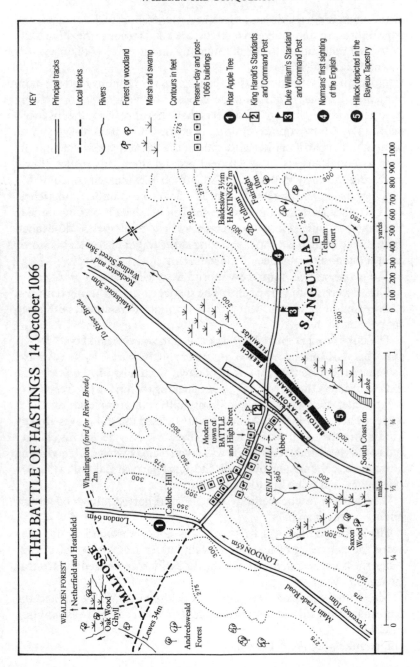

THE BATTLE OF HASTINGS 14 October 1066

KEY

|||||| Principal tracks

- - - - Local tracks

Rivers

Forest or woodland

Marsh and swamp

····275 Contours in feet

Present-day and post-1066 buildings

1 Hoar Apple Tree

2 King Harold's Standards and Command Post

3 Duke William's Standard and Command Post

4 Normans' first sighting of the English

5 Hillock depicted in the Bayeux Tapestry

yards 0 100 200 300 400 500 600 700 800 900 1000

miles 0   ¼   ½   ¾   1

WEALDEN FOREST
Netherfield and Heathfield

MALFOSSE

Oak Wood Ghyll

Andredsweald Forest

Lewes 34m

London 64m

Caldbec Hill

Whatlington (ford for River Brede) 2m

To River Brede

Maidstone 30m

Rochester and Watling Street 38m

Modern town of BATTLE and High Street

SENLAC HILL

Abbey

FRENCH FLEMINGS

SANGUELAC

BRETONS NORMANS

SAXONS

Telham Court

Baldeslow 3½m HASTINGS 7m

Fairlight 10m

Telham

Saxon Wood

Main Trade Road

Pevensey 10m

LONDON 65m

South Coast 6m

Lake

in the open air by Odo and Geoffrey, the bishop of Coutances, the crusading spirit had revived when, before all his troops, the duke hung the sacred relics about his neck. Standing on the dais, William's words had rallied his silent host.

'No matter,' he boomed, 'that the English who bar our road are more numerous than us. Your courage is based on your superior fighting qualities. The English are no soldiers, have never resisted the invader's sword. You know you are fighting beneath God's standard' – and he pointed to the papal banner fluttering in the evening breeze behind the altar – 'Your cause is just.' He had praised them, his glance slowly traversing the army at his feet. With masterly timing he concluded:

'There is no turning back. Ahead of you lie plunder and riches. Behind you lurk death and shame: the English fleet is waiting outside Hastings harbour.' He paused again while a total silence descended upon that waiting host: then, shouting at the top of his voice, his words reverberated in the silence of the gathering dusk:

'We march at five, tomorrow morn,' he cried. '*We win or we die!*'

They cheered him to the echo. The silence of the gathering darkness had seemed more intense when the short night descended, with sleep not coming to many.

The duke arose at four. After a personal mass celebrated by Odo, the duke, his staff and the advance party were on the march by five o'clock, half an hour before the first streak of dawn. And now Fitz could see the endless trail of the battalions, each snaking behind their respective knights and following the gonfalons fluttering from each standard bearer. The tail, which must be a league behind the duke, was already winding up the hill from Baldeslow. The Steward wheeled his charger and urged the animal to a trot. It was seven o'clock when, after weaving through the columns, he overtook the ducal party at Baldeslow beacon where they had reined in to await him.

'The tail's a league behind, sire,' Fitz reported. 'In good order, singing on the march.'

The duke grinned. As he turned his horse westward again, they heard the pounding of hooves growing louder from the track ahead. When the horse reared in front of the duke, Fitz recognized the scout as the knight, Vital.

'Sire!' Vital reported, pushing back his helmet. 'We've sighted the English forming up – under two leagues from here. They're assembling on Caldbec Hill.'

The duke's sigh of relief was audible:

'King Harold?'

'Difficult to be precise, sire: his housecarls are concentrating between us and Caldbec Hill, on the slope dominating the marshy valley. It was still dark, so my sergeant couldn't be sure: but he thought he sighted the king's standard and bearer.'

'Two leagues, you say?'

Vital nodded. He wiped the mud from his bespattered face. 'No further, sire.'

The duke was already sliding from his saddle.

'Arm for battle, my lords,' he ordered. 'Fetch my destrier: sir knight, my armour.'

Fitz nodded to his own squire. Two men-at-arms helped the Steward don his suit of chain-mail, then handed him his shield and sword-belt. Lacing tight his chest flap, he mounted his war-charger. They handed him his old friend, his trusty sword which had become part of him over the long years. He fastened it to his belt, checked it free in its scabbard, nodded to his groom to slip the bridle. He felt that stab of excitement, that touch of fear which he'd never been able to shake off when riding into battle. All men, his sons told him, felt the same . . .

They were leading the duke's magnificent Arab stallion forward, a gift from Alphonso of Galicia. Walter Giffard, a hero from the battle of Mortemer, had been sent down to Campostelle to fetch the splendid animal. They were dressing William in his massive suit of gleaming chain-mail and he was already into the long leggings. His dressers were struggling to ease him into the tunic which extended to below his knees, when the duke stumbled suddenly. The heavy suit slid from his left shoulder: they were donning the suit the wrong way round! The troops who were marching past gasped, shaken by this inauspicious omen before battle was even joined. Duke William was struggling upright and bellowing with laughter:

'A sign of future developments,' he roared. 'From being your duke, I'll become your king!'

Ten minutes later he was in the saddle, armour donned, helmet fitted back on his head. He touched St Peter's relic about his neck before they laced up his chest-piece. They handed up his shield which he slipped round to his back. Today he would direct the battle unarmed, holding only his baton, the acknowledged symbol of command.

'Raise my standard,' he ordered briskly. 'Hold high the papal banner.'

This instant, when the great red banner with its two golden leopards fluttered in the breeze, always sent a tingle to the nape of Fitz's neck. And he smiled as he watched the unfortunate youngster, le Blanc, lifting high the white and yellow banner of Rome. The duke had awarded the honour first to Ralph of Conches, then to Walter Giffard. Both had had to use all their guile when tactfully declining: they preferred to wield their swords than hold a standard aloft for hour after hour . . .

'Forward, my lords.' William lifted his baton, nudged his charger to the trot.

The barons fell in behind, Fitz in the centre, the squires carrying the duke's sword and lances. As the party overtook the marching infantry, the cheering troops parted before them. Fitz had fought many a battle since his youth, but never had he seen the soldiers in such buoyant spirits: if morale was a weapon, the day had begun well – but neither William nor his commanders must underestimate the Saxons.

The housecarls were the steadiest and most disciplined fighting men in Europe. The duke's army contained a considerable porportion of mercurial, Latin mercenaries. But it was difficult to believe that Harold's *fyrd* was as well armed and equipped as this Norman army. And as the Steward trotted past the exuberant soldiers and along the wooded track which crossed these rolling hills, his heart rose: he had recognized a detachment from his own Breteuil battalion. The common foot-soldiers were bearing themselves proudly: their leather jerkins were reasonably clean, even after these weeks of foul weather; the thongs about their stockinged legs were neatly bound, their sandals in good order. Carrying their ash-shafted spears, their slings and their cudgels of holly wood, they marched bare-headed: helmets and caps were badges of rank reserved for the knights, for the archers and the men-at-arms.

These last were the back-bone of William's army; the men-at-arms were in the thick of the in-fighting. Their weapons were clean, the iron tips of their spears gleaming, the cutting edges of their short axes keen, daggers and broad-swords sharpened by the blacksmiths. Most wore chain-mail shirts and their iron caps gleamed in the early morning sunlight filtering through the trees. But it was the archers who were the élite, those lithe, broad-chested men in the pointed caps.

Too unwieldy in chain-mail tunics, the bowmen had to be mobile and able to respond swiftly to the unexpected. On this October morning they wore woollen jerseys over their leather jerkins. The short yew-bows were slung across their shoulders; some marched with bulging quivers jerking at their belts, while others leaned forwards, the leather arrow-baskets slung from halters about their necks. These archers could shoot fast, could reach a hundred and fifty paces with their iron-tipped arrows. The ammunition wagons, loaded full with reserve arrows, were following among the baggage train now wending up the track from Baldeslow. But, efficient though they were, these men were disliked in the army. They were arrogant because of their indispensable talents, but it was the stocks of yew from which they fashioned their bows which made them unpopular: too many horses and cattle were accidentally poisoned by the lethal wood and its berries.

The duke's advance guard was reaching Vital's scouts concealed in the woods of the hamlet of Telham, when Fitz was astonished to hear the sound of men singing – hundreds of voices chanting their camp version of the Song of Roland which their forebears had sung when returning from a Spanish crusade. And leading them, juggling with his glinting, naked sword, was the troubadour, Taillefer, who had been granted by the duke the privilege of striking the first blow for Normandy. Fitz loosened his own sword in its scabbard, wished that he could share this exultation evinced by these younger men striding so joyfully towards death. But, as always, no one ever assumed that the unthinkable could strike him personally . . .

Following the prancing Taillefer, the duke and his commanders reached the edge of the wood stretching up the hill to their right. The track was starting to descend when, at the curve by the edge of the beeches, Vital reined in ahead of the duke. He was pointing across the shallow valley to where a lozenge-shaped hillock, gold-topped with gorse and broom, straddled the track westwards. The mound was about a thousand paces ahead and was the same height as the slope on which the duke had halted. A dark mass was trembling like a colony of ants upon the summit of the hillock; as the duke waited by the fringe of the trees, Fitz saw two large banners slowly rising from the green turf. They flew there defiantly, on the crest of the hill, streaming in the easterly breeze and brilliant in the fresh sunlight: one, the red Dragon of Wessex; the other, Godwineson's own standard, the Fighting Man. The duke glanced at Odo, grinned at Fitz. He rode his destrier forward, clear of the trees. Across the marshy valley echoed a bellow of Saxon voices, unintelligible, but full of derision as they sighted their Norman foe. William lifted his baton.

'I'll command from here,' he said, turning to his commanders. 'I'll deploy as soon as the rear-guard catches up.' He pointed to the right where a stream trickled north-eastward from the marshy meadows; then to the left, where another rivulet and its boggy morass encircled the foot of Harold's defensive hill.

'Follow the track between the streams,' he told his commanders briskly. 'You've a difficult deployment, my lords: you'll have to march in file then turn into line, left and right on the far side of the streams.'

'Dangerous, sire,' Alan of Brittany remarked, 'if Harold attacks before we've turned back into line.'

'Be swift, my lords. Deploy with all haste: Bretons on the left flank, French and Flemings on the right, Normans in the centre.' He tapped his thigh with his baton. 'Hurry – and we'll catch Harold before he's ready.' He turned to the count of Boulogne: 'Eustace, set up my command post here. Raise high the standards. Stick with me, Steward.'

The great banners streamed in the breeze. The duke dismounted, his seneschal leading the white stallion back to the beeches. Slipping from his own destrier, Fitz joined Eustace by the duke's side. Another roar echoed from the hills across the depression, as Alan's Bretons began filing towards the gap between the streams.

It was eight o'clock already. A thousand Breton voices lifted, the ancient Song of Roland reverberating from the foot of the valley and mingling with the continuous hubbub from the Saxon host.

Almost an hour had elapsed while the duke and his two aides, Eustace of Boulogne and fitz Osbern, watched with impatience the agonizingly slow deployment. But Alan Fergant was now holding his banner aloft on the left flank; Robert of Mortain with the main body of his four thousand Normans was in the centre; and on their right, Roger of Montgomery's standard was flapping briskly from among his French mercenaries and the Flemings. It had been a nerve-racking hour, for if Harold's *fyrd* had been organized, it could have attacked down the hill and cut the deploying army to pieces.

Instead, the housecarls were still painstakingly joining up, their shields before them, left shoulder forward, to form an impenetrable wall below the crest of the hill opposite. Fitz could see them plainly – and a captured spy had just confirmed William's estimate of King Harold's intentions.

'They're almost ready, sire,' Eustace croaked, wagging his puzzled head. 'See, there're no gaps now in their wall of shields.'

'Harold's on the defensive,' William snapped. 'Sound the attack as soon as Roger's ready.'

From where the Steward stood beneath the banners flapping above his head, the Saxon king's standards were only seven hundred paces distant across the diminutive valley. Fitz Osbern could see the king's two standards, the personal guard of housecarls shoulder to shoulder around them on the crest of the hill. Fifty paces below these banners, a line of motionless shields stretched horizontally across the hill, a stockade of interlaced shields, edge to edge, along the whole width of the rise: over fifteen hundred, Fitz estimated, fifteen hundred huge, hairy Saxon housecarls, the majority armed with long-handled, half-moon axes, the remainder with lances, spears and swords.

Behind this human phalanx a quivering mass of infantry was darting about, still trying to form ranks behind their housecarls. Fitz counted eleven such ranks, each shoulder to shoulder, jostling for position, stumbling over their assortment of weapons: javelins, slings, short axes. A few carried small round shields, and Fitz could spot bill-hooks, forks and scythes in the rear ranks. In contrast to the silent Normans tensed below in the valley, the Saxon army was buzzing like a swarm of bees.

'How many d'you reckon, Fitz?' the duke snapped. 'You're better at numbers than me.'

'Foulques' information isn't far wrong, sire. Seven thousand, I reckon; two thousand housecarls.'

The duke nodded. 'We judged Harold rightly, Fitz, having fought beside him at Dol. He couldn't stand back and watch his Sussex burning.' The muscles in William's leathery cheeks twitched as they did when he was holding himself in check.

'He should have waited in London for you to attack him, sire,' Fitz said. 'His *fyrd* has not had time to concentrate.'

'They'll be tired: fifty-eight miles in two days from London: they can't have slept much after their arrival late last night.'

'His impetuosity has played into your hands, my lord,' Eustace said. 'You've got the early fight you've always wanted.'

William nodded. 'I'm certain he intended to keep the offensive, by using the same surprise tactics he sprung on Hardraada.'

'See him now,' Eustace said, pointing to the Saxon host on the green and gold hill opposite. '*That's* a defensive disposition. I see no archers yet – nor many *fyrd* foot-soldiers.'

'His bowmen are probably still in the north,' the duke said. His head jerked to the right: 'See,' he rapped. 'Roger's ready!'

Montgomery's lance was lifting, his red pennon fluttering from its tip. From here, Fitz could identify him clearly in his gleaming chain-armour, his huge destrier stamping in front of his division. To Roger's left, the French abutted the right flank of Robert of Beaumont's knights from the Risle. Fitz smiled grimly: war made strange bed-fellows of ancient enemies.

Each of the three divisions was now holding high their commanders' pennons. In the front ranks, the archers and the foot-soldiers with their spears and slings; behind them the men-at-arms in their chain-mail tunics; and at the back the orderly squadrons of cavalry, with their snorting steeds and bustling squires, the grooms with the reserve horses.

The duke lifted his baton:

'*Sound the trumpets!*' he roared.

As the notes echoed across the combe, a mighty roar burst from the bastard duke's army, from one end to the other. The great host quivered: the battle for the gorse-topped hill had begun.

Obeying the yells of command, the front ranks detached themselves, the archers stepping briskly forward. Half dropped to one knee, the others standing behind them. The short bows bent, the arms drew back as the bowmen took aim - and then that dull twang! as thousands of bows loosed.

Fitz recognized that unique flutter as the hail of goose-winged arrows clove the air, streaking uphill straight towards the motionless wall of shields. Again and again the volleys sped between the opposing armies, the arrows thudding into the limewood shields of the housecarls glowering down upon the Norman host. Then, the quivers empty, the duke again lifted high his baton.

The three commanders acknowledged the signal and above the clamour Fitz could just distinguish their shouted orders. The archers sprang aside, waiting for their opponents to return the fire; the foot-soldiers and men-at-arms stepped forwards, drew their weapons and began surging up the slope towards the enemy. The Bretons on the left were soon drawing ahead of their neighbours, because on their left flank the slope was less steep. Within minutes the whole line was struggling uphill to the age-old Norman battle-cry of '*Dex aïe, dex aïe!*'

To Fitz, they seemed to make little progress as they crawled step by step upwards, the distance between the two armies diminishing agonizingly slowly. He pushed back his helmet, letting the sharp breeze blow through his thinning hair. The clouds were sweeping across the cold blue sky above the weald and the woods were turning gold ahead.

A flight of pigeons flapped from the beeches to his right, alarmed by the cacophony exploding in the valley. The men-at-arms were moving like ants, so slowly did they climb; and as Fitz watched them, he saw the anxious archers waiting in exasperation for the enemy's retaliatory salvoes: with empty quivers, they were waiting to collect the Saxon arrows they were expecting to plummet into the turf – but none came. The Saxon bowmen could not have marched down yet from the north: after a battle like Stamford Bridge, thousands of arrows and broken bows took time to fashion and replace. Fitz could see runners scurrying across the combe bottom towards the ammunition wagons. The archers had *not* softened up the defences, ready for the men-at arms to breach the shield-wall: the first phase of the duke's battle-plan had failed.

Instead, the lines of chain-clad infantrymen were clambering painfully slowly up the steep slopes. They could not be more than thirty paces below the silent housecarls waiting impassively above them, shields shoved forwards, the long axe-handles gripped in their fists. But at twenty paces, bedlam broke loose . . .

'*Ut! Ut!*'

'*Dex aïe!*'

'*Ut! Ut! Ut!*'

The sky above the struggling Normans darkened with a rain of missiles: swishing javelins, quivering where they stuck; hurtling short stone axes; jagged flints propelled by hand-held wooden catapults. Fitz had suffered most battle surprises, but never had he witnessed anything like this: the air throbbed with this terrible man-made hail. Even the bowmen at the bottom of the hill were being struck.

'See, Fitz,' William called. 'Alan's advancing too fast: he's separating his right flank from our Norman centre.'

'The slope's easier for the Bretons, sire,' the Steward shouted. 'The others'll catch up soon . . .'

But the Bretons were already grappling with the first line of housecarls. Fitz could hear the grunts, '*Ut! Ut!*,' from those gigantic, bearded men as they shoved and battered with their shields at the struggling, flagging Norman men-at-arms. The axe-heads glinted in the sun; the sickening screams of cloven men pierced the combe as the long-handled weapons scrunched through bone and flesh, cleaving the Norman shields in twain, like tinderwood. Chain-mail flew apart, swords shattered, mounted knights were severed in two, the skulls of their horses split asunder. Fitz turned away, sickened, as the Breton knights wavered, backed, then stumbled down the hillside whence they had battled upwards against the dreadful onslaught.

'God in Heaven!' the duke shouted on Fitz's left. 'Alan's Bretons are panicking!'

Fitz held his breath. Thousands of Bretons were balanced a few paces below the yelling horde above them – first ten, then fifty, then a hundred Bretons broke; turned and were suddenly fleeing downhill, stumbling over themselves as they ran.

'Your Normans, sire,' Eustace yelled from the duke's left. 'Look, sire, they're unhinged.'

The left flank of the central Norman division was suddenly unsupported. Step by step, it was giving ground, the division being bent remorselessly by the furious onslaught from above. On the right flank, even Montgomery's division on the steepest part of the hill was being forced back; it was fighting every inch of the way, but if it broke the whole of William's line would crumble . . .

'My horse,' the duke roared. 'My sword!' He tossed his baton to his seneschal. 'Stick here, Eustace,' he shouted at the count of Boulogne. 'Mount, Fitz! Follow me.'

The Steward's heart raced: once more he felt the tingling through his veins, that feeling, half-fear, half-exultation, surging through him. He strode towards his charger and they legged him up into the saddle. He swivelled his shield round to the front, adjusted his left forearm through the strops into the battle position; he felt for the pommel of his sword, swished the blade free, pulled down his helmet.

William's opening tactic had failed. The jeers of Harold's troops yelling in derision from the hill-top taunted Fitz as he cantered down the slope towards the valley bottom. His eyes fixed ahead on the fluttering banner jerking from the standard-bearer's mount, for the first time the thought of possible defeat pricked Fitz's mind.

The battle was opening disastrously, William's and Odo's optimistically naïve tactics torn to shreds: first, the duke's archers to soften up the enemy's wall of shields; next, the attack by his men-at-arms to carve out breaches from the housecarls' stockade; finally, the duke would deploy the weapon he was holding until the moment was ripe – his disciplined cavalry to exploit the gaps hacked out by his men-at-arms – but God in Heaven, how swiftly was William's plan crumbling . . . and as Fitz charged behind his duke down into the bottom of the combe, the magnitude of the disaster was instantly apparent.

With howls of triumph, the English foot-soldiers were breaking out from behind the housecarls. Chasing the fleeing Bretons down the hill, they were hurling their javelins, flinging their stone axes. And as Alan's troops panicked, taking their mounted knights with them, the demoralized division became bogged down at the bottom, in the marshy ground through which the stream trickled. Horses fell, rolling upon their riders, asphyxiating them in the mire. Infantrymen dragged down their cavalry, grappled frenziedly among themselves, unable to distinguish friend from foe when the English levies fell upon them, hacking, stabbing, scything . . .

Seconds later, stirrup to stirrup with his duke, Fitz was at it, parrying with his shield, feinting, at close-quarters using its lethal edge to split wide the enemy skulls . . . his sword-arm ached but, closing with a burly English soldier, the grimacing face concealed by a mass of flaming red beard, Fitz was so hard-pressed that the pommel-guard of his sword was wreaking deadlier execution than the blade . . . He slammed at the stupid face, heard the crunch of bone . . . hacking, thrusting, Fitz was barely holding his own, when from the corner of his eye he glimpsed William slithering from his saddle, his destrier sinking to the ground, its throat spurting gore, its hamstrings sliced by the English levies.

'Dex aïe!' Fitz roared, searching desperately for aid – and, parrying, cutting and thrusting, gradually he began pushing back the baying Englishmen as his own knights hacked a path back to his side. Young Beaumont was here, God be praised; his own son, Roger, was approaching, grinning behind his nose-guard as he sliced his way towards his father. And as Fitz relaxed his aching arms, eased back his horse, to give place to his saviours, he heard the despairing cries of defeated troops, the unique wail which spelt only defeat.

'The duke is slain! Our Bastard's fallen!' they were chanting. 'Flee! To the sea! To the sea!'

Terror was contagious. Soldier after soldier began discarding his arms the better to keep his balance down the slope, the better to run . . . and even Fitz felt the stab of terror that a sword could in seconds split him wide, an axe plunge between his shoulder blades. Holding his horse's head up again with the last of his strength, his senses reeling, close to his left he heard that bellowing roar which he could identify anywhere:

'Your duke lives!'

Fitz glimpsed William in the reeling mêlée . . . He stood squarely against his fleeing troops, beating them with the back of his shield, flailing them with the flat of his sword as they stumbled over themselves. And as he straddled back into his saddle on the fresh mount, he lifted his helmet. His ruddy face was streaming with sweat, his eyes flashing with rage:

'See, all of you – *Your duke is alive!*' he cried. And as he hacked his path back up the slope again, the pursuing Englishmen checked, hesitated, then began backing up the hill.

'If you flee,' William bellowed at his troops, 'no man will escape slaughter! *Fight back!*' he bellowed. 'Follow me to victory!'

Suddenly the overwhelming tide of disaster was stemmed. The soldiers around the duke rallied, stiffened, began fighting like devils . . . '*Dex aïe!*' they screamed once more as in those vital minutes the duke's most valiant knights beat their way to their duke's aid. Eustace of Boulogne, realizing the calamity, had charged down from the command post; Bishop Odo, his club flailing like a threshing stick, was cleaving a path through the English levies, wide enough for Beaumont, Fitz and his sons, Roger and William, who had moved across from the centre, to plunge in with swords and shields amongst the enemy. They were wreaking terrible havoc and already the English were scurrying uphill, back to the sanctuary behind the wall of shields. Then, as the Normans neared the crest of the hill, Fitz dimly heard the duke's horn, calling them off.

The Steward lowered his dripping sword, shoved his shield behind him. He eased his aching back, leaning across his destrier's neck as he wiped the blood from the horse's clotted mane. He trotted down after the others, thankful for the respite. The duke had restored the situation at the critical moment and now the sun was past its zenith. The Steward had never felt so weary. His sword-arm outstretched and limp, he reached the bottom of the combe. Stricken, screaming horses still flailed in the morass; dying men and wounded soldiers, untended and ignored by their comrades while the battle raged, still moaned pitifully in the gory mire.

Slowly the Steward forced his snorting destrier up the opposite side of the valley, back to the command post where the duke and his commanders were already revising their battle-plans, their helmets pushed back, their squires refurbishing their arms. Fitz accepted the wooden bowl, allowed the wine to trickle down his throat: he felt the kick of alcohol, sensed the pain diminishing in his weary limbs.

'I'll exploit their indiscipline to our advantage, Fitz' William told him. 'But we ourselves will need all the skill and discipline at our command.'

Then, while both sides regrouped and regained their strength, the duke and his commanders relaid their plans.

The sun was already losing its warmth, was well past the meridian before Duke William was fully ready to re-start his attack. His knights re-horsed, the men-at-arms rearmed; the archers' quivers stocked anew from the ammunition train; his exhausted troops and cavalry fed and watered – the issue would be decided before sundown, and after the morning's near-catastrophe the duke was leaving nothing to chance. The confident, braying English were ready too, the wall of the housecarls shortened, the gaps stopped.

Steward Osbern, ordered by the duke to remain with Eustace of Boulogne in charge of the command post, did not relish the responsibility which devolved upon him: from here he could only watch the punishment. He was waiting for the critical moment to release the cavalry battalions stamping impatiently in the hollow of the combe behind the Norman division. The counter-attack would be led by the duke himself. Fitz could see his standard plainly, red and gold, streaming high above the jostling chargers.

'It's going worse than I feared,' Eustace growled. 'I don't like it, Fitz . . .'

Both men watched with growing anxiety while the flower of the Norman knights stormed again and again up the blood-stained slopes. The cavalry charges were losing their impetus: this was the fifth assault since the resumption of the battle and each time the leading horsemen reached the solid wall of shields, a murderous hail of javelins, spears and stone-headed axes rained down upon them. The jibbing horses pranced, off-balance on the hill, as their riders tried desperately to pierce the Saxon wall.

'It's futile,' Eustace grunted. 'They've been at it for over an hour now.'

And when the Norman cavalry began to waver, the dam above them broke: the English *fyrd* burst from behind the shields and grappled with the unbalanced cavalry. The Norman knights, trying to ward off the attacks at their backs, began retiring down the hill: the retreat began again to have the appearance of a rout.

'Wait, Eustace,' Fitz rapped. 'Give it a few more minutes.'

And while the two barons watched in agonized suspense, the English began cascading down the hill after the retreating Normans: the housecarls were yelling at the disorderly mob and beating them back into line with their swords, with the hafts of their axes – but the English foot-soldiers continued to stream triumphantly after their foe, the torrent of pursuers growing to a flood.

'Now!' snapped Fitz. 'Now, Eustace!' They lifted high their swords. Their squires behind them raised the gonfalons of both the Breteuil and Boulogne houses.

Down in the hollow the duke's seneschal jerked upwards the flaming standard with its two golden leopards. The duke's destrier sprang forwards. Fitz could see William clearly, his sword raised, his shield lowered before him as he led his crack battalions into the charge – it was a stirring sight, lances lowered, banners and gonfalons streaming. There was no shouting, no war-cry, only the beating of the hoofs rolling into a thunderous crescendo. They charged in squadrons of between twenty and forty knights, in diagonals across the hill, galloping into the rise – then up and over the sloping shoulder. Then suddenly, even from here, Fitz heard the duke's battle-cry, *'Dex aïe!'* distinctly audible even above the thunder . . . The cry was taken up by hundreds of voices, and then the cavalry was in amongst the rear of the pursuing English foot-soldiers.

The levies did not sense the cavalry charging down upon their flank until it was too late: while the mounted knights butchered the wretched English rear, the fleeing Normans turned. The ill-disciplined *fyrd* was caught in the jaws of the closing trap. The slaughter took twenty minutes: Fitz counted on his fingers the numbers of English who managed to scramble back to the safety of their lines. The slopes of the hill were invisible for the piles of English dead.

By the time the Norman cavalry had regained their assembly-point behind the Norman division, the housecarls had shortened their line by drawing in their flanks. Was Fitz mistaken, or were the Saxons bunching more than before, concentrating more closely about King Harold's standards still fluttering on the crown of the bloody hill?

Twice more the duke repeated his tactics. Twice more the *fyrd* broke ranks to pursue the retiring Normans' cavalry; the savage hand-to-hand *mêlée* swayed back and forth on that gory hill.

It was during the second cavalry charge that Fitz learned from a terrified prisoner that, during the first critical assault at noon, Harold's brothers, Gyrth and Leofwine, had been cut down while pursuing the Bretons. The impetuous Harold had launched his counter-attack much too early and the deaths of his two brothers had grievously affected the *fyrd*'s morale. Harold, his brothers killed, was now on the defensive, shortening his line, consolidating his defence, waiting on William's initiative . . . and at three o'clock, when the carmine sun was dipping towards the shoulder of Harold's hill, the duke returned to his command post.

'This is our chance, my lords,' he told his commanders. He was grey with exhaustion, his chain-armour splashed and stained with gore. He had shoved back his helmet. His blue eyes were hard and devoid of feeling.

'We'll attack in concert, throw him off balance.' He glanced at his weary commanders.

'Eustace: have the archers recharged their quivers?'

The count of Boulogne nodded. 'They've emptied the ammunition wagons, sire.'

'Spread the bowmen along our whole front.' He glanced at Montgomery and Alan of Brittany:

'I'll give you plunging fire. Stand by to attack with your infantry and dismounted knights, as soon as the archers have emptied their quivers.' He clapped both commanders on the shoulder:

'To your divisions, my lords – but wait for my trumpet before moving into the attack.' He smiled as Eustace and Fitz buckled on their swords: 'You can go this time. I'll stay here.'

Moments later Fitz had mounted and was trotting down towards the hollow with Eustace and their knights. It was good to see the duke up there in his command post, legs astride, rock-like beneath his standards – and as Fitz reached the boggy hollow he knew that this must be the decisive moment of this interminable day. The slopes were quivering with the mass of stricken wounded writhing amongst the slain.

The approach of the October evening was bringing its strange solace: wisps of vapour were curling over the monstrous heaps disfiguring the bloody hill, a gigantic shroud rising with the chill of dusk. The Steward shivered, tormented by the cruel paradox.

The woods were touched gold behind him; the bracken was turning crimson; the fleecy clouds drifted overhead. Why, in God's name, *why* did man have to butcher his neighbour in order to settle a dispute? The final phase of the battle was imminent: before that red sun sank much lower, either Harold or William – not both – would be remaining alive to ponder the futility of this horrendous slaughter.

Fitz's thoughts were interrupted by shouting through the lines. He heard the *twang!* then that unique fluttering as the arrows sped high above their heads. He'd never seen such a hail of arrows, flight after flight whistling high, the bowmen on one knee, their arched bows canted upwards . . .

The trumpets were sounding, the infantry and men-at-arms moving forwards in a vast straight line up the slope towards the shrinking wall of housecarls who, swords drawn and battle-axes in hand, were holding their shields above their heads. Upwards the Normans slogged, yelling their war-cries – and then, as they clambered over the mounds of dead to close with the housecarls, the Bretons began to bend the western extremity of the housecarls' wall:

'*The King has fallen!* King Harold is stricken in the eye . . .'

The cry flickered like summer lightning until it reached the Norman lines. The rumour might carry truth, thought the Steward: the western flank of the *fyrd* was wavering, was giving ground before the first cavalry charge pounding up the slope towards it – and the clash echoed through the valley. The Saxons were giving ground as the Normans' second cavalry charge thundered up the western slope. Again the *fyrd* reeled, gave ground, began inexorably to roll backwards. The Norman cavalry plunged onwards, the horses stamping to pulp the mounds of wounded, while their Norman riders strove to grapple with the lethal hail of axes and spears.

Then, to Fitz's left, the duke himself was sizing up the disintegrating situation as the Saxon left flank quavered. William lifted his command baton, cantered towards his waiting reserve of cavalry.

'Eustace, Fitz – attack along the eastern slope. Take Montgomery's cavalry with you along the shoulder. Attack Harold's eastern flank. Roll it back – *this is our chance!*' Stabbing his spurs into his destrier's rump, William swung round to watch the outcome of his decision.

Fitz could see the enemy's two standards drawing nearer, faster and faster now as Eustace and he cantered up the eastern slope, five hundred of Montgomery's horsemen behind them. In groups of forty, stirrup to stirrup they charged towards the Englishmen swinging desperately to reform behind the piles of dead, to turn and face the fresh attack hurtling down upon their left flank. The pounding of hooves, the maddened snorts of the horses – and then the war-cries of the group of knights galloping alongside him . . . Though Fitz registered it all, he felt strangely remote as, sword at the ready, he charged into the fray.

The smells revolted him, the stench of steaming entrails, of blood, stinking excrement – even after all these years he was sickened by the filth of battle. He was suddenly amongst the English foot-soldiers, scything their spear hafts in two with his sword, splitting wide a skull with the pounding edge of his shield. He did not know for how long he battled, but those two standards of the English king were creeping nearer, those proud banners fashioned from golden thread, the Fighting Man and the Dragon of Wessex.

Fitz and his battalion fought with precision, each supporting the other, the leaders hacking, stabbing, clearing a path; holding the ground, waiting for those behind to close up, to exchange roles; then, flailing onwards again, each section taking its turn, moving through those ahead. The Steward checked his charger once again, lowered his sword-arm while his supporting knights hacked their way past him. And as he drew breath he saw that, fifty paces ahead, Eustace's leading section had succeeded in cutting off Harold's personal guard from the remainder of the housecarls: they were now fighting desperately as isolated units.

Some thirty Saxon warriors had encircled the two royal standards which sprouted from the growing mound of Saxon corpses. Shield-to-shield and back-to-back these bearded giants were fighting with desperate ferocity to repel Eustace's relentless attack; and, inch by inch, the Saxon warriors were forced to cede ground, to reduce the perimeter of their defensive circle. The mound of dead grew in height. So fierce was the fight, so close to each other were the housecarls battling that their dead remained upright, unable to fall.

At the rear, on the highest segment of the circle, several of the king's guards were crouching over a bearded figure lying propped against a pile of corpses. The fallen warrior was helmetless and clad in blood-soaked battle-dress. A huge Saxon was bent over the stricken Harold – from his fine apparel, the wounded warrior could be none other than the king. The shaft of an arrow protruded from the agonized king's eye. The others were holding him rigid and the housecarl was trying to pull the barb free. At that instant, when Fitz heard the terrible cry of agony above the din of battle, the human shield of Saxon defenders quavered as the housecarls bent to the fury of the Norman assault. Once again the circle tightened as the diminishing number of housecarls were struck down, fighting to the last man about their prostrate leader. Battle-axes still flailing, the shafts slippery and untenable with blood, the gallant band was growing smaller and smaller – then suddenly the ring broke . . .

At the head of forty of Normandy's finest warriors, Eustace, with Montfort, Walter, and Guy of Ponthieu's son, was bursting through the human wall. Deliberately and methodically, they cut down the exhausted housecarls, one by one. They overwhelmed the last of the royal guards and, sliding from their saddles, they sought out the English king from amongst the piles of dead and dying. They fell upon the prostrate Harold and butchered him to pieces. They stood there an instant, looking down, leaning on their dripping swords. Then, remounting their destriers, they grabbed the blood-soaked standards and wheeled back whence they had come. Their triumphant shouts that the English king was slain rang above the battlefield.

The slaughter was not yet ended. Groups of housecarls were still battling to the death: though now leaderless, they were frantically striving to reach the edge of the forest behind Caldbec Hill where they were desperately mounting a defiant, last stand.

The sun was creeping below the distant woods. The English *fyrd*, chased by the triumphant Normans, was vanishing into the misty dusk. Human vultures were already about their grisly task of extricating mutilated bodies from their valuable chain-mail suits, when Fitz saw Eustace rounding up any knight he could find for the duke's final pursuit. William, a broken lance still in his hand, was waiting impatiently for the force to muster, when Fitz nudged his charger towards the wheeling cavalry.

The October sun had vanished behind the woods. Streaks of crimson slashed the western sky when at last the duke's force was ready to deliver its final blow. The surviving housecarls were formed up along a four-hundred-yard front: their right flank was against a steep bank overlooking a stream; their left, protected by a web of rivulets and bog. Here, barring the duke's advance on London, in this position half a mile north of the oak tree from which Harold's scouts had first sighted the invader's army, the surviving housecarls were ready to fight – they would take as many Normans with them as they could before they died.

William had dispatched two separate forces to cut off the enemy: one, by way of the broken-down causeway which crossed the defensive hollow; the other, led by Eustace, across Caldbec Hill and down the far slope towards the enemy's position.

The light was almost gone when Fitz nudged his horse behind his duke: twelve hours had passed since climbing into the saddle this morning and twilight was at last casting its shroud upon the horrible evidence of this victorious day. And as the Norman horsemen cantered wearily down the slope behind their duke, mixed were the feelings of his followers: the butchery was not yet done because, in spite of resistance from his knights, William was determined utterly to destroy this English army. His victory must remain indelibly imprinted into the minds of these stubborn Englishmen . . . and Fitz recognized that sullen, cold stare in William's eyes that signalled, for good or ill, that he was determined to realize his objective – even if there was more killing to do. Wearily, his muscles cramped with exhaustion, Steward Osbern pricked his failing destrier, felt the protesting animal breaking into the gallop down the easy slope, a descent which disappeared into the darkening vale concealing the enemy's last resistance.

Half an hour had passed since the last streak of twilight had merged with the rolling clouds of night. There was no moon until midnight: only the reflected glow from the last glimmer of sunset touched the dark woods, flecked the turf ahead of the pounding cavalry. The going was dangerous, even for these superb horsemen. It was difficult to see three strides ahead and Fitz instinctively gripped his steed more grimly, held the rein more firmly as he pounded after the eighty knights. The leaders were disappearing into a dark combe below the lip of the hill, when a crescendo of war-cries shattered the stillness of dusk. A group of horsemen reared suddenly from out of the shadowy scrub of gorse and broom. At their head Fitz recognized the stocky figure of Eustace, the count of Boulogne.

'Halt, sire!' the warrior yelled. 'Turn back . . .'

Looming from the darkness, fifty knights confronted the duke. Gasping for breath, Eustace spilled his report. Fifty paces ahead and hidden by the long grass, a gaping void awaited them: over two hundred Norman knights had been ensnared into the hideous trap, the cavalry riding full gallop into the dark ravine; hurtling over the cliff, the heavy chargers and their chain-clad riders crashed one upon another into the shambles at the bottom of the rocky crevasse. Those who had not broken their necks or been crushed to pulp by the remorseless tide of oncoming horsemen were finished off by the rocks and missiles hurled down by the concealed housecarls on the far side of the ravine.

'It's a bloody massacre, sire,' Eustace gasped. 'Turn back. Call off your pursuit.' He handed over his horse to his squire while his force dismounted around him. The duke glared down at his commander:

'Get back into the fight, my lord,' he commanded, not deigning to conceal his contempt. 'Cut them off at the causeway, while I roll them back from the right-hand end of the ravine.' His voice rose in anger: 'Leave no man alive who resists, d'you hear me?'

Fitz was watching the stocky count of Boulogne as he paced sullenly towards the dark scrub whence his squire had walked his destrier. Eustace was stooped in dejection, and was re-strapping his chest armour when there was a commotion from the bushes. A huge Saxon leaped from the shadows. Roaring defiance, his sword arm swung. Fitz heard the clang of the blow on Eustace's helmet, the count's cry as he fell to the ground. By the time the astonished squire and several knights reached their pole-axed master, the concealed housecarl and his defiant soldiers had darted back into the darkness.

'Does he live?'

The duke was gazing down upon his aide, even as he drew his own sword from its scabbard.

'A blow to the head, sire,' the young Beaumont called. The cadet knight was on his knees and lifting the shoulders of the stunned count. 'He's breathing, sire.'

'Take him from the field.'

The duke pulled down his helmet, turned to Montfort:

'Hugh, lead Eustace's knights to the causeway. Attack when you hear my horn.' He lifted his sword:

'Follow me, my lords. To the right – to the other end of the ravine.' He pricked the belly of his charger. 'At the trot and in close order. There's still work to be done before this night is out.'

'Un mauvais fossé . . .'

At last the day of battle was done, the killing ended. The action in the terrible ditch, which became known as the Malfossé, was over, the last housecarl, fighting to the death against hopeless odds, finally slaughtered. The remnants of the *fyrd* were slipping away, gliding like shadows into the dark forest. Even William was satiated, had no more taste for vengeance. Those of his knights who survived the catastrophe of the Malfossé had found their way back across Caldbec Hill, on foot and in the saddle, to the bloody hill where thousands, Normans and English, now lay cold and stiff in the companionship of death. Riding across the corpses, the weary Normans reached the hill crowned by the mounds of slain housecarls who lay intertwined, stiff fingers crooked through arrow-studded shields, cramped around blood-congealed axe staves. Down the far side, layers of Norman dead sprawled across the slopes like the leaves of autumn which were beginning to smother this terrible battlefield; at the combe bottom, thousands of Bretons and English lay asphyxiated in the boggy morass by the swampy pond. Fitz rode in silence at his friend's side, watching isolated knights and groups of men-at-arms limping back to find the remnants of their army. A camp for the night was being set up on Telham Hill, on the opposite side of the combe from the blood-soaked hill upon which the fate of England had been decided.

Duke William was reining in his weary stallion, his fourth mount of the day, the others all killed under him.

'*Sanguelac*,' he murmured.

Lake of Blood – and Steward Osbern halted alongside his duke on the summit. Amidst the highest mounds of dead, where the corpses of the housecarls and Normans lay inextricably mixed, where Harold's standard had proudly flown, the two men surveyed the ghastly scene.

'Stay with me, Fitz.'

The Steward dismounted with his friend, sheathed his sticky sword. Their squires had halted fifty paces behind, were waiting for orders. Down below in the combe, torches were flaring as the bivouacs began to cluster. Shadows darted like quicksilver among the cadavers, the human rats plundering the priceless chain-mail.

William gazed at the twisted corpses at his feet. Already the stench of death was tainting the valley.

'I shall sleep here tonight, Fitz.'

'Here, sire?' Fitz asked. 'Amongst the dead?'

'Send for my tent.' William was searching about him, picking his way to a less encumbered space at the summit. He drove his sword into the blood-soaked turf:

'Pitch it here.' He removed his helmet, tucked it across the pommel of his sword. He pushed back his chain head-piece, leaned wearily upon his shield.

The evening breeze ruffled his matted hair as he stood in silence and listened to the wind moving in the trees. His massive silhouette was bowed against the lingering glow in the western sky . . . and fitz Osbern watched him, this enigma that was William. What was it that made him tower above his fellows? What spirit drove him, half-devil, half-divine? What force had driven this man, from bastard birth to the summit of his powers at thirty-eight, to cross the seas and invade this stubborn island? And then he heard Duke William posing the unspoken question in the Steward's mind:

'This England,' the Bastard murmured softly, 'for whom so much blood is spilt . . .' He was twisting the point of his sword in the soil. 'How much more must be shed to subdue her, Fitz? How hard must we fight to keep her?'

PART IV

❧❀❧

. . . AND ITS SHADOW

21

UNEASY CALM

As the dead king had declared, God had judged . . . but, rotting here in camp outside Canterbury, five weeks of misery in the slush and frosts of an English winter were not conducive to the maintenance of morale, even in a victorious army. Fitz Osbern felt as frustrated as everyone, but recovering from his turn of dysentery in his sodden, stinking tent, he knew that his depression was due mostly to his weakened health.

The dawn after the victory of Sanguelac Hill broke grey, silent and cold. The housecarls had vanished, but among the prisoners the victors were surprised to find Turkish mercenaries. That sad Sunday, 15 October 1066, had brought home to the Normans the cost of their victory as they sifted their dead from the English. The task of burial was a gruesome business, for the human jackals had even hacked off heads and limbs to denude more easily the torsos of the valuable suits of chain-mail. The first tally that night of the Norman army's dead reached two thousand four hundred knights and cavalry; over three thousand archers, men-at-arms, and foot-soldiers – it would take days to count the number of wounded.

The duke left the English dead where they lay, prey to time and the birds and beasts. On the Monday, he moved back to Hastings where for five days he rested and re-formed his cavalry and troops.

Not until he was secure in camp did he allow the Saxons to bury their dead: the drama over the identification and burial of Harold caused Fitz considerable aggravation. If only the English could have accepted their king's death with the same realistic brevity as did William, Fitz would have enjoyed more sleep. While the duke waited impatiently for the English barons to submit, the Steward was dealing with the flood of English pleas to find Harold's body. A mutilated and naked corpse, the face horribly unidentifiable, was found near the bodies of Gyrth and Leofwine. The body was of Harold's height and build.

There was only one person who could certainly identify the

horrifying evidence: the Saxons induced the distraught Edith, the Swan-neck, to carry out her distressing duty. Among the stinking remains of the English dead, they forced her to search for the intimate marks which only she could recognize on the body of her one-time lover. They led her from the hill, too shocked even for tears, but they had found their king.

The old mother, Githa, having seen her whole family wiped out, offered the equivalent weight in gold for her son Harold's body; but the duke, aggravated by the whole business and fearing that the English would forge a legend of the usurper's death, refused Githa's request. Determined to quash the dangerous nonsense and recalling the murder of Alfred by Harold's father, he sent for the Anglo-Norman, William Malet, who at Pevensey had previously tried to forewarn the duke of Harold's invincibility:

'I do not sell the dead,' he told Malet. 'Harold was excommunicated: he cannot be put underground with Christian rites. Bury him on the beach near Hastings.' He added grimly, 'There he can watch my coasts for ever.' Harsh words, thought Fitz, but Harold dead, if the legend was not nailed, could be more dangerous than Harold alive.

The weary duke had then turned his mind to the myriad details demanding his attention . . . First, he was profoundly affected, despite his bluff exterior, by the ghastly slaughter of the flower of Normandy's youth. Picking his way between the grisly corpses, he'd stuck his sword into the soil where Harold's standards had flown:

'In thanks to God, I shall keep my vow to the pope: here shall my monastery be built. Let the place be called Battle. Mark well the spot, my lords.' And on the way back to camp that morning he had confided to Fitz of his fears for his beloved daughter, Agatha. 'She'll never recover from this, Fitz. In spite of everything, she'll never relinquish her love for Harold.'

'She was engaged to him for so short a time,' Fitz added.

William deliberated: 'I'll try her on Herbert of Maine. 'Twould bring peace to our troublesome border.'

Fitz shook his head. 'She'll never marry now, sire.'

William had not spoken again during the rest of the ride back to Hastings. Victory won, the eternal problems of state were already claiming his thoughts. He was waiting for the great lords of England to approach him in submission.

Those next few days, while his army rested and refurbished, brought disillusionment and a flurry of problems. The weary duke's hope that the great men of England would flock to pay him homage was swiftly shattered when the surly Northern earls, Edwin and Morcar, disgusted by the defeat of Harold, returned to their bleak fastnesses. Already there were rumours that Archbishop Stigand was rallying support to adopt Edgar, the atheling, as England's legal monarch; but, despite the Londoners' enthusiasm, Morcar and Edwin's backing seemed half-hearted. The realization that by English law William was entitled to all the lands and possessions of the dead man he had vanquished (Harold and his brothers had owned most of southern England) did little to alleviate the duke's anxiety. It was on Wednesday evening, 19 October, that his patience ran out.

He would march the next day, his objective being the heart of the island: London was where all roads concentrated to cross the Thames. With London in his hands, all he needed to preserve his lines of communication with Normandy was the fortress port of Dover.

Leaving Hastings garrisoned under the capable Humphrey of Tilleul, the duke moved at dawn for his twenty mile march on Romney: its citizens had slaughtered the entire crew and passengers of the invasion ship which had made her landfall too far to the eastward on the morning of 28 September. Allowing his soldiers a free hand, the duke sacked the town with ruthless cruelty: as at Alençon fourteen years previously, he wanted details of the horror to precede him. Sticking again to the coastal tracks and bringing his fleet with him, he moved on Dover, calling upon its citizens to surrender. They would hand over the keys forthwith provided the Normans spared their town. The duke agreed and forbade pillaging by his troops.

Some of his knights and a section of the foreign mercenaries felt cheated of their spoils and, disregarding their commander-in-chief's orders, proceeded to fire and loot the port. Before William could quell the mutiny, several houses of the town's prominent worthies were burnt to the ground. Finding himself in this embarrassing position with the Dover citizens, the duke promptly forced the mutineers to pay full indemnity for the damage they had caused. Truculent Norman and apprehensive Englishman took the example to heart.

The duke rested for two days in the vital port which now safe-guarded his link with Normandy, but it was here that the first cases of dysentery manifested themselves. Leaving the sick to recover in the castle, William began his march northward along the Roman road. He sacked Sandwich and left a garrison in the old Roman castle of Ratupia at Richborough, thus securing the other vital port in Pegwell bay.

Turning west and living off the sparse frosted countryside, his army made for Canterbury.

The cathedral city rendered homage without resistance, but by now the ravages of dysentery, encouraged by lack of food and by the abominable conditions of the campaign, were reducing the invaders to impotency. Wallowing in the mud outside the walls of Canterbury for over five weeks, the duke himself was struck down. He became seriously ill and it was during this long, frustrating wait that Foulques' spies confirmed the duke's suspicions: Stigand's efforts at rallying resistance were bearing fruit.

The men of Kent were fleeing their villages and streaming northwards to the capital city. Earls Edwin and Morcar had at last decided to throw in their lot behind Stigand, impelled by the knowledge that their sister, Edith, was now carrying her first baby, the dead Harold's child: the unborn babe could be presented as the legal heir to the throne of England. Leaving their sister at Chester, they decided to march south and join forces with the resistance building up again in London around Stigand's candidate, Edgar. With such a concentration of troops in the city, the capital was growing short of food, for William was now controlling the roads from the south.

Lying convalescing in his rotting tent, Fitz was very much aware of the slump in the Norman army's morale. This wretched immobility in the filthy slurry and freezing fog of the fields outside Canterbury; this enforced wait without action and the spoils of battle were not what had been promised. There was little glory in dying in such revolting conditions, hungry, wretchedly cold and wallowing in human excrement. But, while they waited for their leader to recover, there had been one satisfactory development.

The duke had sent an emissary to Exeter, the capital of the West, where Edward the Confessor's widow was now installed: the Normans would spare the city and the South-West if Edith would surrender Exeter and pay homage. On 28 November her reply reached Canterbury: Edith and her lords were capitulating – and with the gifts which she was sending, arrived too the news that Winchester, the capital of Wessex, was also paying homage. William now had nothing to fear from the South-West.

The news revitalized the duke and his army. Learning also that the half-hearted Northern earls were returning to their fastnesses (they were convinced that William would never dare cross north of the Severn into their earldoms), the convalescing duke called his council of war. London barred his route to the North, and must be taken. But, though only fifty miles from Canterbury, the capital with its ten thousand troops and inhabitants was too formidable for direct assault. He would encircle the city, cut off its food supplies and give its beleaguered citizens time to reflect on their grim choice. On 30 November, the Steward was in the saddle again, weak but recovering swiftly as active campaigning began once more.

The misery of November was behind them when, on the first day of December, Rochester castle fell to William's advance battalions. Pushing on to the southern end of London Bridge, the Normans were surprised by Edgar's troops who had attacked from across the Thames. To deal with them, the duke dispatched five hundred of his crack cavalry: Edgar's men were severely mauled and, leaving them to scuttle back into their city, William put Southwark to the torch. Sweeping westwards south of the Thames, he allowed his troops free rein to pillage, loot, rape and burn, hoping that the news of the atrocities would bring Stigand and his followers to their senses.

On 14 December the amazing news arrived that Conan II of Brittany had died of poisoning: the duke's last anxiety for his home base had thereby been resolved. He turned north, crossed the river at Wallingford then marched east across the Chilterns, his army creating havoc wherever it passed. To the duke's relief, he then learned that Archbishop Stigand, backed by his faltering clergy, was ready to submit. The realist had smelt inevitable defeat, so was hastening to become the first of England's notables to kneel before the Conqueror: William might perhaps overlook the past, might possibly support Stigand's attempt at *rapprochement* with the pope? While the duke simulated interest and waited for the English to come to him, he ordered his troops to continue laying waste to the shires of Buckingham and Bedford, as his army remorselessly drew the net tighter around the capital.

On 16 December, the English court, headed by the atheling, was congregated thirty miles north of London, in the town of Berkhamsted. Edgar and the Witan, with Archbishop Aldred of York, the Northern earls and the bishops of Hereford and Worcester were waiting to pay homage.

The sheriff of London was offering to surrender the city, but William was in no hurry. Sensing the resentment of the local English and expecting trickery and tough resistance when later he pushed further north, he called his war council together: what did Odo, Robert of Mortain, his Steward and his commanders advise? Would it not be wiser to wait until the spring before accepting the crown which these English were now undoubtedly offering him? By then the Norman army would be rested, refurbished; its notoriety would be widespread and the English would have had time to reflect on the wisdom of accepting a strong, powerful king able to restore order in their land? Furthermore, when William was crowned at Westminster, his queen should be at his side to share a joint coronation. If the crown was accepted now, there was insufficient time during these winter gales for Matilda to cross the Channel to London.

Fitz admired his friend at this important moment. Many of the Norman barons suspected their duke of prevaricating for political ends, but the Steward knew him better. The thin and emaciated duke missed his wife, needed to share this portentous moment in their lives. But many of his council were against his argument, the *vicomte* of Thouars volubly carrying the majority with him: surely it would be more prudent to act swiftly, before the English could change their minds? Once the duke was crowned, the status which kingship carried would demolish any further opposition . . . Thouars omitted to hint that the conquering barons were impatient for their spoils.

Accepting the will of his council, the duke issued his ultimatum to the Berkhamsted court: if the English crown was being offered to him, he would accept it on only one condition. The throne of England was his by right: Edward the Confessor had bequeathed the crown to him. No other condition was tenable, least of all the contention that the English had elected him. He would be crowned by Archbishop Aldred of York who was recognized by His Holiness the Pope. The coronation would take place on Christmas Day in Edward's abbey of Westminster.

The ultimatum was accepted. Despite the protestations of the Londoners, who complained that they had not been consulted, the Norman garrison was dispatched ahead immediately to prepare for the coronation. It was already the twenty-second of December.

'Fitz,' William said, the hard lines about his mouth relaxing, 'see that everything's as it should be in London. I'm going hunting in Epping Forest.'

A dressing of snow carpeted the fields outside the city walls. On this crisp Christmas morn, 1066, the roofs of the huddled houses still wore their caps of white; and the banks of the river Thames were lined to the tidemark with icing – a beautiful, serene setting for this coronation day.

The Steward of Normandy was smiling to himself as he followed behind the duke on their ceremonial ride from the palace to the Confessor's abbey at Westminster. Like his friend, no doubt, his thoughts were of home, of how Adeliza would be coping with the grandchildren on this Noël morning. Preparations for the Christmas feasting were in her hands, but when Fitz had left home the sight of food was nauseating her. She was losing so much weight and he was sick himself with worry for her, now that news from Vaudreuil came so erratically . . .

At ten o'clock this morning the great men of England, led by Stigand himself and the two Northern earls, had set out from the city to fetch Duke William from his palace. And now, falling in behind the Norman knights, they were following the procession through the mystified people who were hurriedly manning the route. Some cheered but most remained silent, gawping at this foreigner from across those stormy seas which had failed to protect them, the seas which through seaborne trade were making this unique island rich. Across the fields, Fitz could see myriads of masts clustered along the banks of the river; as far as the eye could see the ships were moored in trots, while the river itself was speckled with small boats, loaded to the gunwales, ferrying passengers from one bank to the other. Traders were making up against the tide, lowering their masts to pass beneath the bridge, while the mill-wheels rattled in every tribulet. It was no wonder that William's Normans felt at home here among these obstinate sea-faring people – both races shared the maritime traditions which the contintentals could never understand.

London was a vast city compared to all other English towns. It was the commercial heart of the kingdom, a lively, bustling metropolis through which trade arrived by sea from all over Europe. Its warlike, rich merchants traded freely, secure behind the walls originally built by the Romans. Jealously guarding their city privileges, they had always managed to keep the monarch and his interference outside the city: Edward's palace at Westminster was well outside the walls. Smithfields and Moorfields bounded the city, providing food, while to the north on the hills, the rich hunted the wild bull, the stag and boar in St John's Wood, in Enfield Chase and the distant forest.

The duke was clothed in his finest linen, his richest cloak. He wore no weapons, was bare-headed, clean shaven, his russet hair short by English standards, cut in a line at the nape of his neck. He rode majestically on his white palfrey which had been especially brought over from Normandy for the purpose. He glanced neither to left nor right, isolated from the barons following behind him. His brothers, Odo and Robert, were leading with Fitz and the army commanders; the remainder, arrogant and haughty, curbed their mounts to the trot as the procession neared the abbey which soared before them, high and white with its new stone.

There was desultory cheering from the crowd which was massing around the Confessor's church, the surging people being held back by contingents of mounted Norman troops and infantry. While the duke was dismounting, the sun was covered by a passing squall and a flurry of snow. As Fitz walked towards the imposing west door, the two archbishops in their blood-red robes sailed forwards to greet them. The trumpeters sounded their fanfare and then Fitz was inside the abbey, the beauty of which astounded him. After all these weeks, perhaps he had been coarsened by the rigours and horrors of the campaign? The fragile lightness inside Edward's abbey was dramatically striking in contrast to the stark solid simplicity of the Norman churches to which the Steward was accustomed.

As the Norman nobility followed in procession up the aisle, Fitz bowed his head to the English clerics and leading men of authority who had helped him organize this coronation ceremony. The proceedings were going without a hitch, so far: the nave was packed with the highest in the land, the English magnates on the left, Normans on the right. They turned as the duke entered, made their obeisance to the massive figure walking majestically up the aisle. At the chancel step, the Chancellor guided the duke to the throne placed before the marble table. Watched by Archbishop Aldred of York, a tall, spare figure of great dignity, with Bishop Geoffrey of Coutances on his left, William settled himself into the throne while the pages arranged the folds of the cloak.

The congregation remained on its feet, for there was seating sufficient only for the highest ranking. Archbishop Stigand of Canterbury slumped grim-faced in a chair to the right of the altar. Fitz sat next to Odo, in the front tier of the half-circle facing the packed assembly. And when the monks began chanting in Latin, the Steward could not prevent his thoughts stretching back across the years to his adolescence, to those terrible times when his father had been butchered in his bed at Vaudreuil; to the days when his mother had encouraged Fitz to befriend the pale-faced boy whom they called 'the little Bastard'.

True, Fate had sometimes been propitious in the extraordinary fortunes of Normandy's unique leader, but the fact that William now sat on the throne of England was due to his resolute will, to his intelligence; in short, to his character. The proof of his mastery over men and events, of his ascendancy in European affairs was best demonstrated by his superior generalship over Harold at Hastings: a superiority largely the result of his information-gathering network headed by Foulques, his agents and communications. And in a few moments, Archbishop Aldred would be presenting the duke to English and Norman alike as their king. The debate about William's adoption of the English crown had, surprisingly, been contentious among his own countrymen: some Norman barons were nervous of the power their duke might wield over their own interests, but finally the majority's decision had been accepted with grace.

William was determined to follow English tradition in the crowning of their king. Though the ritual of 'crowning' would often be instituted at great official ceremonies, only once in a king's life was he offered the crown of England and anointed with the symbol of sacred oil on his forehead – the instant when kingship began.

By the French Carolingian tradition, the king was enthroned by divine right. Many in the Anglo-Saxon Church resented this assumption, because the people accepted their anointed king naturally as head of their Church. But after William's experience of his ecclesiastics in Normandy – and with his friend, Lanfranc, backing him – he was determined to control the power of his clerics: he himself would appoint the bishops of his choice. Never again would he be ridden by the likes of Mauger, or by this enigmatic, devious charlatan, Stigand . . . and the Steward had to bring himself back to the present as the ceremony approached the moment of presentation. The duke was rising to his feet.

The figure in the rich blue cloak towered above them all. He was addressing the congregation before him in his native tongue – simple and to the point: as their new king by legal right, he would devote his life to the welfare of his English and Norman peoples. He ended abruptly and remained standing.

Archbishop Aldred and Bishop Geoffrey of Coutances were moving forward to the step below the altar, to face the silent throng. Aldred spoke first in English, then Geoffrey in French, both inviting their English and Norman congregations to accept the man standing before them as their lawful king. As each prelate ended his presentation, a roar of assent from each side of the nave reverberated through the abbey, echoing to the vaulted roof, reaching the crowds outside.

This was a moving moment in Fitz's life: and as he watched that silent, impassive man of thirty-eight, majestic, solitary, the crown of

England on his head, the silence inside the abbey was suddenly drowned by an uproar of screams and yelling from the people outside. There was a jostling at the western end, the smell of fire and the harsh commands of soldiers. The congregation began surging towards the doors . . . and minutes later William's seneschal was jostling through the press, back up the aisle, shock on his face.

The nervous and tense troops outside the abbey had taken the shouts of acclamation from inside as a trap: the English lords were murdering their duke. An officer panicked and set upon the crowd, driving them backwards. The stampede spread and in minutes the demoralized soldiers were firing the wooden houses. Then the looting began: these pent-up soldiers, so long used to pillage were once more soldiering in the fashion they understood . . .

The reflections of the flames were dancing through the abbey windows. The contagion of panic seized the packed congregation. In minutes the nave was void. Stigand and the half-circle of Norman nobles were alone in the abbey.

For once, the impassive William was moved. He had visibly paled and was making the sign of the cross, as were his companions. Fitz, too, felt the sinister premonition: was this God's warning to the ambitious, callous duke who had crossed the seas to grab the English throne by force? Fitz saw it himself, for a few seconds only, the trembling of William's fingers as he took the proffered sheet of parchment from Aldred's hand. Then, slowly mouthing the traditional words he barely understood to an echoing, empty church, William vowed solemnly in the English tongue to observe the customs of the land; to enforce the laws of England; to rule with justice and to uphold the Mother Church.

Only the crackling of flames from outside disturbed the awesome silence as Archbishop Aldred strode forwards. Dipping his fingers in the sacred oil, he anointed the forehead of the man kneeling before him. As Aldred stepped backwards, his steps echoed through the empty church.

King of England, Duke of Normandy . . . 5 March 1067, six months since sailing from here, Bonneville-sur-Touques, to join his invasion fleet for St-Valéry; three months since the crown of England was placed on this head, her husband was lying asleep on her breast . . . Duchess Matilda stroked the russet hair of the man she loved but could never quite understand. For him, ambition came first in his life, even before his love for her, she was certain – though he *had* insisted that he'd tried hard to have her crowned as his queen alongside him at

Westminster. Her priorities were different: her love for him and for her children was paramount. She'd tried her best to rule the duchy for him in his absence, but six months was too long to be without his arms around her.

He'd planned his triumphal tour of Normandy about their favourite castle at Bonneville-sur-Touques. And tonight, after their family supper, with only Agatha with them, they had strolled down to the quays at Touques before retiring. Their heart-broken daughter could not reconcile that it was her own father who was responsible for her betrothed's death; it was useless trying to explain the inevitability of the conflict, once Harold had chosen the course he had pursued. As the sun vanished behind the coastal hills on this lovely July evening, they had together taken their beloved fourteen-year-old girl up to her chamber, where they'd tucked her into bed like the child she still sometimes was. Then hand-in-hand William and she had strolled across the lawns from Charlemagne's tower, bade goodnight to the guards in the towers on either side of the drawbridge overlooking the river, and gone straight up to their room.

In the fading twilight he'd taken his time, as she liked him to do. While he slept across her, she lay revelling in her serene content, still glowing warm with the feel of him, while she lazily watched the last carmine streak merging into the night clouds. In her mind she relived the tale he'd taken these weeks to tell her, in the sharing of which he truly found happiness, she felt sure.

He had explained to her the significance of the symbolism with which he was crowned king of England: the knowledge was important to her, should she be widowed. By accepting the Anglo-Saxon customs, he had merely stepped into the shoes of his predecessor. He had to gain the confidence of the defeated Englishmen, and by adopting their customs he could use their administration without hindrance. Immediately after his coronation, he took his army to Barking whence he could survey the city while preparing plans for the rapid construction of his castles – and particularly the Tower which he was building on the banks of the Thames.

He had been surprised at the speed with which the great men of England attended him at Barking to pay him homage, and to promise co-operation in the administration of the land. He had smiled at her when he'd told her he'd decided to return to her at the beginning of March, only three months after his crowning; even if the country had still been in turmoil, he'd said, he could wait for her no longer . . . But England was surprisingly calm, its leaders split up and reeling from the shock of events.

He'd taken no risks when, in the guise of guests, he'd 'invited' the greatest men of England to accompany him back to Normandy. He wished to display to his duchy, he'd told the English, the wealth they owned. So leaving Fitz in charge at Norwich, Odo at Dover, with many of his best barons to support them, William had marched south from London on the start of his triumphal tour.

Matilda smiled to herself in the gathering darkness as she recalled her husband's description of his sullen 'guests'. The hostages, for in reality such they were, were headed by Stigand and the Northern earls, Edwin and Morcar. In the van of the procession rode Edgar, the adolescent atheling, with Waltheof, the enigmatic son of the long-dead earl of Northumberland, Siward. Deliberately choosing the route through Kent and Sussex, the king's procession must have been singularly impressive to the peasantry watching from their daffodil and primrose hamlets in the shelter of the Downs. The treasure, the booty, all on ostentatious display, was carried by a heavily escorted mule train, past the port of Hastings and the battlefield of Sanguelac which they were now calling Senlac Hill, a hideous place where the bleaching bones of the English were still heaped. Skirting the freshly-dug footings for the intended abbey, the cavalcade led on to Pevensey where William had first set foot ashore. In the harbour the fleet awaited its illustrious passengers, the sails already hoisted and brailed, white canvas for victory and peace, a symbol not unnoticed by the hostages.

She had waited for him in Rouen where they spent their first night together after nearly seven months – a very different home-coming to Rouen from that of sixteen years ago. Then, he had returned to a hostile capital, having barely saved his head after defeating the rebel *vicomtes* and retaking Brionne. It was Lent when this time he came home. During those few weeks, with their family around them, they planned together the route he would take on his victory tour. They missed the quiet, competent Fitz, but the Steward was indispensable in England.

They invited all the notables of Europe to the monastery at Fécamp, where together they gave thanks in the Easter mass. It was a splendid, unforgettable moment for her. These, the most powerful personages on the European continent, had come to share in the achievements of her husband. 'King of England, Duke of Normandy . . .' – she could still hear the ringing pride in the voices of the abbot and old Archbishop Maurilius. The gold and silver, the jewelled goblets and the tapestries, all from England; the European courts had been astonished too by the richness of the banquets she had organized. Then they'd ridden down here to their haven at Bonneville, where he could revisit Dives whence his fleet had set sail. Jumièges was next, where it was plain that the old archbishop was not much longer for this world. When he died, William intended that the bishop of Avranches, John, should replace the grand old man. He talked only to her of his plans, but never again would he allow others to appoint the bishops.

Her man grunted beside her, reaching in his dreams for her. She caressed his shoulders, feeling a motherly protection new to her. She too had changed, but not so much as him, she thought. Throughout this victorious cavalcade, the people had rushed to acclaim him, to touch even the hem of his cloak. For them too, their duchy had sprung from the dark, blood-stained years, to become the land of the most feared and respected people in Europe. They were sharing with their duke the splendour and honour he had won for them.

This adulation, the spontaneous warmth of feeling was new to him. But with the glory came the awesome responsibility – and it was this realization which had changed him most, giving him a new-found confidence. He was less aggressive, more tolerant of fools; to her he showed more tenderness, was gentler with the children. Even Robert, William's sad disappointment, had grown closer to his father, even when being dispatched for his final session to the despairing clerks who were trying to educate him. And Matilda shared her husband's anxiety for their son and heir . . .

Robert – Richard – William . . . 'Only Richard has the possible makings of a king,' he'd told her this night, this wonderful night. He longed so intensely for a son in whom he could have confidence for the future of his duchy and kingdom – and he'd poured his seed into her time and time again this night. He'd fallen asleep in her arms murmuring, '*Henry*. We'll call him Henry.'

The euphoria could not last. Her king was at the summit of his career, thirty-nine and in the flush of astounding success. There was only one way now for him, she realized all too well: downwards was the only direction from a pinnacle. The world was watching England. Already Foulques' men were reporting that Sweyn Estrithsen was mustering his Danes for an all-out invasion, timed for the new year of 1068.

How much longer could she hold him? She hugged him to her, kissed his forehead, the tears welling. He'd make her his queen, he'd said, probably in the spring . . . Dear God, what mattered her crown, so long as she always had him? And as the dry sobs came, the summer lightning flickered across the northern sky along the coast.

22

❦

STAIN OF SHAME

The euphoria existing in William's Normandy did not last long. In England, the two regents, Bishop Odo and Steward fitz Osbern had been allotted an impossible assignment. It was inevitable that a conquered, proud people would resent the insensitive Norman military, an army trained in living off what it could grab from the peasants it was terrorizing. By the autumn of 1067, sporadic resistance was breaking out – and the vicious circle was complete.

In England, an influential Devonian land-owner, Edric, whom they called 'the Wild', rallied the Welsh princes, Riwallon and Bleddyn, to support his attack on the Norman garrison at Hereford. Though creating mayhem, they were repulsed, vanishing into the Welsh mists to await another day.

In the south, the men of Kent – those born east of the Medway – had, a year previously, strewn the Conqueror's route with green branches to welcome him on his march to London. In gratitude, the king had consequently recently confirmed the ancient Anglo-Saxon privileges they had always enjoyed by alleviating the burden of taxation; it was therefore a shock for Odo, who was in Norwich conferring with fitz Osbern, to learn that these men of Kent had caught the contagion of rebellion. They had invited one of the leading warriors of Senlac Hill, the count of Boulogne, to cross the Channel and take command of their insurrection. More astonishingly, Eustace agreed, possibly because he had never forgotten his humiliation in 1051 at the hands of the citizens of Dover; but, more probably, because the restraining hand of his overlord, Baldwin, was no more. On the first day of September, Matilda's father died in Flanders; though Baldwin v had never opposed his son-in-law, his support had been equivocal.

Though Eustace, who had recovered from his head wound, sacked Dover town, he could not reduce the castle. His force being slashed to tatters, he hastily re-embarked and sailed back to Flanders – a ridiculous end to what had been an honourable career . . .

But the greatest threat to William's new kingdom during the late autumn of 1067 came in the consistent reports that the legendary Danish king, Sweyn Estrithsen, was rallying European support for his invasion of England, a campaign overtly supported by King Malcolm of Scotland.

Leaving his duchess to rule Normandy (Matilda was four months with child) King William, refreshed and exhilarated after his triumphal tour, hurried back to his kingdom. Exploiting the disunity of the English and the support which he was receiving from many of the Anglo-Saxon bishops, William decided to deal with the insurrections separately, before the expected Danish invasion. He at once had to deal with the rebellious men of the West Country, their independent spirit fired by Edric the Wild.

Exeter and its battlements controlled the South-West. Garrisoned by its sturdy citizens and by many Bretons from across the Channel, its resistance centred about the person of Edith, Harold's widow, who had given birth to a daughter Gunhild, now three months old. Failing to gain support from its neighbouring thegns, many of whom backed their new king, the city drew up its drawbridges; agreeing to pay its taxes, it nevertheless refused to swear allegiance.

Taking the ultimatum as an insult, the king rode westward from London with a handful of Norman knights. For the first time summoning the local fyrd, he was met near Honiton by several burghers of the city who were prudently preferring to negotiate. Returning to Exeter, they found the gates barred to them, the defenders having decided to continue their resistance. William thereupon laid siege to the city and took several of the locked-out burghers as hostages.

The eighteen-day siege collapsed when, beneath the battlements of the city, William put out the eyes of one of the hostages. The atrocity had its desired effect and, after dissension among themselves, the men of Exeter capitulated, on condition that their taxes were not increased. The king, pressed for time with the impending invasion, agreed; commanding the immediate building of a castle, he lifted the siege and departed for London. The subjugation of the remainder of the West he left to his Norman commanders. Cornwall was subdued and Robert count of Mortain was installed as its overlord.

The West Country was rapidly joining its new king: Gloucester and Bristol submitted and, when Harold's three bastard sons invaded up the Bristol Channel from Ireland, the men of Somerset, helped by the citizens of Bristol, flung them back into the turgid waters of the Severn. By the early spring of 1068, the West Country was secure.

The king meanwhile had invited the highest in the courts of Europe to *share in the forthcoming coronation of his queen at Winchester. The daffodils were nodding gold, the primroses scenting the April air outside Winchester palace, when there began a week of pomp and ceremony which would long be remembered in Europe. The magnificence of the king's court, the sumptuous banqueting on gold plate, the display of jewels and tapestries – such wealth could not but impress the high-ranking guests who had travelled so long and so far to share in William's pride. And there on 11 April in Great Alfred's capital, the diminutive figure of Matilda, swollen with eight months of pregnancy and dwarfed by her massive husband wearing on his head the crown of England, stood at the High Altar. Anointing her, Archbishop Aldred then placed the smaller crown upon the dark tresses of the tiny head. The* laudes *to Pope Alexander, to the royal couple and to Archbishop Aldred floated to the vaulted roof. Duchess Matilda was Queen of England.*

Behind her stood Richard, her son, already at fourteen his father's favourite and growing daily more like him. Their difficult Robert, sixteen and a half, was performing for the first time his duty of ruling Normandy during his father's absence. Under the wise Roger of Beaumont, Robert could not harm the duchy; but William was perturbed by Robert's growing friendship with Edgar the atheling of England, who was of Robert's age.

This ostentatious week and the hearty collaboration with the Anglo-Saxons did not please all Normans. William had wisely not interfered with England's traditions, preferring to govern through its tried administrators. Many such men were collaborating and William continued to draft his royal charters and commands in the native tongue of the island. Chief among the English leaders who supported William's policy of reconciliation was the wise, old Archbishop Aldred. But, though William allowed many Anglo-Saxon prelates to remain in their sees – Stigand was still at Canterbury – his tolerant policy caused division between both sides, especially among the suspicious, hard-faced Norman barons who were waiting impatiently for William's favours.

To them, William seemed to be fawning for the vanquisheds' approval: he was insisting upon using the Saxon Chancellor, Regenbald, to teach his Norman Council the Anglo-Saxon court procedures and administration. The king also seemed to have developed an admiration for the young earl Edwin: William had even offered him his daughter, the pining Agatha, to wife. Many observant Normans were convinced that Edwin's cautious approach to the offer was merely a political and cynical ploy. But even more unpopular was William's determination to continue using surviving house-carls in his personal guard: this seemed, to many Normans and English alike, an inexcusable provocation.

The English resentment first manifested itself during the coronation, perhaps because of the humiliation they felt for the ostentation flaunted at the Winchester ceremony. One powerful lord after another began slinking from the king's court, particularly after Edgar had slipped quietly across the border, with his mother and sisters, to join King Malcolm of Scotland. Then Earl Morcar disappeared back to his Northumberland. His brother, Edwin, thereupon claimed his fiancée, Agatha, from her father, an action considered by many of the king's closest advisers as tantamount to blackmail. While William dithered and Agatha tearfully resisted, Edwin himself resolved the matter by leaving the royal court and returning also to his mist-enshrouded earldom. It was evident to all England that, north of a line between the Severn and the Humber, William, the Norman, had singularly failed to gain allegiance.

In spite of Archbishop Aldred's influence at York, a concerted resistance against the king of England was swiftly forming. Edgar the atheling and his family were succoured by King Malcolm of Scotland; and, though Sweyn Estrithsen had not yet struck across the North Sea from Denmark, relations between him, the Scots and the Nordic descendants of Northumberland were sympathetic and close. In this climate, Earl Morcar had little difficulty in rallying support from Gospatric, the natural leader of 'St Cuthbert's land' north of the Tees.

Leaving his queen to await her confinement, William, sensing that Malcolm was merely playing for time while awaiting the Danes, marched swiftly into East Anglia. These fair-haired descendants of so many Norse invasions were unashamedly sympathetic and impatient for Sweyn Estrithsen's long ships to appear over the horizon. But at Lincoln, Cambridge and Huntingdon, the king's will prevailed when the local leaders bowed the knee – and were forced to put in hand the building of their king's overpowering keeps and dungeons, grim reminders of their allegiance to the new, disciplined order.

William had created Robert of Commines an earl, and commissioned him to enforce the royal authority in the defiant North. Hardly had the king returned south to be with his newly-born fourth son, Henry, than he learnt of a direct challenge to his authority: on his journey north, Robert of Commines was warned by Ethelwine, the bishop of Durham, that a band of assassins was plotting to take his life. To make an example, the earl callously and brutally punished several local thegns before breaking his journey at his official residence in Durham. But he was assaulted in the street and forced to take refuge in Bishop Ethelwine's house. That night, his assassins were secretly admitted to the bishop's quarters; and in the early hours, these *determined Northumbrians pounced upon the Normans in the bishop's palace and slit their throats. The earl and his personal guard escaped to a nearby house but the rebels put torches to the timber: Commines and every Norman guard perished in the inferno.*

York was only four hours gallop from Durham. Two days later the men of York set upon the detested Norman garrison. They slaughtered the king's sheriff, but a messenger escaped to the south to alert the king.

Anticipating Edgar the atheling's march southwards from his Scottish sanctuary to support the York rebels, William reacted with immediate and characteristic vigour. Following Harold's tactics, he force-marched north to York, reaching the city gates before Edgar arrived. After retaking the ancient city and cruelly punishing the rebels, William commissioned the overlord of St Cuthbert's land, Gospatric, to extend his authority southwards in order to control the whole of the rebellious province.

The king would never have dared to move south again had he not been convinced of two factors: first, the divided English lords were incapable of mounting a concentrated campaign against him; second, he had the support of the English Church, whose leaders' priority was reconciliation. With this groundswell of support behind him, William could, with only a relatively small efficient force, deal with each uprising as it occurred.

The English resistance remained uncohesive because of the scarcity of leaders, so many having perished at Fulford Gate, Stamford Bridge, Hastings and in innumerable skirmishes. As the months slipped past, more and more of the English thegns and men of influence began siding with the stern and incorruptible administrators of the king: the dream of a United Kingdom under the rule of Law could become reality under the authority of this conqueror from across the seas.

Many of the English prelates, including the bishops of London, Bury St Edmunds and Wells, were committed to the king; and when Wulfstan of Worcester and Archbishop Aldred of York courageously declared for their new sovereign their example had a profound effect. With this support rallying behind him, the king was extending his rule throughout the land through the agency of his earls. In 1068, these powerful men were responsible directly to their king for the execution of his policy throughout their vast earldoms. These provinces were sub-divided into shires which were administered by sheriffs who, in turn, held their positions through their earls. It was to the sheriff that the thegns of the 'hundreds' were responsible for order, the payment of taxes and the mobilization of the fyrd.

Before 1066, the dispensation of justice had been slipping more and more into the hands of the private lords holding sway over the Hundred courts. But

King William, through his earls, sheriffs and inspectors was now remorse-lessly reversing the process. Common law was reverting to the people. The juries were made up of free men who represented the individual and defended his rights according to the king's law, without fear or favour. The inspector was the king's man: his role was to ensure that the sheriff did not abuse his power; the earl of Hereford himself, William fitz Osbern, once reversed the judgement of a court by reducing a fine it had imposed on a minor knight.

It was through the omnipotent and impregnable Norman castles, now being frequently built of stone, that the earl and his sheriffs exercised their control of the countryside. These brooding, sinister symbols of the Norman conqueror sprawled over the land like a gigantic octopus: to subjugate the capital, the footings of the king's Tower of London, designed by Gundulf, the bishop of Rochester, were being dug on the northern bank of the Thames.

In June 1069, William hurried across the Channel to present his queen to the duchy. Then, leaving Matilda once more to govern Normandy in his absence, he hurried back to his new kingdom: the long-awaited Danish invasion was imminent.

The king of Denmark, Sweyn Estrithsen, had left little to chance, had spent months organizing his invasion: his fleet of two hundred and fifty ships were commanded by his brother, Asbjoern; his two sons, Canute and Harold, led the invasion force which included mercenaries from the Baltic, Poles, Frisians, Saxons and Danes. This redoubtable army was awaited eagerly by King Malcolm of Scotland, by his protégé, Edgar, and by the men of northern and eastern England in whose veins ran so much Nordic blood. During that long summer, the Norman king and his superb but smaller professional army stood to in East Anglia waiting for the Danes to strike.

William was hunting in the Forest of Dean when the host of coloured sails billowed over the horizon in the strait of Dover. The garrison of Odo's men in the new fortress crowning the white cliffs repulsed the intended landing; then watched the invaders wearing round to North Foreland before disappearing into the haze of the Thames estuary. Still uncertain where the main blow would fall, William held his army in check . . .

Next, the men of Ipswich, then of Norwich, fearing more for their skins than for freedom, hurled the probing raiders back into the sea. The king's garrison at York was by now fully alerted, when Asbjoern's fleet finally made its landfall at the mouth of the Humber.

While the king force-marched across Mercia, Edgar Atheling swept down from Scotland, gathering Gospatric's men of Northumberland en route. The enigmatic Earl Waltheof, with his men of East Anglia, then rallied to

277

Gospatric. The Danish invasion was sparking rebellion which was threatening the existence of the new kingdom and jeopardizing all that the Normans had ventured and risked for so many years.

The aged Archbishop Aldred died on 11 September, close to the minster he loved. Eight days later, after being overwhelmed in their castles, the two Norman garrisons tried to deny York to the invaders by setting the city aflame. The Danes, having slaughtered the 'French'*, quit the smouldering ruins and returned to their ships in the Humber where they turned the island of Axholme into their fortress base. Thus established, this invasion army, gleefully reinforced by Edgar's Scots, Gospatric's Northumbrians and Waltheof's East Anglians, ravaged northern England.

Parts of the kingdom, sensing that their new Norman despots' days were numbered, insurrected in rebellious support. For centuries the English had lived side by side with their tolerant Saxon invaders whom the natives had gradually absorbed and under whom the islanders enjoyed relative freedom: and with Sweyn Estrithsen's invasion receiving such support from Gospatric and Waltheof, there was a real chance of replacing the hated Normans by the Danes whom the English at least understood.

The men of Stafford rose up, followed immediately by those of Chester, to slaughter every Norman they could ferret out. Cornwall rebelled against its lord, Robert of Mortain, the men of the West Country attacking Montacute where Robert was building his castle. Though Dorset followed suit, the business-oriented leaders of Exeter surprisingly held for the king, until help arrived from Bryan de Penthièvre. Montacute was relieved at the last moment by the energetic Geoffrey of Montrai who, galloping west from London, collected a loyal contingent of the fyrd from the towns through which he rode.

The fall of York, capital of the North, was a lethal blow to the king's authority. When the messengers appeared before William, he exploded with such rage that he ordered the immediate mutilation of the envoys. The witnesses of the atrocious cruelty meted out to these innocent bearers of bad tidings were left in no doubt that treason did not pay: William's obsessive fear of treachery became notorious and was to remain with him all his life.

Leaving his earls to deal with the lingering insurrections, the king quit the Welsh border where he had been suppressing Edric the Wild's latest uprising among the Welsh princes. Force-marching towards York, he slaughtered every male, human and animal alike, razed to the ground every dwelling, put to the torch the winter granaries. His savagery was deliberate: the tactics of Alençon repeated once again.

---

* Only William Malet, commander of one castle, and his family escaped and survived.

December 1069 was bitterly cold, wet and miserable. The bridge across the swollen Aire above Pontefract had been swept away when William's avenging force arrived. Faced by the Anglo-Danish force on the opposite side of the river, William was held up for three weeks, before one of his knights, on a reconnaissance patrol, discovered the ford at Castleford which he forced with his determined band of cavalrymen. King William, outflanking the disorganized allies, swept northwards into the smouldering city of York. He divided his force into two: the first, under his command, for York; the second, to attack the Danes in the Humber.

News of the king's approach had preceded him and split the Anglo-Danish allies. Edgar retreated north into the North Riding; Gospatric to 'St Cuthbert's land' and the wild Northumberland moors; Asbjoern weighed anchor and crossed to the northern bank of the Humber.

William had had time to reflect. His army and his previously irresistible cavalry were proving ineffective against this enemy who, having command of the sea, retained the initiative, striking when and where he chose, then disappearing into the mists. Since Hastings, the king had neglected his navy which was now non-existent. The omission was one which he was immediately to rectify.

The roving bands of Scottish marauders sweeping across the borders were led and fostered by a king in whose word William could no longer trust: Malcolm was contemptuously playing with words and time, while succouring England's enemies. His latest brilliant political move was to marry Edgar's sister, the astute Margaret, and thus ally himself directly to the throne of England. Malcolm had spent his youth at the Confessor's court. When, later, he wrested the Scottish throne from Macbeth, he was able to use to advantage his understanding of the English mind. This second marriage of his to the saintly Margaret could be the move to unite the two nations against the Norman Bastard. To Margaret's welcoming court across the Border fled thousands of Saxon and Nordic exiles with renewed hope.

King William, now forty-one, sensed that all he had achieved was about to slip from his grasp. If he and his valiant band of companions were to survive; if his dream of a unified Normandy and England was to become reality, this menace from the chill mists of the North must be eliminated utterly. But with only a few thousand Normans under his command to subdue the whole island, and with his previously invincible cavalry ineffective against the elusive enemy, how could the threat be destroyed for ever?

At York on 25 December 1069, King William and his knights heard mass together to celebrate the birthday of Jesus Christ. If his mind was tormented, he showed no sign: he had made his decision. On the morrow, he would issue his orders to his commanders. King Winter would be their ally. Combined, they could teach this treacherous, fickle foe a lesson it would never forget.

Through the open doorway of the stone hovel, Steward fitz Osbern heard the blizzard screaming through the bare branches. It was only three in the afternoon and the light was failing already. The stunted trees were ghostly skeletons where they bent to the prevailing wind: their frozen branches rattled like the bleached bones which the army had already passed on its homeward journey – grim evidence silently accusing the Norman murderers.

Gilbert of Erchembald, the Steward's faithful ex-*fidelis* who had stuck by him throughout the years, came stumbling through the low doorway, stooping to avoid the lintel. He was now thirty-six, his beard unkempt and already flecked grey. He kicked off his sodden boots, knocked the snow from his shoulders and began kneading his toes. Without a word, he collapsed on the heap of dung in the corner, the only spot where the snow had melted inside the hovel. In seconds he was asleep.

Fitz stayed on his feet, the only manner to remain awake while awaiting William. Occasionally peering outside, braving the cutting, driving snow, he could not now see the far side of the bridge: the blizzard was driving its flakes horizontally, like a shower of shining darts . . . the king should have returned by now, at least to shelter from the filthy weather.

19 February 1070: the last five weeks of horror had dragged like a nightmare with no ending – it was a month and a half since Christmas at York. The following day, William had summoned his commanders: they were to divide into sections, each leader being responsible to him personally that no man, woman, child nor beast was left alive. His orders were a licence to kill.

During that first half of January, several brave bands of Danes and English held out, but resistance soon crumbled. From then on, the retreat developed into a rout, the chase to a hunt, and finally, like ferrets after rabbits, became a sickening butchery. Leaving the East Riding to his commanders, and taking only Fitz with him as his deputy, William and his large force scoured south-west of York.

Sweeping south to Selby, then curving up to Saxton and Wetherby, he and his troops, with bloodied hands and loaded down with loot, were back in the city on the fourteenth. Four days for the armourers and blacksmiths to refurbish the equipment and then they were off again, up the Vale of York to Durham.

Those sixty-five miles to Durham were indelibly marked into the Steward's mind: it had been a hard march in atrocious weather. The bloody killing lasted almost a week, six sickening days of pitiless hard work, for butchery was a demanding job – hovels and barns were difficult to fire in this appalling winter. The least exacting days were when the weather was crisp and clear, but on that march to Durham the blizzards had howled throughout the long, terrible slog.

Nothing that moved was left alive: humans, cattle, even the fowls and dogs were slain. The swath of devastation cut by the Normans was forty miles wide through the Vale. Working in separate bands led by their mounted knights, the executioners left a scorched land of utter desolation behind them, driving their human quarry before them, leaving reserve patrols behind them to finish off any who had escaped. A soldier's work was a hard business, but this massacre, though vital to William's plan, was a disgusting, frightful affair . . . and fitz Osbern dipped back again into the hovel as another gust howled outside. They'd soon have to get the fires going or there'd be more dead soldiers in the morning. They could not risk slaughtering more horses for meat, because this ride across these merciless hills of the Pennines was taking a savage toll.

The king had decided to cross England through Wensleydale, joining the old westerly track at Leyburn, then to Aysgarth and up the river Ure to Hawes. The hardest section would be across Baugh Fell, before the track dropped off the Pennines and down into Sedburgh. He would then turn south, take the Lune valley down to Kirkby Lonsdale which he must reach before the end of the month, if his army was not to starve to death – and Fitz huffed on his numbed fingers, stamped his feet, by movement trying to prevent his leaden eyelids from dropping into sleep . . .

Today was his beloved daughter's birthday. Thank God Emma had not yet married Ralph of Gael; though she was twenty-two, it was not too late for her to change her mind. Her mother needed her now, with her health deteriorating so rapidly in Vaudreuil. Fitz did not trust Ralph: an upstart, too big for his boots. He had inherited last year the earldom of Norfolk from his father. But in spite of the obvious advantage the union might accrue, Fitz felt uneasy. Ralph was domineering, flamboyant – and Fitz's second son, Roger, was too easily influenced by him. The Steward shrugged his shoulders in resignation: Roger was a disappointment, as were so many of these youngsters. They were riding to riches upon the shoulders of their ageing fathers who had borne the heat and fury of the past ten years . . .

Fitz had seldom felt so low. Disgusted by this cruel campaign, ashamed at the part he was forced to take in it, it would have been more bearable if he could have news of his wife, Adeliza. Even this bloody campaign would be tolerable if only reports from home could be better. Strangely, morale had not entered William's calculations.

The sojourn in England had proved longer than the more staid married knights and troops had contracted for: four years had passed since the invasion fleet had sailed from St-Valéry. The wiser, like old Roger of Beaumont, had remained in Normandy, refusing to leave their homes. The lure of plunder and aggrandizement had overcome most, but these men had not calculated on losing their wives.

In Adeliza's last letter, though not actually complaining herself, she had listed those of her respected friends who had succumbed. Many of the proudest in the duchy were now cuckolding their errant spouses: more of a gambit, wrote Adeliza, to goad their absent husbands back to Normandy, than for the craving of the flesh – but Fitz had read between the lines.

Widows were marrying again, within days of the news from across the Channel of their men's death. Several respected lords in England had demanded repatriation: Hugh of Grandmesnil, the governor of Winchester; Humphrey of Tilleul, at Dover – brave men both. *'Vide chambre fait dame folle'* was all too true – and William had let them go. Many others were chancing to luck, finding solace in the arms of these fair-tressed, doe-eyed maidens who seemed eager enough to comfort their new masters. Normandy was a world away . . . and Fitz's mind was switching to the rumours of the king's fondness for the priest's daughter, when the white curtain outside the doorway darkened.

King William stamped on the frozen floor; with numbed fingers he unclasped his sword-belt, flung it against the wall, the clatter merely causing Gilbert to grunt 'midst his snores.

'They're getting a broth warmed up,' the king snapped. 'What the devil are my officers doing, if they can't get the men to look after themselves?' He turned angry eyes upon his friend, as he blew on his fingers: 'Fitz, I know you well: you're against me too, aren't you, over this march?' And throwing his outer cloak upon the muck, he collapsed against the wall, his feet stretched in front of him. The iced-up nose-guard of his helmet had formed a stalactite, a long white dagger before his face. Wearily he wrenched off his head-gear. 'Speak, my friend. Let's have the truth.'

Fitz held the ice-blue eyes:

'You know how to kill, sire.'

'What d'you mean?' William snapped back. 'I'm a bloody murderer?'

The Steward did not reply directly:

'Unlike me, you're capable of killing in cold blood to achieve your object.' He added softly, 'Sometimes it's your last resort.'

'Often it *is* the only way.' The king shouted the words against the howling tempest. 'By the time I've dealt with Chester, the North'll never rebel again.' He slumped, his huge head sinking on his chest. 'Don't think I'm liking the butchery, Fitz.'

'Sometimes, I wonder,' Fitz murmured, blowing on his fingers. 'You put so much effort into killing. Even the children . . .'

The king looked up, held his friend's gaze; then looked away, staring moodily through the darkening opening. To Fitz, the king seemed ten years older than the duke who had landed at Pevensey. There was no spare flesh on him; his frame was as tough as a wrestler's; his muscles like bands of steel, he could stay in the saddle so long. He was greying at the temples and there were white patches in his rusty beard which was frosted along the moustache and below the cracked lips. William was sinking into one of his moody silences from which nothing could rouse him. Fitz slid to the ground in weariness, sprawled upon his up-turned shield. He'd sleep while waiting for the squire to appear with the broth, but his mind would not rest in spite of weariness. They'd be up again before daylight, trudging south and west for Wensleydale: even William could not march through this night.

After Durham, where he'd left a garrison to start building the castle,* the king had taken his avengers south to the Tees. Thousands of the wretched rebels were dying from cold and starvation in the forests and on the moors. Fitz had seen their corpses, stiff where they fell, frozen in ice, as the Normans marched south again. Those who escaped were stumbling across the border into Scotland to be received by Malcolm's men; they were selling themselves into slavery, rather

---

* Only a quarter of a century later, the cathedral and castle at Durham were completed: proof of Norman energy and of continental influence.

than perish of starvation or be hacked to pieces by Norman steel. Others were scrambling south to reach the succour of the monasteries before weakness drove them to their final sleep. Marching south, William was already paying dearly for his punitive expedition: the scorched wastes could provide nothing off which his army could live. How many years would elapse before life could start again here? Fifteen, twenty? And what bitter memorial . . . could these English ever forgive, ever collaborate after this heinous campaign?

The king had been surprised during his two weeks of slaughter in the valley of the Tees. At the end of January, first Gospatric, then Edwin and Morcar had thrown themselves on William's mercy. Though still allowing the butchery to continue in the surrounding countryside, the king listened to their appeals but remained silent. And then at last the man for whom he was waiting demanded pardon, swore his allegiance: Earl Waltheof of Northumberland, the respected son of Siward and the natural leader around whom the men of the North were rallying, finally capitulated. There, where the banks of the Tees were white with snow and frost, Waltheof bent the knee in homage.

Perhaps the king had been nauseated by the savagery of his deliberate campaign? Whatever the real reason – and he had taken Fitz's advice – the king granted pardon, on condition that the rebels caused no further insurrection and departed peacefully to their homelands.

Once more, Fitz had witnessed this extraordinary side of his friend's character – ruthless cruelty being replaced by an impulsive magnanimity. Conscience perhaps, fear of divine retribution? Inexplicably, William offered the sanguine, crafty warrior the hand of his niece, Judith, in marriage. Arlette's grand-daughter was to unite Northumberland and Bernicia to the hated southerners of England. Waltheof was in no position to refuse. An emissary was already galloping south to Dover to fetch the girl from Normandy.

And so here was the king's army on the nineteenth of February 1070, on the safe side of the Leven. If the king could reach Chester before Edric's rebels installed themselves in the castle, the Normans would have achieved their object. The traditional Nordic freedom, especially that of the freemen 'to go with their land', would end under the yoke of Norman feudalism. The king, through his law officers of state, could enforce his will. The age-long separation by the Danelaw in the east and north-east from the king of England would be annulled for ever; more immediately, the North could not, for a long time, rebel again. A breathing-space long enough, William hoped, in which the English could be bludgeoned to adopt the *mores* of their Norman overlords. The king had already drawn up the structure of his *curia regis*, the legal system through which he would enforce his rule. The English already had their shires, their hundreds and their respective courts through which justice and law could be administered. William would sensibly continue to rule through them, with his Justices of Assize and Justices in Eyre who made their circuit every seven years. But Fitz and many of the senior barons were worried that the king was proceeding too rapidly, was over-confident of his ability to harness Anglo-Saxon sentiment. Several of the Norman lords had approached the Steward already, complaining that the king's intention would be restricting the barons' power. They had agreed to back the Bastard on his invasion, only if their careers and fortunes would benefit, had they not? To many barons, only the king's family and closest friends were benefiting – and hugely . . . William stirred, was turning his morose gaze upon his friend:

'I can read your thoughts,' he grunted. He propped himself on one elbow. 'Sometimes you go too far, Fitz. You're making it all too clear to others that you disapprove of this campaign.'

The Steward nodded towards the other occupant of the bothy. 'Gilbert's there, sire,' he whispered. 'We'd better continue the discussion on the march.'

The king nodded, his eyes on the prostrate form in the corner. 'Gilbert's got stamina,' he remarked quietly. 'He rode straight up from Dover. They sent him on from York with the dispatches.' William was hesitating, about to add something, then thought better of it. Too obviously, he was switching the conversation:

'What d'you advise, Fitz?' he asked, glancing from beneath his guarded eyes. 'Do I punish the mutineers, or don't I?'

Each day several mercenaries and now even a few Normans were refusing to continue this pitiless march: the malaise could become contagious.

'If you punish, sire, you'll only be harbouring resentful men among the troops. The disaffection could spread.'

'I have no need of cowards,' William snapped. 'Let 'em desert.'

Fitz nodded: 'Winter'll take care of the deserters.'

William was looking up again with that guarded, secret glance. Suddenly, he seemed to come to a decision. Clumsily he climbed to his feet. He stood before his friend, staring him straight in the eye:

'Gilbert – ' he said softly, jerking his head towards the recumbent body on the floor ' – I told him to wait for me before handing you the letter.' He stretched out his arm, laid his hand on Fitz's shoulder. 'Emma's written to you.'

The Steward noted the pain in his friend's eyes, a fleeting emotion, seldom seen. Fitz felt the jab of fear, the thumping and quickening of his heart. For so long he'd rejected the inevitable. He'd loved her so deeply, perhaps because they'd shared so much together for so long. So she had left him, then, to make her last journey without him? He felt an irrational anger surging within him:

'Adeliza's dead?' He posed the question brutally, taking a perverted pleasure in watching this man, this tyrant whom he knew as friend, being forced to display some human emotion.

'Emma was with her,' was all William could mutter. 'Adeliza gave her the letter for you, just before she lost consciousness.' His hand dropped listlessly from his Steward's shoulder.

''Tis nearly five years since . . .' Fitz could not go on. He swung on his heel, pulled his cloak about him and with blind eyes stumbled out into the driving, darkening blizzard.

By the time the king's force reached Mossdale Moor, all thoughts of harassing the countryside had vanished. The villages, hearing of the avenging army's advance, were deserted, even the women and children vanishing into the snow, rather than have to face the detested enemy. Barns were empty, bothies void, sheep loosed into the drifts. The perpetual gales howling across the tops piled up the snow into twenty-foot drifts, blocking the track in the open stretches. The king's foot-soldiers were dropping like flies, to be left where they were, swiftly freezing solid, carrion for the prowling wolves and circling buzzards, let alone the crazed dalesmen. If it had not been for the food which the horses provided, the Norman army would never have reached the shelter of Sedburgh and the Lune valley – it was only that meat and the relentless determination of their indomitable leader which finally brought to an end the terrible march across the Pennines. The struggle to remain alive snapped Fitz from his bout of depression after the news of his wife's death. When at last the army reached Kirkby Lonsdale on the last day of February, he had shrugged off the last trace of self-pity.

The king's priest celebrated mass in that serene, deserted town and then, without waiting for the sick, William's force pressed on south to Chester which they reached before Edric the Wild and his Welsh rebels. The astonished citizens of Chester readily capitulated. William left a garrison to start building the castle and then, on 5 March, swept south-eastwards for Stafford. His speed again decisive, the surprised rebels surrendered the town to him on the seventh of March.

The devastated countryside through which he had marched was devoid of food, having been laid waste by his troops only ten weeks earlier. Resting, refurbishing and laying down his plans for the inevitable castle took thirteen days. On 20 March, William set forth from Stafford on the final stretch of his punitive campaign. Ignoring the putrefying corpses from his earlier massacres, the king led the survivors of his Norman army to Salisbury which capitulated on 25 March. Dispatching Roger of Montgomery as earl of Shrewsbury, and Gherbrod, the Fleming, as earl of Chester to subdue the Welsh border, William completed the last act of his expedition.

The Danes were realists. Realizing that all English resistance had been quelled, Asbjoern cannily agreed to quit the Humber in return for William's bribe of gold and booty. A fragile peace existed for the first time throughout William's kingdom. He could turn his mind to the synod he had organized three months earlier to convene at Winchester, but one final act remained. He dismissed his exhausted army, but punished the surviving mutineers by retaining them for an additional forty days. On 26 March the king and his commanders left Salisbury for England's ancient capital. He arrived at Winchester on the evening of 27 March, which allowed him a week to prepare for the significant changes he had so long intended.

The synod opened on 4 April 1070. Steward fitz Osbern, who had been involved with organizing this ecclesiastical assembly even during the campaign, had never admired his friend more: addressing this august assembly was not the arrogant, ruthless commander, but instead, the suave diplomat, conciliatory but firm. First, he dismissed the loathsome Archbishop Stigand, using the accusations of his fellow prelates as condemnation. Taking advantage of this ecclesiastical climate, William also rid the Church of other dubious Anglo-Saxon bishops, replacing them with Norman clerics in whom he could place his trust. To head them all, he invited his trusted Lanfranc from Caen to become archbishop of Canterbury, an appointment which could not fail to please Rome. The humiliated Stigand was allowed to depart for the sanctuary of Malcolm's Scotland.

But even before the synod was ending at Winchester, news arrived that King Malcolm was again sweeping south into Cumbria and

Cleveland, ravaging and pillaging, determined to fill the vacuum left by William's carnage. In co-ordination, King Sweyn of Denmark decided to cross and join forces with his brother, Asbjœrn, who had returned to the Humber now that the Scots were loose. Sweyn sailed his fleet down to the Wash where he landed to fortify the Isle of Ely. The men of Lincolnshire, roused by their leader, Hereward, a dashing *thegn* whom they called 'the Wake', swept south and put Peterborough and its abbey to the torch. East Anglia and the Fens were rallying to this charismatic outlaw, when William succeeded in bribing Sweyn to leave the English shores for good. The Danes sailed back to their land, their ships loaded to the gunwales with treasure and booty.

King William of England, duke of Normandy, had more pressing anxieties on his mind than the subjugation of an outlaw in the Fens. In his duchy across the Channel, the news was disturbing: Maine was in turmoil, a revolt having dangerous overtones. King Philip I of France, now reaching adulthood, was displaying the deviousness in his character by exploiting to his own advantage the absence of his powerful neighbour. It was in the late summer of 1070 that King William sent for his earl of Hereford, his most trusted friend.

'Fitz,' he announced, 'I've got to deal with Malcolm, put an end to Hereward. I can't leave my kingdom.'

The grey-haired earl smiled. He never volunteered directly.

'Things are quiet on my Welsh border, sire,' he said. 'Gilbert has things in hand. He's content now that his lady's joined him.'

'How soon can you cross the Channel to aid my queen? To supervise the duchy, restore order in Maine?'

'When you command, sire. I've no ties now.'

'Give my love to my lady Matilda, Fitz,' William said. 'Tell her I wish that I could come myself.'

The distinguished earl with the silvering hair clasped his friend's hand:

'It's as well my queen loves her king,' he smiled. 'A lone widower is a dangerous emissary.'

The king watched his companion leaving the chamber. The great earl was humming happily to himself as he disappeared through the silken curtains. It was the last sight of the friend he had known from childhood which the king was to have.

23

A STAR EXTINGUISHED

'Can I go back with the others, uncle?'

A gentle smile creased Steward Osbern's face as he glanced at the boy on the piebald pony trotting at his side.

'Yes, Arnoulf. Stay on the path. Tell 'em I'll halt in the woods before we reach Cassel.'

He reined in his mount, watched his new ward cantering back to the small force, the same ten knights he'd brought up with him from Normandy. He nudged his horse forward again across this iron-hard, frosty flat plain of Flanders. He needed to reconnoitre this region thoroughly, because the decisive fight between the Frisian and himself must surely take place here. He chuckled aloud to himself, as happy a warrior as ever he had been, even without his Adeliza, for her memory was fading with time. Whoever would have dreamed that he'd find himself up here, in this dreary province, on a cold January day of 1071?

When William had dispatched him back to Normandy to help Matilda, he'd not realized how serious the state of affairs in Maine had become. The queen and her ageing counsellor, Roger of Beaumont, were at Rouen, but Fitz had moved her down at once to Caen where he could keep a closer watch on developments at Le Mans, the centre of the trouble. He wished William could have dealt with it, but Malcolm in Scotland and Hereward in the Fens were threats too dangerous to be left to anyone but the king.

True, William had, through the dubious quality of brutal ruthlessness, just survived the first organized resistance to his Norman invasion of England. By the end of last year, not only were the principal cities in the kingdom safely in his hands but the North was cowed: it would be only a matter of time before Hereward's outlaws in the Fens would be brought to heel. Though Morcar had deserted to join the East Anglian rebels, William had been deeply grieved that the English earl whom he admired most, Edwin, had also for the second time departed the king's court to escape to Scotland.

On his ride north, Edwin's escort had betrayed him, taking him prisoner and hoping for reward when they returned the earl to the king. On the return journey south, Edwin escaped with twenty of his followers to ride furiously towards the sea. His pursuers hot on his heels, he had taken an erratic route towards a river estuary which, being a spring tide, he could not ford. Turning at bay he fought until the last man, until finally overwhelmed himself. His pursuers sliced off his head and with it rode to London to the king's court. To their chagrin, William hurled them from his presence and flung them into life banishment. On seeing the horrible evidence of his friend's death, he broke down, the only occasion his courtiers had ever seen their king weeping.

The fortunes of the duchy and the kingdom were now inextricably linked, the successes of one counter-balancing the failures of the other. Thus, while William was succeeding in subduing his kingdom, his continental enemies were profiting by his absence in stirring up trouble on the frontiers of his duchy. It was only William's energetic reaction to these threats from across the North Sea, from the Channel and Flanders, from over the Scottish border – and his unchallenged cavalry – which gave the king the means of holding together his condominium.

The citizens of Le Mans had first revolted in 1069, due to the ambitions of a Ligurian noble named Azzo. His wife was Gersendis, the long-dead Count Hugh of Maine's sister. With little difficulty and much bribing, Azzo managed to persuade the influential confederation of Angevin barons to support the rebelling citizens of Le Mans; and to adopt his young son, Hugh, as count of Maine. Geoffrey of Mayenne, his eye always on the Normandy border, eagerly joined the insurrection which the Norman garrison at Le Mans was incapable of crushing. In this fight, Duke William's representative was killed; and the rebels banished many Norman knights, including William of La Ferté-Macé, Odo's brother-in-law. The king of England and duke of Normandy could not now ignore the threat to the duchy.

Azzo returned to his sunny home in Liguria, leaving his wife and son at Le Mans, under the guardianship of Geoffrey of Mayenne. Gersendis promptly became Geoffrey's mistress. But even under Geoffrey's rule, the insatiable men of Le Mans revolted a year later to form the first *commune* in history. Geoffrey was forced to accept the new development but, after treachery from both sides, finally re-entered Le Mans in December of 1070, with his new countess, Gersendis. Maine was now a formidable base from which the enemies of the duchy could be attacked. A month later Fitz had arrived in Normandy to deal with the dangerous situation.

His first meeting with Matilda after five years had shocked him. She was, it was true, now thirty-nine, a difficult age for any woman. Henry, her last child, born in England, was toddling, but it was more the affairs of state than her lonely responsibilities in the upbringing of her large family which had aged her so much. Her lithe figure had thickened and, with her dumpiness, the spring seemed to have gone from her step – and the fire from her spirit. William had sent her back to Normandy a grass widow, more as an example to the majority of the randy wives who were openly cuckolding their errant husbands in England, than to rule the duchy. And she, a hot-blooded woman if ever there was one, now resented her role: she was longing for the comfort of her absent partner. During those long winter evenings, the lonely queen had poured out her heart to Fitz.

Later, one hot May evening, leaving her court behind her in Caen, she'd taken the bridle path with him, down the Orne to the estuary to the sea. She'd talked to the boat-builders in the little tidal haven of Bénouville where they loaded the stone, chatted with the fishermen on the shore at sandy Houistreham which the Saxon visitors still called 'Wester Ham', the hamlet on the western side of the estuary. She called on the abbess there, and investigated a complaint about the failure of the townsfolk to light the beacon on the church tower for the fishermen at night. On the return ride, they had spoken little, the feeling between them vibrant with longing. Had he not been her husband's firmest friend, he could not have resisted her unspoken invitation. The next day he had left for Le Mans, the problems of which were to embroil them both for all that summer – and then had sprung this amazing development which was responsible for him being here in Flanders today, 22 January 1071 . . .

On 16 July, died Baldwin VI, the count of Flanders and William's brother-in-law, only five weeks after Sweyn had finally sailed from England's shores. Baldwin's widow, the gracious Richildis, was left with their two young sons, Arnoulf and Baldwin and – inevitably – the horny problem of succession. Baldwin VI's brother was Robert, the Frisian who had married Florence of Holland whose province abutted the eastern border of Flanders. The Frisian was claiming to be the rightful count of Flanders and would remain so until his young nephew, Baldwin, became of age. Richildis scornfully rejected the

Frisian's presumption: she would remain the regent of Flanders until her first-born son, Arnoulf, reached manhood. To reinforce her determination, the spirited Richildis sought help. First, she turned to the king of France: the wily Philip was only too pleased to stir up trouble along Normandy's eastern borders . . .

Trotting serenely towards the woods ahead of him, Fitz smiled wistfully to himself. He had never realized that his reputation had traversed the duchy's borders: apparently, Richildis had never forgotten him since those meetings in their respective courts before she married Baldwin VI. Though she was thirteen years younger than Fitz, she had always cherished a tender corner in her heart for the lean, chivalrous Steward, and once again Fitz nostalgically recalled the day when the long missive arrived from her, the same evening when he'd discussed the extraordinary proposal with Matilda.

Richildis was proposing marriage with William fitz Osbern: she would make her young Arnoulf Fitz's ward, until the boy was old enough to become count. Would her trusted friend come to her assistance, marry her and defend Flanders against the rapacious Frisian?

Though she could hardly write thus of herself, she was a lovely creature in the rich bloom of womanhood. So Fitz, for too long a solitary widower – and the friends of his own generation becoming scarcer – had welcomed Richildis' proposition. King William had concurred with Fitz's decision; but Matilda had not concealed her misgivings when he had set out gaily from Rouen a fortnight ago with ten of his younger warriors, a knight-errant himself, a song on his lips, and with love and adventure beckoning him from Lille . . .

Fitz reined in as the sunless edge of the wood neared. He leaned on the pommel of his saddle, turned to wait for the troop of cavalry trotting a mile behind to catch up with him. His years of campaigning had taught him the basic discipline of warfare . . . and the delicious memories of these last few days and nights flooded into his mind.

He had thought that his meeting with her would have been embarrassing. But Richildis, far from being the demure widow, had welcomed him with spontaneous fervour, her courtiers doing all they could to entertain his small contingent of knights and squires. And she herself? Again that warm glow seeped through him: perhaps it was the age difference, the *démon de midi*, but he'd never known before such passion as she had offered him. Adeliza had been a good wife and mother; Richildis was adding that element of joy to his life which he

292

had always dreamed could exist between man and woman, but which had evaded him until he'd met his new bride. She could still give him a son – and teasing him, she had reminded him of the other reason for his journey to Lille.

The Frisian was massing his forces in Hainault and, yesterday, contingents of his had been sighted advancing brazenly up the right bank of the Yser. Fitz had already started moving the Flemings north-westward towards Cassel which was the reason for today's reconnaissance of the countryside. And beckoning the young boy, Arnoulf, on his pony at the head of the small troop, Steward fitz Osbern nudged his horse towards the leafless trees.

He felt the dank chill of the plain enveloping them as they were forced into single file by the track through the thick wood. The further he entered the narrower became the track until, spurring his mount through a boggy morass leading to a fork in the bridle-path, he asked himself whether it was worth persevering. As he reined in, he heard shouts behind him.

For an instant he sat rigid, waiting for the squire behind him to appear through the scrub. As he turned, he heard the smashing of branches, the squelching of mud. He heard the clash of steel, a boy screaming. As he grabbed for his sword, wrenched to turn his horse, an excruciating pain stabbed between his shoulder-blades . . .

They found the body later, face down in the slush, the haft of a spear sticking upright: twenty paces behind him, the remains of the boy, Arnoulf, hacked to pieces alongside his pony. Of the ambushed troops, only two knights escaped to carry the news back to Lille.

The distraught countess buried William fitz Osbern, earl of Hereford, Steward of Normandy, at Cormeilles. On 22 February 1071, her Flemish army was defeated at Cassel by Robert the Frisian, who became count of Flanders. The demented Richildis took the veil and remained in a nunnery for the remainder of her mortal days.

24

LE DÉMON DE MIDI

King William was himself without the solace of his partner when the news of the earl of Hereford's death reached England. William fitz Osbern, William's staunch companion and counsellor since childhood, was no more. With characteristic stubbornness and perverse loyalty to the memory of his friend, King William refused to acknowledge Robert the Frisian as the new count of Flanders.

Philip I of France, seizing the opportunity to exploit the difficulties of his powerful neighbour, the king-duke, promptly supported the Frisian, albeit temporarily. While Norman knights were crusading on the continent for the pope against the Saracen infidel, William still had not succeeded in bringing peace to his kingdom.

Though his palatinate earldoms of Chester, Shrewsbury and Hereford were successfully keeping the Welsh at bay, the anarchy north of the Tyne still posed a major threat to England, in spite of the Danes' final departure during the summer of 1071. King Malcolm of Scotland's marriage to the saintly Margaret and his sustenance of her brother, Edgar, the atheling, at the Scottish court posed a continuous challenge to William from across the undefined Scottish border. William's devastation of the North during the winter of 1069-70 had left a void north of the Tyne which King Malcolm was already exploiting. Cumbria and Northumberland were, Malcolm claimed, part of Scotland.

During that summer and autumn of 1071, William consolidated the peace he had imposed on England by finally crushing the revolt in the Fens: by October, Hereward the Wake had been vanquished and calm returned to East Anglia. But this condominium was now being threatened on more than one front – from Scotland and from Maine. Taking his brother Odo, now the earl of Kent, with him, in the new year of 1072 the king crossed the Channel. He found the situation in Maine worse than he had feared. Geoffrey of Mayenne and Gersendis were incapable of subduing the intractable citizens of Le Mans who, it seemed, were inviting 'The Requin', the odious young

Fulk, count of Anjou, to replace their governor. Fulk, no replica of his doughty predecessor, Geoffrey Martel, was nevertheless a dangerous threat: Philip I was backing him.

William was facing the same dilemma as had King Harold – and the Bastard reacted similarly. Speed was the essence and, by Easter, William was back in London. Risking all, he would deal first with Malcolm.

During that summer of 1072, King William prepared his astounding combined operation against the Scottish enemy. He rebuilt his fleet which sailed at the end of August to rendezvous with his army in the Firth of Tay. Leading a large force of Norman knights and English thegns, William advanced through Durham into Scotland, hoping to bring Malcolm to action in the cavalry-country of the Lothians. But the Scots melted into the mists, ill-disposed to co-operate with William's strategy. Fording the Forth below Stirling, William struck north-east up Strath Allan to unite with his fleet sheltering in the lee of Mugdrum island, at the mouth of the Earn river in the Firth of Tay.

King Malcolm, convinced of the futility of further resistance in the face of such a bold combined operation, was relieved to treat with the English king at Abernethy, within sight of the fleet. As proof of his recognition of William as king of England, including Cumbria and Northumberland, he handed over hostages to the English king; for good measure, he also banished the Atheling and his family who thereupon took refuge with the Frisian in Flanders. Before the Christmas of 1072, William's condominium stretched from Lothian in Scotland to Le Mans on Normandy's southern border, a distance of six hundred miles north and south; from Flanders to Brittany, east and west, three hundred: a vast territory to defend. With his northern border now secure, he raced south again to deal with the trouble erupting in Maine.

During his march, he halted on 1 November at Durham to confer with the Lorraine priest he had made bishop of this turbulent town. The energetic and diplomatic Walchere had brought peace to the region by bringing Anglo-Saxon and Norman together; in particular, he had fostered amity with his volatile neighbour, Waltheof, the recently appointed earl of Northumberland. Satisfied, the king continued south to raise his army. In January, 1073, he crossed the Channel with his combined force of Normans and English to march directly on Maine.

Philip I was succeeding with his subversive politics. Backed in the east by the Frisian, Philip was now actively supporting Fulk's advance on Le Mans whose citizens had finally flung out Geoffrey of Mayenne and Gersendis. The king-duke's duchy was now menaced from east and west.

William struck swiftly.

During the last week of March, Le Mans fell to his joint army, his English contingent having acquitted itself with honour. Fulk slipped back into Anjou where during that summer he, Philip and the Frisian combined against William.

The king was forty-five years old, his queen forty-one when, on his march back from Maine, they enjoyed a rare interlude together in their castle at Bonneville-sur-Touques. But, though conceiving her last child there, (Matilda, to be born in the New Year of 1074) the serenity they had always enjoyed in this, their favourite home, had not materialized, their happiness soured by worries over their first-born son.

Robert was now twenty-one and of age. His disappointing behaviour was blighting their love for each other – and, for the first time, Matilda sensed that the rumours she had heard of her husband's dalliance with an English priest's daughter, might have foundation. The seed of jealousy germinated at Bonneville, began to poison her feelings for the man she had loved for twenty-two years and for whom she had borne nine children. Coupled with her distrust was her abhorrence of her husband's cruelties; punishments perpetrated, he'd insisted, to impose law and order throughout his kingdom.

And then, for the remainder of that year, after the succession of the great Gregory VII to the papacy, William had been totally involved with state affairs: against all the pressures exerted by Gregory, William had insisted on the right of the king of England to appoint his own bishops, a policy which Lanfranc at Canterbury had genuinely supported.

In 1074, King William's enemies began to act in concert, ably orchestrated by the wily king of France. In 1072, Philip had deliberately forged a closer link with Flanders by marrying Bertha, the Frisian's half-sister. Then, in 1074, after Malcolm had invited Edgar back to his Scottish court, William realized that, combining their attacks at either extremity of his condominium, his foes were determined to destroy him. Philip of France gave Montreuil-sur-Mer to Edgar who thenceforward possessed a port on the Flanders frontier whence he could mount a Danish-inspired invasion against England.

To counter the threat, William returned briefly to England. He extended a hand in friendship to Edgar by inviting him, his wife and family, back to the English court. Philip, his threat foiled, seized upon the promising opportunity which then presented itself in Brittany: one of the king's most powerful barons, Ralph of Gael, earl of Norfolk, had decided to revolt in Brittany where he was a considerable land-owner. The earl belonged to

Philip's rising generation: Robert, the king's son and now officially duke of Normandy; Edgar, the atheling; Fulk, the Requin; the dead fitz Osbern's son, Roger of Breteuil, who had succeeded his father as earl of Hereford – all were frustrated and resentful of the control which their ageing fathers exerted over them.

Ralph of Gael was a natural leader, a flamboyant young man around whom the new youth naturally rallied. Having caused trouble in Brittany by inciting his Bretons to overthrow William's governor, Hoel of Cornouailles, Ralph decided to emulate in England the success he was enjoying in Brittany. He would rally the new generation to his side; to grasp the rights the Normans should be enjoying in England but which were negated by the King's policy of co-operation with the Anglo-Saxons, Ralph would overthrow William, who in 1075 was forty-seven years old and growing corpulent.

The new earl of Hereford, Roger of Breteuil, had a sister, Emma, whom Ralph was determined to marry. The intended match was forbidden by the king who could not tolerate the union of his principal earldom to that of the rebellious earl of Norfolk.

Ralph, who had an inflated opinion of his own influence, decided to persevere, and persuaded the weak Roger to continue with the disastrous plan. His northern neighbour was the illustrious earl of Northumberland, Waltheof, whom the king held in such high esteem. With Waltheof's inexplicable connivance, at Exning, ten miles north-east of Cambridge, the first act of the rebellion took place. Ralph married Emma, among the secret witnesses being Roger and Waltheof. Open revolt was breaking out.

The king was in Normandy, having left his kingdom under the regency of his great archbishop of Canterbury. Lanfranc thereupon dispatched a messenger to his king: William should remain in Normandy to deal with Maine, while allowing his English lords to crush the rebellion of the Northern earls. Through the action of both the English and Norman bishops, earls and barons, Lanfranc succeeded in containing the two rebellious earldoms and prevented them from uniting. Ralph was almost trapped in Norwich, but managed to escape to Flanders, leaving his wife in command of the castle of Norwich. There he expedited the support promised by Canute, Sweyn Estrithsen's son, who had become king of Denmark on his father's death. Ralph then returned to Brittany to whip up further support for his revolt against the southern wing of the Norman-English condominium. Emma, after resisting valorously, finally agreed to cede Norwich castle on condition that she would be allowed to depart with dignity to rejoin her husband in Brittany.

Canute, having arrived with an armada of two hundred ships off

Yarmouth, found that he had made his landfall just too late, Norwich having fallen. He thereupon sailed north to the Humber where, after plundering York and the East Riding, he returned to Denmark, his long ships laden with booty. Archbishop Lanfranc and his loyal Norman-English had coped with the crisis without the presence of their king.

Before dealing with Ralph and his Bretons the king returned to England during Christmas week of 1075 to punish the rebels, to dispense a justice most certainly to be heeded by all his people. He jailed the foolish Waltheof at Winchester while pondering whether this great earl should pay the ultimate penalty. Those of Ralph's Bretons who had crossed the sea to support their lord's rebellion were ruthlessly executed.

At first, the king could not bring himself to punish the feeble Roger, son of his life-long friend, William fitz Osbern, with the severity meted to the other traitors. Roger of Breteuil was deprived of his lands and his earldom, but was allowed astonishing latitude in the restriction of his liberty: the king hoped that with the passing of time he would be able to restore freedom to the dead Fitz's son. In one of those magnanimous gestures of William's, at Easter, before returning to Normandy, he visited the young man. The king carried with him the gift of a magnificent silk-lined fur cloak: this unspoken gesture would be understood, he hoped, by the ill-advised Roger for the regret it represented. But the perverse son hurled the cloak into the blazing fire. In a cold fury at the insult, William thereupon committed Roger to close imprisonment for life.

Before the king sailed back to Normandy to deal with Ralph's Bretons, rumours were confirmed of Waltheof's involvement in the earls' rebellion. With the earl awaiting sentence in Winchester gaol, his wife, Judith, approached her uncle to disclose that Waltheof had, in fact, been present at Exning for Ralph's marriage to Emma where plans for the rebellion had been finalized.

The legendary warrior had been broken by the suspense of his solitary wait in Winchester gaol. Confessing his guilt, he swore life-long allegiance to his king. He abjectly bartered for his life by promising to exchange his huge fortune for the pardon he craved. Despite Lanfranc's intercession, the king's obsessional fear of treachery decided Waltheof's fate: the earl whose qualities William had admired so much was to pay forfeit for his treason with his life. Leaving the execution to Winchester's military governor, the king departed forthwith for his campaign in Brittany.

The man the soldiers dragged from Winchester's dungeon on 31 May 1076 was unrecognizable as the once-proud earl of Northampton and Huntingdon. Emaciated, parchment-faced, the scare-crow grovelling at his executioners' feet once more craved pardon, implored for his life. The military men, who for months had considered the traitor's existence as a potential danger to the kingdom, hauled the stumbling, pathetic prisoner to the top of St Giles' hill. There, as the sun rose above the downs to the east of the town, he besought his captors time in which to recite his last pater noster. He fell to his knees, his lips murmuring the prayer. He reached the word temptation when the sword blade flashed, severing his head from his body.

The English, as with Hereward and many of their resistance leaders, wove a legend about their colourful martyr who had fought like a beast of the forest in defence of their homeland. His decapitated body was buried in his native Lincolnshire soil, in the abbey of Crowland. Years later, the monks were recounting that the decapitated head had continued to recite the pater noster until the end of the prayer.

King William, secure now from possible rebellion, was forty-eight when he crossed the Channel to ride with his combined Anglo-Saxon and Norman force against the Bretons who, under Ralph of Gael's leadership and with Philip's support, were attacking the duchy's western flank. In September, Fulk had advanced from Anjou to join the rebels. Ralph had moved north to support the Breton lord, Geoffrey of Granon, against Hoel of Brittany who had dispatched a messenger to England for immediate aid from King William. The rebels installed themselves in Dol to await reinforcements from Philip 1: the French king was himself marching from Poitiers to relieve Ralph and Geoffrey who were by now encircled and besieged by the king-duke.

It was essential for William to crush this serious threat to his duchy: if he failed, not only would Normandy's western border be exposed to a powerful, allied invasion force, but a failure in his duchy would once again encourage enemies in his English kingdom.

Supervising his siege of Dol, William's thoughts must have been particularly bitter when Philip was first sighted at the head of his vast army marching to the town's relief. It was only twelve years since he and Harold Godwineson had together also laid siege to this strategically important town. William had come a long way since then – but now, all for which he had fought was at risk. He had not foreseen this massive French intervention. For the first time in twenty years he was compelled to retire. He lifted the siege of Dol and retreated, leaving behind him many dead, casualties and prisoners. Humiliated, the bastard king-duke retraced his steps dejectedly into the interior of his duchy, after twenty victorious years.

He needed his Mahault desperately: she was the only living person to whom he could turn and trust totally – and she would give him the *comfort for which he yearned. They would escape again to Bonneville together – was it already two and a half years since at Bonneville they'd conceived their little Matilda, his 'second Mahault', as he called their last child? And seeing again, from the summit of the Thury track, the great plain of Caen opening before him, windswept and bare on this dreary November evening, he hoped that his messengers had reached the queen in time: he longed to see her tiny silhouette again, waiting there to welcome him at the drawbridge of the castle's great gate overlooking the river Touques. She would have, as usual, everything planned as he liked – but on this occasion, he'd command no fuss, no pomp. He needed her, no one else, however disloyal he'd been to her at times.*

It was one of those brittle, sunny days in March which Matilda loved so much. Here, in Roger of Calcège's castle-home at l'Aigle* in the green, rolling country of the Ouche with its valleys, silver trout streams, budding woods and gorse, William and she were trying to snatch a few days of relative peace after the depressing winter; and (who knew?) this could be one of the last and rare occasions when she could enjoy the presence of most of her family around her. She could hear them rollicking, like the wild brood they were, in the warm sunlight of the courtyard. Queen Matilda of England and duchess of Normandy lay back on the long couch by the window, revelling in this moment of serenity while her husband strode up and down the balcony with Roger Calcège. From time to time they would halt and William would point to his brood, most of the family of ten she had given him, all conceived in love, excepting the last whom William had insisted on christening after his wife – the result, perhaps, of her jealousy after his last long separation in England from her. She'd tackled him about the gossip she'd learned from Robert (was he *really* twenty-*five* already?) of his father's friendship with the daughter of an English priest. She'd managed to conceal from William the burning jealousy she'd suffered, and her own consequent lapse during those long years, especially with her devoted squire: young Samson, the Breton with the slow smile, the broad shoulders and slender hips – and Queen Matilda drowsily bathed in the seductive sunlight, listening to the first bees working in the creeper, hearing the happy cries of her children . . . Little Matilda, the result of their reconciliation at Bonneville on his return from suppressing the first Maine rebellion, was talking now and was playing happily

* The town of l'Aigle was named after a giant eagle's nest found in the adjoining forest.

with her nurse on the balcony, out of the wind and under her father's proud eye as he conversed with his host.

The older she became, the swifter the months slipped past: six years since her devoted Fitz had been killed – and, already, four months since that dreadful evening when she'd welcomed her husband back from his defeat at Dol. The dreary chill of that November dusk at Bonneville would remain with her for ever: who could guess, watching William here in the sunlight, laughing with Roger, that the first serious quarrel of their marriage had flared during those two days in what had always been their favourite retreat? Instead of giving him the comfort, the reassurance he craved after his Dol humiliation, her jealousy had welled to the surface again; their mutual unhappiness and disappointment with their first-born, Robert, had worsened, each blaming the other. William accused her of having spoilt him; of having failed to check Robert's arrogance and ambition; of condoning the dissolute and irresponsible friends with whom Robert surrounded himself. With bitter recrimination, she had retaliated that their eldest son's conduct was due entirely to lack of a father's love and influence. Though Robert had since 1063 been officially the count of Maine, and though in 1067 William had consigned to him, under his mother, the peaceful ruling of the duchy, Robert had, like any self-respecting spirited youth, resented his role of representing only his father's shadow . . . and Matilda sighed when she heard her first-born yelling angrily at his brothers and sisters outside in the courtyard.

Robert was *too* likeable – tough, short-legged – which was why even his father sometimes affectionately called him 'Short-arse' – he could never say 'no' to even the most obvious scroungers among his companions. He revelled in popularity, hated remaining his father's puppet. Of course, the subtle and ambitious coterie with which Robert had surrounded himself was only too eager to manipulate him to their advantage. And, through warnings from the older men, the fathers of this up-and-coming generation, William was very much aware of the direction in which the wind was blowing.

Matilda's heart ached for her husband's understanding. She longed to conciliate these distressing differences within their family – but how could she combat the constant influence of Philip I who, professing to be Robert's friend, was now bracing his muscles as king of France? Philip was enthusiastically urging Robert to stand up for his rights against his father; was revelling in welcoming Robert's wild friends to the French court – their long hair, their manicured hands, their effeminate concern with appearances, a flagrant contempt for tradition led by the unwholesome Fulk of Anjou, the Requin, with his fashionable long, curling-toed boots. And sick at heart, Matilda sighed again, worn out by the futility of it all: appearances *did* matter at court and it grieved her to watch the new generation ridiculing their fathers, those men who had gained the wealth and power which their sons were now enjoying, exploiting and squandering.

In her day, too, youth's ardour was satisfied joyfully by the eminently satisfactory Danish Custom. But now – ah, now . . . ! and she twitched a twisted, secret smile. Joy had turned to lust; the liberty enjoyed in youth had now become licence for the pursuit of pleasure, spontaneity had become calculated debauch; fun of the chase bored depravity, each young blood frenziedly trying to out-shock his fellow. Fulk had started the blaze; Philip fanned it, grinning while the others fluttered like moths around their pliant leader – the charming Robert, prospective heir to the duchy of Normandy and the kingdom of England.

It was not unremarkable that so many young gallants swarmed to 'Short-arse's' amusing court. Edgar, the atheling, with his wife; Ralph of Gael and his Emma – Fitz's daughter – who were now rebelling again in Brittany; William of Breteuil, Fitz's elder son; Hugh of Grand-mesnil's two sons; Robert of Bellême, son of Roger of Montgomery and the disgusting Mabel; Hugh of Châteauneuf. Rémalart, Robert of Bellême's brother-in-law, had even lent two castles in which Robert's friends could disport themselves – sad, but inevitable, reflected Matilda. Great men's sons – history had a habit of repeating itself, from Nero onwards – but watching the sickening process was destroying her happiness.

Robert's ambition was menacing the stability of England and the duchy. His supporters wished to see Robert Short-arse in complete control of Maine and Normandy, a policy in direct opposition to all for which William was striving and for which she struggled for so long in his absence; the union of Normandy and England was her king's dream. Last week, he'd enjoyed immensely the ceremony of Lanfranc's consecration of St Etienne, William's great church for his Abbaye-aux-Hommes. And watching the king so happy and carefree there on the balcony, it was difficult for Matilda to accept the reality of her husband's deep anxieties.

William was such a strange paradox, even to her, his wife whom he trusted absolutely. She was the only human being in whom he could confide. At one instant he was, as at this moment, the devoted father, tending his brood; the next, the greedy despot, concerned only in attaining his objective, through callous and brutal intimidation, if needs must. His suppression of the earls' rebellion two years ago was still too raw in people's memory – and did he *have* to execute Waltheof, the valorous earl whom the English revered?

Often, she thought, watching the man to whom she devoted her life, William was his own worst enemy. It was, she knew now, his appalling childhood which had sown the bitter tares: he could never grab enough and what he won he would never willingly relinquish. Land, money, gold, jewels, his predilection for banqueting and pomp, all were of the same pattern, but the latter trappings of dignity were certainly augmented by his own, naturally impressive presence. And she smiled indulgently as she watched him striding along the balcony, his long arms clasped behind his back, his huge head jutting from his short neck, his russet hair was now flecked white at the sides; aggressive, suspicious, his tanned face was grained, leathery – but the half-circles at the corners of his wide, full mouth still lent an air of benign amusement to his expression. A stern, hard face which naturally men feared.

Even she was wary of his sudden outbursts of rage which, unhappily, exploded more frequently now that Robert was spending these days with them: William was convinced that some motive lay behind Robert's unusual wish to be under the same roof with his father. And Matilda asked herself: if her king was a master at bending the most obstinate of his great lords to his will, he should surely be able to tame the first son she had given him . . . ? He was certainly treating Robert gently at the moment: had the accident last year to their second son, Richard, in the New Forest, brought home to him the fragility of a parent's hold on his sons? After the shock of Richard's death, he had spoken to no one but her, for three days.

His passion for the hunt would be his undoing, she had often thought. The English were foretelling that the ruthless measures he was taking to protect his deer and game in the New Forest which he had created in Hampshire would bring God's vengeance upon his house. *Why* did he insist on making so many enemies merely to gratify his love of the chase? It was this extraordinary streak of cruelty which she found difficult to reconcile with his gentler nature, his genuine love for his family.

These days were hard, brutal times, she knew – and it was the way of the world in which they existed: mutilation of hostages; brutal, disgusting punishments; and merciless treatment of prisoners; but *surely* he could control the poaching of his deer in the New Forest without such Draconian forest laws?

Putting out a hungry peasant's eyes in punishment for the theft of a hart did not win a conquered people's respect, though it was one way to enforce order. As William pointed out, he was merely enforcing the ancient customs of the Royal Forests which the Confessor and Canute had initiated before him. But the English people could not forgive their king for the destruction of villages and the ousting of thousands of peasants from their homes, merely to provide sport for the monarch and his court . . .

Matilda picked up her needlework, shielded her eyes from the sunlight when Roger Calcège pushed back the curtain. Her portly husband stepped into the chamber, then broke off his conversation to smile down at his queen:

'Enjoying your peace, Mahault? We've a noisy brood outside.' He nodded towards the courtyard. 'Roger says I mustn't worry too much about Dol.' He was glancing across at his host. 'Eh, Roger?'

'Saving John from le Réquin's attack on La Flèche has restored some of your lost prestige, sire. Fulk won't try that again, for some time: his wounds will keep him at home with his women.'

William shook his head: 'Ralph of Gael's master of Brittany now. He'll not rest: his cronies will see to that.'

'You did well to settle with Philip in January, sire. At least, he's accepted that Robert is count of Maine.'

William remained silent, deep in thought. Then he said, 'Philip's young, ambitious – a schemer. He's consolidating his hold on the Vexin. Last week he was right up to the Epte.'

Roger Calcège shook his head in disbelief, smiled at his duchess. 'An extraordinary business, my lady, even for these days . . .'

Matilda nodded, smiled up from her needlework: 'Your duke would not have acquitted himself as did young Simon of Crépi.' She laughed gaily. 'I would not have permitted him!' The young count of the Vexin's impulsive decision had been an amazing event.

Simon had inherited the Vexin and had done his best to hold it for his duke against the sporadic incursions of the French. He fell in love with the count of Auvergne's daughter, a demure girl called Judith. He married her, but on their first night he impulsively decided to quit his bemused bride for a life of celibacy in the abbey of St-Claude in the far away, mountainous Jura. Philip at once marched into the Vexin. William was now biding his time and when he was again strong enough, would throw Philip's Frenchmen out from the neighbouring Vexin. It was murmured that, to underscore his ascendancy over William, Philip was about to give his castle at Gerberoi, near Beauvais, to Robert and his friends. From this rallying-point outside the Norman frontier, attacks on the duchy could be mounted when the king-duke was forced to return to England.

'A despicable brat, that Philip.' Roger Calcège spat his words. 'Slimy toad.'

His words were lost in the shouts coming from the courtyard. Hearing William's laughter mixing with Robert's furious yelling at his younger brothers, Matilda put down her work to join her husband who had moved back again to the balcony.

'See, Mahault,' William roared, as he encircled her shoulders with his arm. 'Our brood has the same fire as its mother.'

She laid her hand on his, while together they watched developments of the horseplay in the courtyard. The third son, William, now eighteen, stocky and red-haired, was egging on his younger brother: Henry, nine years old, was developing into a lithe, well-built boy – clever, but thoughtful, he was less impulsive than the others. From the balcony, these two had emptied a pail of water on their elder brother. Robert, in his neatly-cut jerkin, with his gaily-coloured hose of red and green and his long-toed, fashionable pumps, was shaking his fists up at them. He was crimson with rage, where he stood dripping in the pool of water, his dapper clothes sodden.

'Shush, Robert!' Matilda called down at him. 'It's not dignified to use such language – in front of the girls, too.' But a smile worked at the corners of her mouth as she glanced up at her husband: 'He's lost his sense of humour,' she murmured, 'like his father.' She pressed her king's hand. 'Sometimes he's very like you.'

'Our young runts instinctively pick the weakest chink in Robert's armour,' William grinned. 'Ridicule's a deadly weapon, Mahault.'

'Short-arse! Short-arse!' Henry's boy-voice called from the shelter of the balustrade. 'Can't catch me, brother Shorty!'

'They're going too far, my lord,' Matilda said. 'Stop them, before it gets out of hand.'

'That will do, Henry,' William boomed. 'Go down and dry off your brother.' He was trying not to laugh to himself. 'You started it, William Rufus – go down and apologize. Dry off your brother. That's no way to treat the count of Maine.'

But, as the unrepentant pair disappeared towards the stairway, Matilda saw Robert pick up a broom-handle, then enter the doorway to the tower.

'You're their father,' she said, pushing her husband to the top of the stairway, 'Robert's furious. Stop it, before he harms them.' Matilda felt anxious: she knew their first-born better than did his father. She heard Robert's roar of obscenities as he bounded up the stone stairway. Rufus and Henry had doubled back, were pushing past their father for the safety of the chamber. Then she saw Robert halting on the steps, his eyes blazing up at the king who was barring his passage.

'Let me get at 'em, father,' he yelled. 'They've gone too far this time.'

'Calm yourself, Short-arse,' William grinned. 'Can't you take a joke?'

The atmosphere was crisp with tension: father and son confronted each other, Robert trembling with resentment.

'For God's sake, my lord!' Robert bellowed. 'Let me pass. For once, stop treating me as a child.'

'Don't behave as one, then,' William said icily. 'If you wish respect, learn to control yourself.'

Once again that terrible silence: Matilda watched her first-born struggling with himself. The pent-up frustration of these long years suddenly loosed:

'I'm not here, my king, to listen to another of your sermons.' He jumped up the next step, violently tried to push past his father. 'By the pope's beard, I'm sick to the gullet with the ridiculous restrictions you're always forcing on me.' He stood panting for breath, the short, stocky young man, glancing up at the towering figure of his corpulent, middle-aged father.

'Robert,' William replied in that steely tone which Matilda knew to be so dangerous, 'when you show me that you are worthy of my trust, I'll give you authority. But, while I've been in England, you seem only to have surrounded yourself with dissolute popinjays who side with my enemies.' But then he gently added, 'Can't you find better friends?'

'They're fine fellows, father. You don't understand my generation: we're as capable as ever you were.' Robert glanced across at his mother: 'Ask my lady, there. I've stood by her all these years while you've been enjoying yourself in England.'

Matilda put her hand to her mouth. The unpleasant insinuation could only infuriate William who, she knew, needed little incitement to burst into violence. This happy morning was disintegrating . . . William was staring at her. She nodded slowly in assent.

'So, my lord king,' Robert barked impertinently, 'make me officially the duke of Normandy, for God's sake! Then I can govern with full authority while you're absent in your kingdom.'

Matilda was watching her husband. She yearned to plead for her Robert, but fear of causing the permanent break between these two whom she loved so deeply held her from intervention. The king was gazing contemptuously at his son who stood shaking on the step below him. Then William spoke, sharply and with finality, his hands on his hips, barring Robert's passage:

'My son, I undress only to sleep in my bed.' He paused then, watching his son and heir turning from him. As the sound of Robert's footsteps pattered downwards, she heard William's terrible words reverberating after him:

'I curse you, my son, for the treachery and disloyalty you are causing me in my duchy. You're destroying my dream, Robert, for a united England and Normandy. Curse you, boy!' He turned slowly to mount the steps and Matilda saw the pain in those blue eyes. 'Yes, I curse him,' he muttered as the shocked Roger Calcège slipped from the chamber. 'Come, Mahault.' He held out his hand for his wife. 'Let's try to recapture the happiness of this day: where're my other children?'

But Matilda, her head erect, was striding swiftly from the chamber, the hem of her skirt swishing on the rushes. She looked neither to left nor right; neither did she accept the hand of her lord, the king.

25

THE SHADOWS LENGTHEN

Queen Matilda, duchess of Normandy, preferred this warm palace of William's at Caen, a fresh, friendly building built from the selected oak trees of Normandy's forests, to anything which Rouen could provide. Here, before the blazing fire, she could in comfort supervise affairs so easily, because the Exchequer building so conveniently abutted the palace inside the castle walls. The roofs of the town houses nestled one with the other, right up to the wall; and there was the friendliness of the jostling people which she never found at Rouen.

She loved the way the river ran round William's tower below the castle, enjoyed the bustle of the markets and the crooked, narrow streets. Even during this wretched cold February of 1080, the people were good to her when she walked down into the town; when she took her ladies up to her Abbey convent of the Holy Trinity of which she was so proud. And she laughed softly to herself at the rivalry which always existed between her and her husband over their respective penances.

Her Abbaye-aux-Dames, though not so imposing, had a warmer atmosphere than his Abbey, she was sure of that. If he arrived back in time (he'd ridden yesterday to Falaise to see his Chancellor and would be calling in on the Exchequer here, before coming home to her) she would take him up to Holy Trinity to see the new altar they were erecting in the crypt – for her the most serene corner on earth. After these last two years of growing tension between her husband and herself, she needed the solace of her church more and more.

As usual, it was Robert's conduct which lay at the root of their differences. William was right, unhappily: who, other than her exasperating first-born, would act so stupidly after the argument at l'Aigle with his formidable father? Ah! That was two years ago, now – her first two years of constant unhappiness, trying to reconcile the husband she loved to the son of her flesh.

Robert had galloped across Roger Calcège's drawbridge without even bidding her farewell. Collecting his friends as he rode (he must have been insane with rage, mad with delusions of grandeur) he thereupon attacked Rouen castle, calling on the astonished garrison to surrender. She thanked her God once again that the king's butler had been alert when the assault was launched. What unthinkable strife would have split the duchy had not Roger of Ivry thrown out the rebels, neck and crop?

The threat to the unity of Normandy was only postponed, for Robert and his supporters then installed themselves in Hugh of Châteauneuf's castles in the Perche, at Sorel and Rémalart, where they paid scant notice to propriety. And she sighed again by the fireside, remembering as if it was only yesterday, when these young men had been but children.

Matilda felt sickened as she remembered those reports filtering back to the king: the debauch, the roisterings, the dissolute court they held down there in the Perche while they gathered their forces. And how she loathed Philip! The French king was behind this treachery, encouraging, even aiding materially when William took practical steps to counter this tragic internal strife.

Ordering Count Rotrou, Hugh of Châteauneuf's overlord, to arrest Robert and his rebels, William considered the seizing of their lands and possessions. Robert thereupon fled the duchy for Flanders, but the Frisian evidently considered it too risky to harbour this cuckoo in his nest. After trying in vain to elicit help from the archbishop of Trèves, Matilda's brother and Robert's uncle, the stupid boy decided to bide his time. Instead of rallying his forces, he and his cronies typically decided to spend the next twenty months seeking support throughout the European courts. They enjoyed a wild, hilarious time, it seemed, being welcomed with glee by William's jealous enemies. It was in the same month, when the saintly Anselm was elected abbot of Le Bec-Hellouin, that William suffered more humiliating reverses: Philip gave Robert the promised castle of Gerberoi, near Beauvais; and it was shortly before this that Matilda herself had been involved in an impossibly difficult situation. Caught between the profligacy of her son and her duty as duchess and queen, God only knew how desperately she had tried to compromise.

Sitting alone and gazing at the blazing logs while the dull February evening closed in, she knew she had acted wrongly and – what was worse – foolishly. There were no secrets at court; facts always leaked out . . . She shifted in her chair, pulled her shawl more closely about her.

Through her trusted Breton friend, Samson, Robert had appealed to her from across the border. His gallivantings were extravagant. He had run out of funds. Could his mother save him from his dishonourable and embarrassing predicament, one which could only humiliate himself, Normandy – and the king-duke? He must have money.

The bond of a mother to her son, however despicably he behaved, was, for her, fundamental. Foolishly, she had personally gone behind the Chancellor's back, riding herself to Falaise to the duchy's second treasury; then back to the Exchequer here, where she also drew upon the duchy funds which her duke-husband had entrusted solely to her. Samson had sworn that the escort, unaware of what was happening, had delivered the money safely to Robert at Gerberoi.

Then, two long months ago, William broke off his punitive campaign against the Perche rebels, in order to bring his son to heel, once and for all time. Without haste, William began systematically his preparations for besieging Robert and his rebel coterie inside their castle at Gerberoi. And Queen Matilda, in her solitude before the crackling logs, closed her eyes to dispel the mortification of what had occurred there.

To bring his watching son to his senses, the king began methodically to encircle Gerberoi by garrisoning all castles in the neighbourhood; the final assault could await winter, by which time William would have assembled an overwhelming Norman-English force. But, only three weeks after the siege began, Robert and his young knights surprisingly sallied forth in an attempt at escape. A bloody, vicious encounter took place, a confused *mêlée* in which William suddenly found himself face-to-face with his son and heir. In the charge, William's horse fell. Robert lowered his lance, perhaps for the mortal thrust, but succeeded only in piercing his father through the arm. William's shocked knights, rallying about their fallen lord, fought like wild beasts to retrieve the initiative. William was saved only by the bravery of the English knight, Toki, son of Wigot, who sacrificed his own life for his Norman king. The besiegers then retired, taking the wounded William with them.

That dreadful day, an episode even more humiliating than Dol, had scarred William's pride more deeply than any physical wound. Leaving the jubilant victors in Gerberoi, the king returned to Rouen. While Matilda nursed his arm and wounded pride, the most influential of the king's council (many of them fathers of the rebels) sought desperately for a reconciliation: the appalling quarrel was rending Normandy apart.

Philip, enthusiastically encouraging the young rebels, was gloating over his success. The great king's humiliation was also noted by Malcolm who, with Edgar, was planning to attack once more from across the Scottish borders. But, God be thanked, last month, in the bitter frosts of January '80, King William was at last persuaded to come to terms with his son – and the jubilant Philip. But the negotiations had taken nearly a year, a terrible year in which William, forced to remain in Normandy for the reconciliation, had impotently to watch Malcolm and his Scots savage the whole of northern England.

To Matilda's immense relief, William had at last confirmed before his council that Robert was officially his heir to the duchy of Normandy. An uneasy peace now existed between father and son; and Matilda wondered, with Philip creating havoc in the Vexin, for how long the truce could last. Perhaps Malcolm's attack on northern England might bind father and son together? William was deliberately trying to coax Robert into leading the expedition against King Malcolm, to rid England for ever of this Scottish menace. Father and son were now busily mobilizing their army and preparing to cross the Channel.

The queen, above all others, knew what Philip had achieved: never again would William be the same; never again would she see that carefree, crusading light spark in his eyes. He had become more moody, introspective, fighting to restore his own self-confidence. Sullen, prone to dreadful outbursts of rage, the quarrel with their son had caused a rift which could never be completely healed. She prayed daily in her abbey to the Blessed Virgin. Odo had agreed to accompany Robert on the Scottish expedition, but it was unlikely that *his* influence would temper Robert's ambition.

She looked up, tensing – were the shouts, the snorting horses, from the king's party? She heard his distinctive voice booming above the others, then hushing suddenly while he paid his last call to the treasury in the Exchequer. She rose, nodded to her lady-in-waiting who was supervising the fires and the lighting of the candles for the night, then walked into her private room adjoining their bed-chamber. She'd just have time, without troubling her dresser, to slip into her evening gown for him. With nimble fingers, she unfastened her outer dress, allowed the embroidered gown with its full sleeves to fall to the floor. Stepping from the folds, she stood for a moment in front of the priceless glass (it had travelled safely half-way across Europe) which he had commanded for her. It was too early yet for the braziers, but the candle flames leaning to the draught were providing sufficient light.

Her minute hands which protruded from the silken sleeves of her close-fitting under garment, pressed over her body, smoothing out the silk – and she grimaced at the peaked face staring at her: large, black irises still burned from those pale saucers, but the half-circles beneath betrayed her forty-eight years. Those tresses coiled about her head were flecked with white hairs. Below her small, curved nose her full lips were compressed; there were lines at the corners – and with the tips of her fingers she tried to smooth away the talisman of her years of self-discipline while ruling the duchy on her own.

Her eyes ran over her figure which, in this silken shift, still proved why she was still attractive to him. She cupped her hands beneath her girl's breasts, smiled at the memories: they had suckled most of her brood, a feat which had always impressed the nurses (she was eighteen inches shorter than her husband, but she had borne him ten children) – and if her bosom sagged now she must rely more on her dresser's skill with her bodice. She *was* feeling her age, but her flat flanks and pale, flawless skin compensated for her wide hips; at least, she had not given up the struggle – she still had her trim shape. The candle flames fluttered. She turned towards the bed-chamber whence she'd heard the swish! of parting curtains. She smiled at him, seeing him there, her William, portly, middle-aged too, legs astride in the doorway of her private room, still mud-bespattered from his ride.

'My lord,' she cried, moving swiftly to him, her slender arms out-stretched. 'I was beginning to fret: 'tis still dark so early.'

But something in his penetrating gaze, the contemptuous curl at the corners of his lips, halted her. Staring up at those suspicious blue eyes, she caught her breath – she had dreaded this inevitable moment. He did not move, barring her way, his arms akimbo. He spoke softly, his guttural voice emphasizing the scorn:

'Matilda,' he grated, 'you've betrayed me.' The dangerous light flickered in his eyes. 'You've made me look a fool: that's unforgivable:'

She wasn't to be bullied, spoken to like a serving wench:

'Come, my lord!' she snapped, stamping her slippered foot on the rich carpet. 'What angers you? Be plainly spoken.'

He banged the wall with his fist, took one stride towards her:

'Why've you cheated me? You've helped yourself to the duchy's funds to pay for Robert's excesses.' She faced him, her dark eyes smouldering:

'What would you have thought of me, if I'd allowed him to ridicule you before all the courts of Europe? Can't you understand, my lord, the position in which I was trapped?' She shouted at him, 'The king's son in debt. His father refusing him money.' Her laugh was bitter. 'It's to your shame as much as our son's, that he's in revolt against his father.'

William ignored the painful truth. He shouted at her:

'Why did you keep it secret? Why did you not refer to me?'

'You'd have refused – Robert's need was urgent.'

'I've trusted you, Mahault, for all these years. And now . . .?' He spread wide his arms, shrugged his shoulders. 'You've made me ridiculous.'

'Sire, you started the process,' she snapped. 'Gerberoi has not enhanced your status,' she added brutally.

She stood rigid, stiffening for his expected blow. His face was scarlet. Before he could reply, she could not resist taunting him with her pent-up jealousies. 'You talk of trust . . .' She stamped her foot again. '*You* . . . you and your English priest's daughter. They're mocking you in the taverns, says Robert.'

She jerked backwards when he tried to grab her. 'And *you?*' he blazed. 'And your Samson?' His eyes burned as he watched her. 'When I was fighting in Scotland . . .' He'd succeeded in gripping her wrist. 'Can you deny the talk? Samson was boasting he'd made the queen his lover.' He choked, the veins bulging in his neck.

'My lord, your words are unworthy.' She tried to free his grip, but his fingers tightened.

'You used Samson as your agent when you misappropriated the funds. Deny that . . .'

'I could trust him.'

'Ha!' He twisted her arm and she cried out with pain. 'I had him brought before me. They'll put out his eyes.'

She felt the blood draining from her face. She ceased to struggle, let her body go limp.

'*You've blinded Samson?*' The hot tears streamed down her cheeks. 'You savage beast – ' She pounded against his chest with her free fist. 'He was only a loyal, devoted subject.' She choked, gasping for breath. 'You're destroying my love for you, my lord.' Her words were barely audible as the sobs began racking her body.

'His friends smuggled him to St-Evroul before my executioners could grab him. He's an ardent monk now, safe in his monastery.' He laughed coarsely. 'You'll have to make do with your husband now.'

Her head jerked forwards to his pinioning twist. Her teeth sank into his flesh. She tasted the salty, hot blood. She flung free, stood trembling before him.

'You're worse than an animal,' she gasped. 'Cold, calculating . . .'

For an interminable instant they faced each other: the burly king, mad with humiliation, confused like a wild bull; the exquisite, tiny queen, injured beyond comprehension by her man's jealous accusations. He lunged for her then, grabbed at her hair. Blinded by her veil, she cried out in pain as he knotted her tresses through his fingers.

She stumbled. He held her by the hair, dragging her through their bed-chamber – then along the corridor, down the royal staircase and out into the cold, cobbled yard before the palace. Bellowing with rage, bidding his servants to witness the shame of his harlot queen, he hauled her through the gate and out into the filthy, muddy lane winding through the dwellings. And, as the astonished townsfolk backed away between the huddled houses, he began tearing at her shift. He flung the tattered silk into the filthy gutters, stripped her naked. The icy wind clawed at her; the mud splashed at her legs.

'See, my people!' he roared. 'Take your strumpet duchess!'

She shrieked at him:

'And you, sire: you shall pay your bastard fee to the King of France's grand-daughter.'

He flung her, moaning, into the mud. She heard his boots squelching, his insane mouthings diminishing while he strode back to his castle. An old woman ran to her and wrapped a shawl about her nakedness.

'*Quelle froide rue!*' she cried out. 'Oh, Caen! Forgive my lord . . .' A sprinkle of snowflakes crowned her head as they carried her, shivering in violent spasms, back towards the castle.

On 14 May, 1080, Bishop Walcher, the monk from Lorraine whom William had personally appointed to the see of Durham, was battered to death at Gateshead. This open uprising in the North prompted King Malcolm's expected attack from across his Scottish borders. The king, involved with his intricate political decisions in Normandy, had already dispatched his half-brother Odo, northward on the expedition to halt the marauding Scots.

At Pentecost, on 31 May, King William assembled his council at Lillebonne, where two important decisions were taken. First, the final arbiter of justice would be the duke of Normandy. In one stroke, the judicial power of his barons was reduced. His second edict was no less fundamental. The illustrious Pope Gregory VII, who, as Hildebrand, had in the past been such an ally of William's, began major reforms of the Church of Rome. Backed by Archbishop Lanfranc of Canterbury, celibacy in the priesthood was being insisted upon, an edict which was hotly opposed in Europe, especially from the German supporters of the anti-pope, Clement III. On 24 April 1080, Gregory dispatched a lengthy letter to the king of England: in diplomatic language, the pope reminded William of past papal support to Normandy, especially during the invasion of 1066. Gregory continued in elegiac terms to insist that the king's claim to appoint his own bishops must be subject to divine grace; and, therefore, that appointments must be approved by the holder of St Peter's see in Rome. All power came from God, so the king must therefore pay homage to His earthly representative, the pope. The second demand was that St Peter's denier – the Church of Rome's tax – be paid by England more regularly.

William, forewarned, had convened his Lillebonne council before the arrival of Gregory's letter. Backed strongly by Lanfranc and William 'Bonne-Ame', the new archbishop of Rouen (an appointment made without Rome's approval), King William courteously but firmly rejected Gregory's first command: the English were accustomed to nominating their own bishops. But, readily he acceded to the demand for payment of St Peter's denier. This courteous reply was the king's second refusal, but by then Gregory was too involved with his own internal problems to force a schism with the stubborn English Church.

Having settled the fundamental conflict over the episcopacy, William prepared to deal with the Scottish invasion of northern England. At Caen, on 14 July 1080, Robert Short-arse finally consented to lead the expedition against King Malcolm. Robert thereupon crossed to England to raise an Anglo-Norman force, William following him a month later: it was five years since the king had set foot in his kingdom.

In September, Robert and his large army, which had combined at Durham with Odo's troops, ravaged northwards to Lothian, where at Falkirk Malcolm was forced to pay homage to the king of England. Robert then returned south to the Tyne where, to protect the northern border, he set in hand the building of New Castle. Once again, a temporary respite in the conflict over England's northern border had been gained.

Robert rejoined his father for the short, repressive campaign against the Welsh. Under the pretext of a pilgrimage to Saint David's sanctuary on the tip of the Pembroke peninsula, the king's impressive force of cavalry rode through the southern region of the principality. In the Taff estuary, William ordered the building of a castle at Cardiff, then, having successfully intimidated the populace, he returned to his capital. The wild Celts would give no more trouble: and the Marcher Earls at Hereford, Chester and Shrewsbury were having little difficulty in imposing order, a process begun by the legendary William fitz Osbern, earl of Hereford.

At the end of this Welsh campaign, when father and son had ridden stirrup to stirrup, Robert was still disagreeing with the king's insistence that the unity of England and Normandy was all-important. To William's intense bitterness, in February of 1081, Robert Short-arse left his father's court to depart for an undeclared destination in northern Europe.

The million and three-quarters population of King William's England was at peace for the first time during the spring of 1081. Scotland was subdued, Wales quiescent. But, yet again, while William was consolidating relations between his Norman barons and the conquered Anglo-Saxons, Philip of France, now that Robert was back in Europe as a potential, pivotal threat, induced Fulk to take up arms once more from Anjou. In March of 1081, supported now by Hoel, count of Brittany, Fulk once more attacked John in his castle at La Flèche, burning it to the ground.

King William, hurriedly assembling a combined Anglo-Saxon and Norman force, again crossed to Normandy. He force-marched down to Maine, determined to destroy Fulk and his Breton allies; but, as battle was about to be joined, the Church dignitaries of the region succeeded in persuading both sides to come to terms: the previous pact of 1077 was confirmed. An energetic Norman bishop was installed at Le Mans; Fulk retired into Anjou and William to Normandy, though Maine still remained restless and a perpetual threat.

The year 1082 began serenely for the sorely-pressed king and his queen. Their daughter, Adela, whom they had married to Count Stephen of Blois two years previously, made them grand-parents by giving birth to a son whom they christened Stephen.* But, already, during the first months of that year, a year in which the king and queen had reconciled their differences, disturbing reports were reaching William in Normandy.

Pope Gregory VII had been physically abducted from Rome by supporters of the German emperor. Gregory's men appealed to Europe for help, but William's political sense prompted him to hold his hand. He had no intention of embroiling his kingdom in a continental dispute, and his sympathies lay with the emperor who had taken a similar stand over the appointment of bishops.

Bishop Odo, earl of Kent, who was now in his fifties and at the summit of his considerable power and wealth (he owned 439 manors; his brother, Robert of Mortain, 793), was diametrically opposed to his royal half-

---

* King of England, 1135–1154.

brother's attitude to Rome; the king forcefully forbade him to meddle in the dispute. Odo then deviously tried secretly to inveigle some of England's most competent Norman barons into his way of thinking: with a formidable force he intended to cross to the continent, rescue the aging pope – and, when Gregory died, offer himself as candidate for St Peter's throne.

Odo, whose amassed wealth was second only to the king's, was feared by Norman and English alike. Rumours of the earl of Kent's ambitions and deliberate flouting of the royal command soon filtered across to Normandy; Archbishop Lanfranc confirmed William's suspicions and, to deal with Odo's treason, the king left his queen in Rouen to cross swiftly to England. Sailing from the new port he was naming Dieppe, he made Culver Cliff his landfall. Clearing Bembridge Ledge, he sailed straight up the Eastern Solent for Carisbrooke bay where Odo's embarkation fleet was assembling. The king went ashore immediately, strode up the fields to confront his half-brother. Placing him there and then under house-arrest, William convened his council there, at Carisbrooke castle.

The king had underestimated the immense prestige held by his half-brother. At Carisbrooke, despite William's fury, none of the solicited barons were prepared to witness against the formidable earl of Kent. Undaunted, the king personally accused Odo of treachery; found the case proven and thereupon sentenced him to be placed under close arrest.

No lord daring to lay hands on the earl, the king strode forwards himself, for an instant standing face-to-face with Arlette's second son. He grabbed Odo's wrists.

'My lord King,' Odo shouted. 'You have no authority, either to judge or to sentence me. Only the pontiff has authority over his bishops.'

William did not loosen his grip. Staring straight at the defiant earl, the king rasped:

'It is not the bishop of Bayeux who stands convicted. It is the earl of Kent.'

The king had restored his authority. His barons closed in, formally arrested the traitor and bundled him down the fields to the ship anchored in Carisbrooke bay. He was transferred to Rouen, where he was placed under house arrest.*

The bizarre events of 1082 were crowned in December by Mabel of Bellême's final sordid appearance upon the stage. Now gross with her last pregnancy, her greed had nevertheless impelled her to seize the property of Hugh of Sangey, a knight of her traditional enemies, the fitz Giroies. On 2 December, Hugh and his two brothers thereupon infiltrated into Bures castle, by the river Dives, where the countess was staying. Though it was

---

* Odo did not return to England until after William's death. He died in Palermo whilst on pilgrimage to Jerusalem in 1097, in the arms of his nephew, Robert, Short-arse.

midwinter, Mabel had bathed in the river and was lying naked on her bed when the avengers burst into her chamber. They lopped off the loathsome creature's head and carried off the horrible evidence. The truncated corpse was carried to the nearby monastery at Troarn, where astonishingly, the child was born: a boy, Roger, he was to live a life as vile as any of his forebears.

Leaving England under the charge of the magnificent but aging Lanfranc, now eighty years old, and his other half-brother, Robert of Mortain, King William returned in the spring of 1083 to deal once more with the cancer eating at Normandy's core: the serpentile Philip was once again rallying rebellion around Robert Short-arse, count of Maine and heir-presumptive to the Duchy of Normandy.

Despite the burning fever and the agonizing pain in her head, Queen Matilda was able with cruel clarity to realize what was happening to her. Her ladies were fussing about her, ministering to her needs; and she could see Agatha, already a lined, self-contained spinster of thirty, bossing little Mattie about as they tore up the linen with which to dab the pus from their queen's blotchy, putrifying flesh: this body of hers, which had so recently been exquisite, even after bearing ten children.

Yes, there was little Mattie with her mass of red curls, her serious frightened eyes. Was it really only two years since she'd taken her little daughter to her foundation at St-Evroult? The nuns and the lady abbess had been touchingly grateful: Matilda had gifted the rebuilding of the refectory, had presented an embroidered chasuble, as well as the cape and the jewels. But what did these symbols matter now? How transient were the world's material values . . .

The plague had struck Caen suddenly. When was it? At September's end, that was it . . . the week before, she had walked through the Bourg-le-Roi, past William's tower and up to Holy Trinity, the church of her Abbaye-aux-Dames. She had deliberately avoided the Rue Froide, as they now called it, the lane down which she had never set foot since that shameful day. The townspeople had pressed about her, touching her cloak, praying deliverance from this appalling affliction. She'd fallen ill suddenly, ten days ago; only today had she been able to think clearly.

Mother of Jesus, why has your Son tortured my lord and me so grievously? Why is it your will to set my first-born child against my husband? When was it that Robert flaunted this last rebellion of his before the cruel, jeering world? Days and weeks were all confusion now – *when was it? When . . .?*

318

'Hush, dearest mother.' The voice was Agatha's. 'What troubles you, my lady?'

'Robert,' she whispered. 'Is he coming home?'

Her daughter's face blurred. Instead, Matilda recognized her abbess, her namesake, standing next to that fine new archbishop, that nice man, William 'Bonne-Ame'. The abbess was holding the cross above her; the archbishop's hands were raised in benison. She watched the movement of his lips, but could not distinguish the words of what must be the Extreme Unction.

She closed her eyes, feeling the weariness welling over her. *Mother of God:* to rest at last! She felt Agatha's hand enfolding hers: 'No, mother – Robert cannot come,' her daughter was saying. 'William and Henry are with you. Adela's on her way from Blois.'

'She's not bringing Stephen?' Matilda whispered. 'She mustn't bring little Stephen.'

Adela – her favourite – the most like herself. And when her eyes opened, a gleam of joy was flickering. Adela was vivacious, intelligent, loved things of beauty; she shared her mother's French, finer tastes. Artists and musicians were flocking to her court: good for young people during these barbarous times . . .

'Cecily and Constance will be here tonight, mother.' Agatha, reassuring again. So they were gathering her family, all save her two men, the two she needed most. It seemed another existence now, so futile, Robert's final definitive rebellion eight weeks ago against his father. Robert was wrong, oh! so wrong. Her ewe-lamb, for such to her he had always been for all his swagger: that French puppet, Philip, had so long exploited the weakness . . .

'Dear Jesus, reconcile my men,' she prayed. Robert's treachery on 20 August had finally broken her heart after she'd seen the effect on her king. It was then that she had given up – and William had sensed her grief. Now she supported her lord totally. Robert was wrong. But even at this last moment, his selfishness was preventing her lord from being with her – just when she needed her William most.

'The king,' she whispered. 'Where is he, Agatha? Does my lord know I am sick?'

The blurred face of her daughter was nodding. 'They've sent messengers to Gournay-en-Bray,' she was saying softly. 'Father'll be with you soon.'

The queen closed her eyes. In the Bray region – ah, yes – not far from Gerberoi. Her William always acted with vigour, especially when danger loomed . . . The images of her life flashed before her and she smiled. She could hear those by her bed whispering, taking comfort from her smile. Yes, she had been the wife of the most amazing man of her generation: what would the world say of him? How would it judge them both?

Energetic, forceful; ruthless, cruel; hard, loving – ah, Mother of God, how they had loved! She still in plaits, he a swarthy, lusty youth, sweeping her up from Lille to be his bride; their marriage the most cruelly condemned in the world; their first night at Eu; Bonneville, during those early years building their family . . . Strange, how only the happiest images were flitting across her memory to obliterate those endless years of terror, while she waited at home as he fought for survival against the traitors.

A shadow passed across her white face; but those two terrible flashes – hers of jealousy, his of mistrust – both were part of the paradox which completed their life-long devotion to each other: on both of those worst occasions, they had managed to forgive, to overcome the schisms. Time had achieved the healing: for the past two years, they had grown together again, closer than they had ever been – in spite of their physical aging . . .

She, fifty-one, was past the difficult years, at last unable to bear children; he, grizzle-haired, hard-lined, with his paunchy stomach about which she taunted him – but as virile a lover as he had ever been – memories, memories . . . That last week they'd snatched at Bonneville in May with the apple blossom speckling the hillsides pink and white; the clouds scudding across the estuary, the flecked blue sea . . . she smiled, clutching the memory, stretching out her frail hands for him, waiting as she had always done . . . She thought she heard him then, his great belly-laugh as he rode over the drawbridge, Baldur's hooves clip-clopping in the courtyard . . . 'My lord,' she whispered. 'My lord, Mahault's waiting . . .' All was peace, the pain easing, the voices fainter. *'My dearest lord . . .,'* were her last, barely audible words.

Queen Matilda died on 2 November 1083, King William arriving at Caen on the following day. He himself supervised the state funeral, the burial of his queen in her church of Holy Trinity in the Abbaye-aux-Dames.

Queen Matilda's tomb was prepared where she wished: she was laid to rest before the altar in the floor of the choir. Her coffin was covered eventually by a simple, black marble slab. It lies there today, almost a millennium later, the engraved Latin inscription still legible.

26

FINAL DAWN

The archbishop with the dark, burning eyes sat at the king's right hand, the only member of the council to be on the same level as the monarch. The remainder of the council were arrayed in a semi-circle about the throne, a step lower on the dais and facing the packed hall of the royal palace at Gloucester, the assembly having been convened for this Christmas week of 1085.

Archbishop Lanfranc of Canterbury did not feel his eighty-two years. The eyes in the swarthy, aquiline face of the Italian flickered with amusement as he watched the final scene of this great gathering of the nation's land-holders. How self-important were the younger generation, the sons of those whose fathers had won this land for them nineteen years ago! Anybody who was anybody claimed to have wielded a sword at Hastings – and Lanfranc glanced to his left: William was still taking an interest, even though this was the final session.

A subtle change had taken place in William: there was now a fatalistic, cynical bitterness about him which had not been there before his wife's death. Unlike many whom Lanfranc had watched entering the last phase of their lives without their partners, the king had not sought solace in wine or women. Instead, in spite of his failing health and obesity, he was forcing himself as energetically as ever to the defence of his kingdom and duchy. As so often previously, he had confided in Lanfranc: his dream was to forge a unified condominium of England and Normandy, at peace within itself and with its neighbours, before death overtook him.

Save for his son and heir, his family had tried to console him at Rouen during that sad Christmas of 1083, but early in the New Year William had crossed back to England to be with his ever-diminishing circle of friends. Lanfranc had celebrated the Pentecost Mass at Westminster with the king. It was then that William had confided in Lanfranc of the extreme loneliness he was feeling. There were not many of the old

321

guard left: apart from Lanfranc, there were Roger of Montgomery, Walter Giffard, and Geoffrey of Coutances – William fitz Osbern was long dead. The king was facing with dignity his loneliness and the distressing subversion from within his own family – Odo imprisoned, Robert banished; and his queen now dead – while preparing to meet the orchestrated threats from overseas.

Odo, though under house-arrest at Rouen, was still a potential menace, a nucleus around which subversive malcontents could rally. William's son and heir was mounting another rebellion from outside Normandy's eastern borders; and in June of 1084, William had been forced to return to Normandy to deal with Hubert of Sainte-Suzanne who, with Philip's encouragement, was menacing the duchy from Le Mans. Fulk was, of course, also biding his opportunity from Anjou; and Malcolm was poised in Scotland, eagerly awaiting his Danish allies whose impending invasion posed the most dangerous threat of all to England. Throughout 1085 reports of a massive and imminent Danish invasion continued to stream into the king's court at Westminster.

The son of the great Sweyn Estrithsen was no less redoubtable than his legendary father; Canute, the new king of Denmark, had as an ally Robert of Flanders, whose sister he had married. Enlisting thousands of mercenaries, together they were assembling a massive invasion fleet. Canute's attack was expected at any moment throughout that spring and summer of 1085, so William, leaving the Maine uprising to his Norman commanders, returned to England personally to supervise the defence of his kingdom. Commanding his earls to raze the eastern counties into a barren wasteland, William mobilized his entire *fyrd:* the vast army was then installed in East Anglia to await Canute.

It was a gigantic operation and, in spite of the king's immense wealth, payment of such a huge number of soldiers was straining his treasury to the utmost. Hence the formidable assembly at Gloucester this Christmas-time of 1085, a gathering which had agreed reluctantly to the council's long-considered scheme for raising taxes to pay for the defence of the realm. Archbishop Lanfranc suppressed the smile creasing his wrinkled, parchment face: perhaps William's greatest quality was his ability to force his will against his hard-faced, stubborn barons?

But first, a detailed inventory had to be compiled of every man, every parcel of land, every house and its contents, each head of cattle in the kingdom. Only then could the people be taxed according to their ability to pay, and the taxes relentlessly collected by the sheriff's men.

Defrauders and defaulters would be punished pitilessly. For the first time, every Englishman would know where he stood: property could henceforth be transferred without conflict, the register having recorded every detail.

The inventory was to start in May next year, headed by the team of commissioners, a powerful band of the king's most trusted companions: Walter Giffard; Geoffrey, the aging bishop of Coutances who had crowned William nineteen years ago; and (Lanfranc was pleased to see) Hubert of Ryes' third son, Adam, who as a lad had saved the duke's life as he fled from the rebel *vicomtes* at Valognes. The census would extend only to the Welsh border and as far north as a line drawn between the Solway Firth and Newcastle. The district juries would collate the records which would be centralized in several great registers. There was certain to be resistance to this survey: they were already calling it the Day of Doom's register – the Domesday Book – but this strong commission was a signal to the nation of the king's implacable will.

Since William's invasion, two new elements had evolved in English society. A fresh, young aristocracy was growing, a loyal, privileged class dependent upon the king's favour; and an aristocratic army numbering some four thousand five hundred highly trained cavalrymen and troops, all serving under the monarch's commanders – a relatively high proportion from the total of some twenty thousand Normans then settled in England. Lanfranc had during these last years watched the evolution, for evolution it surely was, despite the harshness of William's rule.

One did not notice the progress, Lanfranc thought: but at the time of Hastings, one man among eleven Englishmen was a slave all his life. Slavery was now a rarity; conversely, the traditional 'freeman' of Anglo-Saxon times had lost much of his status in society, with the dominance of the newly developing feudal class.

Lanfranc allowed his gaze to wander across the vast assembly in the hall. He could understand the aging barons' resentment which was shared by the king, a distrust of this up-and-coming, effete society which had developed. The effeminate fashions launched by Fulk of Anjou and mimicked by Robert Short-arse and his cronies, raised their fathers' blood-pressure to boiling point; the traditional savagery of the past was now considered vulgar; though Lanfranc had succeeded in reforming his clergy, and though Pope Gregory (he had only recently died at Palermo) had succeeded in reintroducing celibacy in the priesthood, the pope's views of morals were having little effect in England.

The new leaders of this generation had become steeped in degeneracy: exaggerated manners, subtle speech and a beguiling tone of voice were the mark of the aristocrat. The girls loved the new life, had discarded all reserve and now shared in their menfolk's discussions and revelries. It interested Lanfranc to watch the king's reaction to his other sons' development: William Rufus, was a coarse youth anyway, but Henry, at seventeen years old, was the king's favourite now. Intelligent, subtle, a charmer around whom the maids fluttered like butterflies, young Henry* had a future before him.

William had already asked Lanfranc to prepare for next Pentecost at Westminster when the dubbing of Henry as a knight and vassal of the king would take place. The ceremony would alleviate the bitterness over Short-arse . . . and now there was this other major event looming, the idea which Montgomery had mooted to Lanfranc and the council last week: every land-owning 'Englishman' would be invited to attend a great assembly, there to swear solemnly before God his allegiance to the rightful King of England. It would take place next summer, 1086, and Salisbury would be a suitable venue. William, who insisted upon impeccable ceremonials, intended to celebrate his Easter Mass at Winchester, so that he could be up at Westminster for Pentecost and Henry's dubbing.

The North Sea was still inhospitable until May, as Canute well knew, so the Danish invasion was unlikely before the early summer of 1086. If the Salisbury Oath, as it was already being termed, could be sworn *before* the invasion, the significant event would allay one of the king's principal anxieties – and Lanfranc grimaced: one of William's least attractive faults was his obsessive suspicion of treachery. He could smell treason, he'd told his archbishop. The old man rose slowly from the bishop's chair in which he sat perched like a sparrow: fragile, but as mentally alert as ever, Archbishop Lanfranc watched his king. William turned ponderously, his pendulous paunch protruding, to acknowledge the final acclamation from this vast concourse of barons and knights from whom he drew his power. The king stood, legs astride, towering above his audience, his eyes flickering about the hall.

He was slightly bowed now, his thick neck lunging forward like a bull's. His grizzled, rusty hair topped the clean-shaven ruddy face, craggy and leathery from the years. Those hard lines told their own

* Note: Henry I, King of England (Henry Beau-Clerc), 'The Lion of Justice', 1100–1135.

story: harsh, cruel, obsessed by greed and the amassing of wealth – the fault most condemned by his barons; generous to the Church, religious, attending mass twice daily if he could. Tyrannical and over-bearing; but respected and revered by those who always suffered most from weak rule, the poor. William's justice was pitiless, but his justice kept the peace, forged unity and a stable social structure. In these rough days the king had to have a merciless side to his character if he was to be an effective monarch. A likeable personality guaranteed anarchy: hard-faced barons despised tolerance, taking it for weakness . . . This inflexible man, Lanfranc realized, stood head and shoulders above all others of his time: repellent he might be, hideously cruel at times; but, with his irresistible will, able to bend the most obstinate baron to the royal command; with his undeviating single-mindedness allied to a fierce courage and amazing physical stamina, this bastard Norman had in twenty years imposed his rule upon a divided, proud people, welding them into a unified nation, whose language he eventually adopted.

Watching the king standing before his cheering barons, the archbishop was once again impressed by William's awe-inspiring presence: massive, dignified, a natural leader of men having that indefinable, indisputable authority few would wish to challenge. His vassals either loathed or worshipped him. Few would deny his atrocious faults: but no one could ignore the greatness of this amazing Bastard King.

Reminiscence, King William realized, was the prerogative of an old man. He grunted, resenting any concession to the limitations forced on him by being in his sixtieth year. Even in this special saddle they had made for him, his piles were agonizing on this sultry last day of July, 1087. It was only Philip's taunting which had forced William personally to command this punitive expedition against the despicable king of France in the Vexin.

'Your orders, sire?'

His commanders were ranged around him, their chargers stamping impatiently on the rise overlooking the Seine.

'Put Mantes to the torch,' the king commanded. He spoke without feeling, his words cold, precise: 'Leave no hovel standing. Slaughter every traitor. Let no one escape.'

He watched them galloping down the slope – then the flicker of flames among the houses along the river bank. How often had he witnessed this familiar ritual? Dear God, he was growing weary of it all

– and he shifted in his saddle to ease the pain, his knight and personal seneschals remaining well clear, behind him . . .

He had learned of Canute's murder in the Odensee church in northern Denmark only two days before the Salisbury Oath at Lammas on 1 August last year, 1086. The Danish fleet at Limfjord had thereupon dispersed – and once again the threat of invasion upon England was lifted.

Hardly had he, William, disbanded his *fyrd* from the Eastern Counties than the news from Normandy had impelled him to cross the Channel once more: encouraged as always by Philip, his son, Robert, was on the rampage again. Odo was a festering sore, a nucleus for revolt; the Frisian was truculently fomenting trouble, and in Brittany, Alan Fergant was refusing to pay homage. Sailing from the Isle of Wight (William fitz Osbern had been its first Governor), William crossed the Channel in October 1086, and immediately led his army into Brittany.

Once again, he failed to reduce Dol. Tired of it all, he had compromised with Fergant by offering him his beloved, fragile nineteen-year-old daughter, Constance, to wife. Temporary peace reigned: William returned to Rouen, where he continued to receive the news from England of the appalling famine conditions. East Anglia had been laid waste last year as a precaution against Canute's invasion, and the country's granaries were now empty. And this year's famine was proving even more severe: inevitably, another epidemic of the plague was scourging his kingdom.

1087 had started miserably for him; frustrated and bored, he had spent the long evenings slumped alone before the blazing fire in his palace at Rouen. Growing daily grosser, he had allowed his physical condition to deteriorate; hugely overweight, the physicians condemned him to diet, thereby denying his one remaining consolation. To relieve his piles, they forced him to lie for hours in hot baths. For distraction, he had dispatched envoys to Asia Minor to find the bones of his father, Robert the Magnificent; they would be brought back for proper burial in their native Normandy.

Two months ago, Philip of France, taking advantage of the 1077 compromise between himself and William, began insolently to ravage the Vexin. Old Roger of Beaumont's son, Robert, who fortunately was as loyal as his father had always been, was now count of Meulan; William therefore decided at once to fling out the whipper-snapper, Philip, from the contested Vexin. But, as always, William first tried diplomacy by sending envoys to the French king's court.

At Poissy, Philip waited until William's representatives had finished delivering their king's ultimatum. He'd learned of the hot baths, the masseurs, the potions:

'So he's in no condition to come himself, then?' Philip sneered. 'Perhaps he'll try again when his confinement's over?'

William shifted wretchedly in his saddle, watching the fires devouring the wooden houses. A lick of revenge lusted through him as he recalled the retort he gave to the terrified envoys, when they reported back to him at Rouen.

'By the splendour of God!' he'd roared. 'Ride straight back to Poissy. Tell the brat this: "The confinement's finished. I'm on my way to Paris for my churching in Notre Dame. Ten thousand lances will be my thanksgiving candles." '

So once more he'd been driven to war when, for final answer, Philip unleashed his Mantes garrison into the Evreçin. Three weeks ago, at the height of the summer heat, William, with Robert of Beaumont behind him, set out wearily to teach Philip a lesson he would never forget: the Vexin would be regained for Normandy and never again be ravaged.

Crossing the Epte, where so long ago his great ancestor, Rollo, had established with King Charles of France the boundaries of the duchy, William sacked Pontoise and Chaumont. Yesterday, 13 August, he advanced on this town of Mantes which had always given trouble. And as he watched the flames leaping skywards in the noon of summer, he exulted in this just vengeance against the French youth who had insulted the King of England, Duke of Normandy.

'By the splendour of God!' he yelled to the knights behind him. 'Follow me, my lords – spread out on either side – Burn, burn! Cut 'em down, every fleeing traitor . . . Kill, kill!' And, despite the pain of his incapacity, he spurred down the slope towards the burning houses.

Ah! So the enemy *was* resisting . . . he glimpsed a band of the Mantes garrison scuttling behind a timber barricade they were hastily erecting across the smouldering street. He lowered his helmet, swept his sword from its scabbard. Once more he'd feel the edge biting deep, once more watch his adversary flinging wide his arms for mercy . . .

'Charge!' he roared. 'Let no man escape.'

Once again, he felt the ground trembling beneath the hooves, watched his knights streaming past him yelling their war-cries as of old. He let them pass, content to rein in, to let the youngsters taste the glory.

He slumped in his saddle, allowed the heavy sword to fall at his side.

He could hear the screams, see the swords flashing in the flare of the flames. The crackling of the inferno was all about him, as he watched the roof of the cathedral suddenly crumpling, collapsing inwards like an over-ripe pumpkin. His charger, terrified by the smell of fire, whinnied, rolled its eyes in terror. Savagely, the king dug in his spurs, forced his steed onwards . . .

The animal leapt forwards. It reared suddenly, its fore-left hoof embedded in glowing embers. William was flung upwards. With a tremendous jolt he fell, a leaden weight, down on to the pommel of his saddle.

His roar of pain brought his knights galloping back to him. And as he slithered from the saddle, moaning from the agony of his pierced abdomen, he heard the hiss of fire, the crackling flames; he smelt the familiar, acrid stench of smouldering timber; and, while his shocked companions gathered round him to roll his huge body on to the wooden litter they were fashioning, the appalling pain in the lower part of his body caused him to scream in agony. He could see their shocked, silly faces staring down at him – the crimson world was whirling about him, shot with sparks, the flames licking, hissing . . . and then, barely conscious, they bore him towards the river.

It is eighteen leagues from Mantes to Rouen. And in the torrid heat of that late August 1087, the tormented king was slowly transported in agony back to his capital of Rouen.

News of the shocking, unthinkable catastrophe swept through the duchy, through France. The great king was defeated, grievously ill, his army retreating from the Vexin. And there, in the palace of Rouen, attended by the bishop of Lisieux and the abbot of Jumièges, both versed in medicine, the king lay, refusing food, vomiting day and night. At last, unable to tolerate the noise of the bustling port beneath his window, he besought his stunned servants to transfer him to the cool peace of the priory on the hill to the west of the city. There, in the priory of St Gervais, the great king prepared himself for death.

It was the nausea which he found so hard to bear. He had not taken food for three days, sipped only water, his ruptured stomach and bowel festering, stinking in this unbearable heat. And William for the first time knew that the end could not be long deferred. All his life he had told himself that necessity had forced him to the cruelties he had perpetrated: but the stark truth was now confronting him. His power, his wealth, his crown of England and his dukedom of Normandy had been bought with the blood and suffering of unnumbered thousands: knights, thegns, peasants, freemen, bondmen, slaves – and William gasped wearily, seeking the solace of his archbishop, his able friend William 'Bonne-Ame'. But even this saintly priest could not convince his realist king that this agonizing end was not Divine judgement.

For five weeks the court had been assembled, summoned to Rouen by the council to watch their king die. They were all here, the greatest in the land, those who had served him best; and those who, like vultures, were waiting hopefully for his last patronage.

But among that circle staring enigmatically down at him, the faces of those he most longed to see were missing: his Mahault, of course; Lanfranc, in England and unable to travel; and his infuriating son, the boy he'd once loved so deeply – Robert was persisting in remaining aloof, was absent, still plotting outside Normandy with his patron, Philip. And the king groaned, more from the pain of his disillusionment, than from the agony of his decaying body.

For five weeks, they'd all been trying to persuade him to reconcile himself with Odo. His other half-brother, Robert of Mortain, was as obstinate in his pleadings as he was dim-witted: could not he realize that Odo's release from imprisonment would be the signal for instant rebellion? Now even Rufus and young Henry were pestering him to free their uncle. 'Dear Mother of Jesus,' he groaned to himself, 'let me rest . . .' Aloud he besought the archbishop to hear his confession; for absolution, while his mind was still clear . . .

He had listened to all the pleadings, heard all the arguments. During the evening of 8 September, he called his council around him. A half-smile twitched at the corners of his mouth, as the whispering clerks scratched with their quills. He could see them all clearly, the vultures waiting for the pickings . . . and he began to speak.

First, he asked the forgiveness of his enemies, those he had wronged. Then he made his bequests, gifts of money to those who had been loyal. Often he paused, correcting some clerk for error. His tired voice droned on until he ordered his final bequest: the rebuilding of Mantes cathedral.

'Release all those I hold captive,' he ended wearily. 'Let Bishop Odo be freed.'

He could do no more. With perverse humour, he had kept his sons waiting until the end. Again, in utter weariness, he would bow to his council's entreaty: to heal the internal strife, Robert was forgiven, but *never* was he to be given the crown of England.

'My first-born son, Robert, count of Maine, is to succeed me as duke of Normandy. He must strive to unite his duchy with my kingdom of England.'

The whispers of relief were like the poplar leaves rustling at Bonneville . . .

'And my next son, William, will wear my crown of England, bear my sceptre, carry my sword.'

The squat young man of twenty-eight knelt by the couch. The king touched the red hair:

'William, the Second, King of England,' he whispered. 'Rule my kingdom with justice. Uphold the Faith.' he noted the secret smile, heard his son's hoarse, embarrassed murmur. Rufus rose, kissed his hand, hurriedly left the chamber.

'Henry,' he commanded, drawing his remaining son to him. 'Your brains are your heritage. To you I bequeath the fortune of money held by the Chancellor – five thousand pounds.' Henry touched the king's brow, then rose from his father's side.

The king's head slumped to the right, on the silken pillow. He knew now with terrible clarity that his dream would never be realized: with Robert, Normandy could never be joined to England . . . The archbishop was moving towards the couch. Holding the chalice in his hand, he gave his king the Last Sacrament.

William closed his eyes, but could not shut out the scenes drifting before him, those far-away flashes coming so vividly back into focus. His last crossing of the Channel from Bembridge to Lillebonne in October last year: the weather was wild, the breakers surging beneath the ship's stern; turning up into the Seine estuary, she rolled gunwales under, almost broaching to: as he'd watched the white cliff of Culver towering down upon them, he'd sensed a premonition that this was his last glimpse of those chalk battlements disappearing into the mists. And the drifting image of Walter Fulbert: his strong, craggy face and kind eyes were some of William's earliest memories; Walter had become a legendary shipmaster, but had made his final 'passage home' twelve years ago now. And then his image was replaced by the face he'd never forgotten, the haughty, vivacious face of the mother he'd adored: Arlette with her wistful smile, her flashing eyes – and father's shadow flickering behind her, a broad-shouldered man in fine clothes, walking with his typical swagger, his laughter echoing through the castle. And now the darkness of the forest, the crouching spectres with their long knives, slinking between the trees . . . the brooding, grotesque figure of Ralph of Gacé with his huge donkey head – he'd disappeared across Normandy's borders into France, never to be seen again. And Fitz . . . Ah! the darkness was brightening – and here was his Mahault, the white hairs streaking her black tresses. Her smile was so serene as she gazed down at the little bundle in her arms: their last, their little Matilda, her tiny fingers curling about the lace trimming of the shawl . . . and he could hear that bell again, tolling, far away somewhere . . . The pain was disappearing at last – must be this high fever. Mother of God, he felt so weary. Could he at long last let go . . .?

'Let me sleep,' he murmured.

They watched over their dying king all that interminable night. William opened his eyes with the first grey sliver of dawn, the ninth of September. A mist was shrouding the great river snaking below the palace. William was awakened by the tolling of a bell down in the city.

'What ringing is that?' he breathed through motionless lips.

'Sire, 'tis the hour of Prime for Saint Mary's church.' William saw the shadowy form of the priest who had remained at his side throughout the night: the clerk was stooping, trying to ladle the cool liquid through the parched lips. The king watched those spectres genuflecting, tracing with their fingers the sign of the cross. Some were on their knees, others whispering in the background. The bishop of Lisieux, Gilbert Maminot, was crouching over him, pinching the tip of William's nose, his toes, the lobes of his ears, but already the extremities were cold, insensible. They were tracing the livid wound on his arm – 'your Gerberoi scar', Mahault called it . . .

A faint smile twitched at the corner of the king's mouth. He whispered, trying to reassure them all, as he had always done, charging into battle . . . This moment was like those glorious adventures: yes, like the first exultation of facing the enemy, charging into the unknown. Now he was starting his last assault and paying for his gross, grievous sins. But he felt not alone: He was there, waiting with the outspread arms, the palms of His hands scarred purple where they'd driven in the nails. Mahault was there, waiting too, shadowy, tarrying close by . . . and William sensed a peacefulness welling through him. He, the Bastard King, they'd called him, was starting his final journey . . . He attempted to lift his hands to touch the face of the praying priest:

'I commend myself to Mary, my Heavenly Lady,' he whispered.

331

'Through her, may I be forgiven by her Son, my Lord, Jesus Christ.'

The Bastard then rendered up his soul. His hand fell to the coverlet, lay still.

The king was dead.

The Bastard Duke had become an institution: for fifty-two years he had imposed his will upon Normandy; for twenty-one, had ruled England as its king. But suddenly the rock was gone.

News of the king's death flashed through Europe. In Normandy, knights galloped home to their estates. Peasants bolted their doors waiting for the inevitable holocaust when the new duke returned to the duchy to claim his heritage. Bishops hurried to their cathedrals, priests to their monasteries. And on that soft September morn, the royal corpse lay rigid, alone in the dark, deserted room of St. Gervais.

Within hours, the vultures had stripped the chamber: the furniture lifted, the gold and precious ornaments stolen, even the royal clothes stripped from the corpulent, rotting body. The thieves left nothing. By the evening, Archbishop 'Bonne-Ame' exerted his authority, commanding that the king's wishes be honoured.

William had ordered that he was to be laid to rest at Caen, the town in which he and Matilda had found happiness, had built their great abbeys. He wished to be buried in his church of St Etienne, in his Abbaye-aux-Hommes; there, in the magnificent abbey which he had built to the glory of God, a monument designed by him and Lanfranc to reflect the genius of the Norman people, William was finally interred.

They proceeded to embalm the putrefying body; they filled it with aromatic herbs, then stitched a bullock's hide around the cadaver. The bizarre coffin was laid on its wagon where it waited for a volunteer escort to transport it on its long journey to Caen. The archbishop called for volunteers, but no knight, no squire came forward to carry out this final, sad duty for their sovereign.

The weather was sultry, the days slipping by . . . Eventually a knight of modest means named Herluin was prevailed upon to take the macabre coffin down to the Rouen quay where, with four servants, he loaded it in a barge bound for the Seine estuary. At Lillebonne the coffin was unloaded, ferried across the estuary and hauled by wagon along the winding tracks to Caen. And as the sad cortège progressed, William Rufus was hoisting sail at Wissant for England when he learned of his father's death; barons were raising their drawbridges; Robert of Bellême was evicting the duchy's men from his estate, an action to be copied swiftly by his neighbours.

The news had spread across Europe: in Calabria, the emissaries whom William had dispatched to collect his father's bones, on learning of the king's death, disposed of the gruesome burden and dispersed, flying for their lives.

When the royal bier reached the outskirts of Caen, the townspeople assembled in the narrow streets. They stood in silence, watching the wagon slowly rumbling by, witnessing the last passing of the great duke who had been their lord for so long. In front of the cortège walked the boys, tinkling their bells for the departed soul; behind, shuffled the chanting monks. The oxen lowed as the wagon trundled past the duke's circular tower by the river; the dark clouds lowered, lightning flashed, the thunder broke. Flames spouted from three stricken houses. Women screamed, men crossed themselves, fled to their homes in panic. Deserted by the terrified monks, the lonely bier arrived unescorted outside the great west door of St Etienne, where the priests were waiting to receive the heavy coffin.

The greatest men of Normandy were assembled in that packed church: Odo, at liberty at last, stood to honour his brother as the macabre bull's-hide coffin was trundled on its trolley up the aisle of the nave. To the mournful chant of *Libera me*, ten stalwart bearers lifted the coffin, began to carry it towards the tomb they had opened in the floor of the choir. The bishop of Lisieux began his eulogy . . .

Suddenly the mournful proceedings were shattered by a man yelling above the ovation, the voice belonging to a Caennais business-man named Ascelin. The clerks tried to calm him, to restore dignity to the occasion. But Ascelin hurled the priests from him:

'This spot belonged to my father,' he shouted. 'The duke seized this land and gave it to you monks to build this abbey.' They tried to grab him, but his wild protestations were echoing to the soaring roof, as his hands tore frenziedly at the coffin. In the uproar, the bishop offered Ascelin sixty *esterlins* for compensation. Calm was restored as the man was hustled from the church.

The panting of the bearers as they lifted their heavy burden was the only sound in the ensuing, shocked silence. Grunting and struggling, they carried the bull's-hide coffin to the open tomb. They crouched, began lowering their load through the bights of their ropes: the masons had erred, had under-measured the corpse's dimensions. Cursing beneath their breath, the bearers began struggling with the bull's hide, heaving, bending, pushing at the feet while they tried to force the cadaver into its tomb. The seams of the hide split suddenly, tearing along its length.

The embalmers had over-stuffed the corpse. The obese, white belly burst: the disgusting stench wreathed through the nave. The bishop was hurriedly sprinkling the holy water, pronouncing the final blessing as the last members of the congregation rushed through the doors for the crisp air outside.

The church was empty:

King William I of England, Duke of Normandy, could rest at last.

EPILOGUE

Almost a millennium later, the Conqueror's tomb still lies in the floor of the choir in the church of St Etienne. There, beneath its marble slab, less than half a mile from the tomb of Queen Matilda, rests the empty sarcophagus of the great king, the Conqueror who gave this England its fabric of law, its justice and, eventually, its freedom of democratic government.

William Rufus was crowned William II of England by Archbishop Lanfranc at Westminster on 29 September 1087. The new king commissioned a worthy memorial to be erected over his father's tomb. In 1522, the sarcophagus was opened by papal order; the remains were examined and the tomb resealed. Forty years later, the Calvin upheaval destroyed the tomb; the remains were scattered, except for one thigh-bone which continued to be reverently preserved as a precious relic. In 1642, the bone was re-interred, but during the French Revolution the tomb was desecrated: in 1793 the last remains of the Conqueror vanished for ever.

The stone slab which now covers the tomb records simply the final resting place of William I, the Conqueror, King of England, Duke of Normandy.

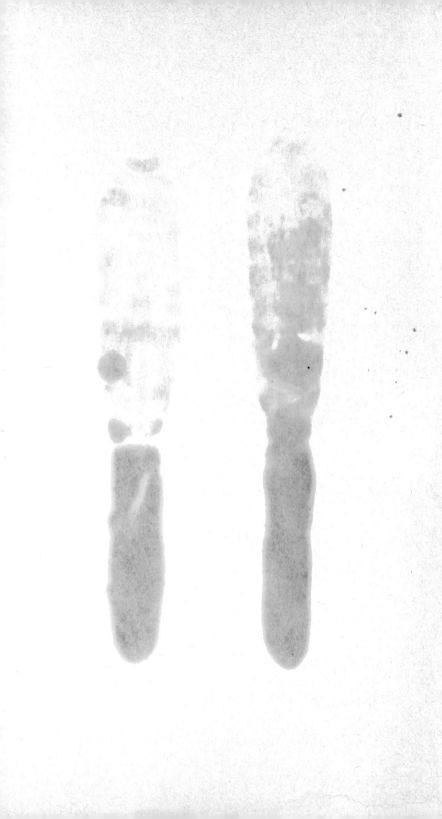

Wingate
  William the conqueror.

                              68005